My Navy Too, *the story of one woman's career in the U.S. Navy, is painted against a backdrop of the drama of the sixties and seventies - the Vietnam War, the women's movement, the confusion of the Cold War, and later, the Don't Ask, Don't Tell, Don't Pursue policy debate. While Vietnam runs its tragic course, Tucker Fairfield fights within the Navy for women's rights and equality against her most implacable foe, "Big Daddy Navy." Tucker's communications with her mentor and friends and journal reveal a complex amalgam of human interactions and conflicts yet to be resolved within today's society. Is it her Navy too? Should it be?*

Here's what people are saying about **My Navy Too:**

How refreshing — an account that is political and personal. I was fascinated by this book and think it should be required reading for women and men who are entering the Navy or any other service.

The Honorable Elizabeth Furse (D-OR)
Member of Congress

My Navy Too is an intimate, compelling memoir of a remarkable young woman's life and loves in a Navy grappling with the growing numbers and importance of women in uniform. Giving her intriguing account great breadth and insight are the words of her friends and family, who shared her adventures but appraised them from sharply differing viewpoints.

Rear Admiral Eugene J. Carroll, Jr., U.S. Navy (Ret.)
former Commander, Carrier Task Force, US Sixth Fleet

Reading this book is a very good preparation for understanding the turmoil that the Tailhook Age has inflicted on our Navy. Tailhook revealed the weakness inherent in the Navy's ultra-masculine bias, and had major costs...*My Navy Too* gives us an exceptionally clear insight into the 20plus years that led up to this turning point in Navy personnel policies.

Lieutenant Colonel Alan Erwin U.S. Air Force (Ret.)
commissioned in the Army Signal Corps upon graduation from U.C.Berkeley, and called to active duty in 1940, saw front line service in WWII. Later, LCOL Erwin was recalled and served until retirement.

As history, *My Navy Too* would be of interest to anyone with a love for or an interest in the U.S. Navy. As a journey in personal growth, it should have a much broader readership.

> Susan Schade Ward
> *Navy Junior (daughter of a retired vice admiral; Navy wife (of a retired Navy captain); Navy mother (of a Navy lieutenant helo pilot); published author.*

This book is strong and has good bones. It is good stuff...*My Navy Too* is a splendid, sometimes astonishing read...If I were a young woman entering the military, this would be number one on my reading list.

> Darrelle Novak Cavan Professor *Emeritus*
> *Mt. San Antonio College, Communications*

A courageous and balanced bio-novel which clearly sets forth the problems faced by both straight and lesbian women in the Navy. This fast-paced story never fails to hold the reader's attention.

> State Senator Jennie M. Forehand
> *Member, Maryland legislature since 1978*

...a moving account of a struggle for women's rights in one of the traditionally most male chauvinist organizations in the world, and the struggle of the protagonist to discover her sexual identity in an organization seemingly paralyzed by fear at any deviation from 'straightness.' What really struck me is how relatively easy I had it compared to the struggles that my sister officers had to, and still have to, go through.

> Captain William Lucas, MC, U.S. Navy (Ret.)
> *Professor Emeritus, School of Medicine, University of California, San Diego*

We have a larger purpose in the world and part of that is to help people coming behind us to understand — *My Navy Too* does that. I like the political Tucker. I would love to see the book used in certain college classrooms.

> Nancy Peterson
> *Oregon State Representative (1985-94) Bookstore owner, mother of a lesbian daughter*

A lived history of a woman in the military — reflecting the true and dramatic changes from patriarchy and paternalism to the beginnings of social change. The curious sexual undercurrent, fear and bias that existed toward women now linger as issues around sexual orientation which remain to be dealt with. A compelling and captivating read especially for those of us who walked parallel with Tucker.

Colonel Margarethe Cammermeyer, U.S. Army (Ret.), Ph.D.

A powerful book. Most impressive to me. Causes a lot of thinking about the issues of women in combat and homosexuality in the armed services. The result of that thinking may, for some, result in a broader acceptance of women and homosexuals in the armed services. For me, the great amount of new thinking caused by the book has only reinforced my previous views. The military services must maintain personnel standards that are completely compatible with and supportive of combat. As for women in combat, the jury is still out for some. But the distractions created already by women serving in combat units leads one to question the role. I cannot imagine a combat commander feeling good about having women in his units, particularly if the outcome of an engagement is questionable.

Vice Admiral Jerry Miller, U.S. Navy (Ret.)
former Commander, US Second and US Sixth Fleets

...packed with detailed, accurate information on Navy policies of the '60s and the '70s. My Navy Too is an engaging book that will inform as well as entertain a variety of readers.

Linda Grant De Pauw, Ph.D.
Founder and President, The MINERVA Center, Inc.
Professor of History; The George Washington University

My Navy Too couldn't come at a better time. It confronts head on one of the most important subjects in American society and politics today, two in fact: how an institution as traditional as the United States military should deal with the issues of gender and of sexual orientation. As the characters here struggle with such questions, we see just how poignant is the impact on individuals, how much the outcome could change our views of ensuring national security. The story — and the stories within it — are highly personal. But in the end, the resolution will have to do with profound values that touch us all. This is a courageous book.

Brad Knickerbocker
Senior Editor for The Christian Science Monitor, former Pentagon correspondent, and former naval aviator who flew combat missions in Vietnam from the USS Coral Sea.

4 September 1997

Anne —
Thank you for your
support. From one Navy
junior & mother!
May you enjoy reading
[Tuck's] journey —
And, may [there]

My Navy Too

healing begin within our
Navy and our country.
Warmly,

My Navy Too

A political novel based on real life experiences

by

Beth F. Coye
Commander, U.S. Navy (Ret.)

With

Marmaduke Bayne
Vice Admiral, U.S. Navy (Ret.)

James T. Bush
Captain, U.S. Navy (Ret.)

Patricia J. Bush, Ph.D.

Kitty R. Clark, M.S.W.

Sandra Snodderly
Lieutenant Commander, U.S. Navy (Ret.)

CEDAR
HOLLOW
PRESS

Cover and page design and production by Dan Schiffer, Digimedia, Jacksonville, Oregon.

The cover flag photo used with permission rights from PhotoDisc. The cover figure used with permission from Commander Kathryn L. Kane, U.S. Navy (Ret.).

Every effort was made to trace and contact copyright holders prior to publication. In some instances, however, this proved impossible. If notified, the publisher will be pleased to rectify any omissions in the next edition of the book.

This is a work of fiction. Whereas the characters involved in the plot are fictitious and are not intended to refer to any living persons, their stories are based on real experiences of the authors and their friends. The incidents described reflect the actual policies of the U.S. military toward women and homosexuals.

Quantitiy discounts are available to Organizations, Book Clubs, Colleges, and Universities. For information, please contact Cedar Hollow Press, Box 23, Ashland, Oregon, 97520, or call (541) 482-6833, e-mail: mynavy2@mind.net, or http://www.mind.net/mynavytoo/.

Library of Congress Catalog Card Number: 97–92277

ISBN 0-9658578-0-8

To a winning team, my mother and my dad,
who united to give me the courage to be myself.

Author's Notes

Given the confluence of my life experience with the current political issues of gender and homosexuality in the military, this book was destined to be written. I began the work alone, but quickly discovered the story would be more powerful, more real, with others to help me. I asked specific friends whose personal experiences and beliefs would be directly significant to the storyline to write letters for individual characters who would be friends and "family" of the major protagonist, Commander Tucker Fairfield, U.S. Navy. I'm grateful we had the right people for our endeavor. While the characters within our book are fictitious, the stories and situations are based on the authors' experiences.

Only I know each of the other authors. They came to know each other through correspondence and e-mail. Some issues required consensus, and for those times I deeply appreciated their willingness to struggle with, and to accommodate, diverse views. For other issues, just as this book's characters see questions and solutions differently, and as the American public and government have reached no consensus, so too the authors maintained their differences.

My experiences and those of many military friends in the last 37 years took place largely under the old paradigm that supported strictly white male values. Now the armed services are undergoing a painful, piecemeal shift to more culturally diverse systems. Throughout this paradigmatic transition, these military systems will demand high standards of integrity and readiness.

Sir John Robert Seely, the nineteenth-century historian, insisted on the principle that an appreciation of history, especially recent history, is essential for the politician. He wrote, "Politics without history has no root; history without politics has no fruit." I strongly believe that the American public and government policy makers, as they examine and evaluate policy issues, need to review the relevant history before jumping to conclusions based on current newspaper headlines. My hope is that My Navy Too is both entertaining as an historical novel and useful as an educational tool toward understanding what's truly behind today's media frenzy centered upon gender and homosexuality in the military, as well as the military's policies and attitudes about sex.

Early on in our project, Admiral Duke Bayne and I talked about the comparison of Tucker Fairfield's story with that of Stockton's The Lady or the Tiger. While the individual characters within My Navy Too write their own views on sensitive, public issues, we intended that, after reading it, the reader would be part of the resolution and make a choice between the Lady or the Tiger.

For those readers unfamiliar with military terminology, a brief Glossary and Acronym List can be found at the end of the book.

Beth F. Coye
August 1997

In Appreciation

The authors of this book had much assistance along the journey toward publication. In particular I want to thank the following people and organizations.

For major editorial help from: Patricia J. Bush, Ph.D., Laura Young, Kathleen Vickery, and Darrelle Novak Cavan, Ph.D. Other editors, both critics and readers, include: Ashland's Tuesday Women's Writers' Group; Ingrid Beach; COL Greta Cammermeyer, USA (Ret.); RADM Gene Carroll, USN (Ret.); CAPT Lee Clement, USN (Ret.); Judith Cope; Nancy Ann Curtis; Richard Davis; Linda Grant De Pauw, Ph.D.; Tomas Firle; Maryland State Senator Jennie M. Forehand and her husband, CAPT William Forehand, USNR, (Ret.); Congresswoman Elizabeth Furse (D-OR); Sabra Hoffman; LCOL Allan Irwin, USAF (Ret.); Brad Knickerbocker; Leon's Writers' Group in Ashland; CAPT William Lucas, (MC), USN (Ret.); VADM Jerry Miller, USN (Ret.); former Oregon Representative Nancy Peterson; Theodore Price; RADM Charles F. Rauch, Jr., USN (Ret.) and his wife Esther Rauch, Ph.D.; RADM Mike Rindskoph, USN (Ret.) and his wife Sylvia; Lucinda Sangree, Ph.D.; Leon Swartzberg's Ashland Writers' Group; Betsy Snyder, Ph.D.; Lee Townsend; Susan Schade Ward; and Jo Whiteley.

I appreciate the invaluable advice from other self-publishers: John Javna and Nancy Parker. The advice and production abilities of the page and cover designer, Dan Schiffer, were exceptional.

Major personal support carried me through difficult times in my author's journey. I'm grateful to longtime friends and family members, including Kay Cutter, Shirley Hall, Nicky Kronick, Sylvia Paymer, CAPT Jane Renninger, USN (Ret.); and CAPT Sue E. Young, USN (Ret.). Special thanks to my mother, Betty Coye, and my father, RADM Jack Coye, USN (Ret.).

My thanks for spiritual support from members of the Rogue Valley Unitarian Universalist Fellowship. Special thanks to Austen Meek, Lou Pollard, and Don Wells of this Fellowship.

My thanks for encouragement from those who are no longer with us: Michelle Abdill, RADM Stan Fine, USN (Ret.), and LCOL Chuck Magness, USA (Ret.).

Thanks for the valuable research support from the fine librarians at the Naval Amphibious Base Library, Coronado, CA; CAPT Dana Koch, USN; CAPT Georgia C. Sadler, USN (Ret.) with the Women's Research and Education Institute (WREI); and the Servicemembers' Legal Defense Network.

I've appreciated my constant Bichon Frisé mascots, Ms. San Diego Sunshine and Lady Love. And, finally, extra special thanks for the continued moral support, encouragement, and sustenance from Esther Bain Bell, my longtime friend and college classmate.

And to all others who have helped us along the path,

Thank You!

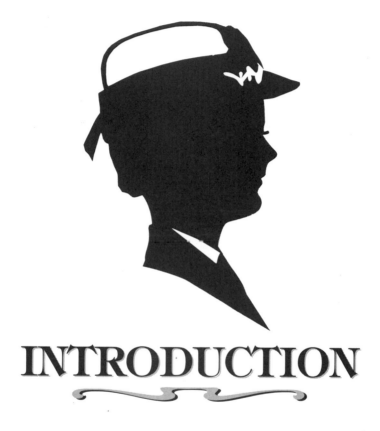

INTRODUCTION

1993

Introduction

The Blow Up

From Tucker Fairfield

15 May 1993, en route to Washington, D.C.

Dear Robyn,

Last night I lost a revered friend and reclaimed my Self — simultaneously. Quite an accomplishment even for me. I blew up at an admiral and vanquished "Big Daddy Navy." And I'm still breathing.

There we stood, in Vice Admiral Arthur "Buck" Buckingham's tastefully decorated Charleston living room, and squared off. I had no right to blast him, not really. After all, he's been a family friend and personal mentor for forty-five years. For so many years, I've loved and admired him. I've learned from him, listened to his advice, benefited from his guidance. Sometimes I resented his views. Why wouldn't I?

But I always kept it inside. You know me, always the reserved, intellectual, respectful Tucker Fairfield.

The evening started out like so many others. The light streaming in through the French doors lit his experienced and handsome face. We held glasses of wine, having just enjoyed an elegant dinner, and began discussing the role of women in the Navy.

Then, he started in on women in combat.

And something snapped.

I found myself on my feet, words spewing out of my mouth — words I've never dared speak to him. He's a flag officer, for heaven's sake! But I'd finally had enough of these self-righteous, conservative senior officers who'd rather push pins around a map than deal with personal issues.

Take's one to know one, you say? You're right. Remember the snobbish, pain-in-the-butt officer candidate from those days in Newport? But I changed, despite the training and education the Navy so graciously supplied. I changed! *Why can't he?*

"I'm a man," he said. "You're a woman. Women to me are precious, valuable, and I was put on earth to protect them. I do not want women on the bow planes when the hydraulic power fails and only pure strength can control the submarine. I do not want a woman topside with me greasing the vents in Japanese controlled waters when the sub has to dive because of enemy planes."

What decade are we in here?

"And I do not want a woman in the intimacy of sixty days submerged at sea."

At least he recognizes his chauvinistic position is no longer acceptable in our enlightened American culture. But that doesn't stop him from saying it. Why can't he see he's only thinking of himself? Why can't he recognize women as equally capable professionals, valuable to the Navy?

His attitude about women, "The military works well without them," epitomizes what I fought and struggled to change during my entire Navy career. Realistically, though, and you know this, Robyn, better than anyone, economic and legal factors forced the military to recruit more women and open up career opportunities for them, or I'd never have been in command. Attitudes, however, are still in the dark ages.

Buck stared at me, his eyes cool and gray. "Why change a winning game?" he asked in his refined voice.

That's what did it! That's when I stopped being the perfect officer and gentlewoman and became a shrieking Harpy straight from Greek mythology.

He even used the same trite words he'd used when we discussed this subject two months ago. He obviously didn't remember, or didn't choose to remember, my arguments.

"I've lived most of my life honoring the Navy's ways. You know the saying, Buck. 'There's a right way, the wrong way, and the Navy way.' " He nodded, slowly, suspiciously.

"Well, I'm going to live the right way from now on. The Navy way be damned. It is the wrong way — sometimes. Big Daddy Navy continues to be smugly self-satisfied about bigoted, classist, sexist, and heterosexist attitudes. You're asking good, honest people to conform to wrong-headed rules and regulations and demanding lies."

In the heat of the moment, I didn't realize what was fueling my rage. But now I know what truly frustrated me. Buck and I'd been sending faxes back and forth for weeks about the gays-in-the-military issue and other matters. I thought he'd "heard" what I was saying. I thought he understood! For over thirty-five years I *believed* that with time and education naval leaders would change their head-in-the-sand views about women, minorities, and gays.

His eyes widened. He looked astonished, like someone who'd just seen a UFO land in his backyard.

I told him that the senior officers judge all military gays, for instance, by the gay community's fringe. "I don't judge *you* by the fringe of the extreme right even though it would be natural to do so given your stodgy position about women and gays. Why punish all gays and lesbians by a blanket policy that says every single one of them is 'incompatible' with the military?"

I took a deep breath.

He breathed in slowly, too. His hands shook and he put down his glass of wine. "Tucker, the new Don't Ask, Don't Tell, Don't Pursue policy will be about behavior, not status. If military gays and lesbians keep quiet, they'll do just fine."

"Dammit, Buck. The policy should be about *conduct* and *misconduct*. It shouldn't define homosexual conduct as merely saying, 'I'm a gay man' and out you go! You're asking young military gays either never to have sex or always to live a double life with shame. You're saying never have a complete, fulfilling relationship. You're asking them to live like priests and nuns. Don't you think that's unrealistic? Plus, you know as well as I do that some commanders will ask and will pursue."

Buck shook his head. "Tucker, gays and lesbians know the conditions of military life when they join the organization. It seems unfair to me to say, 'I'm going to join your outfit, but you have to change the rules because I don't like them.' Besides, the military is *absolutely not* the place for homosexuals. The environment is too close, too charged with intimacy, too conducive to revelation, too dependent on bonding."

Sound familiar?

"When I joined the military," I said, "women were restricted to 2% of the force. Today, we're at 11%. Restrictive, prohibitive rules preventing women from going to sea have been changed, Buck. Why can't the rules change for gays and lesbians? Why?"

The light in Buck's eyes dimmed a little. "It's late. I need to get to bed. You're pushing the boundaries again, Tucker." He sounded weary. "You did it with women's issues and now you're at it again. Let it drop. You won't win this one, so stop wasting your energy."

I left the house. No matter how angry Buck gets, he remains a gentleman. He walked me to my car. Neither of us spoke. We had no more words, I suppose. Just feelings. We barely said goodbye. Buck's face was a mask of determination.

Robyn, I know what I said was right, and I know I had to say it to Buck. I refuse to be denied my personhood by Big Daddy Navy. But that doesn't take away the pain. My life in the Navy has been part of me — parent, brother, friend. It told me how to dress, whom to see, what to be when I grew up. Well, I have grown up. And I have to tell the truth, no matter how much it scares me. Someone has to. A real sailor goes ahead with the fight even when terror strikes. That's what courage is.

I know all this. But, oh god, it hurts. How ever did I get to this place? Without a Navy, my Navy, without a stately ship, without an anchor.

And how do I *leave* this place? I think I need to go back to the beginning of my story.

My love to you and Ned. Will phone from Washington, D.C. I'm off to visit Tom Parker and his family.

Tucker

PART ONE

1948 – 1973

Chapter One

Navy Junior

From Tucker Fairfield

November 4, 1948
1100 Shenocossett Parkway
Groton, Connecticut

Lieutenant Commander A.R. Buckingham, U.S. Navy
Commanding Officer, USS *Seaperch*
New London Submarine Base
New London, Connecticut

Dear Captain Buckingham,

Thanks so much for taking us down under the water in your submarine last Saturday. I never knew the Navy let children go on submarines.

When Daddy said I could go if Mother went too, I was so excited I accidentally slapped my spoon down in my mashed potatoes, and they splattered all over my new dress. It was dry by the time you saw me, though.

Captain Buckingham, can girls serve in the Navy? Can they be aboard submarines like sailors? I didn't see any girl sailors. It would be exciting and fun to work on a submarine. I'd be scared in a submarine when a war is going on, as Daddy and you were. I don't mean Daddy was afraid. Nothing ever scares him. But he said the Japs and Germans dropped depth charges on top of him and his submarine in the war. That would scare me a lot.

My favorite part was when you let me turn the wheels that make the submarine go up and down. Daddy says those were the diving planes, and they make submarines go like that, right? Like underwater airplanes.

Thank you very much for the wonderful ride. I really did love it!

Oh, and thank you, too, for the surprise party celebrating my eleventh birthday. I hope I'll get my birthday wish. I wished someday girls will be able to work on submarines!

I hope you can take me down in the *Seaperch* again soon. Thanks again.

Sincerely yours,

Tucker Fairfield

One week later, 11 November 1948

Lieutenant Commander A.R. Buckingham, U.S. Navy
Commanding Officer, USS Seaperch
New London Submarine Base, New London, Connecticut

Captain Henry Fairfield, U.S. Navy
Commander, Submarine Squadron Eleven
New London Submarine Base, New London, Connecticut

Dear Commodore:

Our Dependents' Cruise last Saturday was a huge success. Twenty-eight USS *Seaperch* wives and children came on board; our guests literally took over the submarine, all within the bounds of safety, of course.

We spent the morning touring Long Island Sound, diving and surfacing and allowing the guests to handle many of the control systems. As always, the periscope was the most popular attraction for kids and wives alike.

It was a privilege to have Mrs. Fairfield and your daughter, Tucker, on board. Mrs. Fairfield, familiar as she is with submarines, was relaxed and delightful as always, though she had quite a job following Tucker around! I was surprised and impressed at Tucker's interest in every function of the boat. She took part in everything, and spent her lunch busily engaged in conversation with crew members about detailed descriptions of the boat's systems. What a bright child she is!

I'm convinced these Dependents' Cruises, which you have instituted, demystify the time spent by the husbands and fathers assigned to the boats, and increase the families' understanding about the long times away from home.

Thank you for allowing *Seaperch* to participate.

Very respectfully,

A.R. Buckingham
Lieutenant Commander, U.S. Navy

Five years later from Tucker's journal

November 5, 1953, London, England

 For the record,

Last night Dad took us aboard his ship, a sub tender docked on the Thames, for a special dinner to celebrate the birthday of the American Ambassador's wife. Mother bought me a new mauve dress.

I sat next to the Ambassador's wife herself...she tells great stories. She actually marched in New York for women's suffrage more than forty years ago!

Sylvia, she told me to call her by her first name, was also polite enough to ask me about my life. And what I thought about London, about traveling, the Navy, school. Everything. Then she told me, in her soft, sophisticated voice, that I would make a difference in the world. Deep down, I prayed she was right.

Then, this morning, a package arrived by messenger for me, and inside was this diary — from her! The note said I should keep a record of what I'm thinking and doing because someday someone will want to know how I got to be who I was. And, I could look back at my diary entries and understand how it all happened, and maybe why.

I'm so excited about what might be ahead for me in life.

So, here I am lying on the bed in our hotel room, writing in this diary. I decided to start off with "For the record" because of what she'd said in her note. Of course, no one will probably ever want to know anything about me, but her encouraging words have inspired me to dream of making what she suggested become real.

The dinner was unbelievable. Dad, because he's "the skipper," was treated like a king, and the rest of us were treated like royalty, too. The table was set with china (white with gold bands and anchors), shiny silver, crystal, candles, flowers, white linen tablecloths. People brought us what we needed almost before we knew we needed it.

After dinner, Sylvia opened her cigarette case and took out a long, thin, brown cigarette and by the time she put it to her lips, a steward was next to her to light it for her! Wow!

Guests talked a lot about the Russian communists. I just listened. I felt overwhelmed with how much I don't understand. Last week, if you said "Russian communist" to me, I would have thought "The Enemy," and that was pretty much it. Now, after last night, phrases about "international economics" and "military strategy" swirl through my head, and I know I know nothing. Mother always says, the more you know, the less you know.

Every now and then someone would say something that made everyone at the table fall silent. Sylvia would tap my hand with her cool fingers loaded with diamond rings (!), and nod at me. I felt like my eyes had never been open so wide.

Tomorrow morning I get to ride on Dad's gig for a short trip around the Thames. Whenever I ride the gig, my senses seem extra awakened. Lying here on my bed, I can already smell the Thames; I can see the clean-cut sailors manning the gig; I can sense the smoothly-oiled machinery, probably diesel run, that is the United States Navy working all around me. Someday perhaps I'll have a place within this machinery.

TF

Six years later from Tucker's journal

March 15, 1959, Wellesley College

For the record,

It won't be long before I graduate. Robyn and I sat at Colley's Cantina last night for almost six hours, sipping beer and discussing what we're going to do with our lives. Of course she and I have debated that particular issue since we hit first grade...I guess we were both trained to weigh the pros and cons of life's decisions. I'm so lucky the college administration assigned Robyn and me to the same room as freshmen. And here we are, four years later, packing up our debris and saying goodbye to Wellesley. It doesn't seem possible.

Robyn's going to be a psychologist. She's absolutely certain. She couldn't avoid it if she wanted to. She'd analyze and try to help people with her insights even if she were never paid. That's who she is.

I wish I were that way. I wish there were something I could do, something I loved to do, regardless of income. My decision would be made for me. But I have to think through and make my decisions for myself. Nothing tells me without doubt what my life work is. All I know is that I must have an impact and make the country I was born in, better for our next generations. When I die, I want people to say the country, maybe the world, is better for my having lived.

How should I do that? I've had an offer from the Director of the League of Women Voters to work for them in their public affairs efforts. I'm tempted and it's a real job offer! But down deep the League doesn't strike the chord within me that says, "Yes. That's my career."

The only thing I've ever really wanted to do is be in the Navy, like Dad. But is that a child's dream? I couldn't be stationed on a submarine, or go to war like Dad, but I could join the WAVES. I could be a senior officer someday. I could affect decisions about the security of our country. What work could be more important than keeping our country safe and strong and FREE?

Or, I could go into academia. I could get a graduate degree in Political Science. I could teach. I know I enjoy teaching.

But no. That's not "it" either. Whether it makes sense or not, the Navy seems closest to ringing the right note in my soul. In the Navy I could use my training and knowledge in political science and my growing skill at strategizing large policies and procedures. And I seem to have a desire, a passion, for using precise methods to achieve what's right, what's best, what's clearest and most useful. Besides, the Navy spells adventure. And I'm ready!

I don't know. Something about the word "Navy" says "Tucker."

TF

One month later from Tucker

Wellesley College, Pomeroy Hall
Wellesley, Massachusetts
April 15, 1959

Captain A.R. Buckingham, U.S. Navy
The Pentagon
Washington, D.C.

Dear Captain Buckingham,

Two months until graduation! I can hardly wait; I'm worn out from Senior Stress.

I'm writing you for a very selfish reason: I'm writing a term paper called "The German U-Boat, A Point of Departure for American

Foreign Policy" and hoped you might give me some feedback on whether my thoughts about this are on track.

My American Foreign Policy prof is great, and more than willing to guide me toward what he thinks about the subject, but I don't want to merely write a "good term paper;" I want to know what happened. I want to discover it, learn it, know it, tell it.

I hoped you could listen to my ideas and tell me where I'm wrong, where I'm right, where I'm not asking the right questions. I didn't realize the United States was unprepared for Germany's decision to use unrestricted submarine warfare, to use the U-Boat. Why?

Admiral William S. Sims, U.S. Navy, writing to the Secretary of the Navy on January 7, 1920, said that prior to 1917, the United States violated several military principles. These included "Unpreparedness in spite of the fact that war had been a possibility for at least two years and was, in fact, imminent for many months before its declaration." Hmm.

I'm concluding that the German decision to resort to unrestricted submarine warfare was *the* point where President Wilson realized we had to shift from being neutral.

My questions to you: Why were we so unprepared for the German U-Boat decision? Was our military as idealistic as Wilson himself? Could the U.S. military ever again be so unprepared for war? Has the United States suspended a Wilsonian idealistic, moral basis of its foreign policy? Are we prepared for the Soviet submarine threat?

If you had been a German U-Boat skipper, would you have followed orders to go to unrestricted warfare? During your service in World War II, were you aware of the importance of the American submarine force to the success of our military efforts?

I hope you and Mrs. Buckingham are well, and enjoying Washington duty. I plan to work in Washington after I (finally) graduate. I've accepted a position with the League of Women Voters in their national office, but I'm thinking about joining the WAVES as an Officer Candidate after my stint with the League. What do you think? Knowing you, you'll have an opinion about me as a WAVE officer. Regardless of what I decide To Do With My Life, I hope to see you soon in Washington.

Sincerely,

Tucker Fairfield

Ten days later from Buck

Captain A.R. Buckingham, U.S. Navy
The Pentagon, Washington, D.C.
April 25, 1959

Dear Tucker,

Wonderful to hear from you! Helen and I had dinner with your parents last week, and we talked a great deal about you. Your parents are so proud. You've apparently taken Wellesley by storm! Vice-President of your class; captain of the hockey team — all this and excellent grades to boot! You shame me; my career at the Naval Academy wasn't nearly as illustrious, though I did manage to graduate as a Company Commander, Three Striper. A "Three Striper" hardly compares with Vice-President of your class, which must rank somewhere between Four and Five stripes in the Academy organization. Maybe you're a "Four and a Half Striper" — quite an achievement.

I always expected you would do well at college. I remember that family barbecue with you and your parents last summer when you were home. I felt positively under siege when you started asking your questions about communism. You have the tenacity of a bull-dog when you want to understand something. A little intimidating at times, a quality that will serve you well as you begin your career (finally! as you say) after graduation.

Tucker, the idea of your entering the Navy comes as a bit of a shock. I'd assumed you'd go to graduate school, following your interests in political science, maybe even study law. I've noticed strong political convictions in some of your letters over the years. I know you inherited a deep Duty, Honor, Country tradition, but is becoming a woman naval officer the best way to fulfill that tradition?

The Navy is a man's world; it always will be, even when there are more women involved than at present. I suspect you will want to move toward the policy level in whatever you do. That's not going to be easy as a Line Officer. The "Warrior Culture" is alive and well in the United States military. In that culture the male protects the female. Breaking that down will be frustrating and will take a lo-o-o-o-ng time. Think about this, Tucker. A military life is not a social battlefield, nor is it designed to suffer change lightly. It has been going on too long.

I'm amazed, though, to hear you're graduating this year. Wasn't it just yesterday when that bright little girl went to sea with me on *Seaperch*. How many years ago *was* that?

I'm flattered you thought of me in your search for "the truth" (a difficult search if there ever was one). The German submarine activity in 1917 was the "cause" for our entry into World War I. But, if I remember my history correctly, if it hadn't been the *Lusitania*, it would have been something else. We couldn't remain on the sidelines much longer.

Why were we so unprepared, you ask. If I am absolutely candid, I will have to admit I really don't know. There are many reasons, all stemming from our government, this constitutional democracy, which does, in fact, draw its power from the people.

The people don't like war.

Franklin Roosevelt was never more representative of the people as when he made his famous "I HATE WAR!" speech. Somehow we seem to feel as a nation that if we ignore war, it will go away. We were unprepared in 1917 for the same reason we were unprepared in 1941, and even later in 1950 when Korea acted up. Until the people literally *feel* they are in danger, elected and appointed officials of government can't spend the money or mobilize the industrial complex to make us ready.

Remember, six months before Pearl Harbor, the Draft Act passed Congress only by one vote. I don't know whether this national reluctance to prepare ourselves stems from political concerns over vote getting, from genuine judgment that national security isn't threatened, or from such a national abhorrence of war that shells have to land on our doorstep before we believe we're threatened. Perhaps it's a combination of all three factors.

My obvious answer to your second question, "Could the United States ever again be so unprepared for war?" is a resounding, "Of course it could, and is." This country has more important things to do than prepare for war. We're not a warlike nation. Despite a general feeling in the country, spurred on by news media and Hollywood, our generals and admirals do not prepare for war. Rather, they prepare to prevent war.

I know no responsible military person who has experienced war in any of its forms who wants to do it again. That's why it's so frustrating when the military recommends a higher state of readiness to have the recommendation put aside on grounds that military people always want more than they need. Of all the world's reluctant dragons concerning fighting a war, the military forces who have experienced war are the most averse. So, their recommendations to get ready are apt to be made reluctantly and should be heard. I'm certain your father would agree with me.

I know I have a military bias when I write like this; perhaps it helps if we understand what a marvelous society we've created in this country, where checks and balances keep us from acting precipitously, sometimes not quickly enough. But once the decision is made, we pull out all the stops. At least that's the way it has been so far. No, we're not as prepared as I think we should be to meet the current Soviet submarine threat which is many times greater than the German capability in either WWI or II. But, should we ever perceive a national need to counter that threat more aggressively, we can outbuild and outfight the Soviets in such a war-at-sea.

Would I have followed orders to conduct unrestricted warfare on American shipping had I been a German U-Boat Commander? Of course I would have — just as I followed them in the Pacific in WWII against the Japanese. That, unfortunately, is what war is all about. War is not neat and clean, obeying Marquis of Queensbury rules. It is brutal, wasteful, nasty, and wrong, which is why professional military people want to prevent war by being strong enough to deter its stupidity by political adventurers. That sounds like military idealism, and I like to think there's a lot of practical idealism which says clearly, "Don't mess around with my valuables, or I will have to hurt you. I don't want to do that, but I won't hesitate if that's what it takes to prove I like things just the way they are."

Ah, Tucker. I got a bit wound up in that last paragraph but you touched a nerve with your question. Many responsible people in this great country don't understand the application of military power and strength. If our submarines ever have to launch their missiles, our primary military mission will have failed. To prevent that failure we have to maintain credible strength. That's not easy to do in a society which hates war and has better things to do with its resources.

The best of luck to you on your paper. I doubt that an historical look at the U.S. response to the German U-Boat in WWI will require much of the philosophy I've spouted, but you asked. I'd like to read your paper when it's done. I look forward to seeing you in D.C.

Warm regards,

Buck Buckingham

Four months later from Tucker's journal

August 9, 1959, Washington, D.C.

For the record,

Robyn and I went searching for some male company last night. We've both been so preoccupied: me consumed with work at the League of Women Voters, Robyn with her work at the zoo. At night, we hole up in our apartment. Robyn studies, and I make zillions of phone calls for the League (I've become quite the political activist!) or work on their newsletter or design and write one of their fund raising brochures. If only Elizabeth Cady Stanton could see me now!

Neither of us has had a date since we moved to Washington. How depressing. We were lounging on the sofa, watching a dumb TV show. During one of the endless commercials, we suddenly realized that two twenty-two-year-old working women were watching television on a free evening. Not a single man in sight. Pretty pathetic if you ask me.

So we got ourselves all dolled up — Robyn even curled my hair and put makeup on my face — and we launched ourselves out of the apartment in search of our dreams (or at least a dance-floor romance).

We drove over to Georgetown and found a little blues bar. It was like walking into another world. The evening light shone outside, but the bar was so dark inside I could hardly see the floor, and the cigarette smoke curled in the air as thick as a gray wool blanket. On the tiny stage, an old Negro man was hunched over his slide guitar, moaning in the air that seemed, as my eyes got accustomed to the dark, full of slow, hidden movement.

I stood at the bar to buy us two drafts, while Robyn miraculously found an empty table — small, round and scarred with cigarette burns, and two hard wooden stools.

I plunked the beers on the table and hitched myself onto my stool. I leaned over to Robyn and muttered, "If they can't even see us, how are they going to know we're just what they've been looking for all their lives?"

She laughed, her greenish eyes ablaze, even in the dark of the bar, excited to be out on the town for a change. "We're female, aren't we? They can see well enough for that."

I said, "Oh, you do give me hope," and took a long drink from my beer. I was going to need a couple of these to deal with whatever might be coming.

The old man on stage sang the usual: love lost, love found, love gone wrong, wrong love found to be good in some strange way...Nothing was happening as far as men were concerned. I began to relax, finally. And to think about my romantic history...

All my life we moved to a new place every year or two. Some places we moved away from and came back to, but even coming back made me the new kid on the block again. I never got really close to anyone, let alone a boy. The closest was to Mary Elizabeth in the fourth grade. It broke my heart when I had to tell her good-bye. And then I went to Wellesley, a women's college. Robyn was the first friend I ever had who was close enough to tell real secrets to. Secrets like — I'd never been to bed with a man, even though I'd dated a lot. Neither had Robyn.

Being perched in a bar for the sole purpose of "finding male companionship" made me nervous. I wouldn't know what to do with him once I found him.

But Robyn was with me. So everything was normal. Everything would turn out just fine.

My thoughts of joining the WAVES flashed through my mind, and I felt guilty. Robyn and I had kind of joined forces in Washington, with the apartment and all. I hadn't told her what I was thinking, because she might see it as a kind of betrayal. Leaving her alone in the big city.

"Robyn," I said, trying to pull the words from my insides to explain to her that my family has a tradition of Navy. At least the men in my family do, and that I needed to continue it.

The words got stuck. I thought about my plan some more. It was beyond rational, this need. It felt like a genetic programming.

I was about to tell her my latest career idea, but before I could, some guy canted himself around Robyn and set his beer on the table and forced his voice over the wailing blues man. "Incredible, isn't he? He's here every Thursday night, and usually so am I. Have you heard him before?"

Suddenly, I felt sleazy. The "what's a nice girl like you doing in a place like this?" line sounded stale.

Shame flooded through me. But Robyn just looked up at him, smiling a smart, catlike smile and purred, "This is our first time. He's wonderful. This is my best friend, Tucker." And she moved her hand out to me, as if she were serving me up on a silver platter. I looked at him and wanted to punch him. Or run out the door.

He sat down next to Robyn and told her his life story. And she listened. This horrified me. This guy was a complete stranger, a man looking for some woman — any woman. I stopped. Wait a minute. That's what we were doing. We were out looking for a man — any man.

Life makes no sense at times. This felt completely wrong though.

"There's a poetry reading two blocks over at ten-thirty," he said, giving Robyn a confident, you-can't-resist-me look. "A Negro woman is reading her work about her life in Alabama. She was raised by her grandmother who was a slave. I've heard her poetry's great. I've meant to go for weeks. I'd love it if the two of you would go with me. I hate going places by myself."

"You came here by yourself, didn't you?" I wanted to say. But I kept quiet. He seemed like a nice guy. What was wrong with me? I was beginning to feel — what? jealousy? Was it because Robyn already had some man interested in her, or because Robyn was interested in some man? I couldn't be sure.

So we went to the poetry reading, and the (okay, okay) nice young guy introduced me to some friend of his, Bill Foster, who was also, I guess, "nice enough." Robyn's young man was named Ned Greeley. He had just finished a Masters in Psychology at Georgetown, and had been accepted into Harvard's Ph.D. Psychology program.

Grudgingly, I had to admit that he might be good enough for Robyn to see once in a while. Not that she would ask me.

Bill was also "nice enough." He was an aide to Senator Haroldsen from West Virginia. He'd graduated from Yale with a degree in Chemistry, but because his father trained thoroughbreds for the Senator, Bill got on as the Senator's aide. Such are the complexities of job-finding. It's not what you know, it's who you know.

"Her soul parched." The poet threw out her arms in a gesture of passion and pain. "But mine. Mine boiled with fresh red blood."

Bill slid his arm around my shoulders. I closed my eyes, and then quickly opened them. What did I feel? Was he the marrying kind, I thought involuntarily? Did I want him to touch me? Did I want him to kiss me? The thought frightened me. And what did that mean, Fairfield? Would I never grow up?

Robyn leaned across Ned's lap to touch my knee and smile at me. "Isn't she amazing? What images!"

I smiled back. I could say nothing.

The poet finished and another took her place. I ordered another dark draft. When the poets finished, the four of us went down the street to a little all-night diner and ordered coffee. I felt isolated. I felt like Bill had gotten stuck with the lesser woman, and I felt sorry for him. But he didn't seem to feel this way and enthusiastically talked with me about his work on Capitol Hill.

Next to us, an attractive, elderly woman spoke quietly with her granddaughter. They were discussing the granddaughter's plans to marry some guy. She patted her granddaughter's hand and said, "I met your grandfather at a dance at the high school. He sold shoes in the next town over. I never saw a man dance as lightly and with so much feeling as he did. He swept me off my feet."

I looked over to see how the granddaughter was taking this news, and I saw she had tears in her eyes. "That's how Jimmy makes me feel, Nana," she said. "When he touches my face and tells me he loves me, it's like music. It's like my heart swells and moves with his music." She lifted her hands to her grandmother, offering up the fragile beauty of what she felt, and her grandmother sat back, raised her coffee cup to her lips, sipped, and set the cup back on the table.

"Well, then," she said.

I can't imagine feeling that way. I can't imagine totally giving up myself to a man, much less feeling excitement in it. I look at men and I see children. Responsibilities. God Almighty, maybe I should just get me to a convent, even if I am Episcopalian!

When we finally got home I spent an hour listening to Robyn talk about Ned Greeley, and how brilliant he was, and how overwhelmed with emotion she was when he touched her.

I wanted to either punch her or punch myself. One of us must be mixed up, or nothing made any sense. If women are meant to be with men, and I am a woman, then what does how I feel mean? Doesn't it matter? Should I just forget what I've read in novels about love? Should I accept that when a man touches me I feel nothing but patience? Well, maybe warmth. Is that what being a woman is? There's a lot of literature that says being a woman is patience, and nothing more. But Robyn says she feels the things I read about in novels. And I don't. So does that mean I just can't feel? Am I emotionally frigid? I don't think so. But I don't understand. I don't understand! I know there's a man out there somewhere who will make me feel all these things — and more. I just haven't found him yet.

I'll keep looking. I have to. And then I won't have to make myself feel what the novels say I should. I'll feel it without even trying.

TF

Chapter Two

Anchors Aweigh

Six months later

Lieutenant Andrea F. Anderson, U.S. Navy
19 February 1960, Recruiting Station, Washington, D.C.

Tucker Fairfield
507 Cathedral Drive
Washington, D.C.

Dear Miss Fairfield:

Congratulations. You have been selected for the Navy's Woman Officer Program. You will report to duty at the Women Officers' School in Newport, R.I. on 1 March 1960 for a sixteen-week course.

I'm enclosing literature that describes what to bring and what to expect in the first week. I want you to know that it won't be an easy assignment. It will test your mettle, but your background as the daughter of a Navy captain should be helpful during the more difficult times, times when you'll wish you were back in D.C. as a civilian.

Call me to set up an appointment to be sworn into the Navy. I encourage you to have your father be the officer who swears you in. I would be pleased to do the honors, but he is the more appropriate person.

Sincerely yours,

Andrea F. Anderson
Lieutenant, U.S. Navy
Woman Officer Programs Officer

Eleven days later from Tucker's journal

1 March 1960, Newport, R.I.

 For the record,

This desk sits under the one window in my barren little room in the Women Officers' Quarters (aka WOQ#113). I can see across frozen Coaster Harbor Island, to the imposing Naval War College which guards the icy water of the Narragansett Bay. A thick covering of snow transforms the bushes along the narrow road running in front of WOQ#113 into mysterious mounds of white. The place looks deserted; everyone must be hiding. The frost has left fragile patterns on the glass of my window. My fingers are cold; my mind feels a little numb. I think I'm in shock.

An inviting picture, isn't it? Just looking over these words makes me want to close this journal, crawl under the blue and white striped thin bedspread, and go into hibernation until I can wake up, fully adjusted to this new way of life. But this is one of those life-altering days, a day when I've taken a step that will affect the rest of my life, and I have to say something about it.

Oh, come on, Fairfield, get a grip! Cold and shock aren't all I feel. Underlying everything is an electricity...a sense of wide-open possibilities. I've taken hold of my life, and I'm shaping it to suit me. And, if it turns around and shapes me, well, that's what I want. I feel this power in myself, this intelligence, this capacity for commitment, and I need to make it real. *I need to make myself real.* The orderly Navy world can force all this from me. I *feel* it, notwithstanding my cold body. And so, underneath the anxiety about suddenly finding myself in a strange world, and the worry that I've bitten off more regimentation than I can chew, I'm filled with a wild excitement!

I took the Jamestown ferry across to Newport, where the school is, and I stood at the bow, letting the cold wind sting my face. The rise and fall of the ferry was like the movement in my life. My work with the League of Women Voters was falling away from me, and my new world, unknown yet filled with exciting adventures, was approaching on the Newport shore that was overshadowed by the War College's graystone buildings.

As I stood there, filled with fantasies about my future, a woman came up and stood next to me. "Going home?" she asked. "Sort of," I said, and by the end of ten minutes I knew everything about her. She's Billie Baker from East Tennessee, taking courses at the Navy's Communications School and soon to be reporting to the Pentagon as a Communications Watch Officer. I told her I had been sworn into the Navy five days ago, and would be spending the next sixteen weeks at the Women Officers' Candidate School. She laughed and told me story after story of her WOCS days; she graduated two weeks ago. She filled me with her optimism and humor. I could hardly wait to get here.

The ferry landed. I drove ashore, parked and stepped out, feeling the New England wind against my body, feeling how momentous this day is. I felt like a bride, preparing to walk down the aisle.

I got back in the car and drove through this old New England seaport toward the Naval Base's Main Gate. My family had lived in Newport for awhile and memories of my senior year in high school flooded me. I remember eying with curiosity, the imposing War College's structures jutting out over the waters and wondering what kind of world-changing lessons and war games took place there. Driving through the Main Gate, I suddenly realized that the Women Officers' School quarters adjoin the War College. One of my dreams, to find out what's really going on in this place closed to outsiders, is about to come true.

It's funny. I remember several years ago telling Mother I wouldn't be caught dead wearing those awful black shoes that the WAVES wore as they marched around the Base.

TF

Three days later from Tucker

4 March 1960, Newport, R.I.

Dear Mother and Dad,

A storm is raging! Actually, the storm wouldn't bother me so much if we could stay inside, but we have to go outside to the Enlisted Mess to eat. I have muffins stashed away to eat during the day, but there's the nightly walk for dinner. Making it ten feet takes ten minutes, climbing through snowdrifts above my knees, perspiration pouring down between my shoulder blades despite the frigid wind, snow inevitably seeping into my boots no matter how carefully I wrap myself up.

As you've said many a time, Dad, "In the United States Navy, we must carry on!" I put on my tough Captain Hank Fairfield face when I say that, Dad...it makes me laugh and feel better.

Other than freezing, I'm fine. I think I'll like the Navy as soon as I can adjust to being a Seaman Apprentice and low man on the totem pole. The set-up is all Navy: commands, clothing, inspections, demerits and gigs (five gigs equal one demerit), and the rest of what they feel we have to learn to be a naval officer. The whole last hour, for example, I've been shining my oh-so-lovely shoes. My fingers are numb and black! The WAVES have a special way of shining, which the middies probably use too. Black polish, hot water and cotton balls — wetting the cotton balls and then dipping them into the polish. Works wonders. Takes forever!

There are twenty other officer candidates in my class. Some are extremely sharp. I probably won't be #1 in studies. On the other hand, some of them aren't too bright. I've clicked with only a couple. Everyone seems so religious...a large number are Catholic, with the rest Episcopalian, Baptist, Congregationalist, and other denominations.

My roommate is, ah, unique. She's twenty-nine (she obtained an age waiver to get in) and, though she's seemingly smart with a Masters in History, she's sooo insecure! Last night Emma regaled me with her many failures in life. She's tried nursing, teaching, church work, and retailing, but, she says, for the last four years she has been obsessed with getting into the Navy! Why the Navy? And why spend four years only thinking about it! Obviously, serving some "good" purpose is important to her. But, if all those avenues, at least as worthwhile as being in the military, couldn't hold her for longer than a few months at a time... I mean, really! On the other hand, maybe she needs the discipline. Maybe she needs to be forced to stick to a goal for two years.

I wish I were rooming with someone I admired, someone who'd push me to be my best, someone like a new friend, Ensign Billie Baker, who makes me laugh, rather than someone who reminds me of how easy it is to lose direction.

Yet all is not lost — there is Lt. Winters. Talk about pushing me to be my best. Tall, slim, attractive, super-intelligent, and absolutely steeped in military procedures and folklore, she's been a WAVE for six years, and is the WAVE rule book personified.

"Fairfield!" she bellows, and my first reaction is always to look perplexed and say, "My God, what is it? I'm right here; you don't have to shout!"

"YES, MA'AM!" I bellow back. It's a struggle. Once I can learn to shout "Yes, ma'am!" without thinking twice, life will be much easier.

My social life looks pretty bleak, at least until we're in the Officer Indoctrination stage eight weeks from now. (what a terrifying phrase: Officer Indoctrination. It sounds like we're all going to be locked in a closet and brainwashed.) Maybe once I'm commissioned I'll have an opportunity to meet some interesting male officers.

I doubt I'll be able to write often; we're too busy shining shoes, starching and ironing our blindingly white blouses, and accomplishing zillions of other trivial little chores every waking minute of the day that we're not buried under mountains of military books. The list of my classes always makes me laugh; back at Wellesley a typical semester included science, literature, humanities, philosophy. Here my classes are: The Individual and the Navy; The Naval Establishment; Naval Correspondence; Naval History and Seapower; and Ships, Aircraft and Weapons. A real change.

At least the food is tasty, except the tin trays nearly spoil it. Boy, am I whiny. But then, freezing to death rarely brings out my true happy, little self!

Is it cold at home? Hope everything is going well. I miss you.

Love,

Tucker

Three days later from Tucker's journal

7 March 1960, Newport, R.I.

For the record,

Today I suffered through my first dressing down. I was selected as the first company commander, an honor for which, I think, I'm grateful. But, I led my little band of women, snow seeping into our boots and winds whipping our new Navy coats in twenty° weather, to the WRONG gymnasium for drill practice.

How was this plebe-type supposed to know that the drill class gym was across the bridge on Coddington Point, on the male officer candidates' grounds? The only gym I knew about was from high school days here. I thought I was so clever. But I sure felt stupid when Lieutenant Hanley, the Military Director, barked at me for not being more attentive to details. "You should've noticed the gym's building number on the Plan of the Day and called for a bus," she snapped.

She's right of course. I feel like grabbing myself by the arms and shaking myself. How humiliating to mess up my first opportunity to show leadership.

TF

Three days later from Mother

10 March 1960, Washington, D.C.

Dearest Tucker,

Oh, I've missed you! I know you had your own apartment and your own life in Washington, but at least you were here! I knew we could see you every now and then.

But now you're in the Navy — adventure, travel, leadership! You've always gravitated toward those things. Dad and I are proud of you, Tucker. You've already accomplished so much for such a young woman. Sometimes I worry that your strong-headed way of charging toward what you want will land you in trouble, but you are without a doubt your own person. Dad and I support your decisions.

When I voiced my concerns over your joining the Navy, I hope you didn't feel that I was trying to undermine your right to direct your own life. In making life's large decisions, considering both the positives and the negatives is important — the pros and the cons, as Dad says. WAVES, WACS, and WAFS all have a difficult row to hoe. I'm concerned that you'll become disillusioned and lose your femininity in an institution that I know, first hand, is managed entirely by men. You are a lovely young woman and I want you to have the best in life.

But judging from the excitement in your voice when you called last week, you're being enriched, not diminished. And so, I'm excited for you.

I know your schedule is fierce and we won't worry if you don't write. But do call us when you can. Everyone is well. Yes, the cold drags on here as well.

All my love,

Mother

Five days later from Tucker

15 March 1960, Newport, R.I.

Dear Robyn,

Two weeks into the program, and it feels like two months! You wouldn't believe the routine I've been immersed in since reporting for duty in Newport. When I get into trouble with all the military protocol stuff (and that's often), I think of you and laugh. You would have walked out the first day, especially if my bunkmate, OC (that stands for Officer Candidate) Emma Landis, had been your roommie! But then, you would never have put yourself here in the first place.

Emma is as far from the WAVE ideal as anyone can possibly be. She's tall, yet dumpy and wears horn-rimmed glasses. Her first words to me were "I need the bottom bunk; I get seasick, and I fall out of bed at night from high up, so I've got to take the bottom bunk. Besides, I have horrible nightmares and have to pee a lot during the night."

Can you imagine this large woman falling to the deck (new lingo) at 0300 (new time) in the morning, screaming with a nightmare, seasick, and desperate to pee in the bargain? "It's yours," I told her as quickly as possible.

Emma and I are both assigned to the pudgy platoon, a fictitious unit filled with overweight OCs. I need to lose three pounds. Emma has to lose fifteen. Seems she lost thirty pounds to join the Navy and in the process she upset her biological functioning. She calls it her "thermostat problem." When it's cold, she's hot, and vice versa. Her problem affects me directly because it's been freezing in (and out of) the quarters, but she has to keep the windows wide open! Boy, would I love to be able to wear my Wellesley raccoon coat! Do you wear yours?

Our main staff person, Lt. Winters, our Company Officer who's in charge of our academic and military performance here, says every Navy WAVE must always look her best because we are so few. She says we have to be the examples, especially for the enlisted women. Did you know that the Navy has only 5,000 enlisted women and 500 women officers, excluding the medical types? No wonder I hardly ever saw uniformed women on naval bases. You know, I hate to admit it, but this constant emphasis on always being perfect is almost hypnotic. I have such a compulsion for being the best anyway; being pushed even harder than I push myself actually feels good, in a way. On the other hand, when I don't see the reason behind the push, I rebel, which is why I've already logged so many demerits for failing to follow military rules and regulations!

This routine exhausts my body and mind. You know how much I hate getting up early and six o'clock is too damn early for normal humans to start functioning. Sometimes I have to get up in the middle of the night and stand a four-hour watch for the quarters. WOQ #113 must be the most watched-over building in the world!

The class work is easy compared with our college classes, but there's an insane amount of memorization, contrary to the way Wellesley professors wanted us to learn. Still, I'm fascinated by

30

some of the subjects. My favorite classes are Naval History, probably my political science bent, and the Individual and the Navy. I also enjoy our Ships, Aircraft and Weapons course, though I often have a not-too-good feeling that WAVES serve in a separate Navy. We're lectured about the ships and past wars, but in the next sentence we're told that our place is on the shore.

Whenever we sing the song "WAVES of the Navy," a sense of estrangement from the "real" Navy mounts inside me. I picture Navy women on the piers waving goodbye to the men as the destroyers, cruisers, and carriers head out to sea with my classmates and me left home to "man" shore desks. We're seen only as a basis for mobilization, the nucleus, should war break out. The staff emphasizes that WAVES are integrated into the Navy, unlike the WACs in the Army. But I wonder. I wish I could have gone to the Naval Academy, but, of course, they don't admit women.

Speaking of Poli Sci, what's going on in the world? I haven't seen a newspaper in over two weeks. There's a TV in the WOQ lounge, but I have yet to find a single spare moment to watch it. How's Senator Kennedy doing in the campaign? He seems like a strong leader, and one to keep the country focused on what's right rather than just what will satisfy the most people. A *real* leader.

How are you? When I called you last week you seemed a little down about your job at the zoo. Is your boss still driving you crazy? How's your love life? Is Ned still in the picture? Mine (love life) is going to be on hold until graduation, although every now and then I run into a new ensign named Billie Baker who swears that someday she's going to take me out on the town and simply force me to relax and have fun.

By the way, I did learn, after 22 years on this great earth, that I tie my shoelaces backwards and thus my damn bow will never be perpendicular to the shoe, a Navy requirement. One more time my left-handedness puts me at a sort of disadvantage. Lt. Winters figured out why my shoelaces were "unsat" and literally retaught me to tie my shoes. Can you believe it?

All for now. Take good care of yourself.

Love,

Tucker

One week later from Robyn

March 23, 1960, Washington, D.C.

Tucker, my friend!

God, it's good to finally get a letter from you! I've thought about you so much, wondering how it's going, especially after all your initial agonizing. Knowing nothing about military ways (except from novels), I've been looking forward to a real-life description.

Tucker, I don't know if you reread your letter (you probably didn't have time!), but you sure dumped on your poor (apparently) unlovely roommate, Emma. I'm wondering why you focused so much hostility, disguised as humor, on her? Her inadequacies seem to offend you personally. You might be projecting onto her your own concerns of living up to your (and your father's) expectations.

You also seem to find the whole experience different from what you expected. I guess a childhood spent experiencing the Navy as an officer's daughter, a Navy Junior as you say, didn't prepare you for the demand to mindlessly follow military protocol. I can imagine the culture shock of that experience. Your father's Navy is probably still there, you just haven't gotten there yet! Be patient.

And Tucker, here's another incongruity that strikes me about your current life arrangement. The Navy's great emphasis on appearance, your obvious disgust with Emma's, ah, shall we say, unfortunate anatomical heritage, and your instant internalizing of the Divine Lieutenant Stewart's propaganda about setting the example for all those lesser beings (like enlisted women)...Tucker, listen to yourself! Tell me, how does placing a priority on *appearances* gel with your ambitious, intellectual, hard-nosed nature? All our lives we've resisted believing that our appearance should be women's top priority. And now you go into the Navy to make the world safe for democracy, or whatever, and right away the Navy tells you to make your appearance a top priority, *and Tucker, you buy into it instantly!*

You finish with one institution, Wellesley, and go into another; okay. You end a childhood spent living in the Navy and start an adulthood living in the Navy; fine. I guess that's where you are today. But you also think for yourself, Tucker. Being the best doesn't mean internalizing the dogma spouted by the people in power. It means seeing what's good and making it better, seeing what's bad and working to end it. And you are the best, you turkey! Don't lose that.

Whew! Enough. On to other things.

Sorry your social life is no-go for awhile. It's easy to get overwhelmed when you don't have down-time. Mine, though, is escalating. Remember Ned Greeley, whom we met that night in D.C.? I hadn't seen him for quite a while, then suddenly last week he called and asked me to dinner. I agreed, though I'd been mystified and a little hurt when he'd drifted off before. But, since I really liked him, I decided to take the risk.

We ate at Hogates, a seafood restaurant on the waterfront. During dinner we talked a lot. Among other things, Ned explained why he disappeared. If you recall, he had been seeing someone before we met. Our meeting kind of jolted his perception of that relationship. He took a few days off and went home to sort out his feelings. The upshot of his soul searching was goodbye to his old friend, a return to Washington, and a renewal of our getting to know each other. A possible downside — he's just been accepted into the Ph.D. program in psychology at Harvard, and he's going to move to Boston within the next couple of months. So maybe it's not as Serious a Romance as it feels like. Or maybe I just shouldn't let it feel so serious. Long-distance romances aren't fun. I've never had one, but judging from the way I feel when we don't get together every few days, I don't think I'd deal too well with six months between visits. And, of course, how could I go to Massachusetts. My job is here, and I love it.

So, here's the bottom line as far as Ned goes: If he's leaving, should I protect myself from getting too involved with him? On the other hand, I do intend to go back to school and get a social work degree as soon as I save up the money, and I suppose Smith near the Boston area wouldn't be such a bad place to get it. But can I get the money together by next fall? I wonder if a scholarship is out of the question? Lots to sort out.

I did tell you, didn't I, that I'm now a "floating assistant" at the zoo? I'm basically assigned where I'm needed. It might be the bird house one day, the baby animal nursery another, pitching hay to antelopes and gazelles on a third. The whole experience is so different! I love the funkiness of saying "I'm a zoo keeper!" To answer your wistful question, yes, I loll languidly around in my raccoon coat at every opportunity. Speaking of apparel, I saw a movie rerun the other day, *Skirts Ahoy*, with Esther Williams as a sexy WAVE. She wore this navy blue skirt and jacket that fitted her boobs and hips like you wouldn't believe. Is *that* the ideal WAVE, Tucker? I looked at that and simply *knew* the real WAVES don't get uniforms that look as sexy as that. At least, I imagine they don't. Do they?

Well, my friend, you'll soon be one of those elite 500 women in the entire United States who are Navy line officers. I hope you're still happy with your decision...you sounded a little unsure. But, Tuck, I know you. You'll go for those gold stripes. And you'll get 'em.

Keep me posted. I can't wait for the next installment! I know you're short on cash, but an itty-bitty postage stamp won't exactly break you.

Love,

Robyn

Five days later from Tucker's journal

28 March, 1960, Newport, R.I.

For the record,

I'm on the 0400 to 0800 watch, so it's quiet (actually dull!) for a change. But, it gives me a chance to catch up in my journal. We're almost three weeks into the training; in five weeks I become Ensign Fairfield! Hooray!

I still haven't adjusted to so many things. The impersonality of the staff (they're lieutenants, but they act like admirals), their fanatic devotion to the Rules and Regulations (the rest of the Navy can't be as precise), being called by my last name. And I'm still having problems using the phrase "ma'am." I'm overcoming that by reminding myself that its match is "sir." Someday I'll be a "ma'am." It's my Yankee background that flinches at ma'am. I'm not sure I want to be a ma'am.

All in all, if the Navy's intent is for me to feel how it is to be at the bottom of the heap, it's working. It feels crummy and inferior. They say we're learning to follow so that we can learn to lead.

The rest of the group doesn't seem to have trouble adjusting. They seem able to laugh with each other over silly requirements, joke about the idiocy of everything, and still feel as if they're all in this together. I wish I could just relax and be part of the group. Why can't you do that, Fairfield?

Their giggles, their horseplay — it all seems so childish. Even as a child, as a teenager, I never did things like that with my girlfriends. Well, of course, moving so much I rarely had many close girlfriends. But at our age...it's just silly.

So why am I envious?

TF

Four days later from Tucker's journal

1 April, 1960, Newport, R.I.

 For the record,

April Fool's Day! And the joke's on me.

I'm sure part of my mood is that I miss Dad. He always played tricks on us today, but here April Fool's Day is a non-event. Or, maybe it's just that April Fool's Day is every day here at Women Officers' School.

Uh-oh. I'm in an irritable mood.

The staff seems to enjoy putting an inordinate amount of pressure on each of us. I think it's because they want to see if we'll break. I'm not about to break. However, things are getting to me — the regulations, Emma, the memorization — then, there's Ensign Walsh.

I went to do laundry last Saturday. The whole room of machines was "out of order." They were rewiring or something. A sign said we were authorized to use one of the laundry rooms in the BOQ next to WOQ#112.

So I lugged my basket of laundry all the way over to the BOQ.

The laundry room was filled with men doing their wash. I went into complete shock.

My first reaction was something like, "God, I've uncovered some unknown cave where men actually do laundry. I'll pretend I've seen stranger things than this." Even though I hadn't.

I went in and found an unused washer and threw my stuff in.

A blond-haired guy came over and thunked his basket of dirty laundry on my machine. "Here, you can do mine, too, honey!" All the guys in the room laughed.

My face burned. "Sorry, that's not my job," I said sharply.

"Oooo!" the other guys nudged each other, laughing, and their attention fully on me, to see what would happen next, which was exactly what I didn't want them to do. I almost wished I'd just let myself get demerits for not having any clean clothes. "You gonna let her get away with that, Walsh?" one guy hollered.

Ensign Walsh laughed over his shoulder at them, and then turned back to me, putting his hands on the washer on either side of me. "Come on. Be nice," he said, smiling. "I didn't mean to make you mad."

As I studied him, I realized he was attractive, fine-featured and tall. I could see he honestly didn't mean me any harm, but whether he meant to or not he'd humiliated me. I didn't appreciate it. I looked him square in the eye and said, "I'm here to do my laundry, not to play some ego-flattering game with you."

"Oh, God, Walsh!" somebody yelled. "Maybe you should arm-wrestle her!"

"Or kiss her. You know that's all women really need," said somebody else.

Ensign Walsh's face was inches from mine. His blue eyes traveled down to my lips and paused there before glancing quickly up to my eyes as if wondering if I'd deck him if he tried to kiss me. I let my eyes tell him that I was off-limits.

Just then, Jane and a couple of other classmates came into the room with their laundry. "What's this?" she declared, "Romance in the laundry room?"

All of a sudden I hated her. Everyone laughed and Ensign Walsh moved away from me. His buddies slapped him on the back as he wandered over to them. I didn't want any part of them or anybody. I left with as much dignity as I could, but I knew they thought I was retreating in defeat. When I got back to my room I leaned back against the wall, and gritted my teeth to keep tears from coming to my eyes.

If I weren't so exhausted from this God-awful routine they've got us on, I would've been able to deal with Ensign Walsh better. And these stupid, and I mean *stupid* regulations that we must accept and conform to without question. I reject some of the more silly ones, like the one that insists that my "admiral," a blanket at the bottom of my bed, be absolutely perfectly folded. Or that, after I've finished ironing, the cord must be wrapped in a certain way. If I don't do these things just so, I get demerits and gigs.

Everything conspires to make me feel powerless and inferior. I fight that feeling constantly. I resist these damn inane regs so much that so far every Saturday I have pulled Extra Military Instruction. And what do I do there? We're told to sit quietly for two hours and write out *Navy Regulations* word for word. Certainly for those of us who are "bad," a more constructive use of the time would be an assignment that asks questions about *Navy Regs*. The instructors delight in harassing us into making mistakes. And I will never graduate at the top of the class (my original goal) because of my military "performance."

This isn't the Navy I've loved all these years. Or, maybe I love the Navy and hate the dumb rules.

And then there's Emma. She continues to be an enigma. I try to be considerate with her, but her personal behaviors are so aggravating. Example: she cheats in her Pudgy Platoon log. Anyone who cheats about how many calories she's eaten, will likely find ways to cheat on a larger scale. She denies that she cheats even when I catch her in the act!

I wish Billie hadn't gone to her new duty station in D.C. already. I never got a chance to discuss much with her, but she always cheered me up. She seemed like me, and not like me. Her focus is on experiencing life; finding good stories to tell, whereas I *must* explore and make real my potential.

Even though she participates in everything, Billie still has the feel of an outsider. And like it or not, whatever the reason, I'm an outsider too. I wish I could talk to her and ask her. Am I being overly sensitive? Shouldn't I be more forgiving, especially of Emma?

Billie gave me her address. Maybe she wouldn't mind if I wrote her. Will also write my recruiter, Lt. Andy Anderson, and blow off steam.

TF

Two weeks later from Tucker

15 April 1960, Newport, R.I., WOCS, WOQ#113

Dear Robyn,

Hey, my friend, for someone who sends me a letter ranting and raving that I'm buying into society's views of what's important for women, you sure are being quick to think about completely rearranging your *entire* life to suit "your man." I know, you would say, "that's a different story."

Anyway, I can't possibly be buying into too much, or I wouldn't have gotten in so much trouble these last few weeks. Lieutenant Winters (you remember "the Divine Lt. Winters") knocked on my door last night and led me off to a small, sterile room down several passageways in the Women Officers' Quarters. She said in her clipped New England way, "Sit down, Fairfield." I sat down.

As soon as she said the words "military performance," I knew I was in for a keel-hauling. She said I've had a chip on my shoulder ever since I got here. She said I constantly fight the Navy's rules and regulations; she cited how I've pulled Extra Military Instruction every week. She topped this off with the results of our OC peer ratings. Seems that many of my own classmates described me as "aloof."

She said that my holier-than-thou attitude had to go. "Your actions, especially with your classmates, reflect a snobbery that'll get you *nowhere* in the United States Navy, or, for that matter, in life. You have innate leadership qualities, but you aren't exhibiting them with your peers. They see you as unduly standoffish and distant. And so do I."

I don't think I've ever felt so scared and alone. I sat there looking at her icy eyes, hearing her cold words echoing throughout the bare room.

I let the anger rise up and then I put my hands on my knees and leaned forward, looked Lt. Winters straight in the eyes, and said in my calmest, most precise way, "You and my classmates are probably accurate in your perceptions. I don't feel like mixing much with this particular group of individuals, and, with few exceptions, they're not the kind of people I'm accustomed to socializing or working with."

Lt. Winters raised her eyebrows, slitted her eyes, twisted her mouth into the most thorough expression of authoritarian disapproval I've ever seen, and said, "Fairfield, the Navy has been in the training business for many years and knows what kind of procedures and training best obtain results needed to qualify someone to be a naval officer. You seem to be unnecessarily resisting these ways."

At the end of our conversation, Lt. Winters gave me what sounded like an ultimatum: "I'll say this one more time, Fairfield. In the Navy we have a saying, 'Shape up or ship out.' Your peers and the staff members have cited your snobbery. I'm not saying you won't be offered your commission. But your snippy, snobby attitude prevents you from taking the leadership position required to become an outstanding naval officer. You're not God's gift to the Navy. You're dismissed, Fairfield."

God, Robyn. Have I made a mistake in joining the Navy? My background and education seem to add up to a mismatch with the demands for sameness and conformity seemingly for the sake of discipline. Individuality is prohibited. So I am aloof. So I feel more intelligent than many of these people. So I'm a high achiever. I expect the best of myself always. I'm an only child, with "only child" expectations. You and I know the high number of Wellesley women who are either first-born or only children. We tend to be leaders, with followers wanting to follow.

I'll have to think more about why I went from one institution to another, especially since I detest unnecessary rules. Wellesley's rules never seemed to trouble me, perhaps because I thought them to be realistic and essential, with student input. Whether they were or not is another issue.

Okay. Change of subject, as you would say.

Congratulations on your "Serious Romance!" What a thrilling, overwhelming experience it seems to be, the kind we dream of all our lives. I'm so happy for you. Send me a picture and complete resumé, transcripts included. I want to make sure he's good enough for my best friend!

And as to rearranging your entire life to make the relationship work, well, Smith would be a great place to get your MSW. Even though being a zoo keeper is funky and cool, you belong in graduate school. Besides, at the rate I'm going, I'll be needing the intensive services of a professional psychologist right about the time you graduate, and I can't afford the fees. Naval officers aren't supposed to need therapy, anyway. You'll give me a discount, won't you, old friend? Honestly, sometimes I wish we could pop into a clinic for some fast therapy like we can for antibiotics!

Let me know what you decide. Or just write me a chatty letter, I don't care. I swear your letters keep me sane.

Love,

Tucker, the snob

Four days later from Tucker's journal

19 April 1960, Newport, R.I.

 For the record,

A few more days to the commissioning. Mixed feelings about the idea of belonging in the Navy. Two pieces of good news — today in the mail I received a whole case of "Endust." Free! The Navy Exchange had run out, so I wrote to the Endust company, asking them to send a few cans COD. Hooray! Maybe Emma and I can get an "excellent" on our room inspections.

Secondly, I rec'd a cheery letter from Andy, my recruiter. Says she has no doubt I'll come through "in shipshape fashion." According to her, the instructors here have to brainwash us thoroughly enough to last our Navy careers.

She writes about what's behind this training: "All this insanity (Navy life) takes lots of discipline, leadership, and respect. You dish out the first two, and you'll get the third for dessert."

She writes about the Navy as a family: "You'll feel a certain pride to belonging to this great bunch of people, like belonging to a big family, complete with family skeletons. Or, better yet, it's like belonging to a team where everyone is pulling for one thing, our country. Don't you realize you're on the scrub crew?"

Andy says to remember it's only four months and the best is yet to come.

I dunno. Hope she's right.

TF

Same day from Billie

19 April 1960, Arlington, Virginia

Dear Tuck,

Of course OCS is ridiculous! For me it was so absurd, it was hard not to snicker at those straight-as-an-arrow, steely-eyed Lieutenants who were so *serious*. But, I bet even they collapse in giggles at some of the outrageous events we pull after they put us — and you — to bed.

OCS, and other officer training programs, are a way to cull those individuals who probably won't last as naval officers. Yet, there's always an Emma. We had Ethel. We called her Ethel-Dammit. "Ethel-Dammit, fix your tie. Ethel-Dammit, march to the music. Ethel-Dammit." And, OCS is an orientation. What an orientation! I know when we're sitting in our rocking chairs at the Navy Retirement Home, we'll still clearly recall those "OCS moments."

Barely five hours after I arrived at WOCS, I was staring at a metal tray full of eggs, beans, potatoes, and toast. And the Master-at-Arms said I had to eat it all! I quickly learned to shout, "No!" before I got more than I could eat.

When I studied journalism at the University of Tennessee, I found out about tabloid or "yellow" journalism. One of the Chicago tabloids, back in the 20's and 30's, ran a story about an evangelist named Billy Sunday. The headline about Billy's exploits read,"Thousands Jerked to Jesus!" I was reminded of that while at OCS. I was *jerked* into the Navy.

Forget your prior life as a Navy dependent. *This* is how you exist, now. The shoes, the uniforms, the hose, (what kind of steel mesh was that anyhow?), the hoods, the havelocks, and the gloves. The jangle of accents, the diverse backgrounds, the various personalities of classmates. At the same time, it was an awesome, overwhelming experience for a SBV (Southern Baptist Virgin), and I reveled in it! I have no doubt that some of my classmates will be long-time friends.

We had to bond in order to complete OCS. We called ourselves the Navy's Secret Weapon as we huddled together in our havelocks and raincoats around the Base. The stupidity of it all! We rolled

our eyes and grimaced as we learned to sit, stand, go up and down
steps and get in and out of the car "properly and ladylike," put on
makeup, comb our hair, and of course wear the uniform. And the
gigs! for Irish pennants, dust, wrinkles, and things askew. I got a
gig for "rubber askew." That scared me to death, until I learned
that's Navy talk for a rubber band!

We could all handle the academics. But the military side of life
shot down some of us. As you've been experiencing, there are those
who just can't march! You and I, Tuck, marched in high school
bands, and I marched in the UT band. So we know right from left
and the cadence of marching to music. But our class, yours too I
bet, had some klutzes. After the lieutenant on watch had gone to
bed, and the student watch turned her head, we all got out of bed,
went to the student lounge, lined up the klutzes and forced them
to learn to march, "eyes right," "hand salute," and all that stuff!
We had hilarious times! We laughed so hard we cried and peed.
We called ourselves the Rockettes of 113. Ol' Lieutenant Hunter's
eyes fell out of her head when one day all of us executed as one!

We decided, as a class, to have midnight ceremonies as we made
it through various "passages" of OCS life. The most satisfying was
at the end of the first (or enlisted) phase. We all put our hose,
those never-run steel mesh hose with seams, in a box, loaded it
down with rocks, and threw it into Narragansett Bay. I bet they're
there still, because they'll never decompose.

Don't get down on OCS anymore. Get to know your classmates
better. Bonding is essential to your welfare. Have some fun! Keep
in touch, and keep those seams straight!

> Billie

Three days later from Robyn

April 22, 1960, Washington, D.C.

My dear Tucker The Snob,

I've been thinking a lot about you since your letter arrived. I'm
impressed that you're not totally reduced to a shivering, stammering
blob. Lt. Winters sits you down, lists your transgressions, and then
as much as says, "Just what do you think you are doing, you bad
girl?"

The entire episode is denigrating, humiliating, and, I would
guess, counterproductive to mature growth. The interchange is not
a dialogue between two adults. Rather, it's some sort of weird ploy

to disempower the trainee, keep her intimidated, and in the control of the Authority.

Two comments or observations about you as well: One is, you're bucking an institution, The System, and therefore such an attack is not personal. You're wrinkling the smooth fabric of the higher power. Good Grief! If every new entrant exercised her thinking potential, her individuality, her personhood, The Omniscient would lose its total authority! God knows what would happen if you turned into a group of women who really didn't care much if their shoelaces were tied properly. O travesty!

The second comment is still more about *you*. Do you feel these allegations are accurate? Are you the person you are "accused" of being? Do you have "a snippy, snobby" attitude? If you are that person and if you do, is that OK? Do you like who you are? Do you want to change? For you? For the Navy? Would you feel compromised by having to adapt in some ways to fit the Navy's mold?

Maybe you have made a mistake in joining this institution. Maybe you haven't. I don't know.

It's a real dilemma, Tucker, and indeed a major one, since we're talking life's major decisions here. See if you can't find someone, not so totally immersed in the process, but who knows what you're going through. Someone who can help you put things in perspective. (Oh, yeah, sure, right. There are lots of folks like that around.)

Work continues to be both fun and interesting. Where else could I go to work in jeans and snuggle pygmy hippos all day long, though thoughts of getting a degree and a real career tantalize me.

Spring is finally putting in an appearance and the brownish gray landscape is becoming bespeckled with purples, reds, and yellows as crocuses, tulips, and daffodils begin to emerge. Ned and I are doing well!

Be sure to stay in touch. Call collect if necessary.

      Love,

      Robyn

Three days later from Tucker

25 April 1960, Newport, R.I.

Robyn, my friend,

Your letter of 22 April was right on. I needed someone to give me perspective on Lt. Winters' chewing out. I'm weary from lack of sleep. Can't think clearly. Between Emma's snoring and the routine of rising at 0600, I'm tired. Yes, I need to remember I'm fighting a Big System and that much of the response is not to me personally. I told you my mother felt that my personality, my individuality, wouldn't fit readily into the military. That's an understatement. I seem unable to go with the flow and accept stupid policies. I feel as if an institution is trying to beat me down into a little robot spouting "yes, sir" or "yes, ma'am" to its policies and ways. The Navy doesn't believe in individuality.

Your second point is more disturbing: do I fit into this organization? Am I willing to adjust? I don't know. I know I can't imagine compromising my integrity and that I intend to be direct with my bosses and not say "yes, sir" when I disagree (at least until the final order comes down.)

Am I a snob? No more so than the rest of our class of '59. I have a feeling the Navy is rapidly forcing me down in "snippiness" by several large notches. That's okay. My intellectualism and the Navy are not a match made in heaven.

But the Navy does seem to want to drive out individuality, and that concerns me. I only have a two-year obligation, which seems long to me at this moment, and I shall monitor this closely. Hopefully in the field we'll be permitted to state our opinions and be heard, though I doubt if that happens much to junior ensigns. We can't socialize with anyone except each other until after commissioning. I do telephone my parents regularly. My questioning of the WAVES' *raison d'etre* and the Navy's institutional ways aren't the right topics to discuss by phone. Dad told me he didn't know anything about WAVES except those that came across the bows of ships. I think he'd not be disappointed if I dropped out. I sense that he doesn't see any need for women in the Navy. I suspect this is true of most senior officers.

Jane Sanderson and I, numbers one and two in our class, respectively, recommended to Lt. Winters that Emma be asked to leave the Navy. We both feel Emma doesn't meet the Navy's standard for the officer corps. Our recommendation was shot down by the staff. This is likely the first of many experiences in which I, the junior officer, will have to smile and say "yes, ma'am" or "yes, sir." Emma will get her ensign stripes unless she falls on her face in the next two weeks. Must go to classes. Take good care of yourself. What about Ned? How are the tigers and bears?

Love,

Tucker

Four days later from Tucker's journal

29 April 1960, Newport, R.I.

 For the record,

It's the last night before commissioning. I'm lying on my bunk bed pondering my future in the Navy. I may not be able to do this. This is a monumental decision, affecting the rest of my life. Jane Sanderson dropped by my room, and we talked a little. I told her, while trying to tell myself, that I have the self-discipline to make it; but is it what's best for me as a person? Does the Navy really care about WAVES or about women in general? What about a Navy that, as in the song, says, "So carry on for that gallant ship and for every hero brave who will find ashore his man-size chore was done by a Navy WAVE?" What about the Navy that says women are not in the "real Navy?"

Does the Navy care about me, about individuals and their rights? Are Navy leaders cold and formal like all of my instructors? Are Navy educational standards all about rote memory and memorization, without concern for thoughtful analysis?

TF

Later,

I can't believe it. Lt. Winters is a real person! She even wears civilian clothes and earrings. I'm just back from a long talk with her in the Main Lounge. At 2200 I'd been asleep for an hour when I was nudged awake by OC Donovan, saying that I should report to the watch immediately. My first thought was that I'd done something wrong, unknowingly and unintentionally — the story of my OC days. One gig and demerit right after the other.

I raced downstairs. I couldn't believe my eyes. Lt. Winters was standing there in a soft, printed skirt, a silk blouse and mauve cardigan. She wore small, gold earrings. She looked smashing!

She said, "I've heard that you're wavering about putting on the stripe." When she spoke, she looked at me with a softness and warmth that I've seen from her only on rare occasions. This was not the tight, disciplined Lt. Winters. Here sat a lovely woman, not much older than I, who seemed genuinely concerned about my dilemma.

I said I might not take my commission. She said she didn't need for me to go into details. She came because she wanted me to know that I would make a fine officer. She said she knew I'd enjoy the Navy. "The Navy is what you make it. The opportunities are great, and only you can determine which ones to go for."

I decided to be honest. "I need to be challenged intellectually, which hasn't happened so far. I'd like to feel free to express my thoughts about matters important to me and to the Navy. The Navy doesn't seem to encourage this kind of person," I said, with a growing sense of sadness.

Lt. Winters listened. "Haven't there been any positives?" she asked.

Suddenly I realized I'd almost forgotten my reasons for joining in the first place. I felt a rush of excitement about wearing that sharp navy blue uniform.

"I've enjoyed the camaraderie," I said. I told her my biggest reason for continuing would be to contribute to my country and all that it stands for. "Maybe that sounds corny, but that's how I feel."

She didn't think it was corny at all. "You'll find out that most people in the Navy feel that way. Giving one's self to the military is one of the best ways to satisfy an inner need to serve," she said firmly.

She said our meeting tonight reminded her of the scene in *The Sound of Music* between Maria and her Mother Superior. She wanted to give me the same advice the Mother Superior had offered to Maria. "Climb every mountain, Tucker. And, somewhere on the path, I bet you'll find your dream."

TF

Six weeks later from Billie

10 June 1960, Arlington, Virginia

Hey Tuck —

You're almost through! Don't let those relentless instructors get you down. All of your Navy superiors will follow the same set of instructions and regulations in the same hard-nosed fashion as those lieutenants. As far as I can see, they can't or won't do anything else.

Have you been to the Viking Hotel, which is the gathering spot for all the male OC's? They seem to be as tense and anxious as we were, you are, about making it through the sixteen weeks.

I know you're working on your Orders Party. It was great fun for our class to roast the staff officers. As a matter of fact, most of those Lieutenants were nice people and I hoped I would meet them socially, at another level. Like every other aspect of OCS, receiving orders is tense and scary. Everyone was on edge about where they were going. Some were disappointed, some were ecstatic. But most, like me, were puzzled and quizzical. *What* is it and *where* is it? The duty stations alone were mystifying. I have an idea, at least from listening to other officers, both male and female, whom I've since met, awaiting orders will always be an edgy, fearful time at any place of a Navy career. Exciting, huh?

Well, duty calls. Keep your tie tied, your collar smooth, your devices right and your chin up! You asked about my job and where I live. Good and good. I'll tell you next letter!

                    Your friend,

                    Billie

Ten days later from Tucker

20 June 1960, Newport, R.I.

Dear Mother and Dad,

This morning is worth writing about:

The whole class has been practicing for our final drill at the graduation ceremony next week. Today we were in the field to the side of our Women Officers' Quarters. Lt. Winters phoned up to say she'd be delayed by 15 minutes or so. Sandy, our class comedienne, brought out her record player and started playing, or more like *blaring*, her favorite record by "Johnny and the Hurricanes," a wild rock 'n roll group. We tried valiantly to march gracefully and smartly to the tunes. No dice. But were we ever having fun!

Then who should drive down the road in her 1959 snappy sports car and swing into the parking lot but our Company Officer. She was mad! I've never seen Lt. Winters so angry. She chewed us out and said that each one of us was "on report for action unfitting to a naval officer." She said we'd be given extra duty, and as far as she was concerned, we might not even graduate next week.

I must say, the Navy doesn't have much humor. Granted, we were right in the line of vision of senior officers who might be coming in the Main Gate. Senior officers such as you, Dad, who were stationed at the War College. So what? What's a little fun and games after 15 weeks of drudgery.

Robyn and my new friend Billie Baker were right. We could use some happy times in our routine. Andy (my recruiter) told me we were going to have fun. There hasn't been much so far; probably some of my own doing.

Love,

Tucker, the almost graduate

P.S. See you next week. Can hardly wait.

Eight days later from Tucker

28 June 1960, Newport, R.I.

Dear Robyn,

I was so sorry that you couldn't make graduation last week. It was great to have my parents at the ceremony. In the Navy tradition, Dad pinned his old ensign bars on me after graduation. You know I'll cherish them forever. Just think, he's not only my dad, but a war hero supreme, and I'm wearing his bars!

I'm still thrilled at having seen the one woman captain in the whole Navy, the Director of the WAVES. She's attractive and so sharp looking with those four stripes on her sleeves and scrambled eggs on her bucket hat. Was I ever excited to have been selected to be our Company Commander for the ceremony. My heart pounded as I marched the troops past her and gave her an Eyes Right in the Pass-in-Review. Even Emma was in step as we marched by the commanders and captains. Maybe someday there'll be more than one woman captain and I can be among them.

I'm pleased I'll be staying in Newport for duty. I wanted to be stationed with the ships and Navy surrounding me. I don't know many people here, but I'm used to that, and of course some of the staff WOCS officers will hopefully become friends.

Keep the faith and will be in touch. What's happening at the zoo? What about Ned and Boston?

Love,

ENSIGN Fairfield, U.S. Naval Reserve

Ten days later from Tucker's journal

8 July 1960, Newport, R.I.

 For the record,

One of our last requirements is to write a critique of the four months' training. I did that and now I want to write down my thoughts. Someday I may look back on the last four months with fondness and affection.

Are my standards too high? Certainly they were met by my *alma mater*. At the moment I'm angry that I and my classmates didn't learn more about the importance of the Navy and the basics of naval leadership. The staff stressed high standards of how to be squared away in one's demeanor and appearance and the curriculum pushed students to their physical limits, and maybe psychological ones too. Rather, I wanted to be pushed to my intellectual limits and finish with a grasp of the big picture.

I'll have to learn that at my first duty station. They say it doesn't matter what job you're assigned as an ensign. It's really about learning the ropes, how to fit in, and how this big organization runs. Onwards and upwards in my new career!

TF

Chapter Three

The Early Years

Seven days later from Tucker

15 July 1960, Newport, R.I.

Dear Mother and Dad,

I'm now in my apartment, only a few blocks from where we lived five years ago. I'm a little lonesome for company, but not desperate enough to look for a roommate. Your idea of a puppy sounds good. It might be hard for the dog to be alone while I'm at work, but I'd take good care of him the rest of the time.

I didn't realize that it's expensive to merely exist. An ensign makes about $350 per month, and I pay $75 for this apartment. You've always said that naval officers don't stay because of the pay. Now I get it.

The new assignment, Assistant Personnel Officer at the Naval Justice School, demands more than an eight-hour day, but that's okay. The responsibilities (and the authority) are large! I'm the boss for 16 men and women. The Chief looks to me for guidance and direction and seems willing to overlook my silly mistakes and to help me find my own answers. I can see what's behind the saying, "The Chiefs run the Navy." I'm constantly getting lots of OJT. My WOCS training is proving more helpful than I'd expected. My job includes writing the first draft of command personnel instructions and notices, using instructions from on high as the basis. (This task has begun to make me appreciate the rules and regs at WOCS.)

All's well with the Corvair. Feels good to be earning a little money again. I'm definitely using the Commissary and Navy Exchange to stay within my budget.

Take good care of yourselves.

Love,

Tucker

One week later from Tucker

22 July 1960, Newport, R.I.

Dear Billie,

I must write about today. I drove around Seven Mile drive today to see Newport's houses of yesteryear with Lieutenant Jennie Winters, my company officer at WOCS. I feel lucky to have a good number of WAVE officers in the area. It's part of the joy of being in the Navy. On one level we're sort of a sorority. Do you have opportunities to meet women officers in D.C., given your communications watch schedule?

Seems a little funny to be out driving with a lieutenant, especially my former company commander. Reminds me of my days dating male lieutenants and seeing them as regular people. Lt. Winters, I can't yet call her Jennie, could become a good friend. She's witty, attractive, easy to be with, and seemingly genuinely enthusiastic about what I'm doing and thinking. We're moving toward being friends, I think, from being just officer candidate and company officer. Strange but nice, too. Felt good to talk over some of my present job problems.

Unfortunately, my immediate boss, Lt. Barbra Hackenback, has some sort of ongoing sickness and is often unavailable. She's not very approachable anyway.

I'd love to hear about your friends in D.C.

Best,

Tucker

One week later from Billie

30 July 1960, Arlington, Virginia

Tuck, Greetings from BOQ Row —

Bachelor Officers' Quarters (BOQ) Row, Columbia Pike in Arlington, runs from the Pentagon to Bailey's Crossroads. (It could run beyond Bailey's Crossroads, but I haven't ventured that far yet.) Columbia Pike is lined with apartment complexes concentrated for a couple of blocks on either side with the more expensive, plusher apartments at the Pentagon end. Then, halfway down the Pike, the squat two-and three-story apartments, called "garden apartments," stretch toward Bailey's Crossroads. I've yet to see a garden, by the way, just a few trees, some sprigs of grass, and lots of bare earth.

The rather seedy buildings teem with people. The more senior officers, with more money, live in the fancy high-rises, and we junior officers, who can barely make ends meet, live in the "garden apartments." At least a couple of thousand officers, from all service branches, live on or around BOQ Row. How many officers do they need in Washington, anyway? We call our complex Forest Ghetto because every apartment is crammed with people. Four or five civil service workers or secretaries, civil service couples with children and teenagers, and junior officers all squeeze into these one or two-bedroom places. I know this must sound depressing, but it's kind of exciting too.

Jennie Winters wasn't on the staff when I was at WOCS. Glad you're finding some women officer friends to bum around with. Oodles are stationed here, as I say, including my two roomies, Niki Simon and Tot Brohm, from my OCS class.

So far, this Navy is good.

Niki, Tot, and I come from homes where everything was done for us — moms and dads who guided our everyday lives and made the decisions, both big and small.

Now we're on our own, facing challenges of existence. Like grocery shopping and cooking. Yuk! We can't buy anything that doesn't come out of a can. We can buy toilet paper and soap without problems, but we just stare at the chicken and roast beef and dream. I can make tuna sandwiches, I learned from helping my mom get ready for her bridge club. And cole slaw. Tot can do waffles and pancakes; Niki can open a can of tomato soup and make grilled cheese sandwiches. It's the details we can't remember, you know, salt, pepper, other spices, cooking oil, even butter. We open the refrigerator or the cabinet and expect everything to be there. How do our moms do it?

BOQ Row is full of delis, liquor stores, restaurants, bars, strip malls, laundromats, drug stores, and grocery stores. Everything a little apartment dweller desires or needs. Niki, Tot and I have found The Red Rooster, a neighborhood bar and grill, owned and operated by a woman named Louise. We call it Louise's Place. At the end of every pay period, when we're strapped for money, we go down to Louise's Place. Louise cooks what I call "Mommy Food" — mashed potatoes, gravy, pot roast, stew, etc. We pool our money and buy a platter of "Mommy Food."

Many women officers live in the Ghetto, and we get together frequently at each others' apartments and really enjoy ourselves! Many talented women. The Armed Services are *very* lucky! Pianists, guitarists, beautiful voices — we *know* we're good! It's a cheap way to socialize and talk about the various jobs we perform (great learning process). For a Southern Baptist Virgin, and the only drummer in the group, it's exciting!

Oh, I gotta mention the three Army second lieutenants (male) who live across the hall from us. Stan, Mike, and Pete are part of the Tomb of the Unknown Soldier guard detail at Arlington Cemetery. So they're the same height and weight, and have *absolutely* the same short buzz top haircut, and they're hilarious. For days (and early evenings) we heard pounding coming from their apartment. Finally, Tot pounded on their door to see what was what. She came back in hysterics and said, "You gotta meet with these guys, and see what they've done." They had taken Falstaff beer cans, cut out the tops and bottoms, cut down one side, pounded them flat, put holes in the top, and hung them on their windows as cafe curtains. Plus, they have footballs, basketballs, volleyballs, workout equipment, a kayak, bicycles, baseball and softball stuff, tennis racquets, and fishing poles — stacked all over the place. In addition they can grill steaks and make a salad!

Must be hard for you, Tuck, not to have roomies to share expenses and cruise boxes!

Gotta go. All about "the job" next time. Come visit whenever you can. Happy WAVES' Birthday!

Billie

One month later from Tucker's journal

31 August 1960, Newport, R.I.

 For the record,

Today will forever be engraved in my mind. The Executive Officer, Captain Jefferson, called me into his office and gave me a royal chewing out about my stupidity and carelessness.

Among my many collateral duties, I'm Officer-in-Charge of the Reserve Officers' Clambake which was held last weekend at the O'

Club. Two hundred or more officers and their guests attended. This was a mountainous job, and I was proud of my role in the "successful" clambake.

Until this morning.

I neglected to set up a proper accountability method, registering who paid for their meals. The net result? The O' Club is short $350, and they want it. Where is it?

As Captain Jefferson spoke to me, his face reddened with every word. I felt as though I had sunk through the floor.

"I expect you to get the $350 from the Reservists within three days or you'll pay the Club with your own money," he barked.

What money? I'm living from month-to-month and barely making it. I'll have to take out a loan.

Then I did what I'm never supposed to do — I cried on the job. I shed only a few tears, but that was too many. Women officers must not cry on duty. Male officers don't cry, so why should we? I've never had a crying problem, but the situation took over. Not only do I not have the money, but I realized this incident would likely be a black mark on my Fitness Report. And I was doing so well.

As I dabbed my eyes, Captain Jefferson began relating the tale of Little Abie.

Once upon a time, Little Abie got himself stuck up in a tree, about eight feet up. He couldn't get down by himself. He cried. His daddy came to the rescue. His daddy told Little Abie to jump and that he would catch Little Abie. Little Abie was happy and jumped.

Captain Jefferson was obviously enjoying the tale. His eyes lit up with glee.

"But just then," said the Captain, "his daddy stepped aside and let Little Abie fall hard onto the ground, bruising himself badly. Little Abie, stunned and shocked, looked up in dismay. His daddy said, 'Let that be a lesson to you, my son, never trust anyone, not even your own father.' "

He gave me an amused smirk. "Take that story in and don't ever forget it, Ensign. You trusted the reservists and got burned by $350. Never trust anyone, not even good naval officers."

I shall not cry again in my career. I shall go to the Reserve Program's senior officer tomorrow and ask for help. I was raised to trust people, unless I'm otherwise notified. Continue to trust people, Fairfield.

TF

One day later from Billie

1 September 1960, Arlington, Virginia

Dear Tuck,

The Pentagon is huge with thousands of people, and I'm convinced no one, no matter how senior, knows a fraction of what goes on here! They wouldn't want to, either.

Hey, I won a medal. I'm an expert sharpshooter! I scored on 48 out of 50 rounds with my .45 "ace," the gun I carry as I make my delivery rounds outside of the Pentagon. Now you wonder what the heck I do.

I'm assigned as a Communications Watch Officer for the CNO and work in an enclosed area right across the hall, oops, passageway, from another 24-hour area called "Flagplot." Tot and I are the only women in our five-officer watch section, plus 38 enlisted men, including a chief petty officer. I have two collateral duties, Division Officer and "Horse" Officer. You probably recognize Division Officer; a "Horse" is a Multilith Press. We have two to reproduce messages. When both are going they sound like horses pulling a stagecoach. I'm the "Horse" Officer because I opened my mouth and announced that I can make mats, ink drums, and set the speed. Now, I've learned the first military rule: If you volunteer, you're "it."

They sent Tot and me to school to learn to encrypt and decrypt messages, and that's what I do. Only officers can encrypt and decrypt Top Secret and various Top Secret compartmentalized messages which represent need-to-know categories. I also deliver messages, personally, to the CNO, the VCNO and SecNav, and all those Deputy and Assistant SecNavs. After we decrypt, we reproduce the messages, every copy accounted for, and then the Flagplot captain assigns them to leather folders for delivery. The CNO uses red ink, and makes notations on the messages for the Flagplot captain, noting actions to take or replies to the messages. I estimate at *least* five miles a watch and I'm down to 98 pounds.

If the message references another message, we attach the reference. Repetitive stuff. I also deliver messages to the White House, the State Department, and an ugly old building called Main Navy. When I make these outside deliveries, I have a car and a driver, and I must wear a gun. Trouble is, the belts are too big and if I don't hang onto the belt, it falls around my ankles. Some quick-draw guard I am!

Tot and I stand nine straight watches — three days from 0630 to 1530; three "eves" from 1530 to 2330; and three "mids" from

2330 to 0630. Then we have 72 hours off. This kind of alienated Niki, because she's a "day worker," with normal hours and weekends off. Our 72 hours rarely fall on a weekend. So Niki has found friends who have hours similar to hers and she leaves notes to say she's here or there.

On the Sunday day watches, I deliver the CNO's weekend message traffic to his quarters at the Naval Observatory on Massachusetts Avenue after it's been screened by the Flagplot captain. I have breakfast with the CNO and his wife, lovely people who treat me as an honored guest. One Sunday the CNO asked me if I knew anything about the WAVES' Chorus. Seems he was hosting an outdoor reception for some visiting Royal Navy bigwigs with the British Embassy and he wanted an all-American affair. He thought it would be ideal if the WAVES' Chorus performed, and by the way, he wanted me to attend in White Dress uniform.

So, the WAVES' Chorus and I showed up for the party. It was beautiful — paper lanterns hanging from the trees, ice sculptures, wonderful food, and the Navy Band playing in the background. The CNO took me by the arm and introduced me to congressmen, admirals, and the RN officers. I guess he sort of showed me off. As the WAVES' Chorus performed, I stood on the side and watched those admirals and I had a disturbing thought: Those guys with the gold up their elbows think of women in the Navy as a novelty — cotton candy, a side show, and we, the women, are *never* going to make it to the Big Top, let alone star in the three rings. Despite the ruffles and flourishes, they're little boys playing with huge toys in their private club house. And it's got a big sign that says, "No Girls Allowed."

Tuck, I think we ought to try and meet somewhere, maybe New York. That's halfway for both of us. A sorority sister lives in an apartment in the upper east Seventies in Manhattan (she's a school teacher), and we can stay with her. There's an hourly shuttle that flies from Washington to La Guardia, and if I wear my uniform it's only $9. We can meet at Penn Station. What do you think? Money's tight, but we need to play. My next weekend with 72 hours off is in September.

Your letter sounded more upbeat. And your orders leave you in Newport! Even though Little Rhoadey is Yankee-land, it's beautiful. Oh, did I tell you Lt. Hunter invited me over to her apartment for dinner after I finished OCS? She's great! So were the other women officers there. See, they're human after all! Be sure and tell me what kinds of jobs ensigns do in Newport.

Your friend,

Billie

Six days later from Tucker

7 September 1960, Newport, R.I.

Dear Mother and Dad,

My life's been full — of work and play. The job presents challenges and fear. At times it feels like I need more advanced training, especially in Personnel Management. The Navy prides itself in OJT. I guess with the high turnover of personnel, tours being no longer than two-to-three years, everyone has to learn fast.

Last week, because of a mistake by me, the command was short $350 when it came to paying the O' Club for a big Clambake. That's the bad news. The good news is that through coordination with the senior reservists, all the money was collected within two days. Trials and tribulations of a junior officer!

Speaking of JO's, have I told you of my auditing responsibilities at the O' Club? As I experience my duties, my collateral ones consume more time than my regular duties. I spend almost a whole day at the beginning of each month inventorying bottles and cigarettes! What a waste of time. On the other hand, someone has to do it, and for now I'm on the Auditing Committee for the Wine Mess. Naval officers drink a lot of liquor!

Newport's so-called summer cottages have become my favorite visiting sights. Cornelius Vanderbilt must have had great fun living in The Breakers, one of the more famous cottages, if you remember. When I'm feeling low, I get in the Corvair, drive around town, and then out to Seven Mile Drive and Fort Adams. Still much wealth here.

All for now. Glad to hear from you via phone.

Love,

Tucker

Two months later from Tucker's journal

15 November 1960, Newport, R.I.

 For the record,

In recent weeks, Lt. Winters — Jennie — and I have been having fun getting to know each other, as well as touring around this seafaring town and environs. But that has come to an abrupt end.

We were sitting out on the rocks overlooking the Atlantic, off Seven Mile Drive. After steeling myself, I said, "Perhaps sometime the two of us could be roommates. I've been having a real struggle in paying my bills and still having money for playing. At the same time, I've been feeling strong connections to you on a deeper level than just a good friend."

Jennie shut down, but I blundered on anyway. "You're someone I'd like to spend evenings with, on a regular basis, though I know your job demands more time than mine, so you wouldn't have that much play time except on the weekends."

After a long pause, Jennie stood up and began walking toward the car. Something was terribly wrong. I followed her. She started to cry. Suddenly she seemed to take charge of herself, shifting into some other person, similar to the cool, aloof WOCS instructor who had chewed me out many months ago. What was wrong? I hadn't thought my idea was so inappropriate.

She then took my hand, looked at me with those wonderful hazel eyes, and said, "It wouldn't work if we were to live together as roommates. I have had a brief relationship with a woman and right this very moment I'm attracted to you, Tucker. One thing would lead to another with us and we wouldn't be just friends, we would become involved in a relationship, a sexual relationship."

I gathered myself together and I told her I had *no thought* in my head about becoming involved in a sexual relationship. My ideas about her involved friendship and sharing expenses. That was all.

Jennie told me I was naive, though, knowing me, that was understandable. My innocence is one of the reasons she's attracted to me. She continued about herself, "While my former relationship was wonderful on many levels, I don't wish to deal with the pressures of being with a woman. Someday I hope to marry and have children."

As an afterthought, she declared, "To live as a homosexual person in the military drives one towards schizophrenia or paranoia and I strongly advise against it, Tucker."

I went into shock. We drove back to her apartment without speaking. We parted with brisk "good afternoons." I almost added, "Ma'am."

I have no idea what will happen with Jennie and me. I just know I'll miss her sharing her thoughts and time.

I've never really thought of myself as a lesbian, or a heterosexual or a bisexual. I'll have to feel out what these things really mean to me. I feel extremely lonely.

I'm scared.

TF

Two months later from Tucker

14 January 1961, Newport, R.I.

Dear Mother and Dad,

What a nice leave I had with you!

Given our discussions about politics, I'm enclosing a letter I wrote last week to the Commandant in Boston. Subject... "Fighting the Cold War."

The Commandant had asked all naval personnel in the District to send him ideas for ways and means by which the Navy can better carry out its responsibilities in fighting the Cold War. He believes the communists' goal is to dominate the world.

As you'll read, I divided my responses into two areas, Problems and Actions. The problems, to my mind, include lack of understanding of and concern for the communist threat; lack of knowledge; lack of actions; and lack of guidelines for the Navy man, both officer and enlisted. As appropriate action, I feel a District newsletter could be vital. We could convince personnel that the freedom and spirit of man can conquer the strong ideology of Communism. They need to understand the present Soviet goal of peaceful coexistence is unconditional economic surrender by the Western World. Also, submission of papers on communism/ democracy by personnel could be a positive action.

Remember how I struggled with my college course, the Soviet Union and its Ideology? The insights I gained there helped me draft the letter. The Soviet public doesn't understand what Karl Marx, Lenin, and Stalin had in mind — too complex for them to grasp. Democracy is much easier. Jefferson and Hamilton had it right!

Hope you weren't too bored with the above. Soviet Communism isn't too far off from Japanese Imperialism, eh, Dad?

I love my little poodle puppy, Gabby. He trained me to put my shoes away faster than I trained him to put all of his feet on the newspaper. I'm also dating several junior officers. Nothing serious, but lots of fun. Take care of yourselves.

Love,

Tucker

Three days later from Tucker

17 January 1961, Newport, R.I.

Dear Robyn,

Had a ball in Boston last weekend. We even got to Durgin Park. Remember the first time we went as freshmen and I absentmindedly sprinkled LOTS of tobasco sauce on the shrimp cocktail? I'll never forget when the waiters came running over after I screamed "Water, water!" This time I splurged on lobster, though dissecting one in Biology 100 — lungs, roe and all — still puts me off. The price is incredibly low off the wharfs in Newport. Even I can afford one occasionally.

Enjoyed our discussion about the the Cold War. You seemed mildly interested in the subject, so I'm enclosing a copy of my letter to the Commandant. I know you were a zoology major and don't follow the Soviets as I have over the years. But I think you should know about their shenanigans, which are really an international conspiracy. Tell me what you think of my letter and its recommendations.

Interesting talk we had about sexuality. I barely ever hear the term lesbian used. In the Navy, lesbianism is as bad as communism or imperialism. The only good "isms" I can think of are socialism and capitalism.

Glad to see you so happy with your job. You're probably learning a lot from the animals that could tell me about the behaviors of the people I work with!

Stay in touch and don't work too hard.

Love,

Tucker

One week later from Mother and Dad

24 January 1961, Washington, D.C.

Dear Tucker,

Your mother and I enjoyed reading your letter to COMONE. I've never known a Commandant to put before a District such an abstract request. We should assume his request was aimed at the officers in the District, although you did say "all naval personnel."

I'll bet a high percentage of naval officers in the First District can discuss with you the meanings of democracy, communism, and their differences...maybe not in the abstract textbook language you learned at Wellesley, but in ways that make sense to them. They might be comfortable saying the major difference is in how resources are used for the good of the individual in a democracy and for the good of the whole (government) in the USSR. Simplistic, you say. Certainly. But this expresses the fundamental difference on which our constitutional democracy is based.

Your mother and I are more hopeful than are you that the strength of individual support for a democratic state will remain superior to the top-heavy supervision required in a Communistic state. We think democracy is the stronger system, and has really little to do but mature and defend its system when necessary. In every wardroom I've seen there's always some pretty deep discussion of "this war for the minds of humanity" that you mention. It's usually couched in terms of weapons to defend against those who might try to change beliefs, but the chitchat is not about weapons for the sake of weapons.

Enough of this philosophizing. We're just chiding you a little for being so serious and idealistic. Maybe you need a break from that tower of intellect you live in. Come on home for a visit and I'll take you sailing.

We love you.

Mother and Dad

Three weeks later from Robyn

February 20, 1961, Boston, Massachusetts

Dear Tucker,

It *was* fun to have you here in Boston and to really catch up. I think it's a tribute to our friendship that each time we get together we can pick right up, though our lives, at least professionally, have taken such different directions.

I still can't believe you chose the Navy. None of our classmates would consider that path. Then again, ninety-eight percent of them seem set on finding a husband and having children, with their career taking a backseat. A Navy woman cannot have children if she's on active duty. Right?

Your letter to the Commandant is well-organized, thoughtful, and well-written. No surprise, you're always articulate and able to analyze political situations of all sorts. I just come at this whole life from another angle. You seem to be intensely involved with goal-directed stuff. I might be, if I knew what I want to do with my professional life. Sometimes I think we have too many choices in our capitalistic system. You've made it easier on yourself in one sense in that you're locked in for at least two years to a structured sort of subculture.

As I said when you were here, I made the right decision to go back to school, but I do miss the soulful eyes of orphaned wallabies in the zoo nursery. Anyway, time permitting, let's get together again. Soon! Ned sends his love.

Love,

Robyn

Five days later from Tucker's journal

25 February 1961, Newport, R.I.

For the record,

This afternoon's major event will forever stand out above all others. I'm still steaming. This morning the intelligence folks, ONI, called me. They wanted me to sit in on an interrogation of one of my young enlisted women in the afternoon. The command's Women's Representative is required to be present during any agents' questioning of enlisted women.

An uneasy energy pervaded the whole afternoon's episode. Seaman Apprentice Brown, one of my best workers and a young, farm girl type, was put through hell by two ONI agents. The underlying motive for their pressuring and almost psychological torturing — accusation of homosexuality. They told me she'd been caught in the barracks engaging in sexual acts with another woman, a senior petty officer. The senior WAVE had been discovered in this situation before and is on her way out of the Navy. Young and inexperienced Seaman Brown knew better, they said, and should be discharged.

They pressed her to the point that she began to sob. At this point, I said, "Ease up on her, guys, right now."

"Before Seaman Apprentice Brown leaves the Navy, we want the names of all other lesbians she knows," said Special Agent Windom. What bothered me most was the viciousness of these agents. Agent Windom seemed particularly evil in intent. He yelled, "Seaman Brown, we want names, *now*." I was appalled.

"Cool it," I snapped. "Seaman Brown is one of my best workers.

This is no way to treat any sailor, male or female." Windom stopped yelling, and Brown stopped sobbing.

After the agents left and I'd dismissed Seaman Brown to her barracks, I spoke with my Commanding Officer. I said, "I recommend Seaman Brown be given a warning and remain on active duty." He vehemently disagreed.

Seaman Brown will be discharged next week for homosexuality. How sad for her *and* for the Navy. She did violate the rules; however, there has to be a better way to handle these cases. She's currently serving as Sailor of the Quarter for the entire Base. Yet she was treated as a dirty, sordid person.

This day is memorable for me for another reason. This date is my Pay Entry Base Date, the day I raised my right hand and swore to defend the Constitution against all enemies, foreign and domestic. (Today those agents felt like domestic enemies!)

This week I had coffee with Bill and played tennis with Steve. Nothing serious.

If ever another homosexuality interrogation happens on my watch, I mustn't be so incredulous. I know agents can be rough during their interrogations. They are, after all, intelligence agents acting on behalf of the U.S. Navy. They have no right, though, to treat Brown so cruelly. It's as if she were their enemy.

Doesn't make sense. But then, I have trouble with other rules and regulations of this wonderful, but sometimes weird, organization. If there's a next time, Fairfield, be more authoritative and don't let them bully anybody.

Having experienced today's grueling experience, I understand why Jennie wants to be with men. I've never thought *not* to be with men. And if a woman wants to live a happy life without fear of agents breathing down her neck, lesbianism is the absolute wrong course to pursue. I definitely will continue to date men and look for Mr. Right before too many years pass me by. But so far I'm not sexually attracted to any of them. Will keep looking. It's hard to believe I've been in a whole year. Am having a ball learning to be a professional naval officer. There's even time for playing and relaxation.

I still can't let go of Jennie and her specialness. She's in my thoughts a lot, but I don't see her very much. Let go and move on, Fairfield. Soul mates meet more than once in a lifetime.

TF

Ten months later from Tucker's journal

Christmas Day 1961, Newport, R.I.

 For the record,

It's a different holiday. For the first time ever I'm having Christmas alone. Because the family is overseas, I'm taking no leave and am doing Christmas with some of my single friends. Strange not to be with family. But I'm an adult. Time to make my own way, wherever that takes me.

My detailer, Commander Hastings, after many iterations, is canceling my orders to the Pentagon. She's sending me to Recruiting Duty instead. Guidance from our WAVE Director states that the best performing WAVES should be sent to "W" billets as part of our career paths. "W" billets include duty at Newport (WOCS) and Bainbridge (Boot Camp), and recruiting duty. The WAVES' supposed *raison d'etre* in mobilization gives credibility to these types of billets.

When CDR Hastings told me I was going to Recruiting Duty in March, I said I'd prefer that my "W" billet be WOCS. "Besides," I quipped, "I'm still a reserve officer and haven't decided whether to go Regular Navy. How can I recruit others if I'm still a reservist in limbo?"

She retorted, "Recruiting duty will either make or break your decision to go regular, won't it, Miss Fairfield? Anyway, we need you in Philadelphia."

Needs of the service, Fairfield.

I can barely imagine living in a big city and being so far from the Navy and Navy friends. Feels scary. What have I gotten myself into? Maybe I should resign. On the other hand, it sounds like a challenging job, with considerable traveling.

I feel alone. What about leaving my friends here in Newport? So many times as a Navy Junior I've said goodbye to best friends. Why doesn't it get easier? The extended family the Navy engenders is the only good part of goodbyes, or alohas. Wherever we go, rules and regulations are the same, and eventually we're stationed with military members from previous duty stations. It's going to take a while for that to happen for me.

Lots to contemplate. Orders are orders, as Dad would say. Not much control by the individual as to duty station assignment, is there? For someone who likes to be in control, Fairfield, you've picked the wrong organization.

Merry Christmas and Happy New Year!

TF

Four months later from Tucker

7 May 1962, Philadelphia, Pennsylvania

Dear Mother and Dad,

It's strange to go to work in a Navy uniform in downtown Philadelphia. I didn't join the Navy to take buses and trolleys and subways to work. Where are the ships? Where's the water? All the male officers at the Station report to work in civvies and change at the command. Seems wrong, but the commanding officer allows it. Part of being a recruiter is wearing the uniform with pride and respect wherever I am. So, I wear the Navy blue to and from work, subways and all. People stare at me. Oftentimes they ask, "What airline are you with?" Sad that the U.S. Navy's uniform isn't recognizable by every citizen. But, then, we have so few women officers. I'll continue to wear the uniform wherever I go. In fact I don't have much choice because of my minimal civilian wardrobe and tight budget.

My apartment is not as large as Newport's, but on LT(jg)'s pay I can only afford a studio. Though small, it's adequate, and has a helpful landlord. The neighborhood's a bit on the low side. That several WAVE officers occupy the same complex made my decision.

I do miss Newport, the Navy, my friends, *and* you. Good thing this job looks to be a challenge, especially in the public speaking arena.

One of my men friends is in town with his ship, our new nuclear powered cruiser, the *Long Beach*, in overhaul at the shipyard. Feels good to know at least one person from my previous duty station. We're going out this weekend.

You seem far away, and you are! But as long as you're well and life is happy for you, I shan't worry. It's hard waiting so long for the mails to make their way across the continents. But at least we're not at war, you're not separated, and you're reasonably safe overseas. How arduous it must have been to endure long, long separations and stresses.

Don't worry about me. I'm happy in the job and will travel to friends as I can. Newport and D.C. are fairly close to Philly.

All for now. Glad you're having good times in *Bella Napoli*. Take good care of yourselves.

Love,

Tucker

P.S. Dad, what did you think about that first live Polaris missile launched underneath the ocean by the Ethan Allen yesterday? Major event for the use of a sub as a strategic weapon!

Two weeks later from Mother and Dad

21 May 1962, Naples, Italy

Dear Tucker,

I remember a time during the War when I was home on leave and took your mother to a nice restaurant. I was standing, in uniform, in the foyer waiting for her to powder her nose, or whatever it is that takes so long when ladies disappear in a restaurant, when a nicely dressed lady said quite politely, "Can you arrange to have the car parked?" Obviously she thought I was the doorman. I've often thought about that — how, even in wartime, our general populace is shielded from the tough stuff. We've never had to fight on our own shores except during the Civil War, so even with the full mobilization we had in WWII, many weren't affected directly and went their own ways.

I understand your annoyance when those you seek to protect don't even recognize you for what you do. "For it's Tommy this, an' Tommy that, an' 'Chuck 'im out, the brute!' But it's 'Savior of 'is country' when the guns begin to shoot." Rudyard Kipling had it right, and you may as well learn to live with it. Of course you can use such occasions to do a little educating, as I imagine you do.

I wouldn't worry too much about the lack of warm winds and following seas. That may come soon enough. This recruiting business seems the hub of the wheel to me. If we cannot attract good people, the cost of training goes way up, and you're so right, Tucker, in seeing that duty in times of peace is so much less stressful than long separations during war when even the mails are irregular.

Your mother and I are in good shape, enjoying life and very proud of you. You sound as though you find the commitment to the Navy satisfying and may want to make it a permanent thing. That surprises us a bit. We thought you would get this out of your system and return to graduate school before marrying or taking a high paying job with a corporation that needs a good analyst or researcher. With your energy, I imagine you can run a family as well as a company.

You do have more ideas than most, you know. The Navy may not always be the best place to air them, for the customs of the service are difficult to change. I don't mean that opportunities for original thought don't exist; actually those opportunities are plentiful. But they have to be expressed using the code, the vernacular, the system of the Navy. And following someone else's method is sometimes not easy for you.

If you're still in Philadelphia when we get back in the States, maybe we could come for a visit and get the grand tour. You'll be pretty familiar with the place by then. Take care of yourself, claim some time for your own and watch out for those "eligible bachelors," if you find any.

> Love you.

> Mother and Dad

Four months later from Billie

> *1 October 1962, Arlington, Virginia*

Dear Tuck —

Now I know why the Pentagon is called the Puzzle Palace. Do you realize that women in the Navy have our own separate chain of command? Not only do these guys think we're a side show, they're afraid to talk to us! I'm flabbergasted. All the male officers on my watch were called in by the Captain, our boss, to discuss their future in the Navy. But Tot and I had to go down to another office and talk to a female Lieutenant Commander whom I've never laid eyes on before! Now *this* is a puzzle!

Anyway, Tot is going to get out of the Navy. She's eager to go back to school, get her Masters, and resume teaching. I, however, can't think of a thing in Tennessee that I want to go back to (yet), so I'm willing to check out another tour.

Despite the terrible hours we work, and the fact that there's a "no leave" policy, I've had fun. Managed to explore Washington and its environs, Baltimore, New York, and Boston. Not bad for a kid from the hills.

Bainbridge was fun, wasn't it? And hey! You're a pretty good tennis player! You creamed that Lieutenant who thought he was so good! Hadn't realized you were in the All-Navy Tennis finals this year.

I think it's absolutely elegant that the Women Officers' Quarters in Bainbridge are not only delightfully old-fashioned in architectural style and turn-of-the-century furniture, but that orange juice, coffee, and sweet rolls appear outside your door every morning! I thought we were really vacationing, didn't you?

I've just received, finally, my orders! Navy Supply Command, Pearl Harbor! My dad can't believe it! First, however, I go to a two-month course called Industrial Security, put on by the Department of Defense at a place in Alexandria called Cameron Station. I don't leave for Hawaii until late February '63. So come on down before I head out. And of course you have an invitation to visit me in Pearl anytime.

I deal with a Captain in SECNAV's office named Buckingham, who says he knows you. We message deliverers have to be familiar to the aides so that they'll recognize us when we have to go to the "inner sanctum."

See you,

Billie

Three weeks later from Tucker's journal

23 October 1962, Philadelphia, Pennsylvania

 For the record,

I'm a little frightened at the moment. Several incidents combined to give me pause. One was on the job, earlier this week. I was driving an official Navy car in Harrisburg and the front end began to spew out steam. I pulled over at the nearest gas station only to learn the radiator was shot. This is the second Navy car incident within the month for me. The first time, the car's brakes gave out in the middle of heavy downtown Philadelphia traffic, with three women Officer Candidate selectees in the back seat! I was terrified.

I'm fed up with our car deal at the Station. Cars are essential for recruiters. When we complain, the commanding officer says we don't have enough money to keep the cars in the best repair. "No preventive maintenance," he says, "just crisis maintenance. The money is reallocated for the fleet, especially nuclear subs."

I understand the need for supporting the fleet as our first line of defense, but when it comes to real personal risk and physical security, I draw the line. My CO says the fleet must come first at all costs. Shore activities get what's left over. Since I'll never go to sea, because of the "combat exclusion law" for women, I'll never be where the money is and where sailors get first-class treatment.

I can't believe we don't have enough money for pencils! They say the Democrats (Kennedy *et al.*) don't care about the defense budget, unlike Republicans who always support us. I don't know. Yesterday I brought my own packet of pencils to work. Sometimes our government screws up its priorities. I'm a Kennedy fan, but...

The other events are closer to home. Last week someone broke into my apartment. I lost only $25, but it's the violation that matters. This isn't the best section of the city, but it's all I can afford. Also, yesterday I was walking Gabby when this scruffy guy exposed himself and came on to me. I raised my billy club at this idiot. Gabby barked but he's too small to scare anybody. The jerk didn't follow me. What to do?

I don't want to seem melodramatic, but I don't like the idea of burglars and perverts running around outside my home. I'm ready to go back to Newport.

Juxtaposed with the President's announcement yesterday authorizing a naval blockade of Cuba, these events seem minor. Real scary stuff down there.

The Navy turned down Emma Landis for Regular Navy, so she'll be leaving soon. May she find happiness and a will to succeed. I still think she represents my shadow side.

Think I'll call Robyn and invite her to the Army-Navy game.

TF

Ten weeks later from Billie

3 January 1963, Arlington, Virginia

Dear Tuck —

Hoo Boy! I don't know if I ever want to be on Recruiting Duty! Sounds like long, lonesome hours. Is that a ticket that all sharp women officers have to punch? Guess not, cause there's Bainbridge and Newport "W" duty as well. Anyway, it was good to see you again. Weren't you impressed with our Early American Bus Station apartment?

I'm three weeks into the Industrial Security School. I'm told I will be a Fire Marshal and a Police Chief in Pearl. I'm certainly learning about equipment, trucks, cars, radios, personnel, in addition to stake outs, interrogations, and combustible materials. I'm the only woman in the class. But my grades, so far, are as good as some and better than others. Everything is "plant." Plant facilities, equipment, buildings, materials. I hope Supply Center, Pearl, already has these plant things clearly delineated!

So far, the Navy is *good*.

If I don't see you before I leave, I'll be aloha-ing you from Hawaii! If I remember correctly, you went to school at Pearl Harbor Elementary, in quonset huts and all.

I'll try to send a note beforehand from San Fran.

See you,

Billie

Three months later from Tucker

10 April 1963, Philadelphia, Pennsylvania

Dear Mother and Dad,

The national news is frightening. *Thresher*, one of our SSNs, sank today, with 129 men aboard. Mother always says, "To live without risk is not to live at all." You're right, Mother, but our submariners go several steps beyond the norm. They deserve every bit of their sub pay!

Every week for the next three months, I'll be spending one or two days of the weekend driving out and about in the cities and countrysides to review parades, mostly in small towns. When we joined the Navy, we were told that we're "on duty 24 hours a day." In Newport I didn't get what this meant. But I do now. My schedule during the academic year (September–May) puts me on the road from Monday 0630 to late Thursday. Friday I catch up on correspondence and my applicants' files and general administrative duties.

During my away time, Gabby stays with a neighbor, another WAVE officer.

During parade season, I attend parades and give PR speeches. At night I often lie awake watching multi-colored fire engines pass by. I don't get to relax enough, but I enjoy the responsibilities. Sometimes I feel like I'm married — to the Navy. Perhaps this duty is like being deployed aboard a ship, Dad. I can see how one's Navy job becomes a way of life, a way of thinking and a true profession. Sounds like a recruiter! I've been sleeping, eating, thinking Navy.

Notwithstanding the not-so-subtle plaintive tone in the above, I love my job. With the exception of the CO, the rest of the officers are not the cream of the crop. Recruiting duty for women is seen as a choice billet; not so for the men. Consequently, the officers' attitudes leave much to be desired. Their minds are on finding a civilian job. This doesn't influence me too much in that I see myself on Independent Duty, doing my own thing. I've about decided to apply for Regular Navy. It'll give me a better shot at being selected for graduate school and getting challenging billets.

Sounds like you're having a grand time overseas. Good! You do seem far away. I miss you.

It's difficult to have a real social life with this job. And even harder to meet eligible bachelors as well. For now, that's okay.

Lots of love,

Tucker

Five weeks later Tucker's journal

15 May 1963, Philadelphia, Pennsylvania

For the record,

Today I made a momentous decision and submitted my application for the Regular Navy. My FitReps are fine. I shouldn't have any selection problems. But one never knows, and I don't know my competition.

I'd planned to stay in for only two years and then go to grad school. But why not have the Navy pay for my schooling? The only drawback is the obligation. For every year of schooling, I must pay back two years, and I'll be 27 before I can be free to leave the Navy.

On the other hand, I love the Navy and seem to have recruited myself further into the organization this past year. I do believe the stuff I tell my officer candidates. The military is one of the few places where American women can have equal pay, as well as have tremendous opportunity for top jobs. Although we can't go to sea and be in the REAL Navy, we have the world at our fingertips and have major responsibilities. The Navy is what an individual makes of it. If you give it your talents and commitment, the Navy will *more* than pay you back.

My first two jobs have challenged my whole Self. This one has forced me to come out of my bookworm shell and give recruiting talks to large numbers of people. Last week I spoke to over two hundred men and women, and the butterflies went away after three minutes. Not bad. I've been on talk radio shows in the mountains of Pennsylvania and can hold my own against the anti-military fanatics.

I have no reason to think that my future jobs will be anything but better than the first. So, Fairfield, take the leap!

TF

Ten days later from Billie

25 May 1963, Pearl Harbor, Hawaii

Tucker — Aloha!

This place is terrific! It's so different — tropical with sweet flowery smells, warm, Asian, Polynesian, wonderful things to eat. I'm gonna have a great time! Plus, I'm an aunt! My sister and her husband last week had a little baby girl. Wait a second, does that make me old?

After the course at Oakland Supply Center, I checked in to Fort Mason in San Francisco to await sailing on *USNS Richard Barrett*. There they put you on duty, then give you liberty until the ship sails. I stayed in the BOQ at Fort Mason, and another WAVE officer, LT(jg) Jean Kelly (she has orders to Naval Station, Pearl) and I had two days and nights to see San Francisco. We even saw a drag queen show at North Beach! Jean is from a small town in Oklahoma, and a Southern Baptist. Events like this are eye-openers for us.

Finally, we received our sailing times. Jean and I had to report for duty aboard the *Barrett*. The passengers' manifest was military officers and enlisted personnel and their families going to be stationed in Hawaii. Jean was assigned to the recreation area where she logged out equipment, games, cards, etc. I was assigned to the nurse and the corpsman to log in patients during sick call. I got really seasick the first night. All the Navy guys teased me about calling for O'Roarke. That's when you hang over the rail and shout "O'Roarke" while you get sick. Ugh!

The crossing was great fun. Not plush, like the *Lurline*, but nice and cozy. There were enough amateur musicians among the passengers and crew to form a band. I played percussion, and we got together every evening to ruin our eardrums. In between, we stood duty 2–3 hours a day, played volleyball, and visited the animals — the families brought their dogs, cats, hamsters, rabbits, iguanas, snakes, you name it, plus a couple of ponies, in big kennels, runways and cages down on the deck. It was a zoo!

When we arrived in Hawaii, we got quite a reception. There was a small band, hula dancers, people with leis, and a spread of finger food. I didn't suspect that for the next couple of years I'd be the officer-in-charge of those receptions. The ships dock at the Supply Center docks and representatives from the passenger's command greet the passenger (and his family). It truly is a welcome.

Now, three months later, and I've had quite a ride. First of all, my boss, RADM Howard Shelton, Supply Corps, is fantastic. One of those people you want to emulate. (I've learned that "emulate" is a word, like "utilize," that every naval officer must know.) He's warm, friendly, genuine, fair, has a great sense of humor, and is totally in command. I'll never make another snide remark about staff officers. The Navy is lucky to have him.

Second, I'm the Administration Department Head. The other Dept. Heads are captains or commanders, and I'm barely into my j.g. bars. Third, I have one of the biggest departments, with over 200 people, and fourth, I have a gazillian collateral duties. Thirty-one to be exact, ranging from Decedent Affairs Officer (whatever that means) to Public Affairs Officer, and I know what that means. Admin. Dept. covers a whole host of things — all the command files, including classified, mail room (the bane of my existence), communications, military personnel, print shop, photography, artist, fire dept, security dept, vehicle pool, and port services — 2 tugs, an admiral's gig and 2 liberty boats. The liberty boats are used to take tourists to the Arizona Memorial! I'm not kidding. I run tourists to the Memorial! Plus, port services has a thing called a "Juicy Lucy," a sort of barge/tug that contains small oil spills. I don't man or run the thing, but it's on my inventory.

Last Friday some of the junior officers at the command and their wives invited me to the O' Club for Happy Hour. There were several of us at the table and we were having a great time, when Captain Stephen Severson, another Dept. Head, staggered over. I mean staggered. The Admiral's aide, LT Bill Mott, said, "uh-oh — here's trouble." He (the Captain) looked right at me and said, "I don't want you in *My Navy*. You might be smarter than me, and more educated than me, but you don't belong in *My Navy*, and I'm going to make trouble for you every step of the way." Then, he wobbled away.

This morning he sent a note to the Chief of Staff saying that I embarrassed him at the O' Club Friday because I was drunk. The CofS came down to my office to discuss the note, and I was embarrassed. I explained to him what happened, who was there, and so forth and he said he'd take care of it. I'm stunned. I feel humiliated. What did I ever do to this guy? Am I supposed to forever tiptoe around these old fuddy-duddies because they're mad at the world and want to slam dunk me or someone else who's a good target? Yuk!

Hey, Tuck! Some great women officers are stationed at CINCPACFLT. They live mostly at the Makalapa BOQ, which is certainly different than the cave I live in. More later. I'll try to ignore the fuddy-duddy.

Best,

Billie

One week later from Tucker

1 June 1963, Philadelphia, Pennsylvania

Dear Robyn,

I must be hung-up on physical security issues. Maybe my budding psychologist friend can give me a few words of wisdom. I've had another unsettling incident.

In conjunction with Armed Forces Day last week, I was assigned duty at the last minute to speak to a group of women about Women-in-the-Navy. The assignment was vague, although my boss said he thought the location, a church, might be in one of the worst sections of town. That was an understatement.

Saturday morning I took off in my Corvair for the Church of the Nazarene. Because of the late assignment, all official Navy cars were unavailable. As I closed in on the church, I became aware of the neighborhood. There were fewer and fewer white people on the streets and in the cars. Soon I was the only white person in sight and the area was *very* rundown. Should I continue on this journey, I thought to myself. My insides were churning with fear. I didn't want to go to the church. But we'd accepted the obligation. Besides, I was probably just having racist thoughts.

I found the church. As I pulled into a parking spot, many young Negro men eyed me and my Corvair. They looked unruly and dangerous. I was hoping they would honor the uniform. I kept telling myself that everything would be okay.

It took all that I had to get out of my Corvair and head for the church. But I did it. I was ticked at the guys at the Recruiting Station who hadn't checked this out. I shouldn't be here as a white woman, traveling alone. Uniform be damned. Those young guys probably thought I was an airline stewardess.

Once inside the church, I felt secure. The people, all women, were pleasant and happy to see me. It was fairly dark. Then I began to feel funny again. I was the only white person in the church.

I felt alone. Not only were these one-hundred-or-so women strangers to me, but they're all Negroes. With every moment I got more uncomfortable. I haven't known many Negroes, except the few at Wellesley. These women seemed friendly, but different. And what about my car? Was it okay?

The woman in charge, Mrs. Bradley, came up to give me information. "You'll be speaking at 2:00 P.M.," she said. It was 10:00 A.M.

I knew I didn't want to be there for four more hours. My main concern was my Car — and my Self. I approached Mrs. Bradley and told her a little white lie. "I need to leave by 12:00. Can you switch the speakers around?" She considered my request, smiled, then changed my speech to 11:00 A.M.

In the next hour I learned about the opportunities for Negro women cosmetologists. Very interesting. My talk went well, though I felt awkward and distant — so it wasn't my best performance.

As I walked out of the church, the bright light of the day awakened me to the outside. The young men were still hanging around my car. I wondered if they hurt the car. The exterior looked fine.

Driving through the city streets, I tried to block out the rundown condition of the immediate surroundings. I reviewed the morning. It hadn't been so bad. My worst fears were only fears. I need to be more at ease with people of all races.

While I suppose I should be happy to have emerged from that event unscathed, what's beginning to eat at me is the risk women must take living in a big city. Have you had similar experiences in Boston? What do you do about scruffy-appearing characters? As I wrote before, I carry a billy club when walking Gabby. Seems a shame, especially for women, that our cities have come to this state.

I will be extra careful as to my whereabouts. I no longer enjoy living in the city. The initial excitement is gone and has been replaced with a growing fear for my physical security.

Have you ever been in a position where you're the only white person in a room? The church experience manifested a weird, uneasy feeling. I now understand how Negro sailors feel as one among many whites. It's a different feeling from being one woman among many men, a feeling I'm experiencing more and more these days. Today's Navy is 98% men.

That's my incident for the day. Hope to have a quiet summer and not face any more security problems for awhile. I'm becoming more and more fond of the Navy, recruiting myself, I suppose. The unnecessary rules and regulations haven't bothered me as much. Must be adjusting.

My love life is minimal here in Philly. My men friends are in Newport or off on deployments. How's yours?

Love,

Tucker, the scared one

One month later from Robyn

July 2, 1963, Boston, Massachusetts

God Tucker!

What an unsettling experience! A couple of questions regarding my favorite compassionate organization, the U.S. Navy, come to mind: In a potentially troubled area of an inner city, it might have been more prudent of the Recruiting Department (or whatever your command is called) to assign two folks, at least one of whom might share the ethnicity of whatever group was to be recruited. Do female recruiters only recruit females, and males, males? Or could a mixed pair be assigned to recruit a mixed group? Did you report this incident to your supervisor (commanding officer or whomever)? And, finally, dear Tucker, why are you getting "more and more fond" of the Navy?

I must say, I'm not really challenging you — more playing devil's advocate. The more I hear, the less and less likely I would have anything to do with it!

My job's fine. I like doing therapy with Inner City kids, and it's a challenge. In a week I'm off on a canoe trip in the Boundary waters of Minnesota. Like you, I can't wait to get out of the city; unlike you, I have (so far) not had such traumatic experiences.

Till soon, love,

Robyn

Two days later from Tucker

4 July 1963, Philadelphia, Pennsylvania

Dear Billie,

You know, Billie, I could be internalizing the rules and regulations of the Navy and becoming a part of the structure more than I realized.

This morning, at the big downtown Philly parade, I just about lost it when I saw Judy, my Navy Nurse counterpart at the Station, carrying a *pink* umbrella. Her hair draped two inches below her collar, two inches longer than regulations allow. I confronted her right then and there. "Judy, it's time for a haircut, don't you think? And what about that pink umbrella?"

She replied, "Tucker, I'm happy with my hair's length, thank you very much. And I love pink."

Nobody else was around, but it was probably not the best place to continue the conversation. Why did I lose my cool? Why does it bother me that Judy carries a pink umbrella and wears her hair too long?

Because. We were taught at WOCS that *all* women who wear the Navy blue must look sharp and stay within the Uniform Board's guidelines. That's why she bothers me. She also annoys me because my boss won't dress her down. He says, "She looks great, is beautiful, so what if her hair is a little too long? Other than her hair, she looks like a recruiting picture. She brings in her Nurse Corps quota and performs well. What more can I ask? So give her a break."

I, as the Women's Representative of the command, am supposed to uphold Uniform Regulations. *A regulation is a regulation.* If it needs to be changed, then change it. In the meantime, if the regs say a woman can only carry a black umbrella, then don't allow a *pink* one! The Navy already makes an exception for women. Men can't carry umbrellas. Why flirt with losing the privilege? If the regs say women's hair is to be a certain length, then it should be a certain length.

A lieutenant commander carrying her pink umbrella with her formal midnight-blue Mainbocher uniform looks ridiculous. I'd better ease up some, Billie. Remember that Officer Candidate who couldn't stand inane rules? Judy sees black umbrellas as a dumb rule. Besides, she's very senior to me. Who do I think I am? Nevertheless, commanding officers should do something about women who are out of uniform.

And how goes it with you in Pearl? Knowing you, you're rolling with the punches about regulations. I find them hard to deal with at times, especially if they're not followed!

Wish you were here, or I was there(!) to talk to you in person.

> Tuck

P.S. Speaking of quotas, the engines that drive any Recruiting Station, my commanding officer and I are in strong disagreement over WAVE enlisted quotas. We've missed our quotas for several months. He says, "You have the bodies." I say, "But they're not qualified." He continually overrides my judgment, thereby lowering our acceptance standards. Perhaps my standards are too high.

Two weeks later from Billie

18 July 1963, Pearl Harbor, Hawaii

Dear Tuck —

You wrote, "A regulation is a regulation." Let me tell ya about that one!

I'm now the new Women's Barracks Officer. It's been eight months since the last barracks officer left and the present Master at Arms has been on board for only six months. She's a very sharp, very pleasant, very aggressive First Class Petty Officer (Personnelman). And, she's also very frustrated. She took me on a tour of the barracks — a WWII type that's been stuccoed over for an outside Hawaiian-type decor — and pointed out numerous discrepancies: leaking roof, leaking commodes, faucets, and showers; stained walls and floors; missing floor tiles; worn and frayed carpeting; and everything woefully in need of paint. The lounge needs new furniture, and the quarterdeck needs all those Navy trappings — you know, shell casings, lines, carpet, and portraits. The grounds, unexpansive but adequate, need replanting, re-sodding, trimming, mowing, you name it. The lanai and the barbecue area need everything.

The MAA and her compartment cleaners keep everything neat, orderly, and sparkling, but her many requests for maintenance haven't been answered. She believes the Chief MAA, the guy in charge of maintenance for all the Naval Station's Barracks, would like to help, but is stymied by several things, especially his apathetic boss, a LT who is also the Port Services Officer.

But her major concerns, other than upkeep, startled me. Her first concern was morale of the residents. Her second was the presence of males in the barracks after hours. She said the two are connected. The second impacts on the first. I asked for a copy of the Naval Station Barracks Instruction that pertains to all the Barracks — eight male barracks and one female barracks. It has the usual stuff (I assume) about MAA duties, compartment cleaners, upkeep and maintenance, inspections and resident behavior.

This is what it says. "Female and male guests are allowed only in the lounge areas of the barracks. Female and male guests are not allowed in individual rooms or passageways outside of the rooms. Female and male guests must depart the lounge areas at 2200 Sunday through Thursday, and 2400 Friday and Saturday. This is to ensure the privacy of the residents."

Then she showed me the watch log since she has been the MAA. Practically every night she and her watchstanders have confronted males in the barracks after guest departure time — in the passageways, in the heads (this barracks has gang heads), the galley, the laundry, and coming out of individual rooms. They, the watchstanders, have been yelled at, shoved, pushed around, and bullied by these guys. The MAA has turned in over 50 report chits and complaints...to no avail. Again, she feels the Chief MAA wants to help, but is reluctant. Seventy-eight of the ninety women in the barracks have turned in written objections to the MAA about the presence of males in the barracks. Yet, a small number of these women continue to open the doors and windows for these guys to come into the barracks every night.

Another aspect of morale, according to "Ski" (Petty Officer Malovski, the MAA), is that the male barracks have command integrity. That's where members of the same command occupy a deck, or a wing, or adjoining rooms of the barracks, and decorate their part of the barracks with command insignias, plaques, and logos. The various commands also supply paint, tiles, carpeting, and other amenities (coffee pots, burners) to "their" parts of the barracks. In addition, these commands provide compartment cleaners and division officers and chiefs to keep their sections clean, maintained, and supervised.

The women's barracks, of course, has none of these things; the residents are assigned to commands all over the Pearl Harbor area. It's the only barracks for women. The commands reluctantly assign compartment cleaners who're also the watchstanders. No CO, Division Officer, or chief from the women residents' commands has taken an interest in the barracks' livability. I tell ya, Tuck, I'm beginning to develop an attitude concerning the males who run this Navy.

After a major learning experience with ONI agents screaming at two young women petty officers accused of homosexuality (you see how my attitude is developing?), I went to the Admin Officer and the Barracks Officer with a letter to the COs of the women residents' commands, asking that a command representative attend a residents' barracks meeting to address habitat deficiencies in the barracks. I explained the problems with maintenance, morale, men in the barracks, and the lack of security. The Admin Officer frowned and said this was unprecedented, but he would check with the CO.

Well, the CO, down visiting my boss on business, asked if he could talk to me about the barracks. He came down to my office. I liked him immediately. He's younger than the Admin officer, has just taken command, and confessed that this is his first command with women, and he needs my help. I laughed and said I'm learning too, and we decided we were both sailing in uncharted waters.

We talked for a half-hour or so about my barracks concerns. As a result, he signed the letter, and we had a very successful barracks meeting. The women residents, a great majority anyway, were ecstatic with the results and gleefully took their command representative on tours of the barracks including their rooms and other areas.

As if by magic, barracks funds were found, and now a transformation is taking place. In a month the women's barracks will be beautiful; already, males in the barracks are down to one or two sightings since the letter, and the women who let them in are awaiting captain's masts. The male barracks MAAs come running when we call, and "Ski" is now invited to the barracks' MAA meetings.

But I'm still upset about the (mis)treatment of the two women petty officers. I learned the "tip" came from the Admin Officer. Out of curiosity I went back through the report chits "Ski" has sent up concerning heterosexual activities in the barracks. Fourteen different male-female couples were sighted together at various times. When I took this information to the Admin Officer and asked why these people weren't charged under the UCMJ and punished, he said, "Homosexuality is a security risk, and those who practice it must be discharged. The others were engaged in a natural act with no harm done."

Well, I'm just learning, Tuck, but as I said before, I'm beginning to develop an attitude. Have you had problems like these?

More from the front lines later.

Your friend,

Billie

Eleven weeks later from Tucker

5 October 1963, Philadelphia, Pennsylvania

Dear Mother and Dad,

Good news! I've been selected for graduate school and should be leaving by March. Am ready to leave *now.* What does that say? It's difficult to keep up the enthusiasm once orders are in hand. Mine aren't yet in hand, but given the scheduling for graduate school, they're fairly assured. More so than the last go-around. I must say waiting for orders can be stressful on both the body and soul. How've you done it for all these years, Dad? One solution is to let go and let the Navy make the entire decision. I would like to have an input in my career, so it's harder on my constitution.

Life has been hectic. My recruiting schedule forces me to be out of the city a lot. Hard on Gabby. I have to leave him with my WAVE friend and neighbor, Marjorie.

The colleges are mostly friendly to us as Navy Recruiters. All the Quaker schools, however, refuse to allow us on campus. If I believed what they do about peace and conflict resolution, I'd probably do the same.

Not much socializing of late. I'm still feeling married to the Navy. Not the best of deals. Most of my best friends from college days are married. You remember Anne, my sophomore roommate whom I introduced to her future husband on a double date in D.C. before I joined? They'll be married next month. I know, Dad, why am I not married? Takes time and energy to find the right man. I'm choosy.

Speaking of D.C., it'll be great to be living there next year. Seems to me it's a cleaner, safer city than Philly, although Philly is doing extensive inner city rehab.

Love,

Tucker

Three days later from Tucker's journal

8 October 1963, Philadelphia, Pennsylvania

For the record,

Today was another alarming event. Must write about it: I'm at the last stop on my errands, the grocery store. As I come out of Safeway, I notice two teenage boys in my car, pulling out my clothes that I'd just picked up from the dry cleaners. My best Dress Blue uniform! Panic. I need my uniform. I can't afford another. I drop the groceries and run to the car, yelling, "God damn. What are you guys doing? Stop. Right now." I make a real commotion. Swearing. Yelling. The young men look startled, drop the clothes in the parking lot and run away.

I can't take many more security-type episodes. Knowing what I know about robbers, in hindsight I should've let those guys take my uniform. They weren't tampering with the car; they just wanted the clothes. My uniform! I could've been stabbed or something worse. Better stop being so assertive, Fairfield. You know that in certain areas this is a not nice city for women.

And where oh where is the grand old Navy? When I signed up, I expected to be stationed near naval bases, usually in small towns.

Instead, I'm about to move from one big city to another. Oh, well. The best news is that I'll be getting a Masters degree. Billie and several of my other WAVE friends will be there. Hooray. Can't wait for March.

Be more careful.

TF

P.S. On the other hand, the security of our planet moved a lot further along yesterday — President Kennedy signed a limited nuclear test ban treaty.

Ten days later from Mother and Dad

18 October 1963, San Diego, California

Dear Tucker,

Many, many congratulations. See, to the victors really do come the spoils. You'd never have been picked for graduate school had your performance as a recruiter been just so-so. Don't worry too much about guiding your career. The key for me has always been to turn in as credible a performance as possible regardless of the assignment. Your service reputation as one who understands "the needs of the Service" are more important than "the needs of Tucker Fairfield" can be critical when selection boards meet.

To Washington, D.C., where it's all decided. How about that! I used to think no matter what was needed, there was always someone in Washington who could provide it, if you could present the need in the right way. I don't feel that way anymore and see those in the Washington jobs as human beings just like me. But it's surely the place to be visible, to get known, and that's as important in the Navy as it is in General Motors.

Your letter sounded a bit wistful about finding someone to marry. I guess that, too, will happen in its time, and you'll surely know when it does. Why are you not married, you ask? Your mother thinks it's because you work all the time; maybe you scare 'em off with your certainty and independence. These days the idea of a man taking care of a woman, protecting her, providing for her, seems to be a relic. Your mother says it ain't all bad, and doesn't ask you to give up your freedom. That notion isn't easy to sell to young people today, is it? Afraid Washington will not improve the male/female ratio in the context of marriage; I read somewhere that the ratio is about five women to every man. Don't give up!

What will you arrange for Gabby when you're in class all day? Can we help? When we talked a few days ago you sounded a bit uncertain over that. Animals, dogs particularly, can establish a demand on your life that seems unreal at times, but they're absolutely unquestioning friends.

It's good to be home. The more we're out of this country the more we agree that no other place on earth can compare favorably with it. Can you come home before you move to Washington?

All our love.

Mother and Dad

Five weeks later from Tucker's journal

23 November 1963, Philadelphia, Pennsylvania

For the record,

Yesterday the world seemed to stop. A darkness swept over Camelot.

I can hardly bear it. To think that we've lost our President. He was one of the greatest, most charismatic leaders of our time. I was swearing in fifteen new recruits when word of President Kennedy's death spread throughout the Station. The city outside seemed to stop breathing. Only blaring radios could be heard. Violence seems to be oblivious to goodness.

JFK pulled us through the Cuban Missile Crisis, but he couldn't pull himself through a senseless killer's attack. I will miss him. The country will miss him. Jackie was so courageous and elegant. And, yes, regal.

I know the country will survive. Yet, something's changed for the country and for me. I feel us all groping for a rational answer to an unacceptable criminal act.

I am much older than yesterday. And confused.

I'm driving to D.C. this weekend, spending time with WAVE friends and going to the funeral. Will be good to see my friends. So many of us are either stationed at the Pentagon or BuPers.

Just spoke with Pierre Dumonte who's stationed in D.C. too. He still talks about his tour with Dad on the *Dallas* as one of his best assignments. Pierre invited me to stand with him (in uniform) at the funeral ceremony.

Pierre mentioned that Lieutenant Tom Parker, a submariner, will stand with us. Wonder what this Tom is like? Pierre said, "You'll like him, Tucker. I know you and I know Tom. You'll have lots to talk about." What did he mean by that?

TF

Two weeks later from Tom Parker

7 *December 1963, Pearl Harbor Day*
West Milton, New York

Dear Tucker,

I just called Pierre Dumonte and thanked him for getting us together; I'd expected to spend my time in D.C. pretty much alone. I was glad to be able to share my feelings with someone who clearly felt the same.

I write on the anniversary of another day of infamy. I was nine then so I remember it well. Surely the one we just mourned will also be forever marked in history. I still feel pretty emotional about the last two weeks. Pierre's a great buddy but politically unconscious; he didn't really get why I wanted to detour to attend JFK's funeral (given I had enough time) from a direct line from nuke school in Mare Island, CA, to the reactor site in West Milton, NY.

Pierre's typical of a lot of academy guys — really great, exceptionally competent officers, but they say to me, "Oh, you went to Michigan. You got an education." I don't truly agree with this. After all, as pre-law, I majored in political science. Of course to catch up to me in history they would have to make an effort. The Navy's making me catch up to them in engineering! All this rambling is to say that I'm really grateful we had our mutual shoulders to cry on over what happened in Dallas.

I'm settled into West Milton to learn the practical side of running a nuclear power plant. We're all working 8-hour shifts here as the reactor never sleeps. Fortunately few enticements exist in this little town to take my mind off qualifying. I can't even indulge in my movie vice. We have only one theater in nearby Saratoga Springs, and it's only open on the weekend! Everyone says wait until the track opens in August — and I think, that's it?

Skidmore College is here, but exploring its possibilities doesn't seem worth the effort, given my (I hope) short stay. And, anyway, the girls sure look young! I hear there's a tavern/bar/roadhouse where people can sit in with the band, so I may check it out. My guitar strings are rusting! But I have a fingernail problem: My pickin' fingers pick better with longer nails. But of course they're unacceptable for gentlemen officers.

I'm sharing a small furnished house with two other trainees. Fortunately for me, they're both whiz nuclear engineers; fortunately for them, I'm a whiz short order cook — one of my college jobs. Did I tell you that as an NROTC student I earned my room and board for two years by waiting tables and helping out in the kitchen at my fraternity? Thus, I wash a mean dish too!

Well, Tucker, write me if you get a chance. This is really to say thanks for staying up with me half the night. We seemed to instantly hit it off and it didn't seem likely we'd ever run out of topics. I haven't talked to anyone else in the Navy with whom I seem to have so much in common — charm, good looks, brains, ambition, wit, no money, no time, etc. Are you sure you're only 26? Well, I guess gals mature faster than guys!

Hey, is Tucker your real name? Mine is, surprise, Thomas, after Thomas Jefferson. My brothers also were named after presidents: Abraham, Theodore, and Ulysses (known as Bram, Ted, and Uly — sometimes by his brothers as "Useless"). My sister's name is Martha, yes, for George's wife. Everyone of them is still in Michigan; my brothers all work for auto makers, the expected career path after high school in Flint and I guess Detroit. Martha's a homemaker with four kids married to a GM tool maker. Brother Ted told me to "join the Navy and see the world" after high school.

I'm grateful to Ted for this, and also to the Navy Chief at Great Lakes' Electronic School, who told me about some exam for "intellectuals who think they might want to go to college." Luckily I had done college prep in high school mainly because in my junior high school shop course, no matter how many times I tried, I couldn't miter corners. Algebra was much easier. I applied to Michigan because it was the only school with NROTC that I knew something about. To be honest, I think I was kind of reluctant to be farther from home too.

I don't know why I'm rambling on so much about myself. I guess because I want us to talk some more, and some of this personal bio stuff may help explain my shortcomings. I realized we spent little time on personal subjects, but talked mostly about Cuba and Lyndon B. and Vietnam and other small things like the role of the US in the UN.

I'm avoiding dealing with the reactor effluent, so I best get cracking.

Warm regards,

Tom

Ten days later from Tucker

17 December 1963, Philadelphia, Pennsylvania

Dear Tom,

What a lovely surprise to receive your letter last week! Felt right to hear more about who you are; yes, we seemed to be simpatico and not to need the perfunctory first-meeting data exchange. I'm still spinning from events of the last few weeks. John John's salute was a fitting goodbye to his dad and to our special leader. There will never be another Camelot, at least not in our lifetime.

Interesting to think of Pearl Harbor and the JFK assassination in the same breath. I don't remember Pearl Harbor specifically, but do have strong memories of saying goodbye to my daddy and knowing that he had to go off to war and "fight the Japs in my submarine." Life suddenly became so different for Mother and me, and he was gone for four long years.

I'm envious of your large family. As an only child, with just a few aunts and uncles and cousins, I sometimes dream of having big family reunions, kinda like the Kennedy clan. Sounds like you could easily have such reunions, with your presidential family! Having a strong sense of family is one of the special benefits of being in the Navy. You and I have both experienced the warmth and support from our fellow shipmates, especially in times of personal crisis.

I was tickled by your comment about Pierre and academy grads. My mother has always said there are two types of officers: those who love and play hard at politics, and those who love to drive ships and submarines, and fly airplanes. Probably too stereotypical a thought, but has some relevance. The second type of officer likes "things," and is the gifted engineer, like Pierre. My dad's personality fits this second arena. He loves boats, ships, and cars and is a true Mr. Fix-It around the house. I'm sure that if one's life literally depended on knowing about his house (*e.g.*, a submarine), he'd learn real fast how to fix it. Certainly Dad's wartime experiences support that theory. He needed to know his boat's every nook and cranny. So I suppose you're now learning about maintaining your "house" as you attend reactor school! Sort of like a furnace and its operation, only on a much more complex scale!

Pierre might surprise you, by the way. At the funeral he told me that he's applied for the same (International Relations) graduate program that I have. Maybe we'll be classmates at American University next fall. Talking with you about international dilemmas confirmed my decision to go to graduate school. I know you too would love to attend, but understand that ADM Rickover has you on a tight schedule for a long while. Will you ever get any shore duty?

I never thought about short fingernails and playing the guitar. Do you think we really inspect for long fingernails? Sounds like OCS to me. I play a mean alto sax and clarinet. We'll have to make some music together.

What was your fraternity? Did I mention I left Wellesley and spent my junior year at Chapel Hill (UNC)? I was looking for less studying and a more natural, relaxed dating atmosphere than at a women's college. I pledged a sorority, Alpha Gam, and had lots of good times but missed the academic challenges and returned my senior year to fewer dates, no football games, but true intellectual stimulation.

My name is actually a family surname, off the family tree on my dad's side. Admiral Samuel Tucker, Dad's great uncle, was one of our famous civil war heroes. So I suppose I'm carrying on the family tradition — just wasn't allowed in the same *alma mater.*

Christmas in Philadelphia is spectacular! The city is aglow with lights and beauty. Would love for you to see it.

Must close for now. I'm way behind with my Christmas gift and card schedule! Thank you again for taking time out from your pressed schedule. Let's stay in touch. If I go to D.C. at least we'll still be on the same coast!

Best regards,

Tucker

Two weeks later from Tom Parker

2 January 1964, West Milton, NY

Happy New Year Tucker,

Greetings from me, still hard at it at "The GE black-ball school." There's a tall, black water tank on our GE reactor site and one of the guys here has a little girl who says her daddy goes to the black-ball school. "The GE" — that's what the locals call General Electric — amuses me. In my native Michigan, people don't work at "The GM," they work at "GM."

Meant to write sooner, sorry. The holidays weren't a fun time. Shift work continued unabated. The married guy I mentioned had a party one Sunday afternoon, and guess what, I had the watch. I did get out to the bar a couple of nights and the band let me sit in; I don't think I let the side down despite my digital handicap.

You're right, I don't get fingernail inspections but it turns out an unwritten rule prevails. On my first West Pac cruise, destroyer duty, I grew my guitar pickers out and twice got remarks — one from the Captain, referring to what shade of fingernail polish would most become me. I decided long fingernails weren't worth the hassle.

So Pierre's putting in for International Relations. The dirty dog never mentioned it once. He's probably thinking "Shore Duty, Shore Duty." I know he'll do well whatever he does. He's a real bright officer. Interesting, your comments about the two different kinds of sailors and the home analogy. On a diesel boat, I'm sure your dad has told you, the officers learn every system inside 'n out. That's the minimum requirement for earning your dolphins. Funny, I'm not handy like my dad was. I can't even fix my car, but I sure felt I could fix my sub if it were fixable. Now they say what's hard psychologically for us diesel boat sailors going to the large nuclear missile boats is we can't know every system inside and out. They say that it's easier for the junior guys who go straight from college to nuke school and thus don't experience anxiety about not knowing everything.

Yes, Tucker, I probably would like grad school, but "I made my bed" and as hard and lumpy as it is sometimes, I'll be lying in it indefinitely. When I was in Pearl on the *Sanddab*, I had a choice of Intelligence School or Nuclear Power School. My natural talents pointed to the former, but getting picked by Rickover was like getting anointed by the Pope. I'd worked hard to get into the program too — taking a correspondence course in calculus, being on his study program (an extra 40 hours a week no less, on top of regular work), and passing his one-on-one, terrifying interview.

So it seemed a real coup for me, a political science grad, to get selected. At the time, Rickover was kind of experimenting. There was a geography major in my class too. But once in, you're right about shore duty chances. Given how fast the nuclear program is growing, and the rate of Rickover pickovers, there aren't enough officers to let any of us have shore duty, period. The closest is shipyard time or building the new subs.

Just reread your letter and realized I'd left out the answer to your important question: my fraternity! It was Phi Delt. What a coincidence! The A Gams were our sister sorority. Living at the Phi Delt house and doing poli sci after coming from a blue collar background combined to make me a liberal. I really began to question the reality of equal opportunity that's such a strong value in our country. I'd certainly been given a wonderful opportunity, but most of my fraternity brothers obviously had an advantaged head start.

Few of my high school friends, some of whom were just as smart as I, were able to go to college. My father had said (but not demonstrated) that anyone who worked hard enough could be anything he wanted, but I know my brothers had worked hard, so hard work alone obviously didn't suffice. Why was it that I was supposed to end up on the assembly line while my fraternity brothers knew from the start that they were university material?

So, I ask, shouldn't the rich be taxed to create programs that could make the disadvantaged more like the advantaged? Not everyone could count on the luck that I'd clearly had. I'm still trying to come to grips with the concept of equal opportunity, especially with the Civil Rights Movement kicking up its heels. Did Wellesley have blue collar girls, or were you all born with silver spoons in your mouths?

I'm one-third done. Can't wait to get outta here. Stay well. We'll have to play together soon, guitar and clarinet and sax. Tell me, how do you play the clarinet and sax at the same time? We can have a trio but I can't picture it. I tried but came up with an image of those musicians who play the accordion and a drum and a mouth organ simultaneously. Maybe it's better for me to take on the two. I can blow and pick at the same time, though maybe only one note!! And that's a note to end on.

Studying is a callin'. When do you hear about grad school? I'll think positive thoughts for you. Have a grand 1964! Hugs from Tom to Tucker, namesake of Admiral Sam. I'm impressed. Guess you've got salt water in the blood!

                    Warm regards,

                    Tom

                    Three weeks later from Tucker

                    23 January 1964, Philadelphia, Pennsylvania

Dear Tom,

And well you should feel anointed by the Pope. Given all the personal horror stories I've listened to about Rickover's interviews, had I somehow screened for his interview, am certain he would've booted me out of his office. Is it true that he uses crooked chairs for the interviewees, to throw them literally off balance? I'm very impressed that you, a non-engineer type, made it through his hoops. You're on your way, my friend. But you're paying a large price in terms of no shore duty.

Me, I'm out in my territory trying to scout up qualified applicants for OCS. We do have a beautiful country and I'm fortunate at the moment to be a "traveling salesman." As you well know, the Navy's requirements are stringent and lately we've been losing a high percentage of our applicant base to physical disabilities. It's remarkable so many enthusiastic young men and women, seemingly perfectly healthy, can't pass their physicals.

Another reality — our Southeast Asia policy seems to be discouraging many college students from joining. I don't know how I feel about our involvement in Vietnam. Will let you know after grad school! What's your take on our policy? Probably you have little time to give it deep thought.

A liberal, eh? We seem to be few and far between within our officer corps. A combination of one staunch New England mother and a Wellesley education turned me from a politically neutral position into a liberal, with a slight lean to the right (from my dad) especially about national security matters. Wellesley, by the way, has many students who come from blue collar families and on scholarship based purely on financial need, not academic achievement. I was on a scholarship and worked in various academic departments.

I imagine there's a strong chance you'll be in New London, home for most of our East Coast-based nuclear subs, and one of my favorite places. Did I tell you I attended both elementary and high school there (with lots of other places and schools in between)?

So good of you to keep in touch. I appreciate your taking time out from studies.

Keep the faith, play when you can, and do keep writing!

> Fondly,
>
> Tucker

Six months later from Tucker

> *8 August 1964, St. Albans Naval Hospital, NY*

Dear Billie,

I'm on the back porch of the Nurses' BOQ at St. Albans, trying to get cool! It must be over 100° and we have no air conditioning so I sleep out here most nights and get dirty looks from the senior nurses (some of whom look and act exceptionally grumpy). In some ways it's kinda romantic and fun to be stationed at the World's Fair. This is an in-between duty stations, three-months deal (TEMDU) before going to American U. Essentially our Navy/Marine Corps unit's a glorified recruiting effort composed of three officers, many senior enlisted and some junior enlisted.

We're exhibiting lots of sophisticated, fun Navy/Marine Corps static displays. The unit is within the Travel and Transportation pavilion and its main attraction is a 12-minute film which we show in a small theater (stand-up audiences of 50), with a concave-shaped screen. Catapulting off a carrier or diving with a sub are so real that several theater goers have called for O'Roarke.

I'm the team leader of one of three watch sections. I stand, and I mean stand, in my high heels and Dress Whites for a good part of the eight-hour watch. (Our area only has two benches. I take my break at the massage chair display around the corner from us and *sit down*. Guess who's bought a chair for her apartment in Virginia!) We're bused back and forth to St. Albans from the Fair grounds. The fun part is we have time to see the whole Fair and its exciting pavilions in our off-duty time. Walking the grounds, you get a real sense of how it is to live in other countries. The difficult aspect is greeting thousands and thousands of people all day or night during the watch. I'm developing crowd-phobia, if that's a syndrome.

My duties as the unit's senior woman have given me a few sleepless nights. These young women, supposedly our best, are also breaking a few regs in their off-hours. Fortunately, a W-1 female Marine, Warrant Officer Sibyl Davidson, gives me full support and great advice.

Just wanted to give you a little taste of the Fair.

How about an update of your times in Hawaii? Bet you're playing hard in your off-duty times.

Soon I'll be a graduate student and won't have to wear these damn high heels every day and pay the constant dry cleaning bills on Dress Whites! The little things in life. Wish you were here.

    Best,

    Tucker

Two weeks later from Billie

17 August 1964, Pearl Harbor, Hawaii

Tucker — Aloha Nui Loa!

You can see that I'm getting proficient in this island-talk. But I've had a few snags: I thought mahalo was the word for trash because it's on all the trash cans, but it means thank you. You can imagine the predicament I found myself in concerning the use of mahalo! As my mother says, live and learn.

The atmosphere for partying is terrific over here. There're some really great people to play with and I'm having a helluva time (well, there are a couple of exceptions which I'll get to later) and overall the Navy's still *good!* The gang I run around with has found all sorts of restaurants, night clubs, little hole-in-the-wall bars and cafes, motels, beach houses, and beaches to visit, play on, or stay in. We laugh and talk a lot and have great times. We also play lots of tennis, golf, volleyball, and go snorkeling. The food's wonderful! I've never had much Asian or Polynesian food before, but I'm getting to be a real fan. I eat rice, saimen noodles, mahi-mahi, teriyaki, sushi, adobo and lumpia like I have eaten it all my life. I act like I've never heard of fried chicken, beans, cornbread or Tennessee cured ham!

There are "haze gray and underway" Navy ships everywhere! Aircraft carriers, supply ships, ammunition ships, oilers, cruisers, destroyers and submarines — not only our Navy, but Canadian, Australian, and British and a few other countries...officers and sailors from all those countries wherever you go. Some of my friends and I are invited regularly aboard these ships for dinner. We receive *engraved* invitations. There's a picture of the Queen in the wardroom over the mock fireplace and we toast the Queen before dinner's served. Aboard the HRM Ships they have booze.

This is the real Navy! Pearl Harbor hums with activity from the shipyard to the docks. All sorts of yardcraft plying the harbor. Ships coming and going and big sendoffs and homecomings with bands and hula dancers and leis. The Pentagon was never like this.

I met a man who's the XO of the *Butterfish*. He's from Savannah, GA, an academy grad, and very much the Southern Gentleman. He opens doors for me, walks me to the door or out to my car, is always on time, makes very good conversation. He's fairly good looking, witty and charming and a lot of fun! We've been to many Navy functions — SUBPAC receptions, parties at my command, CINCPACFLT shindigs. We've also been to plush restaurants and concerts. He's almost too good to be true. I have a gut feeling he's spoken for, as in married or engaged or something. My female officer friends agree. I'll let you know. His name is Charles Edward Osborne, III. "Trey" (as he's called) has invited me to go on his boat for a guest cruise in a couple of weeks. I've never been down in a sub before — adventure awaits.

Now to those couple of exceptions. One is BOQ life: The Pearl Harbor BOQ is an old WWII wooden barracks-type building. Two stories, community heads, a swimming pool, and a closed mess. There're two VIP quarters, and the two women, assigned to the BOQ occupy the VIP quarters. (Again, the Navy isn't sure what to do with women.) Some of the male officers who live in the "Q" are stationed at Pearl — Supply, CEC, some line, etc. They go about their business in a professional manner and are friendly and accepting of me.

But, the Neanderthals are those guys who are TAD from ships and squadrons, attending courses, schools, or other projects away from their commands. They're loud, belligerent, malicious, drink way too much, stay up all night with loud music, roam the passageways beating on doors, unscrewing light bulbs, and tossing empty bottles around. Weekends are absolutely impossible. When I go to the mess for breakfast they sneer and make lewd remarks about my size, shape, what I wear under my skirt and what I can do with my breakfast items. They're so boorish and childish and ugly. Do these people ever grow up? Not all are like that, mind you, but the majority are, or at least they act like it because they don't want to seem different. I don't stay in the Q on weekends any more. My room has been broken into twice, each time to leave a vulgar *Playboy* centerfold picture on my bed and a note saying, "That's all you are. You're not an officer in My Navy." Some of these guys probably expect to command ships someday. Wow!

The other exception is that old fuddy-duddy. Remember I told you about him, Tuck? Well, apparently he's been asked to put in his retirement papers, and he claims I'm to blame! He came to my office the other day and told me that I'd embarrassed him because I spoke to the Chief of Staff about the incident at the Officers' Club. He really got kind of nasty and vehement. My secretary, Margaret, was shocked. So I asked him to leave, and he wrote me up for disrespect! Is it the way I look, the way I talk? Is there something wrong with my attitude? And, of course, I had another little talk with the CofS. He told me not to worry, that it's not my fault. He apologized. Still, to be yelled at by that Captain is upsetting.

You can see I'm getting an initiation into the Navy. But, so far the good outweighs everything else and I'm having a terrific time. Your Fair duty sounds fun. We read about it over here. And to think, I *know* someone there!

Your friend,

Billie

Chapter Four

A Student Again

One month later from Tucker

30 September 1964, Washington, D.C.

Dear Mother and Dad,

Thanks for the check. I'll make it through, but it's great to have a little extra to buy furniture for my apartment. I would've been strapped to pay for first and last month's rent without the Dead Horse from disbursing. Second time I've had to draw one.

I could've roomed with another woman officer, but I'd rather have my own place in light of my need for peace and quiet to study. This next year will mainly be devoted to attending classes, studying, and writing. My undergraduate education will pay off. If they taught us anything at Wellesley it was to think and write with clarity and logic!

This International Relations degree at American University will require much writing, and surely lots of profound thinking. A real change from my last two jobs. That's why I love being a general line officer. The billets permit genuine diversity in the assignments.

The course work looks fascinating. It's an exciting time to be alive, given the challenges of the Cold War. By the end of the year I'll have an opinion on most U.S. policies, I'm sure. My focus will be on contemporary international relations, IR theory, and national security policy. Good background for a Navy job in the fields of politico-military affairs or intelligence, right Dad?

As you know, D.C. teems with cultural events and historical places to see. I can't wait to explore.

Good talking with you last night. I'm happy you're in the good old USA rather than far away in *Napoli*. I'm upset about having to give you Gabby. Though I know he'll have the best of homes, I shall miss him terribly. As we agreed, my schedule's just too hard on him. Hopefully he'll be as special for you as was François, his father and your "son." That's all for now.

Lots of love,

Tucker

Two weeks later from Tom

15 October 1964, USS John Paul Jones
Upkeep in the Holy Loch

Dear Tucker,

I'm frustrated about being unable to coordinate our leave times, but we'll keep trying. In the meantime, I'll write, and hope you'll reciprocate, 'cause I do enjoy your letters. I'm envious to think that you and Pierre are in National Security Policy classes together.

Scotland sure is beautiful. Interestingly, in contrast to the Pacific ports I've been in, the locals don't make much effort to part the American sailor from his dollars. Sadly, I haven't had any time to part with mine anyway.

I need to tell you another reason why I think I turned down Intelligence School and went for Rickover's program. Haven't really said much to you about Marilyn, my ex-wife. When I first decided to stay in the Navy, Marilyn had wanted Intel School instead of Sub School. She dreamed of entertaining ambassadors and attachés and living in foreign countries with lots of servants!

If you and I are going to be long-time friends, I guess I should tell you more of my marriage and what I regard as a personal failure in judgment. I don't know what Pierre has told you. It's hard for me to talk about in person and not so difficult this way.

I met Marilyn at the Norfolk O' Club between Med cruises of my first ship, a cruiser. She (Marilyn, not the ship) was a knockout, and I was, well, an ensign. She gave all the signs of really liking me. She worked as a clerk-typist at a local department store and talked vaguely of going to college. I think we hit every good beach, club, and bar in the area, and even had time for some home-cooked meals with her folks. I really liked it when my fellow officers said, "Wow, who was that (dame/dish/doll/broad) I saw you with last night?"

During the cruise, she wrote faithfully, and I never noticed the topics ran solely to her family, the weather, her co-workers, and her girl friends. In fairness, my letters were probably mostly about my work, my shipmates, and what I thought of her baby blues, with maybe a smattering of comment about a visited port. By the time the ship returned to Norfolk, and I was in a state of high delusional horniness, I'd convinced myself that she was my lifetime playmate.

The rush to the altar was hastened by my orders to the Office of Naval Intelligence, D.C. This kind of rotation wasn't uncommon for NROTC types. BuPers knew not many of us would remain on active duty, so when they needed a junior officer ashore they tended to take us, preferring to leave the academy grads at sea until they qualified as Officer of the Deck.

I can't say we didn't have a good time in D.C. — lots of parties, going to Ocean City or down to VA Beach, and free things to do, outdoor concerts, museums, the zoo. I took the LSATs, applied to Georgetown Law School, was accepted, and planned to go when my obligated time was up. Marilyn was looking for a job.

Then I got a call from an officer at BuPers who said to me, "Why don't you stay in the Navy? We need you. Your country needs you." Or something like that. Well, there's no feeling like being wanted, so I countered, "I might consider it as a submariner." I knew the elites were aviators or submariners, and I didn't fancy landing a jet on a bobbing postage stamp. Submariners I'd heard got better pay and ate well! The BuPers guy countered, "Well, they won't take you unless you're a qualified Officer of the Deck. We'll send you to a destroyer so you can qualify and then you can apply to sub school. Let me see what I can do... Wait a second, you're in luck. There's an opening on the USS *Crandall* in San Diego right now." I talked it over with Marilyn who got excited about driving across country, and no doubt also realized her work obligations to put me through law school had disappeared.

Marilyn's enthusiasm renewed my own enthusiasm for her. By then I'd observed she clammed up when the subject of what was going on in the world came up, and as you well know, when you live in D.C. that kind of subject comes up often! People read the *Post*, then discuss what's in the *Post*. I'd begun to find myself short-tempered with her when I realized she simply tuned out and didn't know what anyone, especially me, was talking about. Sex, I'd begun to think, wasn't everything.

It wasn't long after our San Diego arrival that the *Crandall* deployed to WestPac for six months. We'd found a great duplex on the beach in Ocean Beach, made friends with the neighbors, made a trip to Tijuana, and that was about it. Six months was too long for Marilyn. She didn't get a job or take a course. She went out. To make the tedious stereotypical story short, she met an aviator and she simply left town with him, sending me the "Dear Tom" letter.

At least she gave me no hassle with the divorce. My family sure did though, because they didn't believe in divorce. Some of them might have been secretly pleased that Joe College had messed up and couldn't hang on to his wife. My Navy friends did turn out to be "family" during the crisis, even those I'd hardly had time to meet. Until the ship returned, the CO's and XO's wives dealt with the practical problems Marilyn had left me such as milk spoiling in the fridge and my car illegally parked.

Enough soap opera! I hope you don't find this saga too horribly boring. Just had to tell you some details of my previous life.

We're having haggis for dinner on the boat tonight as we're hosting the mayor. Look it up! Yecch!

Keep those letters coming. Sounds like you're really pounding out the papers.

                    Hugs,

                    Tom

Three months plus later from Tucker

                              15 January 1965, Washington,D.C.

Dear Robyn,

I'm deep into graduate work. It's a pleasure to have full time to delve into political questions. Impossible to do well in night school and carry on with a Navy job, in my opinion. Many do, nonetheless.

I'm truly beginning to appreciate the meanings of political terms such as "balance of power," the school of "realpolitik," and the great traditions on the Nature of Man. To study ideas in the abstract, as we did in our undergraduate days, is one thing. It's another to have served some years in the military and combine Navy policy background with academic ideas. I'm quickly building the so-called "conceptual framework" for comprehending our international relations and policies.

The professors are outstanding, with foreign service experience scattered in their resumés. Several of the hot-shot professors, what I call armchair professors, argue for pretty aggressive foreign policies, seemingly without understanding the consequences (like committing the U.S. and its military to war). They should spend several months at the Pentagon to get the feel for how a military man must support and defend such aggressive policies, whether he truly believes in them or not.

I'm doing well scholastically. Am fortunate to have a solid educational background and a mind that enjoys the work, including *lots* of papers. At the moment I'm in the process of writing a book review of Kenneth Waltz' *Man, The State and War*. Analyzing the theories, assumptions, and values behind national and international actions and policies is vital to policy analysis. No doubt the Navy feels the same, for it granted us a year off from our regular duties for such purpose.

I know you're uninterested in this stuff and would probably rather think about animals and their unique behaviors. As a U.S. citizen, however, you should be concerned about the "little war" we're gradually escalating in Vietnam. I can find no compelling reason for us to be in Southeast Asia, the domino theory notwithstanding. Maybe by the end of the academic year I'll be persuaded otherwise. I doubt it.

My social life goes well, though I still can't seem to find that special guy. What I really wish is that my penpal, Lt. Tom Parker, stationed on a sub out of New London, were here. In the meantime, I've been dating several officers, including LCDR Pete Williams, a university classmate.

Do you remember Lt. Jennie Winters? Well, now Lieutenant Commander Winters works for the Chief of Naval Operations at the Pentagon. I've set up a double date: Pete and I, and Jennie and Captain-selectee Pierre LaMonte, another classmate who's a real gentleman and brilliant student. Jennie seems excited about going out on a double date.

What's new with you? I may be a bore, but will be a lot wiser about U.S. National Security Policy by the end of this course work.

Take good care of yourself.

> Love,
>
> Tucker

Three weeks later from Robyn

February 7, 1965, Boston, MA

Dear Tucker,

It sounds like you've found something you can really get into at last. I don't mean you haven't been involved and absorbed in the

Navy for the past five years or so, but it seems that now your intellect is challenged and you can put together theory and practice to a greater extent. I'm pleased for you!

I agree with you about armchair professors or generals or admirals, or whoever dictates what the little man on the line is supposed to do. Only I think your theoretical profs, and the military leadership, ought to go not to the Pentagon but over to Vietnam and live the life of the soldier, sailor, or airman — ducking bullets, slogging through mud, enduring heat and mosquitoes, experiencing the wasting of men, women, and children, and all the attendant horrors of the game called war. Instead, they sit in their comfy offices and war gaming rooms planning strategies as intellectual exercises. YETCH! Why are we there? I never meet anyone anymore with the tiniest conviction that this is the right thing to do.

Ned and I continue our relationship — no status change, at least in the short term until he gets his degree. The clinic continues to be interesting. I really like the team approach and love working with kids.

Love,

Robyn

One week later from Tucker's journal

15 February 1965, Washington, D.C.

For the record,

Received a brief phone call from Jennie today, telling me how much she's enjoying dating Pierre. Turns out he has a real romantic streak. Yesterday he sent a dozen red roses to her at the office! She was a little nonplused about "combining my profession with pleasure," but said she enjoyed the envious looks that came her way.

Jennie suggested that if Tom gets to town anytime soon, it would be fun for the four of us to go out again. I agreed!

She sounds very happy with her new beau; they're going to the symphony this weekend. I'm truly pleased for Jennie and Pierre. Hope it's a match, though I will always think of Jennie on another plane.

TF

Easter time 1965 from Tucker's journal

For the record,

An odd, *very* frightening thought crossed my mind today. I seem to be interested in one of my classmates on a level beyond friendship. It's like electricity is in the air when I'm around her. Her name is Donna Whitman, and she's in my Theories of International Relations class. I've been drawn to her since semester's beginning. Think the feeling's mutual. We teamed up to report on IR simulation and game theory. The professor suggested a tough book. We each took opposing sides. She's good, *very* good, at analyzing and writing.

We're getting together tomorrow to discuss our in-class presentation. She's a State Department officer, renting in the Georgetown area. Hope I can find my way to her house without getting lost. Wonder why I feel drawn to her? She raises feelings similar to those I experience with Jennie. I've tried to squelch my feeling toward Jennie.

Who could I be? Maybe I *am* bisexual. I sense the feeling toward Donna could easily shift to the physical aspect, and that's frightening. Her whole being appeals to me. Just think, I might prefer women. Certainly would explain my sexuality crisis. My double date with Pete was innocuous. But the tension wasn't there as it is with Donna.

Why am I feeling scared? No doubt some paranoia about woman-to-woman sexuality and the Navy.

TF

From Tucker to Mother and Dad

15 May 1965, Washington, D.C.

Dear Mother and Dad,

I'm about finished with course work. Just need to take the three comprehensive exams. Am not looking forward to them, but should do all right. Should I type or hand write? Think I'll hand write, legibly.

One of the more provocative mental exercises I've conducted these past few months is analysis of Vietnam policy from many directions. To think through national policy in terms of options, assumptions behind the options, and outcomes makes sense. I'm unconvinced that our policy makers always do so. Have been studying the history of Southeast Asia, of our Western involvement, and our alleged U.S. national interest in the area. No matter how I think through the choices, I know we're choosing the wrong option by continuing a military buildup in Vietnam. Do you realize we have over 29,000 U.S. personnel in S.Vietnam?

I can't argue in favor of the United States build-up there. Neither can anyone else I've listened to. We don't have any business fighting a guerrilla war. The generals and admirals are being hoodwinked by the politicians, I think.

If my comps maintain my class ranking, I'll be number one among the 37 naval officers in our class. I feel proud for myself and for Navy women. My classmates have been super supportive. What pleases me most about the possibility of being at the top is that no one can say, "You're using your dad's influence to get good jobs and fitness reports." The School of International Service at A.U. couldn't care less that my father is an admiral. As we've discussed, being a Navy Junior produces both positive and negative effects. One of the negatives for me is the perpetual prodding from lesser lights who think I can get what I want through Dad's power and influence. Far from the truth, and I detest the inference.

I'm excited about where I might go for the next duty station. Hoping for the Naval Academy. They have two billets open in the History Department. Keep your fingers crossed for me!

Your trip to Alaska sounded magnificent. I'm jealous. Hope to see you soon and catch up.

Love,

Tucker

Three Days later from Mother and Dad

18 May 1965, San Diego, CA

Dear Tucker,

It's hard to realize your graduate studies are about done (unless a Ph.D. looms before you). Seems such a short while ago we were trying to buoy you up when recruiting duty seemed trying. We're so very proud of you. You seem to take whatever they throw at you in stride; number one in your class! I cannot remember a time when I was number one academically in anything — your mother maybe, but not I. Hearty congratulations!

The assignment at the Academy seems made to order for you, but as I remember those assignments, they were pretty desirable and you may have male competition. How're you going to feel if a guy gets the job? We'll keep our fingers crossed for you. Don't let the fluff about being a naval officer's daughter bother you. Such statements are usually from individuals who want excuses for their own less-than-topnotch performance. Frankly, I wish I could do something about getting you the assignment you want, but we both know any attempts to do that might well ensure that you wouldn't get it.

Your mention of Vietnam is interesting. Your mother and I discuss it a lot. The news seems to indicate there are things we don't know concerning the manipulation of other governments by our various agencies. But it seems to me the French have proved that getting deeply involved militarily in another country's search for identity is risky. Your comment that the generals and admirals are being hoodwinked is amusing. Civilian control of the military is the name of the game in this country. Whether hoodwinking is the term to use or not, I'm not sure. When political decisions are made, generals and admirals have little opportunity for debate except to express their military capabilities to carry out the decision. You wouldn't want it any other way, would you? I can't imagine there was anything in your National Security studies last year that suggested otherwise.

Wherever you go for your next assignment, remember this beautiful West Coast atmosphere, and come home occasionally to soak it up. We love you.

Mother and Dad

One Week later from Tucker

25 May 1965, Washington, D.C.

Dear Tom,

Sure is tricky keeping up with my nuclear submariner on the *John Paul Jones!* Let's see, according to my calendar, you came off your two months' patrol with no communications on 3 May, are on leave until 3 June and then start your one month's upkeep and two months patrol cycle on 4 June. Hard to explain to civilians about Blue and Gold crews and the need for two crews per one boat.

I'm hoping you'll get this before you leave the Holy Loch. Right now you should be on your well-deserved leave in the British Isles, hosting your big family of brothers, sisters, and nieces and nephews. Great fun!

You remember I wanted that Naval Academy billet — teaching political science and naval history. Tom, you won't believe what the Academy said. The powers-that-be turned me down flat because "she doesn't have enough gray hairs." They told my detailer, CDR Ruth Rhoades, that from my official picture I'm "much too attractive" to teach middies. They'd be *looking* at me and not thinking about what I'm saying about naval history or political science. "Have her try again in ten years." Don't you think that's about *the* most discriminatory reason to turn down a naval officer for a job?

I know our leadership sees active duty women as largely needed in times of mobilization and call-ups, but this is such an absurd excuse. Here I am the *top* Navy graduate in my class, supposedly able to select the billet of my choice in my grade. The Academy has a lieutenant's billet open in its History Department. I choose that billet, and "they" turn me down for good looks (more precisely for my *gender*). The Academy faculty doesn't allow women officer instructors and doesn't intend to. What a bunch of jerks. Their loss. Must sign off early and finish last minute studies. We're having a farewell party next week (all of us naval officer students).Wish you were here to be my escort!

Hugs and warm wishes,

A madder-than-hell Lieutenant

One week later from Tucker's journal

31 May 1965, Washington, D.C.

 For the record,

I'm feeling both sad and glad about my "goodbye" to Donna last night. I did the best I could, but probably was too aloof. I told her our times together had been more than wonderful, that she brought out the best in me, allowed me to be who I really am, and that my playful, fun side comes out when I'm with her.

We both agreed that to have explored Washington together had been extraordinary. We recalled the paranoia and fear we'd both experienced when we walked into that downtown women's restaurant and bar...yet what a comfortable feeling it had been to be with women enjoying each others' company, and how quickly it had become our favorite spot.

We agreed that fate seems to be saying that our last few months were an aberration. Certainly our society and respective institutions tell us that women coupled together, except as friends, is abnormal. And "queer." (My mother always used that word. Seems so excluding.) I think of Donna and me, individually and as a couple, as neither abnormal nor queer.

From all that I know within my heart, I love Donna. I love her in a deeper way than I've been able to love any man. And Lord knows I've been seriously dating many men these last years. Yet I haven't been able to say "yes" to getting in bed with any of them. It was a natural thing to do with Donna. Hope I'll feel this way when I see Tom again!

It's best that Donna and I part for a while and consider ourselves as just friends. For me it seems too stressful to live a double life, a life of deceit and lies insofar as honoring and obeying Navy policies toward homosexuals while simultaneously loving a woman in my private life. Donna doesn't seem to have as much trouble living two lives, the professional and the private. She's perhaps better at compartmentalization. But then, I don't see the State Department as threatened by gays and lesbians as is the United States military, though Donna did relate some horror stories about State and gays in the 1950s. My blood pressure problem, "labile hypertension," has been more prominent than usual these last months for more reasons than anxiety over final exams.

I promised to write her. Wish I were going with her. I don't see any possible billets for me overseas right now. The Navy doesn't permit women to serve as attachés, and intelligence is my selected specialty field. Navy women could be great spies I should think. Remember Mata Hari? Think of the cocktail party gossiping! Would make for great intelligence reports.

Donna and I were a special couple and I'll always have her in my heart. I know she'll find someone else to love.

Wonder what the Ambassador's wife would think of this entry?

TF

One day later from Tucker

1 June 1965, Washington, D.C.

Dear Robyn,

I'm wiped out physically and psychologically. I need to fill you in on what's been happening. Am wondering why I haven't heard from you in a while. Hope all's well.

At the moment I'm disgusted with the Navy. My body is tired from studying for my comps, but the real fatigue comes from stewing over what's happening in both my professional and personal life.

First the professional: looks as though I'll be #1 in our class of naval officers. Wellesley would be proud of me — the only woman among 37 officers. That's the good side. I should be assigned to a great billet because of my standing.

But so far I've had two strikes. The first — the Naval Academy turned me down because I'm too attractive and distracting for its middies! The second strike hit today — I've been excited ever since my detailer called and said it looked likely that I'd be sent to the Pentagon in the Navy's Politico-Military Affairs Division to a billet that no woman had ever filled. I'd essentially be a briefing officer to the Chief of Naval Operations (the CNO, the Navy's head guy) for a certain area of the world, like Southeast Asia or Western Europe. Hard work, long hours, but terrific experience and great career opportunities. She said my record had been sent up the flagpole and had passed all desks and chops except the CNO's office.

Robyn, you're not going to believe this: the CNO's office immediately responded "No!" to my name. The main reason — the big wigs want to be able to use "shit," "fuck," or any other four-letter word, whenever and wherever they wish. To have a young female lieutenant in CNO's briefing room would deter them from using such expletives. Wonder what Navy they think I've been in for the last six years? So, no go for Lieutenant Fairfield.

I'm devastated by this second low blow dealt by the Navy. I've worked so hard for six years, and to be turned down for just "being a woman" is wrong. These guys couldn't say, "you're not qualified." They could only make up dumb excuses. It feels like I (and women officers in general) will never be given a card or key to the REAL Navy.

Second, the personal. I don't know how to write about this without blurting it out to you. The last few months I've been having a special social life with another classmate, who happens to be a woman, Donna Whitman. We've had great times, including in bed. I don't know if that news shocks you. I doubt it, or I wouldn't be writing it to you, I'd tell you in person. After all, you're a New England liberal, and we've sorta discussed the subject through the years.

The outcome of all this — major stress for me and Donna. She's a neat woman with a fine mind (and a great body). We've had incredible experiences, in between class work and exams. But throughout this I've had tremendous conflict over what my heart tells me is okay and what my conscience tells me is not okay. My conscience is driven by societal and parental norms, as well as Navy policies. My conscience has been winning in the last few weeks. Fortunately (or not), it looks as if I'm going to be stationed in the D.C. area and Donna's headed for Oslo. To carry on any meaningful relationship would be impossible. Two days ago I told Donna that I couldn't continue with her other than in a friendship. One of the most discomforting scenes I've ever experienced.

As you can sense, my friend, life's been full and stressful. Hope yours has been more peaceful. I plan to get back to dating men and get in the swing of things once I finish with comps and report to a new duty station.

What *do* you really think about same-sex relationships? In college none of us truly discussed the subject, probably because society keeps it so secretive. I must say feeling equal in a relationship is a great feeling. I've not felt that way with men; there's always the so-called sex roles underlying the relationship. Sometimes I enjoy what that implies, but the inequality of it all bothers me. Guess who's the less equal?

Enough deep stuff. Let me know what's happening in your life. My correspondence with my submariner friend, Tom Parker, has picked up. He's a most appealing man, too!

Thank you for letting me blow off steam about the Navy. I'm thinking more and more that the powers-that-be have their head in the sand about Navy women and our capabilities. After all, we women line officers have been around since 1942. Peace be with you.

> Love,
>
> Tucker

Two weeks later from Robyn

> June 15, 1965, Boston, MA

Dear Tucker,

Wow!! We get out of touch for a few months and ZAPPO! All kinds of stuff surfaces. I hardly know where to start.

First off, I need to express my indignation that you, an educated, intelligent, knowledgeable, highly motivated individual, are denied a totally suitable position because some exalted officers want to say "Goddamn," or whatever. Tucker, *why* do you continue to put up with that garbage? It's one thing to say a woman can't serve in combat situations, chauvinistic though it is; but to be denied an appropriate, responsible position so someone can swear is insane. Bizarre! Unnatural! Outrageous, weird, and outlandish! The men and the organization sponsoring them are truly beyond belief! Do I make myself clear? GOOD GRIEF! Why ever would you want to get a card into the REAL Navy?

On to your letter's second dynamo. You're right, we never did discuss same-sex or same-gender relationships in college. We were probably so busy trying to fit in and date and go to mixers and go steady and get pinned and get scarves from this and that college that we never even considered such a phenomenon. Since school, I've known several people involved in same-sex relationships, actually a couple of men and a woman friend. They're not having an easy time. Two of the three haven't yet come out to their parents. Most keep their relationships secret, sharing lifestyles only with close friends. All three are wary of anybody at work finding out. One couple lives in a suburbanish-type area and is very anxious about neighbors. In fact, they may soon move because the stress factor is so high.

More. What do I think about same-sex stuff? Am I shocked? Do I disapprove? Ultimately on some level I suspect you're wondering if our relationship will be altered by this information. I would assume, Tucker, that you know me better than that. But I'll assure you anyway! The only thing I think is a huge — well, tragedy — is the way we as a society are so fucking intolerant. (You don't scare me into not saying fuck!) And, Tucker, knowing how hard it is for my friends to cope in the outside world with this lifestyle, I can only imagine the torments for you and others in the Navy and other military services.

Again, I cry, "What is it that keeps you battling such primitive, irrational odds in your chosen career?"

I don't suppose all this shrieking has been particularly helpful or supportive. I want you, however, to know I support you in every way. But, as you might have noticed, I've become increasingly less enchanted with your outfit as the years go on.

Me, I'm fine. (I always am in the summer. I dislike with a passion the cold Boston winters.) Ned's fine, got his degree a week ago. And now, with that behind us, we might consider some lifestyle changes. AHEM!

Hang in there, my friend, and let's stay in touch.

Love,

Robyn

Five days later from Tom

20 June 1965, The Holy Loch
USS John Paul Jones

Hi "Madder-than-hell (and still are I bet) Lieutenant,"

How would you expect leering, lecherous, lascivious sailors to keep their minds on the great battles of the sea with you in front of them? That's really the problem with you women. You don't understand that it doesn't matter whether we men fully appreciate your brains, talents, and skills. We can't keep our dirty minds off your body parts. Even if we do, through great dint of effort, we're still going to be afraid of our reactions to you and of our inability to understand what the rules of engagement really are.

The way we can protect ourselves is to stick together as guys and find reasons to keep you out! Perhaps letting you become an instructor might work if we followed the custom of costume in some of the more forward thinking middle-eastern countries. You could wear a floor-length black bag with heavy veiling or perhaps lecture from behind a curtain. Off duty you might be allowed to wear your uniform if you promised not to put it on until you were well-cleared from Annapolis and the juvenile lust of midshipmen.

Jokes aside. Will it help if I tell you I think you've been royally screwed and have every right to be pissed off? You have and you do. Can I tell you what to do to change it? No, I can't. Let's hope this is an isolated incident for you. If, in fact, it typifies the way you're to be treated, well, only you can decide if it's worth sticking.

I managed to survive my stint as travel guide for my family. No, I don't mind going to the Wax Museum for the umpteenth time. I swear, the last time I went, Lord Nelson recognized me and winked. "No, Tom, the kids probably don't want to go to the Royal Ballet, but we'd all sure love to see that Agatha Christie play, *The Mousetrap*. Hasn't it been running for the last hundred years? Why do the English drive on the wrong side of the road? How can we get to see the Queen? Don't those guards ever speak? How much money is a pound? What do they call the really public schools if a public school is a private school? Why are their cars so small? Why do they say spend-a-penny when you have to put in a shilling?"

So, Tuck, sure it was fun, and my family's great right down to the weeist bairn. But don't succumb to the only-child trap of over-romanticizing big families; they have their downsides too.

I'm grateful every day that I'm not on my way to Nam, but instead "going on guard on the perimeter of the free world"— that's our stock answer to the nosy civilians who ask where we go when we go on patrol. In fact very few of the crew has any clue to where they are once we deploy. The water looks the same down there and when we come up again we're just outside of The Holy Loch.

You're studying international relations now. Isn't it customary to have some kind of objective in mind in a war? What's ours exactly? It's clearly not about keeping the commies from rowing ashore in L.A. How do we know when we've won? What I regret is seeing our military (Us. You and me, kid, too!) lose respect, not only in other countries, but at home. I hear that when one of our off-crew officers visits a campus NROTC unit to talk up the nuclear power program, he calls ahead to the officer-in-charge of the unit to see if it's OK to wear his uniform on the campus! A buddy of mine recently got back from visiting Harvard and they told him it wasn't! He went in mufti! Great word, huh! I used to think it was what a British Raj wore in India. Another childhood illusion smashed.

Hey, Tuck, how about you making it over here my next off-crew, 4 Sept–3 Oct? I'll take pleasure in showing you the sights so long as you promise to visit the Wax Museum on your own! If you can't get leave, why then I'll visit you in D.C., maybe the first two weeks. Then I'll have to visit my parents and maybe make a couple of these campus visits for ADM Rickover.

Playing any tunes? I've learned a few Scottish ballads and I'll play 'em for ye ere I see ye agin.

Keep the home fires, etc. I'll look for a letter before it's "Dive Dive" and incommunicado time again. Wives and parents send familygrams, a very limited number of words in a message to the boat that can be read by the whole fleet! I hear the officers' wives on the *Lincoln* got together and sent, "One of us is pregnant."

Sorry to have missed your farewell party. Would've loved being the one who beat out the others to be your escort. If you're not going to turn on the middies, where are you going? I need to know!

Your ever lovin', lonesome,

Tom

Five days later from Tucker

25 June 1965, Washington, D.C.

Dear Mother and Dad,

I'm so glad you're enjoying San Diego. Do you know it's the second largest contingent of any Navy in the world?

I've lost confidence in the Navy's personnel system. It will take a while to restore my trust in detailers. As I told you last night, I'm reporting to a counterintelligence job here next week. Don't ask me any more about the billet because my detailer said she couldn't tell me. When I asked her the meaning of counterintelligence, she said "it's too classified to answer." Hmm. The dictionary says it's the part of the intelligence business that spies on other intelligence services.

Dad, I think the Navy sees its women as useless appendages who are only good for mobilization in war time, and who have only administrative skills. My administrative skills are okay, but my analytical skills are pretty damn exceptional. The Navy doesn't want to deal with me other than as an attractive being who can fill administrative billets. What an archaic view! The Navy has spent money educating me. It ought to want to *use* my education. What a waste of womanpower. It's going to be a long row to hoe for military women. We can't mutiny. Perhaps we should consider revolution. Jefferson recommended a revolution every generation!

Feels great to have the comps behind me, and I received my finest fitness report ever. Lot of good it did me in getting a good job.

The D.C. humidity seems the same as Philly's. Not so fun. Fortunately I can at last afford a fully air-conditioned apartment.

By the way, for my own peace of mind, last night I dropped a note to Buck Buckingham, telling him of my distress with the Navy's personnel ways. He shouldn't attempt to change my assignment, but he should know the details from my perspective. And I'd like to know his view.

Will keep you posted. Must get some sleep.

Love,

Tucker

Six days later from Mother and Dad

1 July 1965, San Diego, CA

Dear Tucker,

How the scene changes. A little over a month ago we were all happy as clams over your performance at graduate school, and now you sound as though the world is ending. Get some perspective. Not getting the assignment you want is more likely to occur than not. Weren't we talking about needs of the service a year or so ago?

Counterintelligence isn't the end of the world and even you admit to good analytical skills. The job's in Washington; you'll be visible. I imagine when your boss, whoever he or she is, catches a glimpse of your record and your ability, your light will not be hidden under a bushel of administrative claptrap.

Some do see women in the Navy as an anomaly. I really don't know whether the fact that I have a daughter in naval service colors my view, but I expect it does. I grew up at a time and during a war when women did certain things. I do wonder how women would've handled the dicey moments in submarines under attack during WWII. Probably my uncertainty's because I use a general term here, "women," rather than speak of a specific woman whose capabilities and interests I know. I can hear you say, "that's because they've never had a chance to prove what they can do." Certainly a lot of logic in that.

I don't think of a position in counterintelligence as a woman's job. Maybe you know something about it you haven't told us. Why is it a waste of womanpower? Your mother and I didn't quite get that one. It just sounds to us like you're mad because you didn't get what you wanted. We know you're smarter than that.

Glad you wrote to Buck. He will understand that your performance will be better in an assignment you really want, rather than one you'll have to learn to like. Maybe he can find a spot with NATO. Stranger things have happened. Hang in there, Tucker, and if you get too weary with all the infighting, come home. Your mother and I will cool you off. Sailing is a wonderful way to clean out the mental attic.

All our love. Mother and Dad

Two days later from Buck Buckingham

3 July 1965, The Pentagon

Dear Tucker,

This is in response to your note of 24 June. Personnel assignments can be perplexing. Sometimes logic seems deliberately not to have been used when we're matched with military tasks. As time goes on, you advance in grade and have a bit more influence over what your next job will be and disappointments like you're experiencing tend to diminish. Even then, senior officers — I mean even admirals — are often surprised when their actual orders are issued.

"NEEDS OF THE SERVICE," that wonderful phrase which says everything and says nothing. It's the fallback position of every personnel detailer trying to explain why expected assignments didn't materialize. In my own view you qualify in every way for an Op-06 assignment. Planning seems to be your forté; you like order and reason, you research subjects thoroughly and draw objective conclusions from your research. You're well-educated in the academic cross-disciplines of political science; you want an assignment there, and I know there are those who want you in Op-06. What more is needed to qualify for such as assignment? I do not know.

It could be that some special "need" reared its head about the time your name came up for assignment. Perhaps someone else had been requested for the Op-06 assignment, and the requester had more influence than the individual who requested you. There's an outside chance the detailers feel it's a "man's job." Such thinking is rarer these days, but we still have a few chauvinists to educate.

I believe the chauvinistic reason is the least likely reason you didn't get the assignment, but it's difficult to repress such feelings when they hit you. If you create noise with a claim that sex discrimination did you in, gradually you'll develop a service reputation of putting yourself first, looking for trouble, and being difficult to please. Although these feelings will have nothing to do with the fact that you're a woman (such reputations are built by men also), they'll be used in an "I told you so" way by those who are unhappy to see women in the military. The objective is to get good, visible assignments where you can contribute and be noticed. Tucker, developing a personal stigma of any nature will hurt your career.

Meanwhile, I'll look into this, discreetly. I'll also begin to ring a few bells around the corridors sounding off about the opportunity missed by not assigning you to Strategic Planning. Maybe that can lay a little strategic groundwork for you and for WAVES in general.

Do not let this get to you. We've all been there. It's a part of the inherent waste in a personnel system which has more qualified people than billets for them. It will always be this way since the military mission is to be ready for conflict if we're unsuccessful in preventing it. That requires a lot of people "in waiting," people who can be seen as wasteful by those who misunderstand the system.

Warm regards. My best to your family when you next write.

Buck

Two weeks later from Tucker

17 July 1965, Washington, D.C.

Dear Tom,

What a lovely invitation! Scotland sounds super! Unfortunately, I'm one of the junior officers, with no priority in the command's summer leave schedule, so I'll have to settle for seeing you in September.

Turns out I'm in a mediocre job, working for a civilian boss (former agent). I've told myself that I'll give it my best shot for a year, and then see what alternatives are available. (Actually I don't have a choice — one year at a duty station before any PCS transfer.)

I read the Intelligence Reports (IR's) written within naval intelligence offices in Western Europe. I can tell you exactly what the admirals and generals prefer in their martinis and old-fashioneds!

Speaking of intelligence, I'm finding it strange, sometimes formidable, not to talk about my job except at work. As you know, this comes with intel business and clearances, but that doesn't make it easy. What a switch from talking freely with armchair professors at the University to completely restraining my tongue after duty hours. Difficult to differentiate between classified and unclassified information. So, I don't talk much, particularly with civilians. At night I talk to myself and the television, sorting out the day and the tasks at hand. It would be great to talk with you in person, even with having to avoid sensitive, classified subjects.

One area that bothers me daily is Vietnam. Can you believe we're continuing to build up our strength there? Seems so wrong-headed to me.

Feels good to be back in uniform. Now I don't have to think about what to wear when I get up.

All for now, my love. Hope you can work out dates.

Love,

Tucker

Two months later from Tucker's journal

15 September 1965, Arlington, Virginia

For the record,

Tom and I slept together last night. At the end of a lovely evening, including dinner at Old Ebbitts Grill downtown. It just happened. Tom drove me home and asked if he might stay the night. Somewhat reluctantly, I said "Yes, let's go ahead. It's time."

But unfortunately what happened wasn't like what I've read or dreamed about. It wasn't magic; it wasn't bells and whistles. What *did* I feel? I felt warmth. I felt special, special to be with an attractive, loving man, with his hairy chest and strong shoulders. I felt loved, for his love was transparent, and he obviously was enjoying me and my body.

BUT, I didn't have a good time. I felt violated. I was frightened that I might get pregnant, although Tom assured me that he would tend to that. I certainly don't need to deal with an abortion.

On the other hand, Fairfield, you do love Tom as a friend, as a caring, loving man. Why couldn't you take that leap of faith and just enjoy him as he did you?

Maybe I expected too much. Robyn told me the first experience is never what it's cut out to be, or, what it ultimately will be. So there, there. The first time isn't necessarily like the novels or the movies.

Life's getting too hard again.

TF

Two days later from Tucker's journal

17 September 1965, Arlington, Virginia

For the record,

Tom and I discussed "serious subjects" last night while on the town. Washington is such a magnificent city. I do love living in the capital.

We'd had a special dinner — Mai Tai's, lobsters, the works, at Trader Vic's in the Hilton, one of my favorite spots. Always reminds me of Pearl Harbor days in the late 40s. Feels like Tom's ready, even anxious, to settle down and give up bachelorhood. Seemingly out of the blue, during coffee and with the *Hawaiian Wedding Song* as a backdrop, he shifted from his usual breezy manner and asked, "How do you feel about children?"

I thought for a moment, wanting to be honest with him. I said, "Part of me wants to share myself not only with a partner but with my very own child; another part doesn't want to take on the *huge* responsibility of raising a child. And, I'd have to give up my career."

He seemed unhappy with my answer. "That's right. You'd have to resign if you became pregnant. Wonder what would happen if women stayed in when they got pregnant? Could be a detailer's nightmare."

"And then again, it could be a woman's dream — to be able to have both a career and a family," I mused.

Tom fits my personal theory about bachelors. They reach a point when they want to have families. Presto. Tom's arrived at this point, now that he's completely over Marilyn and all the trauma she caused him. The question is — is Tom in love with me or with the idea of marriage? Another, harder question — am I in love with him? I've every reason to be. He's such a great guy...self-assured, one of the most physically attractive naval officers I've ever met, caring, funny, and dedicated to the Navy. For heaven's sake, Fairfield, what more could you ask for?

After the children question, Tom asked me my general thoughts about marriage. I was honest with him by omission. "I've always wanted to have a companion to grow old with," I said. (What I left out is that I'm unclear about the *gender* of the companion. A big omission, I admit.)

He said, "I agree with you and I'm ready for a permanent companion."

I changed the subject. "You must be getting itchy about your next duty station?" Tom seemed all right with the shift.

I'm unwilling to discuss my inner struggle over homosexual feelings with Tom, even though he comes closest to my ideal partner. But these feelings don't seem to go away. To follow that unaccepted path, however, will inevitably lead to real pain and conflict.

Tom and I slept together again after our deep discussion. Still no bells and whistles. Yet being close to him felt good.

Stupid kiddo. I know very well that Tom would be a faithful, wonderful husband. He'd take good care of me, probably the rest of my life, something not to dismiss lightly. I truly love the feelings when he holds me closely. It's very comforting.

But why am I not totally comfortable about marriage? What is it? What's the barrier? I'd better figure it out soon.

TF

Two weeks later from Tom

2 October 1965, The Holy Loch

Hi Tuck,

Greetings from the land of lassies, kilts, and scones, and my favorite, haggis! I'm not sure I care if I ever hear another bagpipe either. Got a laugh last night though. I was having a wee pint at one of the locals and also there were a couple of Scots in full dress celebratin'. One of our boys sang out, "Oh, what does a Scotsman wear under his kilt, awang, awang" and quick as a flash one of them pointed at his companion and responded, "I don't know what he wears but as for me, I wear nothin' and I'd be pleased to show you and all these lassies right now."

I'm just starting to feel that my ear is tuning into the fine Scots' brogue and well, well, I've got orders. I'm to be Exec of *Starfish*. She's overhauling in New London, and I'm to report 7 Jan. I don't get back from patrol until 3 Jan so alas, there will be no time for T & T to make merry between the sheets between my duty stations. And make merry we certainly did, didn't we?

BuPers must have a spy whispering, "Hey, that Tom Parker is getting overly fond of that Tucker Fairfield. He's having much too good a time with her — better those two should pay more attention to Navy business. You know what happens when officers get carried away with sex. Their minds start to wandering when they're supposed to be preparing the crew for passing the reactor safety inspection and writing papers on the political instability of the Ottoman Empire. Let's fix it so he can't possibly get to D.C. on his way from Scotland to New London."

I can only hope you're as disappointed as I. We did have a swell time, didn't we? A great meeting of the mind and a damn good collision of the bodies. God, I do miss you. Those legs, those eyes, those lovely breasts. Delicious!

It seems I'm disappointing the locals (the people, not the pubs) by my schedule. There's a tradition here called "first footing." On New Year's Eve, if a tall, dark, handsome man (me!) carrying a lump of coal is the first person to cross the threshold after midnight, why then the family has good luck for the coming year. I've had a batch of invitations. Too bad, it would've been fun running from house to house bringing people luck.

We sailors continue to be well accepted here, though some groups have held protests and don't want either the tender or the subs here. In some ways I sympathize and secretly admire their acting on their concerns so long as they're neither violent nor interfering in our ops. They worry we'll pollute their harbor and leak or dump radioactive coolant, and that our presence makes them a prime target. The Scots seem more ambivalent about the cold war than we. A lot of them don't seem to care that much if Scotland gets overrun with commies. They've always been concerned about being overrun with the English and see us as being imposed upon them by London. In some ways the protests are like the ones against Vietnam at home. This activism is truly a change, isn't it? My generation of college students did nothing. I recall a small campus effort to free the Rosenbergs which consisted of a booth on the Michigan diag with a petition to sign, but nothing akin to holding a sit-in in the ROTC buildings.

Time to get this in the mailbag if it's going to get off the boat today. And time to check out what movies we've got for patrol this time. Did you know we take a different one each day? Funny, there's often one or two that we watch over and over and language or action in it becomes part of our at-sea social life. On one patrol it was the Beatles' *Yellow Submarine*. When something on the sub quit working properly, the crew would sing, "Well, we all live on a yellow submarine," as though that explained it. You might try this mid-patrol madness out on your psych friend, Robyn. Maybe she can explain it. Is it the essentially serious business, the underlying fear, the confinement, or what?

Tucker, I hope you can arrange your schedule to come to New London early in the year. I'm rather surprised that I'm missing you as much as I am. I thought I had developed a considerable amount of rhino-hide resistance.

Give yourself a hug for me...well, more than one. Kisses are okay too. I can imagine you leaning way over forwards and backwards trying to reach the areas that I plan to.

Love, love, love, and more love,

Tom

Eight months later from Tucker's journal

14 May 1966, Washington, D.C.

For the record,

You've rediscovered something today, Fairfield. Your trust in the goodness and human side of the U.S. Navy.

Today I spent time with my WAVE detailer, CDR Rhoades, outlining to her why I need to leave my current billet. She finally understands. It's a misuse of my energy and training. CDR Rhoades said, "Go speak to the Intelligence community's detailer, CDR Bill Johnson. Since you want to stay in that business, he'll detail you next." I was a bit confused. I thought I was detailed by her.

Since I was already in BuPers, I decided to find CDR Johnson and schedule an appointment to explain my predicament. He not only was there, he was available. Turns out he'd worked for Uncle Joe in Naples as his intelligence officer, so we had much to talk about. It's finally becoming a small Navy, as I'd anticipated.

CDR Johnson didn't mince any words or waste any time. He called for my record.

After he looked through it, he said somewhat crossly, "You're *definitely* in the wrong billet."

"No, I'm in the wrong community. This intelligence business is not for me."

He quickly retorted, "You're in the right community. You're ideal for serving in many types of intelligence jobs." He laid out several jobs I could fill and even presented a mini-career track for me.

"You'll be out of your current job by the end of the summer," he said. "I'll be calling with some possible billets for you." I didn't ask how he'd get me out from under CDR Rhoades' thumb. I just knew he would honor his word. For the first time in a long while, I feel as if I *belong* in the Navy, the Navy that cares about its people and takes care of them whenever possible.

It's been a hard year. But it feels as though I've paid my dues and can move on.

One saving grace — Billie's friendship. Since her arrival in D.C. in December, we've had many WAVE get-togethers with stimulating conversations about Vietnam, our jobs, WAVE politics, and the new women's movement. Billie's having troubles at work.

TF

Four months later from Tucker

12 September 1966, Washington, D.C.

Dear Jennie,

I'm so pleased that you and Pierre are engaged! He's a very special, sensitive man, as well as a fine naval officer. And such a handsome fellow. You're lucky. And so is he. Will you stay on in the Navy and try to be stationed together? That's a tough road, as we know. Even though the detailers try to assign couples together, it's tough to find them both a good billet. And what about children?

Someday the Navy will change its policy that we women can't have children. But not for a while.

At least initially you'll be together in Norfolk. Maybe the Navy can keep you both there indefinitely. (Doubtful!) Speaking of Norfolk, I may be stationed down there with you in a few months. The intelligence detailer has been working diligently to get me to the Joint Staff at the CINCLANT/SACLANT compound. The next step is approval by the Deputy, Vice Admiral Richardson. Any WAVE officer assigned to a joint staff must be especially approved by the local command.

They do treat us with kid gloves, don't they? Wonder what they fear? As you told me several years ago, we women must be extra sharp and work doubly hard, for we're role models, blazing the way for others to come. I'm tired of being assigned to break down the barriers to equal opportunity! How many women have gone before? Will it be better in ten years? Hope so.

Washington duty has been okay, though not as challenging as I would've wanted. I'm ready to go back to being around the seagoing Navy. Even though we can't serve on ships, feels right to be close to them, smell them, and be around guys who serve on them. Someday I bet we'll serve on ships. At least the non-combatants. What do you think? I know Pierre is open to the idea, as are many of my other male officer friends. The real question, is the country ready? If the public thinks it's a good idea and civilian leadership agrees, the Navy will change and have women serving aboard ship or fighting in war zones.

Tom and I are having an affair via correspondence. Somehow that's less threatening than if he and I were stationed in the same city. Tom meets all my "requirements" for my right mate. Whether we're ready for marriage, we'll see. By the way, does Pierre know that Pete Williams, our classmate, is married! One of Pete's best friends told me. He sure put on a good front with me, including not wearing a wedding ring. And I was thinking he's such a great guy. Here I'd been trying not to be so cynical about men and then this happens. What a jerk!

My very best to you and Pierre. When's the wedding? Take good care of yourself.

Love,

Tucker

Three weeks later from Tucker

1 October 1966, Washington, D.C.

Dear Billie,

So sorry you had to hurry home on emergency leave to be with your family. To have lost your dad so quickly to a heart attack, and so early, is a real nightmare. I'm thinking about you a lot. You certainly didn't need family problems on top of your work situation.

Billie, you tend to keep your problems to yourself. Time to share with your buddy. Maybe if you vent by mail it'll help resolve your issues. My problem now is "the big wait." Waiting and waiting for PCS orders affects my total life outlook. Our Navy, our detailers, seem to thrive on crisis management and that's not my style. I never pulled any all nighters in college during finals. Did you? I bet you did.

Planning ahead and setting goals, that's my nature. For the first time in my career, work isn't fun and challenging. But that's natural in that any moment I'm expecting word of a new assignment. Still...

I'd like to know *now* whether I'm "qualified" to be on a Joint Staff, whatever that means. Why do WAVES need special consideration?

On a happier note, I love getting letters from Tom Parker. Just received another one with an update on his life at sea. Wonder where we're headed?

I miss my play-time buddy. You know you keep me sane and less serious.

How's your mother holding up? Miss you. Write, if you can.

Love,

Tucker

One week later from Billie

9 October 1966, Washington, D.C.

Dear Tuck —

Thanks for your expression of sympathy to me and my family. And your flowers are beautiful. What a shock! I expected my Dad to be here forever. You know, we could grow old together, he could play with his grandkids, go to football games, go fishing with me. I'll miss his intellect, his wit and humor, and the warmth and comfort of him just *being there*. I know he wouldn't want me to mourn very long, or to be overly morose (and, I don't want to, either), so I'll be back in D.C. by the 20th, back to the old proselytizing routine.

During these last two weeks, in the southern tradition of providing comfort to the bereaved, my relatives and family and friends have brought us much food — good old-fashioned southern cooking — ham, chicken, chocolate cake, every salad in the world, gallons of iced tea. No one goes hungry with a death in the family.

My thoughts are slowly shifting back to D.C. and my job. I want to take the time to write more than a note. First, I need to write something about the growing anti-military movement on several campuses. I sometimes have a problem expressing my thoughts about personal negative situations.

Live and let live, at least until something is directed at me.

Just before my father died, while we were on a U of Maryland recruiting visit, a group of students, both men and women, approached us and turned over our tables. They scattered our recruiting materials, poured a red liquid (signifying blood, I assume) on our blue and gold Navy tablecloth, while calling us "prostitutes," "bitches," and "whores." I told my team to forget the recruiting materials and the recruiting because we were leaving. When we got outside, the campus police had just stopped another group from overturning our car!

This kind of stuff is scary, a form of terror. If you shout or shove back, you're just as stupid as these idiots, plus, you could get hurt. And for what? Should we be on campus in this sort of atmosphere? Is it worth it? Do they give medals for recruiting duty? Recruiting should be scratched. It's low budget, anyway.

Just before I left Hawaii, a civilian ship unloaded 5,000 metal caskets to ultimately be shipped to Vietnam. What're we doing? Five thousand caskets? I know very little about Vietnam except what I read or hear from the media. But a growing group of violent protesters are pointing their fingers at me as if I were the culprit. Because I wear a uniform, they single me out. I know I probably sound like a cry baby, but I'm very disturbed. Also angry, embarrassed, upset.

While I've got recruiting on my mind, I'll relate another run-in with a horny CDR. This happened on an extended recruiting trip and I didn't get a chance to tell you before I came down here. The nurse recruiter (LCDR, you've met Maria), our Yeoman 1st Class Gail Nelson, and I were visiting the U of KY in Lexington and we were joined by an Airdale recruiting crew out of Memphis (Millington) and a surface group from Nashville. For 3 days we made quite a little Navy show. Good prospects, too. We stayed at a Ho Jo's not far from the campus and we girls had a two-room suite.

The Airdale CDR invited Maria, Gail, and me down to his room for drinks. We said sure, that'd be nice. He fixed the drinks, we toasted recruiting, and then he said he would like to take us all to bed, one at a time! I stared at him with my mouth open. Maria stood up and said, "That's not funny, Commander," put her drink down, started for the door. Gail, who's older than I, gave him the finger as we exited. Outside, Maria and Gail started to laugh and I joined in. We collapsed into giggles and when we got back to our room we could hardly talk. That's what I'm gonna do from now on. I'm gonna laugh at these dominating, horny, proud-of-their-anatomy fools. *Who* do they think they are?

Again, thanks for your sympathy and thanks for listening to my recruiting woes. I don't recall you had this sexual harassment stuff or the anti-war situation (too early in the war) in Philly.

> Your friend,

> Billie

P.S. You'd asked about "Trey." He forgot and wore his wedding ring one night. Can I pick 'em or not? I recall you had a similar experience.

P.P.S You'll have to tell me how serious you are with Tom. Somehow I can't feature you (or me, for that matter) married.

Five days later from Tucker's journal

15 October 1966, Washington, D.C.

 For the record,

I'm qualified! Commander Johnson called and said, "Admiral Richardson gave his blessing to your orders. You'll be leaving within the month. Start packing."

At least the Admiral gave me a fair break, unlike the Academy and the CNO's office. Perhaps these are the orders I was supposed to follow all along, and it took a year to get them. Who knows? What I know is that I must wrap up many loose ends before departure for Norfolk.

The only negative — I'd hoped to take leave to visit Donna in Oslo. Will have to scratch that idea. Maybe go in the spring.

Hot dog! It's a new day! Life will be good again. Thank you, CDR Bill Johnson. Thank you, U.S. Navy.

TF

Chapter Five

New Horizons

Four months later from Tom

14 Feb 1967, New London, CT

Dear, Dear Tucker,

YES, YES! At last we can stop pretending this is not an impossible relationship communications-wise. When I was on the *J.P. Jones* I couldn't get letters or phone calls two months in three. Then when I did get off-crew, the Navy had something else for me or you to do. No wonder the married submariners say the 7-year itch doesn't roll around for at least 14 years. This shipyard duty is almost worse: the crunch to complete the overhaul of *Starfish* has had us working round the clock. At least the shipyard workers have shifts; we officers are available 24 hours a day. Leave?? Only if you can say your work is done, which is never.

BUT my news, and worth popping a cork for, is that I'm going to be a new construction XO of SSBN *Farragut* (Gold) in Newport News. She's scheduled to be based in Charleston. And, unless I put the missiles in upside down or scram the reactor or some such, I should be promoted to Commander at the end of this tour. But who cares, who's counting?

What's off the Richter scale (I started to write Rickover, I guess reflecting the monumental impact he's had on my life) in earth shaking importance is that I'm going to be virtually on shore duty for a year and just a hop, skip, and bebop through the Chesapeake Bay Tunnel from Norfolk and my favorite Lieutenant. Hot Damn! I'm already imagining sweet sojourns in Williamsburg, Yorktown, and Virginia Beach. How did BuPers manage to screw up and allow us to be so close? Must be a new batch of detailers.

Speaking of your duty — note how I'm selfishly always writing about me — I'm totally pleased that you're enjoying your SACLANT duty. I'm looking forward too to getting your opinion on why this damn Vietnam war isn't over. What the hell is LBJ thinking of? How can we have a "Great Society" with our country being torn apart? It's like tic-tac-toe — a no-win situation. The Squadron Commander's son just went to Canada rather than be drafted and you can imagine how painful that is for him and his wife.

And so, my girl, I'll be on a plane this afternoon for a brief visit home to see my folks — my dad is quite bad I hear. Sounds like he's developing dementia. I'll call you from the family homestead in Flint. I can't tell now how long I'll be needed there. My brothers and especially sister Martha have had all the burden of my parents so I need to help out. But then look out. I plan to descend on Norfolk and you prior to reporting 15 April to Newport News.

Make plans! Tune up your instruments. Uh huh…all of 'em. It's almost harmony time.

With lustful thoughts and max anticipation, Tom

Five weeks later from Jennie

20 March 1967, Virginia Beach, Virginia

Dear Tucker,

Pierre and I thoroughly enjoyed our honeymoon in San Juan, P.R. The city is lovely; the weather was balmy and we actually swam in the ocean as it lapped up on the beautiful white sandy beach. We indulged in marvelous rum drinks and specialty foods, including *arroz con pollo* — a chicken and rice dish with delicious saffron seasoning. The moonlight flooded the beach and trickled into our honeymoon suite.

Have you ever been to our Base there — Roosevelt Roads? "Roosey Roads," our largest naval base in the world, served as a training facility during WWII. In '55 it became a guided missile training center and was redesignated a NavSta. Its beauty is breathtaking — tropical flora, palm trees, hibiscus, and plumeria surround it. A beautiful beach, golf course, tennis courts, and a recreational services area where folks can rent sailboats, fishing boats and gear, and snorkeling equipment.

The O' Club, decorated in the Spanish style with interior patios and a swimming pool overlooking the nearby water, has three small intimate dining rooms. Pierre and I dined in one and ordered our own special meal and champagne from a waiter who served just the two of us! We had *paella*, a seafood with rice and peas dish, with saffron too, on a big platter. I found baby squids hidden in the rice! Good, actually. For dessert we had guava paste with cream cheese. Yummy.

One day we went snorkeling for longustina (sp?), a small lobster, and then came back to the O' Club where they cooked our catch for us. You pry those little guys off the reefs with a special tool.

I'm backed up with housecleaning and unpacking, but I did want you to know how happy we are. It was wonderful having you and Tom at the wedding. From the looks of it, I'd say things are going well between you two. Pierre and I drank a toast to you both on our first night in San Juan. You know, we do owe this happiness to you and Tom, my dear. So thank you. Remember that night in D.C. two years ago? Who'd have thought it would end with a honeymoon in Puerto Rico.

So pleased you're geographically closer to Pierre and me.

Fondly,

Jennie

Two weeks later from Tucker's journal

3 April 1967, Norfolk, Virginia

For the record,

God, life's a dilemma. Tonight Tom asked me to marry him. He wants us to be engaged NOW!

We'd had dinner at the Norfolk Officers' Club. We both were having a good time. Had seen lots of old friends. Tom looked at me with those marvelous, deep brown eyes. Suddenly he became serious. "Tucker, I want to marry you. Will you marry me?"

Though I was somehow expecting this, I was stunned by his question. When he actually proposed, I was unprepared. And my feelings cascaded around me.

An overwhelming thought predominated. I decided then and there, I needed to confront my doubt, my demon. Lucky for me our table was in a corner where no one could hear. "Tom, I don't know how to tell you this, so I'll just blurt it as best I can. For many years

I've been attracted to *both* men and women. Actually since my ensign days."

Tom stared hard at me, his face cold, set. His eyes filled with disappointment. He turned away. In a barely audible voice I heard, "Nice going, Tom." He turned back, stood and said, "Let's get out of here."

Neither of us spoke as he drove me home. After turning off the key in my parking lot, with both hands on the wheel, staring straight ahead he said, "It's okay, Tucker. You can make a choice. You can decide to be with me. You're a strong, independent-minded woman. You clearly can make a choice. You can choose me. You can choose us. I love you very much."

"I love you too," I said.

He turned toward me and said, "Why don't you sleep on it, and I will too. I know it shouldn't bother me that you're attracted to women. Hey, it's understandable. So am I! I'll get over my negative reaction. It's not like two men. I'm absolutely certain that if you make the choice to marry me, you'll stay the course. I think too that you're concerned about my wanting children. Don't worry, we'll work that out. It'll be fine."

He got out of the car, opened my car door and walked me to the door of my building. He didn't suggest that he come in. He didn't even touch me. "I'll call you," he said and left.

It's three o'clock in the morning, Fairfield. You're *never* up this late. Can't sleep. Can't think. Okay, just write.

In my heart of hearts, I believe I don't have a choice. Repeat, *I don't have a choice.* While I love Tom deeply, I'm not *in love* with him. I don't have the same sexual thoughts or feelings about him as I've had with Jennie or Donna or other women. Face it, I've always been more attracted to Deborah Kerr and Esther Williams than to John Wayne and Alan Ladd.

Damn it, there's a missing piece. Everything else is right. That's the rub. Tom offers me his love, his desire to take care of me, as a person and wife. He offers a life society says is right, and potentially magical, a life that my immediate family, and my Navy family, say is correct. In fact, they would see living with another woman as damaging to our American values.

And, yes, no doubt we can work it out about my career ambitions, and about children. But that's not a clear area either. Shouldn't I feel a stronger pull toward Tom and marriage than toward the Navy and my career ambitions? Shouldn't I be more willing to give up this great new job and have children?

Am I willing to go with my heart or am I going with what society, my family and the Navy say is befitting? What is my heart saying?

Down to the wire. It's not fair to Tom to delay the decision. But, nobody to talk to. Robyn's in Hawaii, vacationing with Ned. She would help me get to my heart. Billie's off to Japan. Jennie would probably tell me to marry Tom and stop struggling about my sexuality. My parents would want me to be happily married. But would I be happily married?

I'm almost thirty years old. I need to stop kidding myself about men and marriage. I detest the words, the labels: straight, homosexual, lesbian. Write it anyway: I am a lesbian — a reluctant lesbian. And, somehow life will be okay even though the path will continue to be tenuous and rocky.

Fairfield, you need to trust yourself. Climb every mountain till you find your dream. Marrying Tom is not my dream. Life somehow will be just fine.

TF

Ten weeks later from Tom

20 June 1967, Newport News, VA

Dear Tucker,

Not the easiest letter I've ever written. Sorry for the silence. I keep looking at myself in the mirror and seeing a guy who's a complete failure at picking women. First the disaster of Marilyn and then a woman who likes other women better than me. What's wrong with me? My ego did a deep six. Without expecting it, suddenly I found I was angry, really angry. It welled up from somewhere destroying my image of myself as always coolly in control. The photo you gave me of the two of us at Virginia Beach somehow got smashed against the bulkhead. Worse, I went out and got really falling down drunk. The next morning I ran into the Chaplain by chance and found myself to my surprise asking him if I could talk to him for a few minutes. Imagine that!

He asked questions and talked about the power of an intelligent person to overcome emotion that's largely ego-driven. That's easier said than done, but I'm trying. Two things really were clarified by the Chaplain's conversation: I really knew you were holding something back all along, although what it turned out to be is a major shock. I'd assumed career or maybe someone else in your past whom you hadn't told me about or just the reluctance of an unmarried "good girl."

The second thing had to do with why I wanted to marry you. And that came down to enjoying you as a companion, as a good friend, someone to bounce ideas off, and to share a common view of the way we would like to see our world arranged and our nation's place in arranging it that way. For sure I didn't again want to marry someone who didn't understand the difference between a political and an economic system. Yeah, and it had occurred to me that I wanted smart children and that to get those having a smart mother would be an advantage. Pretty obvious!

I concluded that the things I most valued in you, in our relationship, were potentially still there if I could turn my head around and just think of you as a best friend. Why should we toss those away merely because I got a bruising? I don't understand these sexual feelings for same-sex persons and whether they're a choice or whether you know in the same way that one knows one is heterosexual. There's a crystal-clear difference between men and women though — men can't fake it! Damn it, did you fake it? You don't have to answer that.

Well, all this is to say that, if you still want to, I want to shake and make up, old buddy. And I'll try to keep looking for the second Mrs. Parker. So, write me or maybe we can get together again if you still want to (as pals!), and together we'll continue to solve the problems of the Navy and the world out there. I sincerely hope you will.

                        Still here, Tom

P.S. Speaking of global problems, that recent attack on the USS *Liberty* by Israeli torpedo boats nearly knocked me out. Thirty-nine sailors killed and 75 wounded. An immediate reminder that we live at risk on the seas.

Three months later from Tucker

                        15 September 1967, Norfolk, Virginia

Dear Tom,

It was so good to see you last week and to know we'll still be friends. I was actually scared to see you. You looked great. I'm glad you're feeling better about our relationship. I still love you. I think you know that.

As you could tell, I'm truly immersed in my job which involves both strategic and operational intelligence. I'm finally using all my capabilities. While it feels good to be stretched to the max, sometimes the long hours are tough. Yet I don't feel pressured as I might in a CINCLANT job. The non-U.S. officers don't seem as dedicated as ours because their working days include more playing (and drinking). Who's to say who is the wiser of the two groups?

I enjoy discussing the international scene with you, even if we must restrict ourselves to UNCLASS. As chief speechwriter for Buck Buckingham, I've discovered, much to my surprise, that nearly 80% of classified information can be found in unclassified material. So why is it classified? I know, bureaucracies love secrets.

We talked only briefly about the Soviets. I've enclosed a copy of the speech that Buck and I have been working on — "The Cold Wet War." He presents a classified rendition in Brussels next month and hopes to obtain approval for a NATO Study Group. Essentially the Cold Wet War represents the Soviets' increasing challenge to the West on the seas.

The American public and much of the military are mostly unaware of the buildup in Soviet maritime strategies and capabilities that Khrushchev initiated in the mid-fifties. Khrushchev and his so-called *peaceful co-existence* not only demanded a new national strategy, but appropriate military tools. The Soviet military was told to develop more mobile, flexible forces which could support Soviet interests on a global scale. The rest is history. The Soviets have their Five-Fleet Navy!

Tracking Soviet sub operations is frightening. Until this billet I hadn't realized the Soviet submarine force had become so huge. At least 375–400! But, then, they have a lot of geography to protect. The Soviets now challenge the West in maritime areas where we've never been challenged. We have to question how much is defense and how much is competition with Western forces.

Why don't more Americans know about this Soviet maritime threat? I know, the Vietnam conflict is foremost in the public's mind and two fronts to think about is one too many. And they just got over worrying about the Arab-Israeli War in June. I suppose that's what we're paid to do in the Navy. We're definitely earning our keep!

Speaking of Vietnam, do you think LBJ will win the nomination next year? Anti-Vietnam sentiments are growing

It feels good to be in the midst of operational planning, as much as any woman naval officer can be at the moment. I like to fantasize that someday women in all countries, but certainly the U.S., will sail on military ships and fly military aircraft, deterring the enemy — whoever it is.

Enough deep thought. Tom, I've been thinking about you a lot. I worry about your long hours and your Exec tasks. How're you coping with being the busiest guy on the boat? I look forward to talking with you next week and being assured that you're well.

I'm also looking forward to our date at the SACLANT Ball. Should be fun to see the international naval officers decked out in their full dress uniforms. And I get to wear my tiara!

> With affection,
>
> Tucker

Two weeks later from Tom

1 October 1967, USS Farragut, *Newport News, Virginia*

Dear Tucker,

I'm sorry I had to cancel our date. Please don't think it's because my ego still is in the dumps, although our relationship certainly isn't what I once anticipated. I think I've learned to settle for geographically close. I would've loved to have escorted you to SACLANT's big do. Tiara and all! But we had a mini-emergency at the shipyard and my presence was *persona* extremely *grata!* How about I try to make it up to you by inviting you to a launching? USS *Winston Churchill*, another big missile sub, a sister ship to my *Farragut*, slides down the ways on the second Sat. in Nov. One of Churchill's American relatives will christen her. There's always a good party afterwards paid for mostly by the shipyard. I'll have a proper invitation sent to you; let me know if you can make it.

I'm interested in your terminology, "The Cold Wet War," since I'm deeply submerged in it. In truth, I don't think much about the U.S./Soviet balance of seapower, so reading the speech was refreshing. My energies are taken up by efforts to work with the shipyard, train the crew, understand as much as I can about how this big submarine is put together, and tend to personnel problems as they arise.

Another thing: We're sure we're the best. We're also sure if the Soviets ever get anywhere near our capability, we'll just redouble our efforts and stay way ahead. We're smarter and technologically more capable and we know it.

You and your intel pals must think there's a fairly big Soviet threat, on and under the seas, because there are 41 of these big nuclear missile firing subs— these "boomers" — being planned, with each one carrying 16 nuclear warheads. Even with 1/3rd of these subs in upkeep and 10% overhauling at any one time, we should always have 25 at sea. The Blue and Gold two-crew concept means we're working the boats at emergency levels without having to keep the crews at sea 9 out of 12 months. In addition, we're building 100 nuclear attack subs, like *Nautilus* and *Starfish*, to tail the Soviet subs, to conduct intelligence ops, and to train our own ASW forces.

As you know, the best way to track and counter a submarine is with another sub. And the Soviets keep building them. Still, when you think about it, we're certainly putting a lot of effort and taxpayers' bucks into the "Cold Wet War" concept, especially when you factor in the number of long-range bombers and missiles in silos. But then that's our current strategic policy, isn't it? The triad with several backup systems. I guess *Sputnik* has us believing the Soviets can do about anything technologically they put their minds to and we're damned if we're going to let them have more or better!

In truth, I'm not as concerned about the Soviet Navy buildup as you and RADM Buckingham seem to be. Without any aircraft carriers or amphibious capabilities, the Soviet's Five Fleets represent no significant challenge to our Navy.

How's my XO job? Actually damn terrific! Did I say I was the busiest officer? I thought I said the b.s. officer! Much of the pleasure of my job stems from my easy-strain CO, who's the nicest guy I've ever known in my life and never appears to get upset, a quality that extends to his home life according to his wife. The crews are, of course, hand-picked from the best, so they're a pleasure to work with too.

The Newport Newsian natives are really friendly. The local country club gives the CO and XO memberships without having to pay initiation fees. I'm forced to take up golf to get my (lack of) money's worth! So far I consider it a good day if I come in with as many balls as I went out with. Imagine my joy last Sunday when I actually came in with more. Probably this frugality is genetically imprinted in depression babies.

Will look forward to seeing you for "launch." And maybe for dinner too? By then I should have my compelling argument together on why I think LBJ's gonna lose. It's something along the lines of the inability to tax enough to have a "Great Society" *and* to win both a hot and a cold (wet and dry) war at the same time.

Your Cold Wet Warrior, Tom

Five weeks later from Tucker

8 Nov 1967, a red letter day! Norfolk, Virginia

Dear Billie,

Hooray for Congress! Hooray for the Defense Advisory Committee on Women in the Services (DACOWITS). The new public law Congress just passed is long overdue. No longer will we women be restricted to only one captain on active duty (temporary at that). Military women will be able to hold the permanent rank of captain and colonel.

I don't know about you, but I've felt the rank restrictions on women were wrong. If the Navy is serious about us as officers, and sometimes I do wonder — many men seem more interested in how we *look* and *feel* than how we think — then it must create women's career paths that lead to the top. For male leadership to give up an admiral's number to the women, active politicking by DACOWITS and women in and out of the military has to start. Personally, I'll be happy to make captain, but the opportunity should exist for women to be admirals.

This lieutenant is excited!

How goes your CHINFO duty? When are you coming down for a weekend?

Love,

Tuck

Three weeks later from Billie

30 November 1967, Alexandria, VA

Dear Tuck —

How goes my CHINFO duty? Tuck, this is it! This is where I belong! I *love* this duty. I can really contribute. Now, I know what I have talent for. (Bad grammar, but I'm excited!) No matter what the Navy gives me to do, I'm content because I have a specialty!

I'm assigned to the Community Relations Department and to public affairs projects. Whether it's a band concert, or a parade, or a fly over, or a static display, or something much more complicated, I plan it down to the last detail. Plus, I get to create new projects. The Navy needs a person like me!

In addition, I'm in charge of the SECNAV Guest Cruise Program. I call community movers and shakers across the country, men and women who can be spokespersons in their community, and invite them on various SECNAV cruises aboard ship. Sometimes they visit Marine Corps bases or naval air stations. The elite guest cruise aboard an aircraft carrier observes all the flight operations. Pretty good for a hillbilly, huh?

I get names for the cruises from members of congress, senators, the White House, from SECNAV, or from admirals. It's such a thrill when I pick up the phone and someone says, "This is the White House, may I speak with Lt. Baker?"

Now, back down to earth. Life in the Pentagon, is, well, life in the Pentagon. I'm assigned as an Asst. Secretary of Defense (Public Affairs) briefer as my watch. Twice a month or so, I go down to the DOD spaces to prepare to brief, a twice-a-day briefing to the press about what's going on in Vietnam concerning the Navy. I brief on ship operations, air strikes, brown river Navy ops, in-country operations and downed aircraft.

I'm appalled at the increasing anti-military reaction of the media reps, the network TV reps as well as major newspapers like the *New York Times*. They shove and push and crowd and try to shout me down with malicious interruptions. They ask stupid questions they know I can't answer, and do everything but call me a liar. They press for more and more information than I have, as if they want me to say something untrue, and then vilify me. They're derisive, and snort and laugh as I try to get through the brief. I'm completely disgusted with them, and dread my briefing watches. Do they give medals for being a briefer! I wish we'd never heard of Vietnam.

Now, for a brighter note — my mother is visiting. She's doing well, but feels lonely now that my youngest sister has finally graduated from U.T. Great Aunt Thelma, rest her soul, passed away a couple of months ago and left an inheritance for each of my sisters and me. Not much, but enough for a down payment on a house. Mom's helping me look, and I think we've found one in Alexandria off Seminary Road. I'm about to become a homeowner! It has three bedrooms and two baths with a big kitchen, a living room, and a fireplace. It's also brick, with a nice yard and on a cul-de-sac. It has a big unfinished basement with all sorts of possibilities. I can't believe I'm about to be domesticated. Mom's thrilled. Now we can party.

I'm with you. I certainly think women deserve to be advanced to higher rank. I would definitely like to command, but I would *not* like to be an admiral — too much politics.

Yes, let's get together. Mom's going to be here through Thanksgiving and she'd love to visit Norfolk. Do you think she

could come? She makes a mean Manhattan and is the best chicken
fryer I know. How about the weekend before Thanksgiving?

Billie

Three weeks later from Tucker

20 December 1967, Norfolk, VA

Dear Robyn,

Happy holidays, my good friend! I have time to write my
Christmas cards this year, thanks to a special holiday leave. Seems
the non-U.S. countries enjoy celebrating Christmas even more
than we do. They believe in taking more time off, so I'm on half-
days for the next two weeks with no leave deducted. That's neat.
Since I've been logging a lot of overtime in my regular job plus my
two additional duty jobs, Assistant for Woman and speech writing
for Admiral Buckingham, I'll take off afternoons without guilt.

Had I mentioned my Assistant-for-Women job before? Each
naval district Commandant (an admiral) is assigned to his staff a
woman officer on an additional duty basis to advise him on policies
regarding Navy women in his area. This is part of what one might
call the quasi-chain of command in the Wavey-Navy. That is, any
shore command that has enlisted women has a Women's
Representative, a woman officer who reports to the Assistant for
Women, who reports to the Director of the WAVES. This additional
duty absorbs a good bit of my time these days (we have over 600
enlisted women in the area). My top intelligence boss, Captain
Asher (British), is somewhat annoyed with me and the U.S. Navy
for this additional time. I want to give myself to both jobs. Probably
an impossible task.

Recently I told Captain Asher what really should happen is each
commanding officer and his respective subordinates should take
equal responsibility for their women, as for their men. I said, "Maybe
someday this will occur with pressure from the right levels and
offices. The quasi-chain perpetuates the belief that WAVES aren't
fully integrated into the Navy." He agreed and wondered aloud
how it was for the British WRENS.

Needless to say, my workload has pushed me physically. About
a month ago, my mentor and good friend LCDR Jennie Winters
Dumonte and I were having lunch at the CINCLANT/SACLANT
mess. She's now married to a great guy, Captain Pierre Dumonte.

Jennie and I were having one of our heated discussions about WAVE policies when suddenly she stopped eating and gave me one of her firm and stern looks. "What's the matter?" I queried. She quieted herself for a moment, and then proceeded to move into her motherly tone with me. Uh-oh, I thought, what next?

"Lt. Fairfield, do you realize you're having a second glass of wine? I think you're drinking too much," she vehemently declared. Then she gave me a lecture on alcoholism and how I might be falling into a deep hole.

"I don't think I have any problem," I said. "It just happens that our division is the most partying one in the command. We have at least one party a week, with some of the best quality of alcohol in the *world* being served. I consider attendance at the parties to be an important aspect of the job. Besides, if you'll look around you, you'll see that almost everyone is on their second glass."

After an intense debate, I realized Jennie was genuinely concerned about my drinking. And, since I respect her wisdom, I paid close attention. Our conversation ended in a bet — that I couldn't refrain from drinking for thirty days. It was a good bet from my standpoint, ten to one. If I lost, I owed her $10; if she lost, she owed me $100.

That was on the 18th of November. What a long month! Mainly because my immediate boss, a Norwegian Commander, was extremely unhappy that he couldn't buy me a drink at lunch, or worse, serve me a drink in his home. One night he got on my case, which he *never* does, and somehow took offense with this 30-day period. "Not even a tiny *creme de menthe?*" he asked in a sarcastic tone. To exacerbate the situation, this was a pre-holiday period, with more than the usual partying.

Robyn, the thirty days drinking fast was a real lesson. I realized that I've been overdoing the lunches and probably the partying. Yes, the military tends to overdo partying. We have a higher incidence of alcoholism (something like 17%) than in the general public. On the other hand, Happy Hour can be an important part of getting to know the people you work with. I'll be more careful to monitor my drinking, thanks to Jennie. She had a very close WAVE friend go down in flames (not get promoted) because of alcoholism and therefore she's extra-sensitive to the issue.

All of the above is grist for your mill as a budding therapist. Sometimes it's helpful to let off the job pressure with drinking. Other ways exist no doubt, and I'm sure you counsel your clients as to these other releases.

On another subject, I still have a strong attraction to Jennie. It seems not to be present for her (toward me). Better not be, for she and Pierre seem happily married. She's hoping to get orders to the Women Officers' School as Officer-in-Charge. Pierre has orders to Newport.

What do you know about bisexuality?

How're you enjoying graduate school? When do you finish? Maybe we can celebrate with a vacation. Are you seriously thinking of marrying Ned?

You've been pressing me since OCS about why I stay in the Navy. Would you believe — I'm beginning to agree with your point of view, perhaps for different reasons. The one that's getting to me these days is lack of career planning and career patterns for women officers. After this job, I'll probably have to serve in an administrative billet. I want to continue in intelligence but the Navy says women can't be "restricted line officers," officers who can specialize in fields such as intelligence, public affairs, or oceanography.

It's somewhat complicated to explain to a civilian. Just know that many women officers want to serve their country yet feel their careers are limited. But you can't fight City Hall and get promoted. So I'm in a quandary. I'm sure you'd support my resignation. Will keep you posted. One of my options is to get out and work on a doctorate. Maybe I'll see you in Boston before you know it. Take good care of yourself.

Love,

Tucker

Two weeks later from Robyn

January 2, 1968, Boston, MA

Dear Tucker,

A fine and happy New Year to you! May it bring some enlightenment to your adored Navy which seems to constantly thwart and frustrate you.

Me, I'm fine. As I said on the phone, I'm really glad you were able to shake off the oppressors long enough to get to the wedding. It's not all that different being married, except that now in addition to being a social worker, I'm identified as WIFE — whatever that means. It was also quite queer to wake up the day of the wedding as Robyn Conway and end as Robyn C. Greeley. But my adjustments are minimal compared to your continual confrontations.

I gather you were kind of shaken up by the whole episode on alcoholism. And maybe not. The important part of that anecdote, seems to me, was your increased awareness of the potential for a problem, especially if folks are drinking as much as you suggest they might be. Jennie seems to care a lot about you and your well-being. In a sense, then, it's not too surprising that you still feel attracted to her despite the fact that she's been able to adapt to the "approved" style of housekeeping.

The whole issue of what is bisexuality, homosexuality or heterosexuality is an interesting and complex one. In general we tend to assume that everyone is either MALE or FEMALE, when in fact I think we're all along a continuum, similar to what Kinsey reported. All of us, whatever our gender, possess both masculine and feminine hormones, traits, tendencies, and attractions. Labels such as bisexual or homosexual just indicate way stations on this continuum. And even within and between and among categories are grades and degrees of maleness/femaleness. These labels are culturally determined and change over time. So, what do you think of all those wise words?

I agree, it's been too long since we've spent time together. Even if it's just a long weekend, let's think of a jolly adventure! My HUSBAND sends love.

> Till soon, Love,
>
> Robyn

Three weeks later from Tucker's journal

24 January 1968, Norfolk, VA

For the record,

I'm thrilled! Buck called me into his office this morning and told me that Manlio Brosio, NATO's Secretary General, has approved a major study which will compare Soviet and NATO maritime strategies and capabilities. Our SACLANT staff will have prime responsibility. Buck, a primary force in getting the study approved, will oversee the project. He's arranged for me to be "Editor," with two or three yeomen working directly for me. I'll report directly to Buck and his executive assistant!

My god, the task is large, but we'll have a year to complete the project. Seems to me the Navy has groomed me for this job. Our offices will be within the Intelligence Division spaces, so I'll still be with my good friends here.

How did I get to be so lucky? Good thing I got myself out of that counterintelligence billet. Think what I would've missed.

Secretary Brosio is right on. The Soviets have gradually increased their presence over the last two years, with almost a permanent presence in Med ports, and forays into the Indian Ocean. U.S. projections of their shipbuilding plans are worrisome. They're even building aircraft carriers! The political implications of these actions need to be addressed. For instance, just as the Soviet Med Force is now providing a counter to the Sixth Fleet, politically and psychologically, we may also need to counter a Soviet Indian Ocean Fleet.

As Buck says, this study will be the perfect vehicle for digging into such matters. Hooray for Buck! Hooray for SACLANT! Hooray for me! Too much attention is focused on Vietnam, and not enough on the Soviets' naval expansion worldwide. Unlike yesteryear, we now have a competent rival on the high seas. I'm working myself into a mental tizzy. Let's hope I get to relax, too. All work and no play…better go whack some tennis balls tomorrow.

Just think. I'll be working full time for my mentor and friend, Buck Buckingham. A brilliant officer and strategist and an extra special member of my Navy family. Who would have thought that this could be?

New subject: I can't believe a U.S. ship has been captured by another government. Yesterday, so it's reported, *Pueblo*, an intel-type ship, was seized by N. Korean patrol boats. What about "Don't Give Up the Ship?" Must talk with Dad.

Time for some good sleep.

TF

Ten weeks later from Billie

11 April 1968, Alexandria, VA

Dear Tuck,

Last week I sat on the BuPers hill and watched our nation's capital burn. Burning! The outline of the Capitol Building and the Washington Monument silhouetted against the smoke and the flames. What's happening? Why have we turned to violence and destruction? Why are we venting our emotions in such a senseless and ruinous way? "We the people" have lost our way.

It's unbelievable that Martin Luther King, Jr. was assassinated last week — in Memphis of all places! I was just leaving the

Smithsonian where I was arranging for a tour of international Boy and Girl Scouts (CHINFO is the CNO's scout liaison and these scouts are camped for a special jamboree at Quantico) when I heard the news on my radio. I was crossing Constitution to F St. NW to "Central Drug" as we call it — Central Liquor Store. I wanted to get Jamison's Irish whiskey for Irish coffee. After I left the liquor store I drove to E St. to turn back on Constitution and saw mobs of people about 3 blocks away, yelling and screaming. They had sledge hammers and 2x4's and were breaking windows and doors of the stores — liquor stores, clothing stores, jewelry stores, delis, and so forth. At our corner is the Hecht Co., and the mobs were headed our way. And then we saw smoke and flames!

Getting out of D.C. was a nightmare. Bumper-to-bumper traffic, people running everywhere, fire in the background. I have Tennessee tags on my car and had a few frightening moments. One guy banged on my windows and another jumped on my hood. But I finally got across the 14th St. Bridge and stopped at BuPers to see the fire. What a devastating sight.

I left the BuPers hill and drove to my home in Alexandria. Most of my neighbors stood on their lawns staring at the fires' glow. Like me, they were shocked and dismayed at both the assassination and the aftermath in D.C. My black neighbors were just as alarmed and stunned as the rest of us. We kept the radios on to give us a play-by-play description of the riot — widespread looting, fires, uncontrolled mobs, beatings, innocent victims, cars overturned and burned, especially police vehicles.

We were told not to go downtown until there was an all-clear. The D.C. police were unprepared for this, and, of course, most of the police force is white. So several ugly confrontations took place. The mayor had to ask for the Army, since D.C. doesn't have a National Guard, to stabilize the situation.

It's hard to explain my feelings. In our U.S. capital tanks are prowling the streets with soldiers on every corner with their weapons, including rifles and sandbagged machine gun emplacements. On E St., every other store is a burned hulk. The Hecht Co. has all of its windows smashed. Bulldozers are clearing debris from the streets — piles of broken liquor bottles, burned clothing, smashed television sets and furniture. Burned cars overturned everywhere. Helicopters overhead. Tanks moving and soldiers patrolling.

Something is very different. I might describe it as a loss of innocence, a sobering passage in my life. Some say America still operates with a Frontier justice mentality — bushwhacking, gun toting, swaggering. Some people make themselves the judge, jury, and executioner. These people roam our country carrying out their own brand of justice. What can we do about that? Our Constitution guarantees us "Life, liberty..." What can I do about it?

And the anger of the black people. They have a right to be that angry after years of discrimination. But do they have the right to destroy, to loot, to steal, to place themselves and others in jeopardy? No, they do not! I'm angry at being frightened, at the destruction around me, at having to flee. I'm confused by my intense feelings of distrust, dread, and fear. I hope I don't always feel like this, but right now I'm suspicious, wary, looking over my shoulder. Angry people can do anything.

Thanks for letting me cry on your shoulder. Maybe next time, although, sadly, older and wiser, I'll be more upbeat.

Billie

One month later from Tucker's journal

11 May 1968, Norfolk, VA

 For the record,

The Navy is a conundrum. Subject: fraternization. We have strict rules that forbid officers and enlisted personnel from socializing or being "familiar." Seems elitist and classist, yet it's the way of the military, with few exceptions.

But people break this rule frequently. At two of my previous duty stations fellow women officers were *married* to enlisted men — in the same command — and nothing was said. Against all the unwritten rules these couples lived together. How can the Navy outlaw love? On a command-to-command basis, the rules crumble.

Yesterday, after a WAVE barracks inspection, Chief Anne Alexander, the barracks Master-at-Arms, asked me, "Will you teach me to play tennis?" I said, "Let me think about it."

This Chief is the epitome of shipshape and 4.0 in military ways. I know that she'd never step out of bounds. Another factor, for the first time in a long while I feel a physical attraction to a woman. Will I get myself in trouble? Unlikely. Between the Navy's unwritten policy on fraternization and its written policy on homosexuality, the name of the game for both Chief Alexander and me will be tennis, tennis, tennis. So go ahead and teach her to play. She's in another command. She'll probably be a better player than you before long and you'll have a real partner. You've sorely missed a tennis partner these days.

Remember: obey the rules despite their irregular enforcement and the fact that they're outdated. Can't seem to get it through my head that the Navy is a highly hierarchical organization, as well as an authoritarian subculture. Always has been, always will be! That's why it so adamantly resists giving women and other minorities their equal place. Wonder what it would do with men and women aboard ships and flying airplanes? Strengthen its fraternization rules of course.

TF

One month later from Tucker

10 June 1968, Norfolk, VA

Dear Tom,

How're you? I'm still reeling from the Bobby Kennedy assassination last week, the *Scorpion* loss in May, and the King assassination in April. What next? Our country can't take much more. Doesn't pay to have charisma, does it.

I'm heavily involved with a major Study Group and haven't found extra time for playing or corresponding. In addition to participating in the study group, most command personnel have been absorbed in "Operation Red Flag," a two-week intensive NATO maritime exercise, including deployment of real ships and aircraft. Because of the operation's CLASSIFIED nature, I can't write much about the exercise. I do, however, need to vent to you about the process.

The operation's debriefing sessions presented my third chance at observing this particular CINC in action. At the end of each day in the war room, the staff gathers together, and often the CINC, Admiral Peter David Morrison, joins us. A man who physically towers over everyone except Rear Admiral Buck Buckingham, he creates ambivalent impressions within me. On the one hand, he's a brilliant strategist, someone you'd like to have on *your* side in any actual war planning and implementation. On the other, the way he treats subordinates, especially captains, leaves a lot to be desired. He's as cunning a leader as he is calculating as a naval strategist. With mere gestures (including nervously tweaking his full red eyebrows) and facial expressions, he chews his captains down to lieutenants, spitting out each stripe with great merriment.

The war room sizzles with Morrison's sparks. He barks, growls, gets red in the face, and spouts profanities. Yesterday I winced when he barked at my boss, Captain Asher.

"Why the hell didn't your people tell the Blue forces they were surrounded by Orange forces with not ten but fifteen ballistic missile subs, not three AGIs but five? Jesus, Asher, how could you mistake a damn Orange force helicopter carrier for a damn cruiser?" Captain Asher didn't have a good explanation.

And to think I was turned down for a job so the Pentagon brass could swear. Surprisingly, Admiral Morrison snarls more softly at commanders and below, and doesn't even bother to acknowledge the presence of lieutenants. RHIP, but we're taught early on to "praise in public and censure in private."

Watching this behavior saddens me. Is this what it takes to get to the top of our Navy? I've heard sea stories of other senior admirals and their ways. What a shame the military encourages these behaviors. Reminds me of my dad's description of the Navy, "It's an autocracy within a democracy. No way around it."

I know some of the barking is a show of force. I also know the respective captains who are attacked regularly by the Admiral don't appreciate the fireworks display. To put the fear of God into them is totally unnecessary. But then, I'm only a lowly little lieutenant, watching the bloody sparks, explosions, and fizzles.

An ah-ha! Remember Little Abie from my ensign days? Admiral Peter D. Morrison probably is Little Abie grown up in disguise and doesn't trust anybody, not even his closest friends. Sad for him, as well as his friends and family members. You recognize the personality type. Recently I've had a second thought or two about Little Abie. What if his mother had been the one under the tree? Would've been a different moral.

Hope the above gives you a sense of my mood. As a former recruiter I know that enlistees have many reasons for joining the military. Inversely, officers and enlisted men resign or refuse another enlistment for many other reasons. At the top of my list is the unnecessarily harsh behaviors and attitudes of some few senior officers.

I'm gradually recognizing that the name of our game in the military is WAR. And, in order to prepare for war, my chosen profession condones personal behaviors that might, or might not, be appropriate in the thick of battle, but are needless in the context of daily operational work.

I'm realizing that the horrific violence, within and outside of our country, saps my energies and enthusiasm for my profession.

We Americans have gone from one assassination to the next, from civil rights protests in our cities to student protests on the campuses, from a few hundred Green Berets and SEALS and a small naval force in Vietnam to over 500,000 (!) military men committed to the Vietnam effort. When will this violence cease? I ask myself, do I want to be a part of this violence by the mere act of wearing the blue uniform? I too am a warrior, who happens to be stationed ashore.

While tracking Soviet maritime operations around the globe stimulates my analytical mind, I must ask myself, is this what my life is all about? Must I stay in another twelve years (till retirement) to make the case that women are invaluable to our military? None of my Ivy WASP friends would set foot in a recruiting office. Perhaps they're the smart ones, and I'm dumb. Who knows?

Spring is in the air. The azaleas are magnificent and colorful bunches of flowers cover the CINCLANT/SACLANT compound. I must say, our Navy does know how to manicure lawns and flower beds.

Answers to the above aren't required. I needed to let off steam about Admiral Morrison and the military's warrior environment. Maybe, just maybe, twenty-five years (eighteen as a dependent and seven as a naval officer) will suffice.

Keep the faith.

        Love,

           Tucker

Three weeks later from Tom

28 June 1968, Charleston, S.C., USS Farragut

Dear Tucker,

You're gonna love this! I went to the Squadron Commander's Farewell Party last Saturday night and the guest speaker was Rep. Mendel Rivers. Well, he must've had a few too many 'cause he got carried away. First, he argued that these Polaris missile submarines shouldn't be called boats, which is, of course, the traditional name submariners give submarines. No, says he, they're large and expensive with big crews so they should be called ships.

Then, he added that the missiles aren't just there for looks; no indeed, someday they're going to be needed by our great nation in a war. "They're gonna be used; they're gonna be fahred," he said. Well, you could have heard a pin drop as everyone stared at the floor contemplating this remark. I wondered later if anyone will ever bring to the Congressman's attention the implications of what he said. It's disturbing to have a person in a position of power who presents himself in such an authoritarian way that everyone over whom he has power is in effect silenced. If the person is brilliant, he can get away with it. I gather that's the way you feel about Admiral Morrison.

I suppose that Admiral Rickover falls into this category too. All of us respect him and at the same time fear him. But, when the person is powerful and says or does stupid things, as did Rivers, it's unpleasant and seems dangerous. He broke the rule, and raised the unspoken questions lurking in every nuclear submariner's mind, questions about our role in the cold war and its contrast to the traditional warrior readiness to fight and kill.

These questions are complicated by the difficulty in answering questions about why we are in the military in the first place. It's nonsense just to say we're in because we love our country and are willing to serve and sacrifice for it. There are too many personal rewards for serving — in my own case, education, responsibility, prestige, variety, and even things like travel, free health and dental care, and an early, quite well-paid retirement. Sometimes I think I just got on the track and so long as I got everything I wanted next, I didn't have any reason to consider getting off.

Polaris patrols are unusual experiences. We never talk about shooting the missiles or their purpose. We talk about keeping our "boat" running safely, retention rates among the sailors, passing exams, next duty stations, promotions, and personnel. We never discuss "the big question." But we do have a lot of time to think.

I often think about being a "nuclear warrior." The whole question of what constitutes a warrior is a little difficult to put in context on a missile patrol. When I think of a warrior I think of a Marine in a foxhole at Guadalcanal. I suppose we are warriors, but if we're required to launch our missiles we'll never see the people we destroy. Our type of warrior is becoming more common: Air Force officers are in the missile silos and the U.S. is developing something called a cruise missile that will have ranges upwards of 1,500 miles. Obviously those on the ships and airplanes who fire cruise missiles won't see their targets either.

If I were unable to play my part in a missile launch, I would tell the Navy. Obviously I wouldn't be in the Navy long after that. I realize our mission is deterrence, and if we have to fire our missiles, either the mission has failed and somebody has attacked the United States, or, it has changed (we've gone to a first-strike posture).

As far as the crew goes, we use the personnel reliability program as a means of determining if they're ready to launch our missiles. We ask them straight — would you be able to participate in a missile launch?

"Of course," they almost always respond. "If we are required to launch our missiles, it means the United States has been attacked, and it would be our duty."

Then, we say, "But you know the United States maintains the right to strike first. Do you want us to tell you whether it's a retaliatory attack or a first strike?"

"No, sir. I trust our government and you."

I often get the feeling some of these people secretly hope the order will come.

The question of whether we should have women on board is thorny. Women could do all the jobs on a missile sub. But I don't know the effect on morale or performance. There's only one value standard on a submarine — you must know the ship. The person who knows it best is the most valuable person. That's why the physician, a highly valued person ashore, is our least valued officer. We don't often need his skills and he doesn't know the ship. If we add women to the crew, we might be adding an unknown value.

For example, say a very attractive woman in the crew likes a certain sailor. That sailor may be the envy of every other sailor regardless of how thoroughly he knows the ship. Be that as it may, we're making plans to have women in the crew, possibly as members of our navigation team. If the decision is made to proceed with having women on board, we'll be in uncharted waters.

Sorry to be so wordy, but these issues require some in-depth discussion. I just scratched the surface. There is one big difference between the two issues: one is never discussed and the other is often discussed!

I'm enjoying my Exec job. The Captain is competent and easygoing. Some think his "no sweat" style will keep him from making admiral. I hope not. I'm very comfortable with him, the crew, and the boat. I know them well, having helped build her. Most of the commissioning crew is still aboard and will make the first patrol.

Tucker, everyone has to come to grips with his or her own role in the military. I can see where that might be especially hard for a woman who wants to have it all and could certainly do more than she's allowed. But would you really want to change places with me? Or, is it that you don't have the chance to turn it down that smarts?

Today I gave five bucks to a freckled-faced college girl collecting money in a bucket that said "Eugene McCarthy for President." I asked her how the campaign was going in conservative Charleston. She said the locals were friendly and viewed it with bemused tolerance. One older woman said to her while donating, "I don't know whether to vote for him or George Wallace." It's an interesting, volatile, and sometimes amusing year politically!

> Warm regards from a very hot (it's 98° in Charleston today) cold warrior.

> Tom

Three days later from Robyn

July 1, 1968, Boston, MA

Yo Tucker —

As usual, first me, and then into the diatribe which your letters always seem to instill in me. I'm not too fond of waddling around like a beached elephant seal. The kidlet is due next month. Actually, it's been a fine pregnancy, except for feeling like such a behemoth! (I've made a series of cartoons of my porcine self engaging in assorted activities. I've named the character Squantum, which sounds appropriately oafish and lumpy!)

At least one thing about your (so far) chosen career — you've never moldered in boredom! Peter (Pompous) Morrison's shenanigans don't surprise me. You present a charmingly convincing image of pomposity, accompanied by snorting, raving, and prancing about. People like Morrison tend to lose touch with the real world of communication, interpersonal relationships, and just plain courtesy. The need to demonstrate personal power becomes overwhelming. And what better way than to wither everyone within earshot?

And then you. Your musings on how you, as a uniformed member of the military, fit into the horrors of war and violence, how the intellectual intrigue of strategizing and tracking juxtaposes with real people on real missions. We've talked about armchair strategists before, as in professors, generals, admirals, and captains and lieutenants. The difference between them and you is that you step back and are sensitive to where it all leads. Whereas, "They" continue to work the puzzle square by square and never look out the window. And rarely look at the *feelings* of those surrounding them. Perhaps it's analogous to a surgeon who avoids becoming too close to his patients so he doesn't have to face that they're human beings who might die.

The military doesn't deserve someone like you, who is both insightful and intelligent. If it wants to behave loutishly, then let it recruit louts! Relatedly, I understand that we're sending an inordinate number of low IQ types to fight the war and letting off the more intelligent souls who desire deferments. Is that true? Is this how our democratic processes play out in crises?

Actually, your focus is closer to mine in human services, as you struggle with the issue of Navy women being equal partners. I don't know what to say about your possible resignation. I do know that, whichever way you go, it'll be a carefully considered decision and not an easy one. I know how much you both love and sometimes hate the Navy. Despite my somewhat less than totally enthusiastic endorsement of the Navy, I do respect your commitment and struggle lo these many years, and hope that whatever you decide, you're not left feeling ambivalent.

Not easy times. Till the next crisis!

Love,

Robyn

Six weeks later from Buck Buckingham

15 August 1968, Montreal, Canada

Dear Tucker,

The international naval seminar is proving both educational and concerning. I sense the participants could not agree on the Soviet maritime threat. The non-U.S. countries will go along with our assessment and force buildup, as long as we pay the bills. Not all are reluctant, but one country gets the other thinking about the urgency of the threat.

Last night, for instance, a very liberal Canadian politician spoke with silver tongue, saying he saw no sense in Canada buying into the submarine ASW program when its friend, the United States, was doing what was necessary to monitor the problem. He was very good, very persuasive. I stayed up nearly all night writing a speech to answer him, modifying our presentation to counter his arguments. The slides in our Cold Wet War presentation need more work, Tucker.

I think I failed miserably, although there were some welcome comments that I was more logical in my "let's work together" theme than he was in suggesting that Canada opt out. Thankfully, the seminar was put back into focus by a feisty Canadian naval officer,

Captain Shorty Hawkins. You probably knew him at SACLANT. Shorty, a short, hard-as-a-rock kind of guy, stood up and said, "I'm not as eloquent as Admiral Buckingham, and not as politically motivated as John Austin [the Canadian politician], but the facts are, as Buck presented so clearly, the Soviets are building one hell of a maritime capability. They say it's 'to protect our Homeland.' That's a bunch of malarkey! So what are they going to use their capability for? Canada is geographically closer to the Soviet potential for blocking seaborne commerce than is the U.S. We have a responsibility to recognize that, support our ally, and get on with it!"

Tucker, we have our work cut out for us. We must modify the Threat Presentation to include a logical argument about Soviet intentions. We will add this to our description of their capabilities and history. Why are they building all these ships, naval and merchant? Defending the Homeland doesn't cut it. One implication of their fast-growing merchant fleet might be as an alternative to the Trans-Siberian railroad.

I'll be forwarding the seminar's Working Papers to you before I head for the Imperial Defense College in England. Be prepared with new thinking upon my return 30 August.

My best to you and your family. It's difficult to believe your dad is retiring next month.

Warm regards,

Buck Buckingham

One month later from Tucker

15 September 1968, Norfolk, VA

Dear Mother and Dad,

What a fun time you had cruising around the South Pacific!

I'd rather be with you now than struggling with one of the hardest decisions I've ever made — to resign from the Navy. I weighed the pros and cons, and came up with "resign." As I wrote in my resignation letter to the Secretary of the Navy, "The reason is simple: The Navy hasn't developed multifaceted career patterns for women officers. It's currently stuck on one path which forces me to fill an administrative billet for the next three years. I can't fight policy."

We know that only civilian leadership and the public can take on the Navy and win.

While the decision seems right for the long term, am somewhat depressed and frustrated at the moment. If I were a male submariner or surface warfare officer or aviator, Dad, I would have challenging career paths to follow and be part of the first team.

I can hear your words now, Mother, "It's the Navy's loss." Thank you for the kind words. But the Navy seems to consume its people. The impersonality bothers me too. A few individuals will miss me, but that huge bureaucratic machine will just keep chuggin' along.

Received my Masters Thesis committee's final approval today. Hooray! While it's been a challenge to research and write about JFK's National Security Policy, I'm ready to move on. So it's back to academia probably and pressing on for a doctorate.

Hope you're both well and happy.

Love,

Tucker

One week later from Mother and Dad

22 September 1968, Washington, D.C.

Dear Tucker,

You've certainly had some emotional swings in the last year or two. Now, you're resigning from the Navy, or talking about it. We really don't know how to respond. You've always been impatient. Things don't happen quickly enough for you. Maybe that's because your mind works faster than most. If that's the reason, that same mind should let you in on the secret that basic change takes longer. You have no logical reason to conclude that appropriate assignments for you are up to you alone, or that you, as a woman invading what has been a man's world, can expect opportunities comparable to those available to men. It just takes longer.

You say you have no clear-cut career path ahead of you, unlike male officers who can choose among several specialties. I assure you it's not nearly so simple as you make it. I have heard male officers making the same bleats. BuPers is all mixed up, or that assignment is "the kiss of death" (a favorite emotional utterance). That sort of thing is no more true for them than it is for you. I understand your frustration about the slowness of equitable assignments for men and women, but your mother and I are surprised when the frustration becomes defeat. That's uncharacteristic of you.

We've never really understood your strong desire to be in the Navy. We've told you that many times; but people do not tell you what to do, Tucker. You know that as well as we do. You've given it a good shot, certainly a much better shot than most. If it hasn't worked, go back to graduate school, get a doctorate under your belt, and become the best political science professor in the country. You will certainly have some unique tickets with your experience in the Navy.

Yes, we're well and reasonably happy, but when something this huge develops in your life we're understandably less happy than we could be. Maybe we should talk this out. Can you come home on leave for a week or so? We love you.

Mother and Dad

One week later from Tucker's journal

l October 1968, Norfolk, VA

For the record,

Processing my decision has been healthy. Time teaches. My resignation touches deeper levels than just job satisfaction:

- Men see Navy women as members of the second team, unable to fill first team seats. This is unacceptable. Equal pay is great, but what about honoring the capabilities and potentials of Navy women?

- Navy policies and attitudes toward minorities reek of bigotry. I can no longer accept this. Since early childhood I've heard damning remarks and jokes about minorities. I've accepted them as okay and part of the service, even though there's talk of "the Navy family." Yet belittling comments relating to lesbians/gays frighten me. I still don't know if I'm bisexual or lesbian. Doesn't really matter, but if I were to stay in the Navy I'd have to be, at least pretend to be, heterosexual!

- Navy personnel standards are only as high as recruiting needs — unacceptable. During this war, right now, because many Americans are draft dodging and angry, we're not recruiting a reasonable percent of the nation's best. Reminds me of my conversation last week with good friend and sometimes date, Lt. Comdr. John Osburn. After exchanging sea stories over a lobster dinner, he surprised me by exclaiming, "Tucker, you *know* in your heart of hearts that this Navy's filled with mediocrity and mediocre people."

I was shocked at hearing this from a dedicated submariner, with twelve years service. "John," I said, "that's so wrong and sad for the country and the Navy."

But at the end of the conversation, I realized that at the moment the Navy is a mediocre organization. That's hard to swallow. I want the Navy to have the high standards I first encountered at Officer Candidate School to apply today. "Needs of the service" and the draft dictate otherwise.

- The Navy allows inconsistencies and sometimes inflexibility regarding unjust, unnecessary policies and regulations. For me, for instance, notwithstanding written policy regarding women's career paths, exceptions should be made to the current, too-rigid policy. "Needs of the service" oppose "needs of the individual."

Feels good to nearly be a free person again, unencumbered by the Navy, George Orwell's Big Brother at its worst, and a benevolent father figure at its best. I shall miss the benevolent father, but not the Brother.

Reckon I'll have to find some other mountains to climb, less demanding and more satisfying.

TF

Two weeks later from Tucker's journal

17 October 1968, Norfolk, Virginia

For the record,

My God. I can't believe my dilemma. Buck called me to his office this morning. "Tucker, I can't let you do this."

"What do you mean, Admiral?"

"Resign from the Navy, Tucker. You're too fine an officer for us to lose. Social forces are pressuring the Navy to change policies and attitudes toward its women. It's the wrong time for you to resign. I have a proposal that I would hope you can't resist."

I'd imagined Buck would be disappointed when he read the resignation letter, but had expected he'd sign off for my sake.

"I recall you'd like to work on a Ph.D.," he said.

"Yessir," I replied, "that's been in the back of my mind for several years."

"Okay, I have a plan. I've just been appointed as President of the Naval War College in Newport, departing January."

"Congratulations, Admiral. That's a three-star billet, isn't it?"

"Thanks, Tucker. It's the billet I've wanted for a long time. I'll find a spot for you at the College. You can simultaneously attend Brown for the doctorate and work for me. It's only an hour away. What do you say to coming with me?"

Startled by this bold plan, I mumbled, "I — I'll have to think about that, Admiral. Thank you for your confidence in my abilities. On one level your plan fulfills my professional dreams, but it doesn't eliminate the reasons I'm resigning." Buck and I hadn't discussed my resignation. He only knew I was discouraged specifically about women's career paths and opportunities.

"Tucker, we all have our crosses to bear. This will give you an opportunity to work on your educational goals. At the same time, I foresee forces will compel naval and civilian leadership to be more open to the idea of military women. You're on the forefront of change, Tucker. Nonetheless, you'll have to accept this offer 'on the come.' Nothing in life is guaranteed, you know."

He handed me my resignation papers. "Newport's a great place. We'll both have a clear stage to make a difference."

I am so confused.

How can I possibly turn down such a fabulous offer? What a remarkable gesture from any admiral. I know that flag officers weigh carefully their use of influence. Remember though, all the reasons you're happy to be leaving the Navy.

Sleep on this. Check in with a few friends. Too hard to decide tonight.

TF

Chapter Six

The Challenge

One week later from Tucker

25 October 1968, Norfolk, Virginia

Dear Robyn,

Thanks for your empathic ear last week. Feels like another big life juncture. I'd like to handle the decision well, or "trust the process" as you say. Admiral Buckingham's orders to be President of the War College and my close working relationship with him have rebalanced the scales — in favor of the Navy.

If I remain on active duty, I can reframe all of my motives for leaving except one, the so-called lesbian question (I despise that word). I can handle this issue too, by suppressing those inclinations while encouraging positive feelings toward men as "the opposite sex." The male dynamic actually stimulates me, and I like being part of an organization where males predominate. But am I turned on by any of them?

To decline a job offer from a mentor I truly admire and respect seems foolish. Following an admiral is like following a President — one yields certain personal desires in favor of "the good of the Navy or the country."

When I spoke with Jennie about "the gay issue," she advised I repress my feelings toward women and encourage the heterosexual side.

"That assumes I'm attracted to men," I retorted.

"Well, if you're not, Tucker, then for God's sake be neat and discreet. I don't want you to ruin your potential for promotion, or your very *career*. We both know women who have left early, or who have been asked to leave, because of their sexual identity. At the same time, we know others who are 'neat and discreet.' *You* know the rules."

"Yes," I said. "I know the Navy boots out gays, but rarely adulterers. Adultery and homosexuality are both allegedly 'conduct unbecoming.' Why are adulterers overlooked and gays pursued? The inconsistency in enforcing the rules smacks of bigotry."

"Tucker, you know I've always said you must 'take the bitter with the better,' " said Jennie.

We ended on this discordant note.

The question is, Robyn, what is my sexual identity? I know I can work through a lot of Navy institutional stuff — bigotry, the second-team status of women, and even the Navy's mediocrity. To be continually stressed out over inappropriate policy toward gays and lesbians, however, whether I am one or not, is asking too much. Besides, people whom I think to be gay, though no one can be absolutely sure who is or isn't, are top performers. They consider their sexual behavior a matter of individual privacy and I agree.

Ah, me. I'll date fiercely and see what happens. I'll probably be so involved at work and study, I won't have time anyway.

How're Derry and Ned, and you? Am thrilled you and I and your family will be together soon.

Love,

Tucker

Two weeks later from Robyn

November 10, 1968, Boston, MA

Oh Tucker,

As soon as you deal with one thorny issue, up comes another one to help make your path challenging. And this one's a biggie! Aren't they all?

I'd call the Navy's persecution of homosexuals hypocritical rather than bigoted. While it cheerfully tolerates, even condones, adulterous behavior, as well as "unbecoming" behavior so often demonstrated by sailors of all rates and ranks, the Navy humiliates, excoriates, and banishes those perceived as gay or lesbian.

Tucker, I don't know if you're a bisexual, a lesbian, or a kangaroo by definition. I don't think it matters. You need to attend to your own biology, your own instincts, attractions, leanings, whatever. I hate that you must repress who you really are. Why should you "date fiercely and see what happens" to please your benevolent Big Daddy Navy, as you occasionally refer to it? Why should you continue to give and give to an organization whose appreciation is muted at best? I hope you know what you're doing!

We're all fine and look forward to our get-together this month. The mouth, so called for obvious reasons, is at a really cute stage — smiling and drooling and upchucking and all the other endearing infant idiosyncrasies! He's also very vain and knows who is the *real* ruler of the Greeley roost!

Much as I do love my new status of Motherhood, I'm glad to be back at work part-time. See you soon,

Love,

Robyn

Six Months later from Tucker

17 May 1969, Newport, R.I.

Dear Mother and Dad,

I must write again about the sinking of a U.S. submarine, USS *Guitarro* at San Francisco's dockside yesterday! How can a sub sink right at dockside, Dad?

With sailboats skimming along Narragansett Bay and the shoreline rocky against whitish sands, Newport is as glorious as ever. My office in the War College Main Building overlooks the Bay. Feels like the right decision to be here.

I'm having real problems with our Vietnam policy, however. Among the staff members from all four service branches returning from duty over there, I haven't found many happy campers. While they don't come right out and say, "I'm against our policy," I sense these officers believe we're marching down the wrong path. Either we should've been given the go-ahead to do the job right, or else we should be out by now. Wish the White House and our politico-military leadership could see the light. President Nixon seems to be worried about U.S. credibility, all the while sacrificing military men and women.

Instead of enrolling in the Ph.D. program in September I hope to be a student in the Command and Staff course for LTs and LCDRs, which is ten-months' duration. There's a track available for staff officers to attend one of the two courses, while simultaneously performing staff duties. Sounds exciting to me and less difficult than commuting to Brown. Besides, the opportunity seems too great to pass up. This campus is where the action is for me.

Dad, you must be relieved to be retired and not have to worry directly about the Vietnam mess, though I understand you'd prefer to be on active duty. If one had to go to war, WWII would have been my choice. The goals and the missions were much clearer than this guerrilla-like war. Who would ever have imagined a brown-water U.S. Navy in 1941?

The American public has little idea about our military's "dovishness." It doesn't fully understand that civilian leaders make the decision to fight, and it doesn't understand the implications of civilian control, with clear lines of authority. Dad, as you've said, LBJ and McNamara micromanage the war from the White House.

My duplex is a block from the Atlantic ocean. Much better than ensign days. Enjoy your retirement!

    Love,

    Tucker

Ten days later from Dad

27 May 1969, San Diego, CA

Dear Tucker,

A submarine can sink anywhere if someone makes a mistake. I have to assume that's what happened to *Guitarro*. The investigation will find answers. Seems a unique occurrence to me.

Today I reread your letter from Norfolk not quite a year ago. What a difference a few months make. Then, you were on the verge of resigning from the Navy; now you sound positively settled and in the right place. I hope Buck has done you a good service by keeping you on active duty in an assignment you like.

I'm not sure you should give up the opportunity to get a Ph.D. from Brown. The War College Junior Course will help in the Navy, but that Brown Ph.D. will help anywhere. Are you determined to stick this out a bit longer? You know things aren't going to happen as quickly as you want them to.

The War College is a fascinating place, and with a person like Buck running it, you should be able to express your own ideas. What comes next might throw you into another deep disappointment. Naturally, we'd like to spare you that if possible, but we support you in whatever you decide.

Answers to Vietnam are no closer in that hallowed place than they are in my morning newspaper. This country is confused over why we're there. Until it understands that, we'll be uncomfortable with it. I, for one, cannot understand why we do not mobilize. We're treating SE Asia as a police action and never letting the people feel that it's really important, yet we're committing more and more resources to the scene. What do they call it, "butter and bullets" policy? It's not bringing the country together in support of our policy overseas.

Newport is no doubt putting on its Spring show for you, but remember from your officer orientation days, its winter can be a real test of resolve.

Your Newport of today sounds so unlike your Newport of orientation days. What has changed, Tucker? You or Newport? Your Mother joins me in sending all our love.

Dad

Two weeks later from Tucker

10 June 1969, Newport, R.I.

Dear Robyn,

To think we graduated from Wellesley a whole decade ago! Our class reunion last week created strange feelings within me. It was wonderful to visit with old friends and be on campus again. Such a splendiferous campus, with lush lawns and flowers, and structures exemplifying the best of academia. Yet it's the college's products (we) who shine. We were smart to have selected Wellesley.

The downside — I felt like the odd woman out conversing with our classmates. Their primary conversational topics were men, men, and babies. Whereas my friends seemed genuinely interested in me, they also kept their distance. Perhaps my profession's the problem, and I shouldn't take it personally. Most of them are liberal and anti-Vietnam. I drove home thinking I'd better hurry and have children, marrying first of course!

What was your take on the reunion? Did you talk about anything other than Ned and your children? Jobs must understandably take a back seat to family commitments.

It's great to be back in Newport, away from the big cities. Will be in touch.

Love,

Tucker

Three weeks later from Robyn

July 1, 1969, Boston, MA

Tucker,

You know, Tuck, you're right on about our reunion and conversational topics. You probably shouldn't take the apparent distancing personally. People talk with relative strangers, as many of us were to each other, about what's immediately of concern, neutral and uncontroversial topics. Once one settles into a conversation and gets to know the person a little, then topics tend to grow deeper and more personal. You're the only one in our class in the military and somehow that profession seems more encompassing, more involving, than many others. It's a profession, rather than a career.

And though you've been in your profession for nearly ten years, it's been an intense time, a real love/hate relationship. Most of the rest of us would've long since peeled off to do something else if we'd had to put up with some of the stuff you've been dealing with. And, of course, you've been working on the whole issue of sexuality in a way that probably most haven't, though it would be interesting to know how many folks have had similar feelings and concerns.

I believe the distancing you experienced was circumstantial and probably affected us all to some degree. I certainly didn't exchange many profound truths, though I did reconnect with a couple of people. So based on our reunion experience, I don't think you need to rush to building a home and raising kids, especially since you'd have to think about resigning again. You did tell me ladies of the Navy couldn't have kids, didn't you? It certainly isn't easy being a female naval person; you can't have children and you can't be gay. I suppose the only viable alternative is to be a straight nun!

Derry's first birthday comes up in a couple of weeks. I think it will coincide with his first tooth and probably his first step!

Till the next time.

Love,

Robyn

P.S. Thank goodness most classmates oppose the Vietnam War!

Seven weeks later from Tucker's journal

20 August, 1969, Newport, R.I.

 For the record,

"Unqualified," because of my *gender*. My anger riseth up again. This morning I walked down to the Command and Staff area, excited that soon I might be enrolled in the course. Captain Lucas, Director of the curriculum, turned me down saying, "*All* women are unauthorized and unqualified to attend this course."

Shaking his head, he continued, "Don't take it personally, Tucker. You don't drive ships or submarines, and you don't fly airplanes. This course is about shipboard tactics and planning. The nuts and bolts of being at sea. You women aren't assigned to sea duty, and I don't anticipate you ever will be."

"I predict we will be at sea someday, Captain, but I grant you that for the moment we are WAVES ashore, supporting the fleet. Proud to do it, too, I might add. In the meantime, your course is also about staff planning. I could definitely have used the staff portion of the course in my last Joint Staff billet. I worked on several OpOrders, for example."

The Captain seemed to be searching for other reasons to reject me. "I hear you're a hotshot in International Relations," he said. "Why don't you apply for the senior course, which is more strategy oriented? I suggest you talk to Captain Hannagan, the Director of the Naval Warfare course."

Captain Lucas was adamant about no women in his course, even though several women officers now fill billets in which his course is a *prerequisite*. Strange times. Navy women are making their way up via outstanding personal performance, with minimal support from "the system" and Big Daddy Navy.

How many women have to crash through the damn barriers before we're accepted in "this man's Navy?"

Guess I'll muster up my courage once more and ask Captain Hannagan tomorrow. As Mother says, "Nothing ventured, nothing gained."

Should I resurrect the Ph.D. idea? The Navy makes it damn formidable for its women. But, then, nobody ever told me the climb would be a piece of cake. And, Jennie merely said, "climb."

"Unqualified!" They're really saying, "*Unwanted!*"

TF

Six days later from Tucker

26 August 1969, Newport, R.I.

Dear Jennie,

How're you and Pierre? Sure would be special if you both were here to console me now and then. In the meantime, I'll have to settle for writing and phoning.

Sometimes assertiveness causes nothing but trouble and dissent; other times it hits pay dirt. Last week I tried to enroll in the College's junior course. The director said, "No, thank you." So, yesterday I took myself and my academic record to see the senior course director, Captain Hannagan. As I walked into his office, the Captain looked at me with a fairly unfriendly smile. I suspect Captain Lucas had briefed him on my request.

"Lieutenant Fairfield, you don't have the right rank to be in my course. This course is for commanders and captains."

"I know that, Captain. But I don't have the right gender to be in the junior course. My academic and military backgrounds dovetail with your course." I suggested he could make an exception to the rank requirement. I told him I understood during this semester his course would have two women officer students for the first time ever, and then handed him my transcripts, mentally crossing my fingers.

He carefully read through the transcripts. "Bob Lucas is right," he said. "You've got some damn fine qualifications. I'll take your case under advisement and let you know tomorrow, Tucker. If I do accept you, you'll be required to fulfill all the requirements, including a group research project."

Jennie, it's an odd and tough time to be a woman in the U.S. Navy. The more enlightened men want to open up the channels for us, but Navy policy says, "No dice!" Some are willing to bend and even break the rules. Fortunately Captain Hannagan struggles with his heart and says "yes" to more equal opportunity for women. As of today I'm enrolled as a student in the senior class with commanders and captains! My participation qualifies distinctly as a form of discrimination in *favor* of women. Usually the opposite prevails. My faith in the Navy is on a roll.

Will you and Pierre be leaving Norfolk soon? Seems it's that time.

Have you heard the latest scuttlebutt about Captain St. Martin? She, as WAVE Director, is fighting with the Medical Corps Director over birth control pills. You got it. She feels birth control pills shouldn't be distributed to "her women." The Medics feel otherwise. Guess who'll win?

What about your decision to stay with or leave the Navy? If you and Pierre can be stationed together, I should think you'd hang in. On the other hand, you both probably want children. Perhaps you should challenge that stupid regulation.

My love to you both. Keep me posted.

> Love,
>
> Tucker

One week later from Jennie

4 September 1969, Norfolk, VA

Dear Tucker,

Congratulations on getting yourself into the senior course at the War College! You do have a way with words, "don't have the right gender to be in the junior course" indeed. You're certainly correct about the frustrations of certain rules and regs. Pierre and I have been talking about our next assignments and how we can finagle getting the assignments for geographical togetherness, as well as for our own personal career advancement. It's difficult and sometimes I resent following him around rather than his following me. Of course, he does outrank me, though he never pulls rank on me. Looking at opportunities at large bases with billets for both of us is a real challenge.

You asked about our plans for having children...not any time soon, maybe never. Tucker, although I'm happy with Pierre, sometimes I feel a loss of my own "identity." I still have goals in the Navy for myself and am pretty sure motherhood is incompatible with them. Once in a while it feels like wifehood isn't either. I imagine you can understand that a little.

Having said all that, we'll probably end up in D.C. in the not-too-distant future.

Take care of yourself. Keep those captains in line!

> Best,
>
> Jennie

Four months later from Tucker's journal

14 January 1970, Newport, R.I.

 For the record,

I'm doing it again. Taking on too much work and not relaxing enough. My nature and the Navy encourage the practice. In the meantime, what an education! This Naval Warfare course gives a bird's eye view of international politico-military relations. Each day brings a new perspective from major Washington players — State Department officers, generals, admirals, high officials. By and large, the generals are the best speakers.

If all goes according to plan, in my staff hat I'll be advisor to a student group research project on Women-in-the-Navy. I drafted the project's proposal, with a bibliography and approach, and both school Directors have signed off to Buck's Deputy on the concept. Group research, Buck's idea, allows for in-depth analysis of a policy area. Lord knows we need policy research on women. It's now up to the students themselves to select a project from the long list.

My regular duty as an intelligence briefer has been disappointing. Minimum challenge. No doubt the President's having created a special billet for me has caused resentment in certain quarters. Figure out something after June. Find a better billet, Fairfield.

The horrifying Vietnam war stories and intelligence reports continue. Each day the news worsens. I can't support the effort, and am not alone among my fellow officers. Limited war is limited war. Given the nuclear context, we should no longer be in Southeast Asia. The Soviets are holding us hostage; *i.e.*, as long as they have huge nuclear retaliatory forces, we can't use nuclear weapons in Vietnam. If we don't use nuclear weapons, we can't win without tremendous losses in ground forces. We're caught, and Moscow, Peking, and Hanoi know that. Political leadership has thrust us into an ungodly mess, with casualties and "body counts" mounting daily.

I'm surprised at the attitude of several staff officers. Yesterday I overheard several instructors arguing about the war. An Air Force colonel yelled, "We should nuke 'em till they glow in the dark." Such a comment brings out the pacifist in me, though I believe in a strong U.S. defense structure.

Part of me wishes I'd resigned. Why don't a few admirals and generals resign? Why don't the senior retirees speak up? They could truly make the point to the public.

Feels good to be working with some of our finest officers. I wouldn't use "mediocre" to describe my classmates.

TF

Six days later from Tucker

20 January 1970, Newport, R.I.

Dear Robyn,

I seem to write you when I'm discouraged. Hope that's okay. My life has been going swimmingly at the College until today. You know I've been excited that our students will be researching Women-in-the-Navy, with me as advisor. No more.

This morning the War College's Deputy, Rear Admiral Jim Taylor, summoned me to his office and said, "No, to your women's project, Tucker." He explained that Captain Marie St. Martin, WAVE Director, had uncompromisingly shot the idea down.

"Marie said the subject is a political football and cannot be studied up there at the College." The Admiral looked disgruntled. "Those were her exact words. I'm sorry, Tucker, but orders are orders. Marie rules the roost when it comes to women in the Navy."

"Admiral, can't we study what we damn well please? Isn't that the beauty of an academic environment? Controversial subjects need to be studied and not shunted aside."

"We need the blessing of the sponsor on contentious projects, Tucker. The WAVE Director's Office is the logical sponsor for this study and she chooses to disapprove. I agree with your inference. It's her loss because the War College offers a perfect opportunity for free, quality research by top officers on many subjects, including the future of our Navy's women. Yours is an idea whose time has come. The women's movement is knocking at our doors."

"Yessir!"

With a sigh, the Admiral sent me on my way. As I left he said, "I regret, but I must honor, Marie's decision. I know you're frustrated, Tucker."

Frustrated. And furious. Robyn, it took some politicking to put this topic on the students' list of research topics, as you can imagine. Given the Navy's conservative nature, women are a controversial subject all right. But why not use the War College's resources and go for it? What's Captain St. Martin afraid of? Wonder how she found out anyway? I shouldn't have been so enthusiastic in telling other women officers about the project. Someone must have told the Saint.

I must let go of my commitment to the women's issue and enjoy my own student group research. Have selected the Indian Ocean as my topic area, with considerable encouragement from Buck Buckingham. Given our relationship and his interest in the area, I probably didn't have a choice; that's okay.

When will we women be seen as equals? It's going to be a long haul, with political fights along the way. Women can be their own worst enemy. Reminds me of the comfortable matrons who are ticked at the burgeoning women's movement in our country because it might affect their status quo.

So what's with you, my friend? Haven't talked with you in a while. Let's get together soon.

Love,

Tucker

Ten days later from Robyn

January 30, 1970, Boston, MA

Oh Dear Tucker,

The Navy chops and hacks and slashes again! This time blame can't even be laid at the feet of the chromosomally disadvantaged half of the human race! What a bummer! Of course it's okay to write when you're discouraged! We've shared back and forth a life time of ups and downs.

I thought admirals were higher than captains, and we know the Navy considers males vastly superior to females. So the question is, why does St. Marie have such power? If it's her department, her decision, why did the Admiral tell you and not St.Marie? Will you have a chance to confront her directly? The question of academic freedom *is* at issue. Her decision seems to be idiosyncratic. Is it possible that St. Marie is being the fall guy for the institution and not in fact simply representing her own attitudes? How infuriating!

We're all fine. The winter slips and splatters in a monochromatic drudgery of gray — dirty gray, ugly gray, brownish gray. Well, you get the idea. Such urban ugliness leads me to our move. We've decided urbia is no place to raise kids and have been looking in Maine. We like its relative unclutteredness and its long coastline. The notion of a seaside town is very appealing. All the better for Derry to join the Navy some year. JUST KIDDING!!

Ned has all but clinched a job in Bar Harbor, and I'll look once we get there. The move will probably happen in the early summer. That leaves plenty of time for you to come up and inhale some "cultcha" before we go.

How about coming up in a couple of weeks and we can eyeball each other directly. Till soon.

Love,

Robyn

Five weeks later from Buck Buckingham

6 March 1970, Imperial Defense College AIR MAIL

Dear Tucker,

Greetings from London. Helen and I have been treated like royalty here, including a grand dinner at the Admiral's House. We toasted the occasion of the nuclear nonproliferation treaty taking effect this week, as ratified by the U.S., U.S.S.R., and other countries. Real progress, Tucker.

The dinner sparked an idea I want you to explore.

Our Naval War College offers an ideal location at which to host an International Naval Dinner. Think of it! We can invite naval representatives, and their wives, from all the NATO countries, plus top officers from the Naval Command Course countries, plus the foreign students themselves from the course. The theme that pops up for me is "The Band of Brothers in Blue." I know, your feminist perspective will balk a bit at that one. But it fits.

Officers will arrive the night before the event and during the next day we'll brief them about strategic naval matters. I'll send a message to the Chief of Staff outlining the event's purposes and tentative schedule, tapping you as the Action Officer for the Dinner itself at the Officers' Club. Please start the wheels rolling on this, Tucker. My schedule has me in Brussels next week and back in Newport on 10 April. I'll speak with you then about the Dinner. Hope the March winds aren't blowing you into Narragansett Bay. Bet you're wearing your havelock!

Warm regards,

Buck Buckingham

Two months later from Tucker's journal

11 May 1970, Newport, R.I.

 For the record,

Don't ever do group research again! Disconcerting. The concept works well if all parties equally contribute. Two of the five group members wrote the study. Enough said.

Buck Buckingham's pleased with our product. "It may well become the Navy's policy in the Indian Ocean area," he said at our final briefing yesterday. He tasked me to declassify the study and get it into the *Naval War College Review*.

Having seen group research in operation, I'm even more distressed that the women's project was canceled. The conceptual framework which group research supports could've launched a comprehensive policy for Navy women. The Saint fears change. As did whoever passed the word to her.

Buck asked me to stay for a moment after the briefing. He seemed down and needing to blow off. I asked him what was wrong. He replied, "Vietnam is wrong."

I couldn't restrain myself from saying that a senior officer or two should take a risk and resign over the matter. He didn't directly respond, but with visible anger and pain he said succinctly, "This is a lousy war and we should not be there." He said the civilians should've defined the war's purposes and then let the military handle it, get it done, or leave. Buck went on to say that from its beginnings strategic errors have been made, because plans and decisions have been formulated by people who have no experience with military operations, no understanding of military life and its complex bonding and leadership patterns. "Vietnam's a huge military problem micromanaged politically."

He concluded, "The country doesn't understand why we're in Vietnam, and most troublesome, neither does the soldier, sailor, or airman being asked to fight."

I must add — and neither do I! Such a waste of money and manpower and human lives. And, with the four Kent State students killed by National Guardsmen last week, I know the country will suffer more angst and turmoil.

TF

Two months later from Billie

15 July 1970, Knoxville, Tennessee

Tuck —

Tried to get you on the autovon my last day in the office, but you were out. This is just a short note to keep you up to date...

My bags are packed, my car is stored in my mom's garage. My house is rented to two really nice WAC officers stationed at Fort Belvoir, and my chartered flight leaves from JFK in 10 days. I'm going to land in Frankfurt and my new boss, Colonel John Clark, USAF, and his wife Amy are going to meet me. They sound real nice and energetic. I've talked to them twice now by phone. They'll drive me to Stuttgart (Patch Barracks), where I'll be temporarily in the BOQ. Soon as I find out my autovon number, I'll call. Can you believe it? I'm going to Europe! All my relatives want to visit. This is going to be my "grand tour."

I'm still peeling from the daily sunburns I received down in Virginia Beach. Dead skin keeps dropping off my nose! That was a terrific condo we rented — slide open the door and step out on the beach! I know the clams, oysters, and crabs were glad to see us leave; they bordered on extinction! You and I have a great group of pals! Glad you could fly down from Newport.

Right now I'm going to relax in the Tennessee sunshine, get my last fried chicken and homemade peach ice cream, visit the family, and tie up loose ends. My sister, who has moved back in with my mother, found a great job with an advertising agency as Art Director.

My mother has really slowed down. Her rheumatoid arthritis is extremely painful. And, I've now been diagnosed with the same disease! Remember when I came down to Virginia Beach and my right wrist was red and swollen? Well, I had a lot of tests done at Bethesda, and the RA factor was in the blood. Oh, my! Right now it's in remission, but it'll be back. Bless my mother's genes!

I've finished two thirds of the Master's Degree at AU. I could only take one or two courses at a time because of my heavy workload at CHINFO. I'm not going to miss the media representatives. I hope their editors spike them all!

Sorry your plan to conduct the Women's Study was shot down by the Saint. If women are to be a part of the Navy we have to pull all the duties, at sea or ashore. We need the same career paths as men, we need to be *equal* partners. If we ever get serious about the subject, it's going to be hard to convince the male Navy that women can be equal.

Find the time to visit me in Germany. We can do the "Grand Tour" together!

             Billie

Two months later from Tucker

                       8 September 1970, Newport, R.I.

Dear Robyn,

Last night I was privileged to be a guest at *the* most elegant dinner I shall ever attend. I mentioned that Buck dreamed up the idea of an International Naval Dinner, the celebratory part of a weekend of strategic planning, hosted by the War College. I've spent many extra hours on the project, and because of its specialness, I must write you (copy to my Journal) of the glittering evening.

The guests, ninety naval officers and their spouses, began arriving in official black cars at the Officers' Club at 1900 sharp to be wined and dined. The scene was like a Hollywood movie, with distinguished naval officers from many countries decked out in their Dress Blues. The Norwegian admiral, Bjorn Martinsen, and his wife Ellen took the prize for the best-dressed couple. He sported epaulets on his boat cloak, and she wore a stunning purple velvet gown and simple gold jewelry.

Perhaps we should've held the dinner at a Newport mansion. The O' Club staff, nonetheless, outdid themselves, and as the guests flowed in, they stood at attention, with twenty tables of eight decorated with blue tablecloths, gold napkins, and bouquets of flowers at each table. Each place setting had gleaming silverware, white plates with gold rims, three wine glasses, and a special place card. Behind the head table stood flags from all the thirty-three countries represented by the guests.

The Club manager met with Helen, Buck's wife, and me for several hours to decide upon the meal. It was the finest dinner menu we could select and the food, cooked to perfection by the Club chef, Jacques, was served by the staff with elegance and charm. Before I continue, let me describe the menu, which was displayed on a printed card at each person's place:

The first course — a Consomme Madrilene, served with a dry wine. The second course — Coquilles St. Jacques. The salad arrived next, mixed greens with avocado and grapefruit. The fourth course, accompanied by a Cabernet Sauvignon, was Filet de Boeuf Wellington. Served on the same silver platter as the filet were Pommes au beurre, Broiled tarragon tomatoes, and Honey-glazed carrots.

Buck stopped at our table about half-way through the event. He said, "Veddy, veddy British."

I replied, "Veddy, veddy special."

Buck said, "I have never experienced an event to match this dinner, even at the White House or in England." He looked so pleased with himself.

Getting full, Robyn? We're not finished. The next course was a spoonful of lemon sorbet served in a small silver compote, to clear our palates for dessert — a magnificent, flaming Baked Alaska (my very favorite of desserts). The servers then carried in platters of cheeses and crackers and demitasse to the seated guests. Then we were served the Port in a bottle for each table which passed to the left. About that time baskets of nuts and mints arrived.

Buck then stood up, raised his full glass of port and gave the following toast, written by Yours truly:

> To you fine representatives of the democratic seafaring countries of the world, welcome to the United States' Naval War College. Thank you for making your long journeys. My hope is that this will be the first annual gathering of our distinguished group. Within the past 24 hours we have accomplished the purposes of our gathering — to come together, face-to-face, to share how we can better protect our countries' maritime interests and how we can prevent any further hostilities on the high seas.
>
> I'm especially gratified that you have given full support to the NATO Maritime Force, the first ever multinational naval force. With good fortune, the force will operate in the Mediterranean within the year. And now, please continue to enjoy this memorable evening.

Next, the senior official present, Admiral Leslie Watersby, the First Sea Lord (Britain), responded with a staunch statement, something about "our Blue Coated Band of Brothers." He seemed to me to be unusually young for his position and terribly bright and secure.

Robyn, as you sense, we enjoyed far too much food, all divine. The outcome, with the wine too, was loose tongues and good "fellowship." The event epitomized the Old Navy, with lots of protocol and pomp and circumstance and ritual. I'm sad that these traditional ways are phasing out of our Navy, with modernity and expediency riding high. In my short eleven years of service I've seen a speeded-up naval life, with fewer times to appreciate Old Navy ways and more times that can only be described as Crisis Management. It's more than a reaction to the war.

Robyn, last night a perfectly planned and executed, magnificent naval dinner came off without a flaw. I felt at ease at being included as one of the guests, knowing that I was blessed to be working for Buck and completely comfortable with "the brass."

My second thought was that I'll never be that honored naval officer admiral, that quasi-royalty of our world navies; nor will I be that admiral's spouse; neither role is my destiny. And that can be hard to accept. My role, maybe my "box" in these moments, seems to be the extra woman, hopefully adding both femininity and brainpower, who is neither totally included nor excluded.

I'm wondering about you and your family? And Ned's new job? How about a short note to fill me in. Hope to get up to Bar Harbor during either the Thanksgiving or Christmas holiday time. I'll be in touch by phone.

Love,

Tucker

Three weeks later from Jennie

1 October 1970, Washington D.C.

Dear Tucker,

How's my favorite (former) lieutenant? Bet you're liking your Newport duty.

Pierre and I are mostly enjoying our new assignments, but the pressures in this city can be a drag. You've heard the old joke, "I work half days," meaning that's half of a 24-hour day, not a civilian 8-hour one. The senior officer controls the hours in the command, or office — if the admiral goes home at 1800, the captains leave at 1815 and the commanders leave at 1830 and so forth. Since I'm usually home by 1930, you know where that puts me on the totem pole. Pierre often gets home even later, and he's on top of his pole! We try not to complain but it's hard on our relationship sometimes.

A fascinating thing happened today which relates directly to Lieutenant *Commander* Fairfield. Which reminds me, how was your wetting down party? Great invitation! I wish Pierre and I could've been there. We toasted you *in absentia*.

Getting back to the matter at hand, I was briefing our Human Resource Management Director, Rear Admiral Stanley Hopkins, on our Leadership Project. Out of the blue he asked me if I'd heard about Tucker Fairfield's War College study about Navy women.

I told him that since Captain St. Martin quashed it back in January, it was a dead letter.

Then, surprise! The Admiral strongly expressed that he, and the CNO believe women must become equal members of the Navy community! He said, "Captain Marie St. Martin is dead wrong and not up to the times if she can't support a research project at the College about Navy women."

I couldn't believe my opportunity here: I suggested he contact you and perhaps resurrect the study. I also mentioned you'd have to have the WAVE Director's sanction to do the job right.

Then he muttered something under his breath that sounded like, "Marie's done enough. It's time for a new broom."

So, my dear, I think you just might hear from the Admiral soon. He remembers you well; says you and he flew a few missions back and forth from Newport to DC several years ago. Guess you and he were taking military hops together?

I hope this will be your big opportunity. Go for it!

By the way, did I tell you it was Lois Lever who blew the whistle on you and informed Marie? Thought you'd like to know. But let it go, Tucker. She's not worth stewing about. No doubt Lois, along with many other senior women, feel the project threatens their futures.

Come see me on your next trip down. Take care.

> Fondly,
>
> Jennie

Three days later from Robyn

October 4, 1970, Bar Harbor, Maine

Okay Tucker — I'm impressed!

Newport mansion indeed! The Officers' Club certainly didn't sound too shabby!

Your party, so elegant and sophisticated, yes, but also stilted, formal, and cool. Tucker, I still don't get what's appealing about that life for you. (Can you tell I love to play the same record over and over?) I don't want to come on as curmudgeonly, but I think you sometimes write me in detail about these events because you like to incite my baser reactions. You *know* I'm not going to cry out in awe, "My dahling! Such ado sets my heart agog, my very nostrils quiver at merely the mention of such pomposity!"

So I'll live up to your expectations and make with the challenging remarks. Before I begin old friend, let me assure you, I'm not knocking you personally, or the others who planned the affair. I know it was a lot of work, and required much thoughtful consideration of detail to bring it off. My concerns, observations, questions are of a more global and philosophical nature.

First, what was the purpose of such a spread? Tucker, the Old Navy notwithstanding, it was lavish and extravagant for officers and their partners. I don't think there was a parallel party happening for the enlisted underlings and their partners. Surely they're stressed out too?

And the cost! Was I (as a taxpayer) paying for the Beef Wellington, three kinds of wine, fresh flowers and all the other stuff, including, I suppose, the Officers' Club facilities and staff. You speak of the "old Navy" and its ways, and regret such traditions are being phased out. Tucker, this is 1970! Do you realize how elitist and classist you sound? All the military, certainly the Navy Elite, seem to live in a luxurious microcosm where different standards and expectations apply.

Now to some of your own concerns expressed in your reflections on the evening. You were comfortable with the brass BUT somehow not one of them — in an odd way, an outsider, never to be an admiral or an admiral's spouse. Somewhat parallel to but more privileged than enlisted persons who do all the scut work, yet never have such a meal or indeed any meal at the Officers' Club. Though more privileged, Tucker, your status is less than theirs since they at least know where they stand. They have a space, as long, of course, as they aren't gays or lesbians.

Again and again I hear the Navy as having designed itself for white, straight men with a hierarchy as rigid as royalty! Elegant (and well-orchestrated by you and others) as that party was, its essence, to me, seems shallow and self-serving for those in power. Hollywood, indeed! I visualize self-absorbed puppets moving tastefully between the palate cleaner and the herbed tomatoes.

Yikes! Tucker, you know when you present this stuff to me I can be persuaded to become absolutely fanatical on the subject. But I'm not attacking you!

Do come to Bar Harbor, and we can get into this face-to-face. Ned loves his new job and we're all happy as Cheshire cats up here. I'll even feed you. How about a clam bake, a specialty of Ned's! But I warn you, there'll be more diapers than golden table napkins around, and we don't care if you're an admiral or an armadillo. You are you and that's good enough for us! See you soon, I hope.

> Love,
>
> Robyn

Four days later from Tucker's journal

8 October 1970, Newport, R.I.

 For the record,

I was taken aback by Robyn's letter. She's a dear friend and I've always respected her opinion but she obviously didn't get it. She didn't appreciate the importance of our International Dinner, which was the celebratory part of the gathering. She didn't understand the symbolism and tradition encompassing the evening, which was planned so that the guests could bask in the lore and adventure of the sea, revel in the differences among the sea, air, and land forces and reinforce their pleasure in being part of the seagoing arm of our countries. She missed the poetry, beauty, history and custom of the evening not to speak of its morale value, from the National Flags in evidence to the passing of the port after dessert.

She took aim at the classist, stuffy sense of the evening and at the military's perks. But don't corporate executives get lots of perks and earn buckets more money for equivalent (or fewer) responsibilities than these officers do? Everyone knows that flag officers often dip into their own pay and foot the bills for social events. I happen to know Buck did just that!

Our guests were some of the most senior ranking naval officers in the Western world. The officer/enlisted dichotomy is the same in industry and academia (faculty/staff) where inequalities abound. Besides, our enlisted personnel have great clubs of their own and great parties too. Also, usually ships have at least one dinner-dance a year for everyone attached to the ship (both officers and enlisted personnel) and their guests and often personnel pay out of their own pockets for these.

Yet her feelings are legitimate and probably reflect those of a lot of civilians these days. I think she has a severe case of "taxpayeritis." Taxpayers, especially in light of Vietnam, believe the military get too many undeserving good deals. Robyn leans toward an anti-military, anti-nuclear stance which may account for some of her criticism.

So, let it go, Fairfield. Remember the dinner as a memorable, lovely evening which you'll always treasure.

When I see Robyn next month at Wellesley, maybe I can moderate her opinion.

TF

Two days later from Tucker

10 October 1970, Newport, R.I.

Dear Tom,

I haven't heard from you in a while and I know you must be somewhat overwhelmed with nuclear engineering studies at Naval Reactors school with ADM Rickover. He'd better appreciate you and your capabilities or I'll come down and tell him a thing or two. Wish you and I were a little closer, but geographical separation from friends and loved ones is one of the disadvantages of our great, large Navy. I've been sending you lots of positive energy though.

Today is a red-letter day for me and I'd like to share it with you. You've patiently listened to my woes of inequality and injustice regarding Navy women, so, in contrast, thought you might enjoy a slice of the upbeat from your feminist naval officer: Yesterday Lieutenant Bud Johnson, aide to Rear Admiral Hopkins (Director, Human Resource Management, in case you've been out of touch) called me from the Bureau and said, "Lieutenant Fairfield, the Admiral wishes to see you in Newport on his Base visit tomorrow. Can you make it at 1400 in the senior officers' BOQ?"

I couldn't believe the Admiral wanted to see little ol' me.

"Of course. What's the agenda?" I answered as nonchalantly as possible.

Bud didn't know. Based on a letter from Jennie, I deduced he probably wanted to know more about my defunct women's study.

At the appointed hour I stood outside the Admiral's BOQ room while he finished a conversation with the Base commander. Within a few minutes, Admiral Hopkins, a tall, gray-haired man with a chiseled jaw line, stepped out of his room, sent the commander on his way and motioned me inside. "Great to see you again, Tucker. You're looking well. Been on any hops lately?" I'd forgotten his warm smile.

"No sir, Admiral. Good to see you, too. My Washington friends tell me you're doing a great job as Mr. Human Resource Management."

The Admiral said my friend Commander Jennie Dumonte sends her best to me. "I've come to realize that we have many of our best WAVE officers in the Bureau," he said, "and she's one of them. Now — to my motive for calling you here. First, would you like a cup of instant coffee? I'm fixing one for me." As he ambled over to a small sink, he remarked, "Hope you don't mind if we use this hot water. It's all that's available."

As you know, Tom, I rarely drink coffee in the afternoon, but I was so surprised that an admiral would be making his own coffee, I said, "Yes sir." The Admiral made us both a cup of tepid coffee and then proceeded to present a startling plan. "Tucker, I understand you're working on a study about Navy women. When will it be finished?"

I explained the study's history, and that the study had been killed. "I stopped the process several months ago at the request of Admiral Taylor, our Deputy. Without Captain St. Martin's approval, it can't be written. An important element of the study, as I envision the work, would be interviews with many women officers in order to provide credibility."

The Admiral looked directly at me and said, "Tucker, you and I both know that a new WAVE Director is being selected this week. You and I know who that is."

"No... no sir," I replied haltingly. "I don't know the outcome of the panel interviews. I did know our mutual friend, Jennie Dumonte, was one of the finalists and of course I was praying for her selection."

"Keep this to yourself, Tucker. It's Commander Eleanor Marit. And, as you might imagine, Eleanor and I are in sync. There's no doubt in my mind that she'll support your effort."

I told the Admiral I was pleased about the choice. "I know and respect Commander Marit and her abilities. A great selection, though I'm disappointed about Jennie."

Admiral Hopkins didn't waste a moment. He said he and Admiral Zumwalt wanted the study done as of yesterday. "Therefore, I'll give you four months. On my desk in four months."

I was taken aback. The Admiral was asking for a miracle! I explained that I had an extensive study in mind, and to give women a fair shot, one year would be more likely, assuming Commander Marit were to give her blessing. "At the moment I have no assistants or student researchers. It wouldn't be a group research project. Further, I've just reported to a new billet on the staff that's a full-time job."

The Admiral looked disappointed, though he seemed to understand. "Okay, Tucker, I'll accept an eight-month time frame or sooner. Get with it, kiddo." He smiled again. "We need this today. August is your drop-dead date."

"Aye, aye sir."

He stood up, cueing me to leave. As I turned toward the door, I said, "Admiral, I would ask you to speak with Admiral Taylor about this special project so that my command is cut in and supportive."

"I'll take care of both Jim Taylor and Eleanor Marit. You have my word. You just write the study. Thanks, Tucker. Thanks very much. I feel very strongly that we must better use our Navy women resources."

Right now I'm both excited and scared. I just hope Admiral Hopkins will smooth the waters. To complete this study could be a lifetime's chance to end years of discrimination and unequal opportunities for Navy women. Yes, women love the Navy, but they're tired of being second-team members. Can't imagine the study would invalidate these feelings. Yet such a large task, and on top of my regular duties! Reminds me of my junior officer days and all those collateral duties. If the study flies, it'll be a *monumental* collateral duty. Good thing I'm a workaholic!

Naturally I feel honored to be tasked by Admiral Hopkins. Hope I'm up to the work for my sake and the sake of other women. I'm reminded of what JFK's father said, "After you've done your best, to hell with the rest." I can only give the project my best.

How about an update from my favorite submariner. How're your parents? My dad had a scare last month. Turned out to be bleeding ulcers. You'd never dream he was the type. Strong, silent, and I guess keeping all his stress bottled up inside. He's okay now.

Don't let the studies and "The Admiral" drag you down. By the way, several of my WAVE officer friends work directly for Rickover and think he's a magnificent officer.

Fondly,

Tucker

Two days later from Tucker's journal

12 October 1970, Newport, R.I.

 For the record,

Large task! My God! To flesh out the initial concept, develop charts and procedures and create chapters. Need some assistance, in the form of actual personnel. Will ask my boss, Colonel Benson, for support. Maybe some reserve officers can help. Ensign Kathy McKennen wants to work on the project. It'll come together, but right now seems overwhelming.

Remember when times get rough, and they will, you originally *asked* to do this, for the sake of future Navy women, as well as for yourself and fellow women officers. Anachronistic policies need to be changed to project Navy women into the present.

The study's first principle: that any future Navy policy decisions regarding women officers must be based on knowledge of the status of American woman in general. Therefore, the first several chapters should cover the changing role of American women (a study unto itself!).

Professor Carol Simpson, M.I.T. sociologist and a War College adjunct faculty member, will be a large support system. Use her skills, her networks, including DACOWITS. Start pulling resources together. Look for available expertise, especially a statistician.

You're not equipped to crunch numbers and develop the questionnaire by yourself. Money is tight though. It'll have to be a small pilot questionnaire.

First task, to refine questions to be asked of women officer interviewees. Then, invite CDR Betty Aldrich to lunch. Lay out your plan. Request permission to interview her staff at Women Officers' School.

God, Tucker, you might be in over your head in terms of the time line. You do have another full-time job.

Go walk on the beach tomorrow.

TF

Three days later from Billie

15 October 1970, Stuttgart, Germany

Gutentag, Tuck —

The Navy is good! I'm having the time of my life! I just moved into an apartment in Beutlesbach, a suburb of Stuttgart, and I'm sitting under a clear blue sky, among some tall pointy trees on the gray stone terrace about to light the charcoal grill. I've got a couple of bottles of Dinklclacker (that's a local beer) sitting in a bucket of ice. From this perspective, Tuck, it's hard to remember frantic Washington, D.C. and the Pentagon.

I love my job. It's a "purple suit" outfit, that is, personnel from all the U.S. armed services and I'm assigned as a Project Head. Right now I'm working on two community projects, one in Amsterdam and the other in London. The U.S. Army Tech Sergeant (he's a terrific photo-journalist) assigned to my staff and I fly back and forth regularly. Can you believe it?! Amsterdam and London! My staff and I do everything for the projects — from layouts of brochures and programs to photography, printing, art work, writing copy, placing the bands, static displays, personnel to march in parades, American flags and other symbols, assisting embassy staff. It's amazing the number of events here in Europe that require an American presence.

Colonel Clark, the consummate professional, is a graduate of Columbia University School of Journalism with a Masters in Public Relations from the University of Missouri (the two best journalism schools in the country). He's so smooth, gets the best out of his staff, and makes the creative juices flow! I'm learning so much. My AU courses, especially in the layout business, have really helped. After this tour of duty, I, at least in Public Affairs, can handle anything the Navy assigns. This is a terrific way to boost one's confidence.

Vietnam is not as much of a presence here, but it's here. From time to time there are anti-war demonstrations outside the entrance of the command. The scary thing is an outfit called the Red Army Faction. They're evil. They've planted bombs and killed people and they target U.S. personnel and we have to take all sorts of precautions. The gate guards use long-handled mirrors to search under my car for bombs. I don't always look over my shoulder, but I do look around. Vietnam has certainly produced the worst within us Americans — hawk or dove, one is as bad as the other.

Once again the Navy has allowed me to expand my epicurean tastes. There are many things to eat here in Germany. I haven't tried them all yet, but I'm making the rounds. Really good restaurants, even the O' Club has good food. Now that I have an apartment, I've been tackling the local food stores. They're different than our supermarkets and a real adventure! Patch Barracks has a commissary and, of course, the familiar foods are stocked, but, you know the old saying, "When in Rome..."

The command urges everyone to travel, and I plan to do just that! Munich, only 118 miles away, is great. Even Stuttgart offers a lot. I want to "see" the Alps, Vienna, Salzburg and eventually make my way over to Spain, Portugal, and Italy. Whatta life!

My apartment's modern, brand new actually, two bedrooms with a nice kitchen. I have a used car that gets me around fine. You have my autovon number now. Call me.

Your friend,

Billie

Five days later from Tucker

20 October 1970, Newport, R.I.

Dear Jennie,

Politics is hell! And I'm not always very politic! Subj: luncheon of LCDR Fairfield and CDR Betty Aldrich. Outcome: shot down.

Since you're partly responsible for the launching of the women's study, thought you'd be interested in my discussion with Betty. As you know, I should interview at least thirty women officers. Since no travel monies are designated, I should interview *all* the women stationed in Newport, the majority of whom report to Betty at the Women Officers' School. Given that Admirals Hopkins and Taylor are on board, for her to support the project seemed like a reasonable request.

Our luncheon at the O' Club started off on a pleasant note. Then I raised the subject of the study and the issue of women officer interviews. Betty asked, "What kinds of questions will you be asking?"

"I intend to ask twelve-to-fifteen broad-based questions that give interviewees a wide berth for personal views," I said. "The study's intent is to open up Pandora's Box and personalize the present-day dilemma of women line officers."

I then read some of the questions that I'd drafted. "What do you think are the Navy's reasons for maintaining women officers today? Are they the same reasons that apply to enlisted women? What kind of career patterns would you prefer ideally for yourself through the rank of captain? The majority of line women officers are in the field of administration or management. Should this continue to be the norm? What officer designator do you feel best fits this present women officer complement?"

Looking up from my notes, I observed Betty's discomfort. I continued anyway, "What specific woman officer personnel policies should be reevaluated, if any? What role do women officers now play in support of the requirements? In light of changes occurring in the Navy and in society as a whole today, what is your estima — "

"Stop, Tucker! I now understand why Captain St. Martin doesn't support the study. You're suggesting that the Navy needs to revamp its policies toward women. Marie and I are in accord. *Now* is not the time to restructure our women's policies, especially during Admiral Zumwalt's tour as Chief of Naval Operations. Look, Tucker, look at the many positive, though gradual, changes we've made and the wonderful career opportunities we already have. Let's not risk bargaining for the moon and losing what we've achieved. We certainly don't want to be forced to go to sea, for example."

Even though Betty is one of our more conservative senior women, she's got to realize that the rapidly changing roles of American women will affect military women's roles. At this point in the conversation I felt thwarted, but I attempted to maintain my composure and remain diplomatic.

"If not now, when, Commander? It's not a matter of bargaining with the admirals. It's a matter of laying out the facts, capturing the views of women who live with the policies, and making recommendations."

She looked at me crossly, but I continued anyway. "Seems realistic, don't you think, Betty? Do you understand why I need your support and that of your staff through the interview process, at a minimum?"

"I understand, Tucker, and I won't give you permission unless directed to by Marie. She's our Director and I know she's against your project. Nothing personal. She just doesn't want it to happen. Neither do I."

We changed subjects, went back to pleasantries, and ended our luncheon quickly. You know, Jennie, Betty maintains a cool, polite demeanor, while objecting to ideas she disagrees with. A good politician (and naval officer). Much more subtle than I.

So, my good friend, I'm in a quandary. I'll proceed with the total concept, but interviews obviously would enliven the study. I consider them an *absolute requirement*. I'm wondering if you have any advice? Feels as if I'm caught between two chains of command, that of the WAVES' quasi-chain directed by Captain St. Martin and my own War College chain. I'll have to wait for the Saint's retirement.

Wish you and Pierre were here, for fun times as well as for moral support. I know you feel as strongly as I that we must work to effect career changes; otherwise, the status quo will persevere indefinitely. Guys have too much else on their minds, and leadership hasn't yet taken it aboard that women are underused.

I'm negotiating for some reserve officers to work on the project. I think I have a lieutenant commander and lieutenant lined up for the statistical reporting, to determine what billets and areas we've filled through the years. Also, we need to develop a properly written questionnaire. We'll need a pilot test. Will only be able to question women this time (and not male officers).

How do you and Pierre feel about Vietnam? Have been so busy that I've barely kept up with the actions. This will be the first war we've ever lost. Vietnam has been a wrong-headed war, with fuzzy objectives at best. But President Nixon and the generals and admirals haven't asked me.

Take good care. Hope the workload has eased for you both.

My love and best,

Tucker

Two weeks later from Tom

5 November 1970, Charleston, S.C.

Dear Tucker,

First, my apologies for not answering your letter. At the time I received it, ADM Rickover and his helpers had my total concentration. During the entire four months of preparation for nuclear command, I didn't find the Admiral's so-called "charm school" very charming. As you know, nuclear engineering doesn't come naturally to me. And that's an understatement!

Fortunately there's a lot more to commanding these boomers than engineering and I don't doubt I'll be successful in my new billet as Commanding Officer of the Blue Crew, USS *Christopher Columbus* SSBN 645. You see, the job's so new I still enjoy saying and writing out the whole title.

Along with getting my command, I was promoted to Commander. Getting promoted at Naval Reactors was a real ego deflator. The Admiral's secretary came into my study cubicle and handed me the piece of paper and said, "Sign here." I said, "Is that all there is? I spend fifteen years working hard to become a senior officer and this is the only ceremony?" She laughed.

Here's another vignette you'll enjoy. After you succeed in going through all of Rickover's "charm school" hoops, you're called into his presence for congratulations, at which time the Admiral gives you a little block of wood with a small metal plaque engraved with your name and his name. It reads: "Oh God, thy sea is so great and my boat is so small." Well, after he gave me mine, he shook my hand and said, "Remember, Parker, you don't have to be a genius to run one of these boats." I was really relieved — here I thought I wasn't going to be able to do it! But the Admiral sure put my mind at ease! I said, "Yes Sir" and fled before he changed his mind!

I'm sorry you weren't able to come to my Change of Command. Some of my family came from Michigan, but alas not my parents. My dad is now hospitalized with dementia, and my mother's in the process of moving to a retirement home. The Change of Command ceremony went well, good weather and a nice reception, to say farewell to the fellow I relieved and I guess hello to me. I counted that reception as also serving as the wetting down party for my new stripe. At least I tried to convince my friends that it doubled as a wetting down/CofC party. Most of them considered it a cheap cop-out. Of course relieving the other Blue skipper is only a ceremony. The real challenge comes when I relieve the Command on board the ship. The *Columbus* will return from patrol in about a month, at which time I'll relieve her Gold Commanding Officer.

We'll conduct a 30-day upkeep and then proceed on a 70-day patrol. I understand she's a great boat. I'm comfortable with my crew. I already knew some of the junior officers and the Chief of the Boat or COB, as we call him. He's a character and famous for his ability to make needed parts appear when supposedly none are to be had. A cumshaw artist, *par excellence*. I've learned not to ask what he traded for them. One nice thing about relieving on a nuclear submarine — you know everybody's well trained; they have to be or they wouldn't be where they are.

I wanted to tell you that I met someone at the reception and we've gone out a couple of times. She's a widow and has two kids, Willy, the baby, and Carolyn, almost five. Joanna's husband, a Navy pilot, was killed in Vietnam when she was two months pregnant with Willy. Her parents live north of Charleston so she came home to have the baby and has recently taken a job at the College of Charleston library.

I don't know why I'm boring you with all these details. Maybe I'm feeling she might be the one, but I know I have to move slowly. Twice burned remember! I also have to make sure I'll be okay with the kids. Anyway, things will naturally move slowly, if they move at all, because I'll be starting my patrol rotations in six weeks. At least upkeep is here instead of Scotland, so I'll be stateside more like two in four months instead of one in four as before.

Your study sounds like it's needed but I wouldn't hold my breath if I were you waiting for action after it's done. The fact that you can only interview women tells a tale doesn't it? A study by women, about women, and for women is likely to end up where most bones do! Or is there some political motive that isn't apparent? I suggest you try to get permission up front to publish it. That might save it from languishing on someone's desk until "the problem" goes away.

Think I'll go sit on a pier and strum the old guitar for awhile. That oughta startle the passing river traffic! I suppose I could grow my pickin' nails out now, at least on patrol. See how power corrupts!

Keep in touch. And best of luck with your study. By the way, let me know if you find out anything about how Nixon's going to extricate us from Vietnam. Where oh where is the secret plan he ran on???

Cheers as always,

Tom

Six weeks later from Tucker

20 December 1970, Newport, R.I.

Dear Robyn,

I'd hoped to see you over the Christmas holiday, but I'm headed to California tomorrow to be with my family. A good change from our wintry, windy New England. It's not as cold as my early Navy days here, but would you believe I have to use an electric heater in my office because we keep our building at 68 degrees in the winter. Saving taxpayers' money can be a drag!

Since my talk with Admiral Hopkins in October, I've been in overdrive *every* day. Have managed to get some help, but the major work must be done by yours truly. The study's general strategy is to recommend direction for woman officers' career patterns. Four or five policy options must be developed, with each option reflecting a set of underlying values, especially beliefs in the role or status of women.

A simple concept, yet requiring much research about Navy personnel policies and the status of women. The Navy must ask the same question our society is debating: What is woman's place, or role in society? As you might imagine, Navy people have mostly dismissed the women's movement as ridiculous or amusing, believing the Navy can remain aloof from the resurgent "feminist movement."

At the moment, I'm researching the movement, trying to understand rationales about woman's place and have arrived at three overall major approaches to women's roles:

- *the Traditionalist viewpoint*, which claims woman's place is in the home.

- *the Neo-traditionalist perspective*, which claims that society must update woman's traditional role, expand and open her horizons of opportunity as long as the changes don't upset men.

- *the Egalitarian position*, which perceives women as capable as men and encompasses the extreme and moderate feminists' views.

The above may sound terribly philosophical but the thrust is simple and important for every woman to grasp, as we each assess our future roles. Depending upon which rationale she selects, she can manifest her role or status in facets of her own life. My immediate task — to recommend future roles for Navy women officers.

Support at the top of the Navy for innovative ideas flourishes. You may have heard that we have a new Chief of Naval Operations, Admiral Bud Zumwalt, who's making sweeping changes in many areas. I happen to know he and Admiral Hopkins are best friends and that both want to bring Navy women to a more equal place. Admiral Hopkins envisions my study as giving them the conceptual framework upon which to launch new policies.

Right now Navy women are treated as a separate "WAVE" corps, with discriminatory, different policies, largely reflecting the Traditionalist's viewpoint. You know most of these discriminatory policies. I've ranted about them to you in previous letters — women are subject to separate laws, including promotion; they can't go to sea or fly airplanes; they can't command except in the administration of women; and their numbers are kept to the minimum.

My basic goal is to help sway this vast and wonderful institution, Big Daddy Navy, toward selecting a policy option that reflects a far less traditional value system. One of the real barriers is senior women officers who fear major policy changes. Feminists today speak about women being co-opted by a system or institution. That's how I perceive some of our senior women who have bought into the Navy's rules and values over the years, consciously or unconsciously. They don't want change. They say, "We've made it to the top, with certain assumptions and values, so you younger women can do the same." The Queen Bee syndrome.

Robyn, I'm wondering if you're finding this same phenomenon among your working women friends, especially those in higher positions. I'm not intimating that all senior women in the Navy accept the male-dominated, or majority system, though many have. But some like being treated as women and are unwilling to move into the egalitarian value structure, fearing loss of their femininity.

Enough philosophy. I'm walking a fine line between the moderate feminist and the conservative naval officer. It's difficult, with flak coming from all quarters. Feels great to have Jennie and Pierre, and several friends here at the college, including its President, Admiral Buck Buckingham, urging me on. Otherwise the task would be intolerable.

My next step is to interview. Will have to wait for WOCS staff members. The Officer-in-Charge, CDR Betty Aldrich, one of those who has been co-opted, so to speak, refuses to grant me permission to interview her staff, and the Saint hasn't been relieved.

All for now. Would like your thoughts re the women's or feminist movement. By the way, I'm not planning necessarily to recommend that women go to sea or fly airplanes. On the other hand, maybe you would!

Love,

Tucker

Two weeks later from Robyn

January 5, 1971, Bar Harbor, ME

Dear Tucker,

And a cheery post-holiday season to you, my good friend. A fun celebration we had on the 28th. Derry's enthralled with those little boats you gave him, though he prefers to have them clamber over mountains and prairies than to situate them in their customary environs! As I said, I want to respond in writing to your letter of December 20th. So here goes:

In many ways the Navy's a microcosm of the the larger world. The world outside, however, is peopled with roughly 1/2 female and 1/2 male persons. While it's largely a male-dominated existence (in terms of power), it isn't totally. Obviously, that's what the women's movement is about. There are enough females to assert themselves and change things. The Navy is indeed a Man's World, a largely white male establishment with such underlings as minorities and women appearing only tokenly. Of course the establishment is threatened. It's terrified that change might really happen, that beings other than upper class white males might actually get to serve in meaningful ways. The senior women you refer to feel especially vulnerable, as they got where they are in the context of the existing matrix. If this system should shift . . . oh dear! Whatever might happen to those currently clinging to its infrastructure?

I don't think higher-up women in the outside world are as threatened, since the system of which they're a part is *slightly* less tight. The "status quo" may not like us, but we can't be retired or discharged from society in the same way as a naval protester can. We don't all work within an up-or-out promotion system.

You're certainly courageous to carry on when on practically every flank (dig the military jargon) you're being shot down (more m.j.). Thank goodness for Jennie and Pierre and Tom and the others who are a wee bit more far-sighted. And, by the way, yeah, why not women going to sea or flying planes? The only place a woman, or anyone in general actually, might be denied access, is to tasks that are physically impossible. It's unlikely that a 110-pound woman could easily lift a cannon on a ship for example. Perhaps required tasks, on the other hand, could be outlined for prospective workers, and they could decide for themselves the feasibility of accepting the assignment. All very simple, you see, what's all the fuss?

My job's great, everything I had hoped it would be. I wasn't sure I'd be able to negotiate the schedule I wanted, but the clinic director ended up being both accommodating and flexible (and a nice person to boot!). So we're settling in, as is the cold weather.

Love,

Robyn

Ten days later from Tucker's journal

15 January 1971, Newport, R.I.

For the record,

Need to write about my visit with Eleanor Marit, the new WAVE Director. Because of the women's study, I was one of the first on her appointments' schedule as Director. She's as stunning as ever and will do the WAVES proud from that standpoint. I do believe that the selection was based on looks as well as record. Sexist. But then, not many bald male captains make admiral. So it's equal discrimination!

We had a wide-ranging discussion. Bottom line: she and I represent opposite poles of the political spectrum. At the same time, we respect each other's opinions and are willing to hear each other out.

"Tucker, you must include enlisted women in the study," she insisted. "After all, there are 5,000 of them and only 500 of us. You're missing that ship."

"I can only do so much by August, Captain. I have doubts it'll be completed on time *without* adding the enlisted question. I fully understand your concern about the enlisted women. You'll have to initiate studies from your office."

Toward the end of the conversation I asked that her office sponsor the study, briefly explaining the Saint's negativity. She said, "Of course you have my blessing, Tucker. Though I may not agree with your recommendations, I certainly believe it's a valid, timely study, and respect your initiative. Admiral Z.'s pushing for a comprehensive review of women's policies, and your work might give us a general foundation upon which to launch our Washington efforts."

"And what about Betty Aldrich's staff," I asked. "I need those numbers for the interviews."

"No problem. I'll call her today and explain my position. She'll support you."

She appeared relaxed, but anxious to move on to settling in. I stood up and said, "Captain, I wish you much luck. It's a big job. Don't forget to have fun."

"Thanks, Tucker. And the best of luck with your study."

Based on our talk, I predict that Eleanor Marit and Admiral Z. will have some real clashes about the future of Navy women. Exciting times!

TF

One month later from Tucker

10 February 1971, Newport, R.I.

Dear Jennie,

Greetings from the cold north. I read that the President closed down the Pentagon and all other Federal offices yesterday, except for essential personnel, due to the blizzard. Are you one who had to wend her way to work? Hope not, though I always think of you as essential to the planet and to the Navy!

The study's progressing well, now that I have access to the Women Officers' School staff for interviews. I've interviewed fifteen women, with about nineteen to go. The data are fascinating. Must tell you about yesterday's interview with Captain Bobbie Garrison, your former boss at the Women Officers' School. I arrived promptly at her office for the interview at 1500. We didn't finish until 1730. The last half-hour heated up to boiling, with the Captain dressing down — scolding — the lieutenant commander.

"Tucker, you're pushing too fast on this project. You don't seem to have a feel for how far WAVES have come since our beginnings in 1942. Slow down! Ease up! You could spoil things for us if you're not careful."

"Captain, I'm doing my best to present a realistic, candid picture of how it is *now* to be a WAVE officer. We must give Admiral Hopkins and his Bureau folks assistance in moving us into the seventies and beyond." She looked worried.

I continued. "We have a golden opportunity now that Admiral Z. is Chief of Naval Operations. For the first time in my career the top truly supports full use of human resources, including women, both enlisted and officers."

"Yes, Tucker, I know. But you haven't lived as long as I, nor have you witnessed the tremendous changes we've made. Let me elaborate."

Captain Garrison then gave me a school teacher lecture on the history of the WAVES (remember she taught for several years before joining). "By the end of World War II," she said, "we had approximately 93,000 uniformed women serving with the Navy. Then, as after World War I, women serving in the Navy had their service terminated. In 1947 and '48 the great debate took place in Congress concerning the desirability of integrating women into all the armed services. This debate," she continued, "culminated with the Women's Integration Act, which legally removed women from their heretofore auxiliary status. This gave us permanent status, even though Navy numbers were capped at 500 line officers and 5,000 enlisted women."

"Yes, ma'am," I said, nodding my head as she resumed her mini-recruiting speech. The Captain must've forgotten that I'd been a recruiter and knew these facts well.

"Tucker, Navy policies are tied to federal laws that we're gradually modifying to reflect the times. We had a major change three years ago when President Johnson signed a bill removing the ceiling on the numbers of women in the armed forces, as well as grade restrictions. That's the reason I wear four stripes today."

I was restless and tired, but still wanted her viewpoint on several key issues. "Captain, what do you see as our role into the future."

She became less pedantic. "We WAVES are both a nucleus base in times of mobilization and a resource base, providing specialized skills to the Navy, especially administrative. The nucleus theory is about dead, but indeed we've proven ourselves invaluable as specialists in management and personnel. I daresay the Navy would be a far lesser institution without us."

It was late. How does she feel about sea duty for women, I wondered. "Captain, you and I know that the essence of the Navy is ships and aircraft operating at sea. We're precluded by the 1948 statute from embarking aboard naval vessels when at sea, except hospital ships. We can't even go on temporary assignment aboard ships and are therefore prevented from serving in many shore-based jobs which require access to personnel aboard ships. Do you see us someday serving aboard ships, say non-combatants?"

"Tucker, there you go again — pressing hard!"

"I think we shouldn't necessarily be aboard ships, Captain, combatant ships in particular. But we need to project what might occur, in light of societal changes and egalitarian leadership, as shown by Admiral Z."

The Captain paused for a long moment. Then she said, "If you're trying to pin me down, Tucker, I'd have to say that we should continue to advance opportunities for women in a *gradual* manner, without revolutionary moves. We won't have women at sea on my watch, but it might happen on yours. Would you like to go to sea?"

"Absolutely, Captain. But unfortunately I'd be too senior to serve, in that, as you know, we need to *grow* our seagoing men and women, starting with officers at the grade of ensign."

"You see, Tucker, I never wanted the opportunity to serve at sea. But I'm not saying the opportunity shouldn't be there. I'm saying, actually advising, that the Navy must move slowly on this one, for the forces of conservativism within are strong. Many influential seniors are still resistant to WAVES as a concept. They think we're taking up cushy jobs ashore that should be given to men when they come off of sea duty. You and I feel otherwise."

Then she abruptly changed subjects and said, "We WAVES have a record of proven performance. That performance was made historically in an environment of national manpower shortages. If the shortages are removed, we're less appealing to the manpower planners. Remember that many, maybe the majority, of Navy leaders would rather we keep a low profile and not rock the boat, so to speak. Admiral Z., Admiral Hopkins, and *you* are rocking the boat. Be careful not to drown in criticisms and sideswipes that surely will come your way."

I thanked the Captain for her mentoring. It felt right to tell her about the hits I'd taken from The Saint and Betty Aldrich. "That's what I mean about moving slowly, Tucker. You serve in an ultra-conservative organization. I know that you're seen as both a threat and a radical liberal by several women whom I know well. Be cautious. I commend you for your enthusiasm and effort, but you need to tread softly."

With that the Captain glanced briefly at her watch and said, "It's time to close up shop."

Those few hours were a real lesson to me, Jennie. I sensed that the Captain wants me to succeed in the project, yet she feels the weight of history. She doesn't want the study to foul up anything for Navy women coming along. I believe, at the same time, she isn't fully aware of societal trends that affect our future as women. She's lived too long in the Navy's subculture, to the exclusion of the larger culture. The Navy may not have the luxury of deciding for itself whether to send women to sea or whether they can fly airplanes or attend the Naval Academy. The women's movement is mounting initiatives, including the Equal Rights Amendment and those who live in the past will feel forsaken and angry.

How're the winds blowing in D.C.? I suspect they're filled with Change, Change, and Change. Admiral Z. is urging Navy planners to keep control of personnel policies and not let outside forces tell him how to run his ship. That's why I think we have a superb opportunity to change WAVE policies from within, notwithstanding the status quo forces.

Well, my friend, thought I'd pass this along to keep you up-to-date on the study. Because you know Captain Garrison well, thought you'd appreciate her comments.

Time for bed. I've been putting in lots of extra hours to keep the study on target. So far it's on track. Sometimes I think the study's mandate is too encompassing for one person and a few reservists. But I'll press ahead. Do I have a choice?

My love to you and Pierre.

Tucker

Two months later from Tucker

21 April 1971, Newport, R.I.

Dear Billie,

How's life in Europe? In a small way I regret that I turned down the opportunity to serve overseas, in favor of non-admin/ communications billets. No major regrets though. I can visit you on leave!

My life has been overtaken by the women's study, which is moving along rapidly. I've finally found the balance between working at International Relations projects (my regular job) and Navy women's future.

The study has come alive since I've completed the interviews...thirty-four women respondents. Much data. And wide disparity in views, as would be expected. As Freud wondered years ago, "Dear, God, what do the women want?" It's clear that the majority of interviewees, from captain to ensign, want *change*. It's a matter of how much and when.

Relatedly, I've mentioned that Ensign Kathy McMennon's assisting with the research and editing. We've had some major disagreements about style and presentation. She wants the study to be more radical in tone. She's a frustrated, restless junior officer, probably similar to that ensign who wanted changes in Women Officers' School policies and curricula many years ago. I've mellowed out some, and want now to set a tone that senior officers will be comfortable reading and acting upon.

Some of my verbiage, however, could be labeled "semi-radical." I describe the milieu in which Navy women live and work, including "channelization" of billets, conservative women's leadership, minority attributes, paternalistic attitude of male officers, and status or role ambiguity. Taken individually these seem harmless. Together they add up to unhappy circumstances for many women, who valiantly try to fit into the Navy and create a myth that they're fully "integrated."

Most interviewees don't see themselves as a minority, yet they have the psychological attributes of a minority including self-rejection and identification of survival with the prosperity of the majority. Most have relegated themselves to *women* officers and a separate officer community, because of separateness of policies, and more importantly, separateness in the eyes of Navy men.

The study's real strength will be developing policy options and their underlying theoretical bases. With our new naval leadership, there's a chance for real change, away from a Traditionalist's view.

I'm receiving a lot of flak from various quarters at the College. Naval officers are trained not to question superiors unless for good reason. I'm questioning the ways of the Navy. Many, including women, are uncomfortable with my study.

Yesterday, for instance, one of our male commander students arrived with me at an outside door to our Main Building and said, "Aren't you the one who's writing that libber study? Why should I open the door for a women's libber?" I was annoyed by his remark, but said with a smile, "It's always your choice to open the door. I understand your conflict over my role. You're wondering, should I treat her as a woman, a lieutenant commander, or a feminist? I don't consider myself a 'libber,' and as someone junior to you I should of course open the door." With that, I reached for the door's handle, but he overreached my hand and opened the door. "Thank you," I said politely.

I'm getting lots of good support too, especially from Washington sources.

Wish the study were completed. But can't push the river. Will brief Admiral Buck Buckingham on the study in late July. He's slated for a new billet in Washington. I'll miss him terribly. Haven't seen him a whole lot professionally, though I'm invited to events at his quarters. He and his wife Helen give wonderful parties. Usually we're in our Dress uniforms and the times are fun and stimulating. Either formal dinners or cocktail parties. Yet a large black cloud always floats through the scintillating conversations — Vietnam, and our continued strong presence. The military is as conflicted over our policy as the public.

Drop me a note, with news of you and your family.

> Love,
>
> Tucker

One month later from Billie

> 20 May 1971, Stuttgart, Germany

Dear Tuck —

From our autovon conversations, and now your letter concerning the Women's Study, (and I'm glad it's back on track) you're definitely on overload. I can hear it in your voice. But, don't despair, I have a feeling this study will be a major breakthrough for future women officers *and* enlisted women. Surely, goodness and mercy, our male-dominated society can eventually see the minds and achievements of women over what they normally see in women, or do I expect too much?

By the bye, I loved your anecdote about the student and the libber! Sounds like a '70s' folk song.

I'm proud of you. I don't know many of us, and that includes me, who would have the guts, balls, effrontery, and staying power to take on a project of this magnitude and take the constant thumbs down sneers, jeers, and outright rejections from our so-called peers. I'm with ya, Tuck, in mind and spirit, if not by your shoulder. If I can help from here, let me know.

When this is over, take a couple of weeks (or more) to relax in Europe. I'm enclosing a schedule of charter flights leaving JFK for Frankfurt. Pick a flight and let me know. I'll do all the other scheduling from here. We have a terrific travel office; and since we're encouraged to travel while here, we can get reservations in Paris, London, Amsterdam, Munich, Vienna. Of course, we pay for everything, but it's the reservations that are important.

It'll be great to see you! I can introduce you to German beers and wines, French wines, London pubs, and Amsterdam everything!

What an open city. They have things in shops on display that makes this Southern Baptist blush!

Hang in there Tuck, don't give up. Hope to see you soon.

Billie

One month later from Tucker's journal

20 June 1971, Newport, R.I.

For the record,

I've been described as an intellectual. I've taken that as negative because the Navy's action-oriented and sometimes anti-intellectual. But it'll take an intellectual to get this study done! If I listen too closely to the emotional arguments for and against Navy women, I bog down. Weighing policy options and their disadvantages and advantages mitigates against the hysterics that accompany discussions of women as equals. Last week I uncovered an old quote from General Hershey which describes the underlying values beneath the whines of conservative military males:

> There is no question but that women could do a lot of things in the military service. So could men in wheelchairs. But you couldn't expect the services to want a whole company of people in wheelchairs.

Most Navy men are too polite to address their emotions so bluntly, but I know down deep direct competition from women threatens male psyches. Many Navy men can't imagine women going to sea or flying naval airplanes.

The majority of women interviewees want an expanded role for Navy women. But only the most junior officers, the ensigns, want exact equality with the men. Five out of the eleven ensigns interviewed selected the policy option that supports the egalitarian philosophy. I personally wouldn't choose that option. That's my conservative streak. Women warriors for the moment are better off fighting on a different front with expanded career opportunities.

Someday, though, the ensigns will be commanders. Watch out, Navy!

Am tired. It's been a long winter/spring without much play time. Hopefully the work will be read and action taken. Admiral Hopkins is now Chief of Naval Personnel. That should help circulate the study.

Time for a spin around Seven Mile Drive to revive my spirits. Always reminds me of Jennie. It's been a whole decade since our conversation on the rocks. She seems happy with her marriage. More specifically, she loves Pierre. She and I weren't meant to be in a relationship, especially in the U.S. Navy!

And then there's Tom, my best friend and more. He's found Joanna, who seems ideal for him. I trust Joanna and her children will bring love and happiness to him, which he so deserves. I truly wish he and I could've been together. But, damn, I'm incapable of being in love with a man, or I surely would've chosen Tom. Who knows, maybe I'm incapable of being in love with anyone.

Strange. I feel pain and even jealousy about Tom being with another woman. I should feel only happiness, knowing he's found a life partner. I must never, never let him know my conflicted feelings. I must give him my support and blessing. I was the one, after all, who declined his marriage offer.

Fairfield, you seem destined to be without a partner. Not what you'd expected out of life.

I feel boxed in, closed down.

TF

Six weeks later from Tucker

1 August 1971, Newport, R.I.

Dear Jennie,

The study is completed! I briefed its Executive Summary and charts to Admiral Buck Buckingham and his staff yesterday. All I can say is we Navy women "have a long way to go" to reach any kind of equality of opportunity.

In the eyes of Washington, Buck has put the War College back on the map, but the process took its toll. He looks and acts tired. The College, however, no longer is seen as a gentlemen's country club, where officer students play for a year in between tough sea duty assignments.

Buck was warm and open in the briefing, at least in the beginning. "Come on in, Tucker, haven't seen you in awhile. Keepin' occupied with that women's study I hear."

"Yessir, Admiral, I've been challenged by the study, but am ready to get back to a routine."

I briefed the five options for women line officers, with their underlying assumptions, as well as their disadvantages and advantages. The briefing turned spirited as I interjected quotations from the women officer interviewees.

After the fifteen-minute briefing, Buck asked, "What option would *you* select, Tucker? You haven't told us your view. How come?"

I told the Admiral that I agreed with Henry Kissinger who, when presenting policy options to the President, never tells him what his own choice would be. Kissinger's rationale is that his choice might bias the President's selection; my choice might bias decision makers in their process.

"An intriguing analogy, Tucker. By the way, before I forget it, speaking of Kissinger, yesterday I received word that the substance of your group research project on the U.S. Navy's presence in the Indian Ocean has become a NSSM. This means our U.S. naval policy in the Indian Ocean will largely be influenced by students' work. That's how I've envisioned our students could truly contribute and ease the stress of policymakers. Good job and congratulations!" The Admiral's face lit up. He looked pleased with himself and with me.

His line of questioning returned to the women's study. "Come on, Tucker, I still want to know your policy choice. After all, you've spent ten months or more thinking about this, plus many years as a woman naval officer. I know you. What's your favorite option?"

I felt put on the carpet, Jennie. Throughout the study's writing I'd not selected an option so that I could argue each option objectively.

I told Buck that, based on my knowledge as well as my personal experiences, I'd have to go with one of the Neo-traditionalists' options. That is, give women considerably more opportunity than they have today, but not total equal opportunity. The sea duty option is of course precluded by statute — 10 U.S. code 6015.

Buck said he agreed with me. He couldn't imagine putting women aboard ships or submarines. "As a submariner, I strongly believe quarters are entirely too confined to allow women serving with men. Given my experience as a cruiser skipper, I'll never support the idea of women serving on any man-of-war. The efficient running of a ship is a demanding task at best. Sexual attachments and attractions that might ensue were we to have mixed crews would be a horrific problem for the commanding officer. Besides, think of the pregnancy problems. No. No, that's definitely not on the horizon."

I observed Buck as visibly worked up over the idea of the Egalitarian option. "You and I, Admiral, and probably everybody in this room, can't envision women at sea."

Everyone nodded.

I added, "But my sense is that the women's movement, the pending ERA discussions, and the All-Volunteer Force, will pressure the Navy into experimenting with women at sea and women flying in a non-combat status."

"You may be right, Tucker," the Chief of Staff, Captain Dick Anderson chimed in, "but I'll fight it, as will most senior officers, male or female. The military is essentially a man's profession, and a *manly* profession at that. The *warrior* image, you know. Guess I must have a more traditional view of women. You know what I mean. Keep the home fires burning."

I was about to respond but Captain Anderson continued, "Besides, much deep trouble can be caused by 'revolution, not evolution' as a strategy. Bud Zumwalt, our leader, is already making too many waves. No pun intended, Tucker. He's got his hands full with trying to integrate the blacks, and he doesn't need to take on you women."

"Bud's imbued with a philosophy of change, revolutionary change, and he's not about to alter his direction, Dick," said Buck. "He already has the women's equality issue on his agenda. To him, as with Tucker, minorities include women. The question is, will he ease up enough to let forces play out their natural strengths? The women's movement isn't strong enough to influence us into sending women to sea. But in time, that movement and other powerful forces will likely move the Congress into action, notwithstanding a conservative administration."

Buck paused, cleared his throat, and continued, "It'll take time, a court case or two, and more women like Tucker to get me and other senior officers to reevaluate our positions."

"Yes," said Captain Anderson, "I read the United Auto Workers and other pressure groups have endorsed the ERA. It's a matter of time before the Amendment passes in the Congress and goes to the states for ratification."

The Captain then seemed to rise from his chair as if on a soapbox. "I've always said, Admiral, let the Congress tell us when to send women to sea, and we will. With any luck the Congress will defer to us as the experts. But, damn, let's not be proactive on the social issues. Our job is to fight and win wars!"

At this point, Jennie, everyone was upset. The atmosphere had become uncomfortable.

"Admiral, if I could interject?" said Admiral Taylor, the College's Deputy.

"Yes, of course, go ahead."

"We need to set distribution on the study, Admiral."

"I don't have the time for that, Jim. The rest of you can make that decision."

Buck looked directly at me and said in a fatherly way, "Tucker, from what you've briefed, my major concern is that Stan Hopkins as the Chief of Naval Personnel, and Chuck Howeland, our Human Resource Management Director, will not have the foggiest idea how to implement your study. You're asking a bureaucracy to think totally differently about a group of people who have been around for almost thirty years as an auxiliary, nice-to-have package."

"But we're giving them a thinkpiece, sir."

"Tucker," continued the Admiral, "Stan, Chuck, and Bud have so many higher people priorities, like retention and integration of blacks. I can't see them moving quickly on this one. As Captain St. Martin told us last year, this is a hot potato and very political. We're not in the political business, Tucker. So don't be surprised if your study collects dust."

We all marched out of the office and agreed that Captain Anderson and the Colonel would decide on distribution. The next day, as I passed Captain Anderson in the hallway, he told me the distribution. He added sarcastically, "Tucker, you know this is a man's profession and it always will be. And, you *ladies* don't belong at sea." I didn't let this one go, as I often do in the presence of senior officers.

"Captain, I'm a woman. Furthermore, I've completed my eleventh year in the Navy. Are you implying that I'm not a woman, or that I'm not a professional?"

The Captain smiled wryly, anger in his eyes, and walked away. Then he turned around, looked at me sternly and muttered, "The Navy can always use a few good women."

Jennie, I had a disconcerting afterthought: The Captain has a chop on my fitness report. Ah, well. That's the breaks. Can't worry about how my every response will affect my bosses' evaluation marks. That's unhealthy.

So there you have it, my friend. It's hurry up and wait for Admirals Howeland and Hopkins to take action. Months may go by. In the meantime, one of our old friends, Commander Louise Shelton, will be attending the senior course and wants me to work with her on an extensive questionnaire about Navy women. Should be fun!

Will see you in a few weeks in D.C. My best to Pierre.

Love,

Tucker

Two weeks later from Jennie

15 August 1971, Washington D.C.

Dear Tucker,

Congratulations on a job well-done and hard fought! But don't count on it being implemented any time soon. As your Captain Anderson said, "God forbid the Navy should be proactive!" The brasses' attitude does make me feel like a second-class citizen at times, except for Admiral Z. Wonder how he feels as he continuously bangs heads with the leadership.

The Navy needs voices such as yours, Tucker. Nothing will ever change if no one speaks out. I do commend you for your willingness to stand in the line of fire. From your OCS days, you never were satisfied with the status quo.

Pierre and I have had several difficult conversations about having children. I'm not ready, probably never. I wish I could feel differently, but am aware that I don't have a woman's usual response to being a mother, at least what I imagine to be usual. Besides, I love my work and am unwilling to give up the Navy. Pierre tries to understand. He's certainly a truly supportive partner, but I feel I'm letting him/us down somewhat. It would be good to talk about some of this with you. Certainly you'd understand where I'm coming from re the career Navy parts especially. Will you be down soon? Maybe you can let off steam re the system and I can bend your ear with my issues. Equal opportunity to share time —

Take care of yourself.

Fondly,

Jennie

Ten days later from Tucker's journal

25 August 1971, Newport, R.I.

For the record,

A month and a half of highs and lows. The study's completion and a tearful goodbye to Buck. Life's extremes. Buck detaches tomorrow and heads for his new billet in Washington in OpNav as Head of Plans and Policy.

Naval officers don't cry; I shed tears in Buck's office. During these last years his omnipresence has been my anchor to family and intellectual challenges and no one will take his place.

Regardless of our philosophical and generational variances, he's my all-time hero. We may never serve together again. Buck personalizes the impersonality of our organization as few others do.

Today Buck and I confronted our differences as caring, intellectual naval officers. An oxymoron. Intellectual naval officers! Eleven years into this remarkable profession and I finally get it — the military *in toto* isn't about intellectual endeavors. It's about driving ships, flying planes, diving subs, firing missiles, and winning wars. The true scholar is a rarity among us, and oft times unpromotable.

Buck and I shared our views of the war. We agree. Vietnam is a lousy war and we shouldn't be there. Then, I uttered a mini-wisecrack, yet at the same time a truth for me. I told Buck that we are a warrior culture and each of us must face that reality. The bottom line is this: The military's purpose is "to kill, to destroy." "Some days I wonder why I stay, why I continue to wear the uniform and why I support those purposes! Do you think about this, Buck?"

Buck's face flushed. He looked agitated. He said he disagreed with my premise of "to kill, to destroy," but had no time to debate with me now. That piece of the conversation ended and we shifted to less charged subjects — my study, his new assignment, Helen and his children, and my parents.

I expect Buck will tell me his views someday. We will write.

How many more times must I say goodbye to the special people in my life?

TF

Five weeks later from Buck

2 October 1971, The Pentagon

Dear Tucker,

My world has changed. No longer does it encompass the relaxed academic atmosphere where most problems belong to tomorrow, and few issues are so critical that they cannot be handled during office hours. Here every single action is urgent and office hours don't count. I arrive at my office by 0700, sometimes earlier, absorb an early-morning briefing on the issues to be discussed in "the tank" (where the Joint Chiefs meet), read and decide the Navy positions on the major papers — positions on budget matters, presentations to the Congress on personnel and figures, base closures or needs, contingency plans for this or that part of the world, latest verifiable figures on Soviet Order of Battle, and responses to whatever political questions are asked during Congressional briefings and investigations.

You would think these events would be considered in the regular order of routine business, but here they seem to take on an urgency far beyond any rational understanding. I'm seldom home before 1930 in the evening, and then there is the interminable Washington social life to endure. It seems Helen and I rarely sit down to a quiet dinner together. A plate left in the refrigerator seems my normal evening repast, unless I stay in the Pentagon so long that I have a sandwich in one of the eating areas...usually standing up. Yet here's where you can see your actual work reflected in what is said on the floor of the Congress next day, or sometimes in the headlines (not always a blessing). Which scene do I prefer? Hard to say. They're both necessary. Surely burnout is more apt to occur in the Pentagon than in Newport, but they're not either/or situations. I like 'em both.

An aside: Several weeks ago, Sarah, my granddaughter, asked me to arrange a tour of the Pentagon for her. I did and she was enthralled. As we left I asked her why she had wanted to see what it was like. Her reply is important to me. "Grandpapa," she said, "all the news people, all the articles I read, speak of The Pentagon as having a soul of its own. I just wanted to identify it for myself." When I asked if she'd done that she said, "Oh, yes. It's part history, part building, part Army, Navy, Air Force, part mystery in those places we couldn't see, and I guess its soul is in those exhibits of the famous people, ships, airplanes, and tanks." I just hugged her!

Tucker, I was sorry to cut you short during our last conversation in Newport. Here's how I view our military's purpose:

Certainly the bottom line, as you stated in August, is "to kill, to destroy." BUT, and the BUT is a major one, that bottom line is operative only after the real purpose of the military has failed. The real purpose, the fundamental concept of military power, of strength, of military threats, of whatever words one uses to describe "the military" in the abstract, is To Prevent War. A strong military is first and foremost a deterrent. Now that deterrent can be wrongly used. Certainly Hitler used his military to achieve ends this country would never seek.

Never have I thought that my part in the military is "to kill, to destroy;" my truth is quite the contrary. That fighting becomes necessary at times is a result of the competitive human condition — when one side or the other is undaunted by the basic purpose of the military forces it faces, forces that support the country's national interest.

This is very important; it's so fundamental to me that I will disown any description of the military forces of this country which says simply they exist "to kill, to destroy." Yes, training is necessary, weapons must be supplied and attitudes honed to enable killing and destruction, but the force's mission is for use only after all efforts to prevent such action have failed.

I admit military training and education aren't the same as that received in seminary, or in a sociology class on human welfare. In this country, nonetheless, all such academic approaches to understanding the human condition start from the premise of prevention of war, and not of its engagement. Surely your good friend Tom Parker would have to agree that, were he to fire his submarine's missiles, his basic purpose would have failed.

Our United States military exists to prevent war, and since 1945 it has done a remarkable job of doing just that. Without a strong western alliance, think of the killing and destruction that would have occurred on this planet, including nuclear explosions. It's not accidental that always, in any public poll in the U.S., the armed forces stand high on the respect and trust ladder. That's not because they "kill and destroy;" it's because they stand against killing and destroying. "Warrior culture" is not a pejorative term; it's respectful and proud. It doesn't need, and isn't readily subject to, dilution by everyone's opinion of what it should be. It exists. It works. Whatever is done to its composition, its fundamental purpose must accommodate to that existence.

Your statement obviously disturbed me, Tucker. I trust you will rethink your own words. I'm off to a briefing prep for Congressional testimony next week. In haste and,

> Warm regards,
>
> Buck

Two weeks later from Tucker

14 October 1971, Newport, R.I.

Dear Buck,

Thank you for elaborating your thoughts on the military.

I agree, the real purpose of a military is to prevent war. But if we fail, then military members and their constituents, must accept that the military's next move is to fight, to destroy, and to kill if necessary. We exist to support the political system and defend our democracy and its interests if so deemed by political leaders. All too often we fight. Right now we're fighting a stupid war. Perhaps that colors my description of the military's purpose. We are killing Vietnamese; they are killing us.

You write, "Never have I thought that my part in the military is 'to kill, to destroy.' My truth is quite the contrary." To me this statement describes the essence of the ineffable facet of the military and its warrior culture. None of us military individuals, potential combatants or non-combatants, likes to address the killing function. Yet it's an accepted, underlying assumption to our mission.

During the Cuban Missile Crisis, while recruiting at Gettysburg College and alone in a motel room watching JFK tell the nation of our dilemma, I realized nuclear war is a real probability. Our drills turn into the real thing all too quickly. And I wear the uniform that carries the day or not.

For others in uniform, only when they start shooting guns or firing missiles does this feeling become real *inside* themselves. Please understand. I'm trying to describe a feeling that's barely recountable and that goes against the grain of good men and women of integrity. As long as men (and a few women) pit ideology against ideology and force against force, well then, so be it.

Know that I miss your presence and leadership. We're carrying on, but...hope to see you and Helen on my next TAD to D.C.

Very respectfully,

Tucker

P.S. And you know that I absolutely support a strong American defense system!

Chapter Seven

Rocking the Boat

Two months later from Tucker

20 December 1971, Newport, R.I.

Dear Tom,

And happy, happy Christmas to you! My calculations tell me you're on leave and not "on guard on the perimeter of the free world." Before I head home for the holidays I'm writing a few cards and notes to special friends like *you!* I trust you're well and still enjoying command. As usual much of my life is about my job.

Life takes funny turns, doesn't it? While the study's in an idling mode with the Navy, sitting in "action" and "hold" boxes in Washington, or desk drawers, my work and ideas have become popular with the other services, who are moving ahead steadfastly with their women's equal opportunity programs. Why can't the good old United States Navy be as enthusiastic and interested? Unfortunately, you and Buck were dead right: Because of its traditional norms, Big Daddy Navy's unprepared to respond to the study's central issue — women's equality.

Part of me wants to expose the macho, chauvinistic attitudes of our organization and write an article for Ms. magazine or *The Atlantic Monthly*. Most of me, however, says stay focused and work inside. So, I'm now editing an abridged version of the study for publication in the *Naval War College Review*.

You and I know turning against the Navy isn't in me, though several civilian friends suggest this action. We, the Navy, if possible, must make our own decisions about women and equality, rather than be pressured by external forces. The people admirals

(Howeland, Hopkins, and Zumwalt) will come around to the women issues. As Jennie says, "Be patient. Relax! Right now retention, recruiting, let alone the Vietnam drawdown, and our Cold War with the Soviets, are much more important than 'the women.' " My women officer friends and I are tired of sitting on the afterdeck!

But maybe we won't have too long to wait. Can you believe Admiral Z.'s sweeping changes? He even took on our "chicken shit regs," dumping stuff like writing out *Navy Regs* during Extra Military Instruction at WOCS, and permitting the wearing of beards and sideburns (that one may come back to bite him, methinks).

Last week one of my BuPers friends passed me an internal memo from Zumwalt to all flag officers that highlights the so-called women's problem. If you haven't seen it, the memo reads that higher echelons have been "sadly enlightened, mainly through the WAVE Retention Study Groups" about how frequently Navy women are still being used as receptionists, coffee runners and such, despite their technical training and competence. "This appears to be especially true in the case of enlisted women, although it is by no means confined to them."

Separate subject: How're you and Joanna and your relationship? I imagine the hard issues for you are your wish to have your very own children, and how it might be to help raise Willy and Carolyn. My social life is fairly quiet, though I've been enjoying some fun parties. Unlike your experience in Rickover's Charm School, our students don't study all the time!

Finally, my good friend, may the New Year of 1972 bring you real happiness and continued good health!

> With much affection,
>
> Tucker

Two weeks later from Tom

3 January 1972, Charleston, S.C.

Hi Tucker,

Thanks for your New Year's card and newsy note. I was most remiss this year and didn't send out any holiday cards, and I'll likely be deservedly punished by losing some friends. We both know all of us military types play a kind of shifting billets/musical chairs game and lose track of friends unless we contact them at least once a year.

Read the missive from Zumwalt and was indeed sadly enlightened. Seems I've been missing out so far and I wonder how I can get at least one WAVE to bring me coffee and run errands. I promise I'll be really nice to her and tell her how pretty she looks while giving her friendly pats on the bum.

Seriously, Tuck, how can I get a copy of your study? Is it generally available, or going to be, for military personnel to read? There's probably not much wiggle-room for accommodating women on the boats right now, but I can keep my eye on what happens on the staffs and when I'm on one myself someday, I'll try to have a modern opinion. So far, except for some heavy line handling during my enlisted time, I've never been asked to do anything in the Navy that a woman can't do. The problems are hormones and historic social and sex roles, aren't they? Questioning women's military abilities is easier than facing up to the challenge of changing social expectations and rules of behavior.

Re Zumwalt's changes, nothing's more change resistant than military tradition. Rigid, unquestioning conformity to dress code, for example, is somehow equated to following orders in battle. That Zumwalt even began to question this link has shocked (and perhaps frightened) many officers who felt secure when they knew the rules. The authority of officers, including COs, has eroded. While the occasional tyrant should be toppled, generally the system has worked well and this erosion is an error. Submariners have always been more casual about dress and regs than the surface Navy, at least at sea. On subs what counts is knowing the boat and your job.

One of my toughest sailors wears a gold cross in his ear and no one bothers him. My crew painted the faring (a kind of exterior sleeve on our periscope) with large black outlines of flowers. I view these actions as a source of amusement, and neither a breach of discipline nor a political statement of "'60s flower children." Of course the flowers are visible only when the periscope's extended, which is normally only when we're submerged and following tradition, as a kind of "salute" when we enter port.

The crew also painted the insides of the 16 missile tube hatches to match the colors of the 16 balls on a pool table! In case pool isn't your game, that's 8 solid colored balls, 7 striped balls, and one cue ball. The hatches are rarely open all at once, but when they are, they sure brighten up the waterfront and perhaps remind those who see them that even nuclear warriors can have a sense of humor. I'm enclosing a photo. Fun, huh?

I've been seeing Joanna about every chance I get. Her kids are great and I'm fond of her folks too. I've told her about you, and I think she was a little shocked at first due to limited Southern womanhood experiences. Not to worry. She's a rational and generous person. In addition, she respects our friendship, possibly because you're not the "other woman" threat but more like a good old Navy buddy. Actually I'm grateful you turned me down. I realize now that I was appraising you as a kind of investment — smart, attractive, lifetime companion, good mother, good genes, common views and interests. All pluses and no negatives. Definitely not a Marilyn type! Now I realize that Joanna has all those good pluses too and in addition, she completely turns me on whenever I'm near her and occupies much of my thoughts when I'm not. It's sorta scary. For sure, I want my own kids too. I can deal with a big family but am unsure about Joanna. Well, I'm not about to rush into anything, and the Navy's hardly giving me time.

Don't give up your efforts for women. I know you probably have to put up with bra-burning remarks from airheads. There's a sea change out there and a refreshing climate of questioning why we've always done things the way we have. Eventually, it'll blow a fresh sea breeze your way. Count me on board!

Warmest regards as ever,

Tom

Five days later from Tucker's journal

8 January 1972, Newport, R.I.

 For the record,

Tom thinks of me now as a "good investment" that turned out not-so-good. Was he never turned on to me? Seems he was fooling himself and me. Or, is he now reframing our relationship into good old buddies for safety's sake? I won't ask!

Why wasn't I born to marry? To have children? To be like other women? The gods decreed this life for me. No choice about which gender attracts me truly. Good thing I'm not a Christian fundamentalist. I'd probably commit suicide! Glad I was born with some good looks. Maybe I'd be better off if I'd been born homely. Men do find me attractive. I suppose I "pass." Sometimes too well. I could do without the sexual nudges and sexist remarks.

Whatever Tom's motives, I live with unresolved heartache and pain about my sexual identity. This won't go away soon, Fairchild, so carry on. Besides, you were born a survivor. Talk with your friends.

I need to talk with someone who cares...

Tom must never know my ache. He's got his own problems and major responsibilities, both Navy and family. And I cherish his friendship.

A Navy psychologist would place a black mark on my official record, heaven forbid. That won't do. Dad, Mother, and the Navy always say only the weak need psychological help. I'm strong. Just isolated.

Dad and Mother would be surprised and displeased. No grandchildren either.

My Navy family demands that I live with a secret, one they consider an unforgivable human "trait," and a disqualifier. Some family. Some Daddy.

Thank heavens for Robyn, Billie, Tom, and Jennie and Pierre. I'll visit Robyn soon.

TF

Two days later from Tucker

10 January 1972, Newport, R.I.

Dear Tom,

I'm delighted you and Joanna are having a great time together. I wouldn't fret about kids yet. Let the cards play out.

I mailed "my baby" (my study took nine months to gestate) to you yesterday. The War College libraries will retain a copy for lesser lights than you. An abridged version will appear in the March issue of the *Naval War College Review*. The *Proceedings* nixed the same article, returning it with extensive sexist comments in the margins; *e.g.*, where I wrote of women's concerns about their uniforms, some editor scratched, "Next thing she'll want is Army-issue girdles. Ha!" Ah, the fight goes on.

I spoke with Jennie and Pierre yesterday. Jennie's pressed to her limits with work on the CNO's Human Resource Management and Leadership Programs.

Joanna's reaction to my different way of being is natural. For me to know this is my path, notwithstanding cultural, religious, and military biases, took eons. This is my true self. I trust she realizes I'm an ordinary soul in every other way!

My best to you and your family. Hope your mom is getting along okay without your dad. At least he didn't die while you were on patrol. It's hard enough to lose a parent, but to come in from patrol to that news must be extra heavy. Or, are you one of those who chooses to be informed of bad news while still at sea? I don't know which choice I'd make. Do most of your crew want to get bad news at sea or at the end of their patrol? It must be rugged on you as the skipper, having to give bad news when you're feeling elated to be back in home port. Speaking of parents, mine are truly enjoying their retirement in San Diego. Dad's many hobbies will keep him going till he's at least 100!

Warmest regards,

Tuck

Ten weeks later from Tucker

24 March 1972, Newport, R.I.

Dear Robyn,

How's my good friend? Am feeling upbeat. Received a year's extension on my tour of duty, so I'll be here until June 1973. Feels as though I lost a year in this assignment because of the study. My calling is probably "teacher," and for the moment I'm really pleased to be both a naval officer and instructor on a Navy campus. Have been teaching a new, and exciting course, "Organizational Development."

An update on the study: Last week Admiral Chuck Howeland was in town and I made an appointment with him to discuss the study and reactions to it. His major comment, "Tucker, how do I know that other women officers agree with you? Prove it to me."

My immediate feelings were deflation and frustration. Then I relaxed and asked, "What would it take to convince you?"

"I want more evidence, Tucker. When I get that, I'll move ahead and take action. Not before."

I refrained from sarcasm…barely. If he'd read the study, he'd know where at least 34 other women stood. An idea popped into my head: "Admiral, an edited version of the study is published in this month's *War College Review*. You could convene a group of 10-12 women officers and ask them to comment on the article."

"Sounds like a winner," he replied. "I need more ammunition from you women to show Bud and Stan the *felt* need for change. Women are the best spokespersons for change, as black sailors are for their causes and concerns. Lord knows we've learned a lot from them since promulgation of Z-66 in December last year."

Then he asked, "What do you think about Eleanor Marit's edict that you're no longer WAVES and that the WAVE Director's office will close?"

I told him I support her goals, but I oppose her strategy and timing. "Right now women aren't integrated and we're a far cry from equal. Indeed, we may always be equal but different in certain respects. *Vive la difference."*

I added, "Captain Marit's creating a major coordination problem with no one office calling the shots for women's policies. Decentralizing the functions of the Director's office looks great in theory, but women are a long way from being an integral part of the organization."

"Lots of politicking going on, Tucker. Admiral Z. and Eleanor don't agree on several key matters."

The Admiral's attention then diverted to the Human Resource Management workshops he was observing. As I turned to leave, he said, "Tucker, I'll be looking for the results of your interview group."

"Aye, aye, sir."

Robyn, this is a crucial moment in history for Navy women. The first tenet of organizational development is this: The top guns must be behind any changes. And guess what? The admirals are finally asking women what they think. It's a first! In the past, they've always gone to the Director of the WAVES. Period. In her own way, Eleanor has helped by disestablishing her office. Still, she's confusing people unnecessarily. We've lost our leader at a critical time. (She's off to become one of our first woman COs of a major command.) We're no longer separate, but we're still damn different, with different personnel requirements. The guys have no idea how to deal with the so-called "women's issues," so they have to ask us.

Exciting times! Navy women now must move into an intensive sales mode. Part of the excitement comes from outside pressures. I'm sure you've heard that two days ago the Senate passed a Joint Resolution previously passed by the House which proposes an Amendment to the Constitution establishing equal rights for men and women. It's been submitted to the States for ratification. A long, long time in coming. We'll at last be treated equally by law.

I'm going to an Inter-service Conference at the Air Force Academy in May for top middle managers. The other services, perhaps because they're not going through such a huge social upheaval, seem to be more interested in Navy women than the Navy itself. The Navy's way below meeting its recruitment quotas and our retention numbers are terrible. Admiral Z. has higher people priorities to think about than equal opportunity for women, like Vietnam, the Cold War, and the Soviet strategic and maritime threats. Nixon's overtures to China bear watching too!

Thought you'd want this update. I've set one of my goals for my last year here as, "to have more leave time." I'm still trying, and failing, to be open to marriage. If I'm going to marry, I'd better hurry. I'm turning 34 in October!

How's life in beautiful Maine? Would love to hear from you.

Love,

Tucker

Seven weeks later from Robyn

May 16, 1972, Bar Harbor, Maine

Dear Tucker,

How great to get an upbeat letter. Congratulations! If not totally single-handedly, you've certainly been instrumental in putting a bee in the bonnets of Them-What-Makes-Policy. They probably wouldn't have even thought about innovative views about women without you and a few other outspoken women as catalysts.

How come the Navy lags behind both in women's issues and other areas? If the rest of the military is doing okay, it must be the fault of individual personalities, not policies. I assumed different branches of the military share a similar conservativism.

Admiral Z. seems to be the most outstanding and reasonable person, male or female, whom you've encountered in all your naval experience. Does he have the power to fight all the reactionary types?

That trip to the Air Force Academy should be fun. Have you been to Colorado Springs before? Take some time either before or after the conference to do some exploring. That latter in reference to "more leave time." If you don't play pretty soon, my industrious friend, you'll forget what "relaxing" means! On the other hand, I suppose you could quote me the ant and the grasshopper fable!

By the way, in the fall Derry will experience the initial letdown that often accompanies the loss of Only Child Status. Hopefully after the immediate shock, he'll be ecstatic to have an in-house contemporary. Then it'll be more fair — two of Them vs. two of Us.

Till next time.

Love,

Robyn

Three days later from Tucker's journal

19 May 1972, Newport, R.I.

 For the record,

This day I forwarded the transcript of the Women's Interview Group to RADM Howeland. Sparks were flying from the briefing folder! The group more than confirmed the study's conclusions and recommendations, with the majority of them, from CDR to ENS, wanting change. As LCDR Margaret Maskell said,"For the last 8 to 10 years I've been hearing that 'things are happening,' and 'changes are in the mill.' But I've seen damn few changes."

A small majority were skeptical of the study's approach and long-term effect, saying things like, "All this pushing for equal rights is going to mess up a very good situation for most women in the Navy. We have equal pay, equal benefits. What do you want, anyway? To go to Vietnam? Well, I don't! I don't!"

I say we can't have it both ways. LCDR Patricia Herr, for instance, was worried the study sounded too feminist. "Most Navy men don't think women's lib is worth a hoot. And let's face it, the people who really have the power to do something about it, right now, and for a long time to come, are men."

This viewpoint was countered by CDR Carmichael,"We must seek changes now, if we're to continue to attract and retain qualified young women. We must march to the beat of the times." (My sentiments exactly.)

Several worry about a goal of true equality. "If this drive for equal opportunity goes much further, women might find themselves ordered to sea." These women feel we're support staff. At the same time, they feel women aren't given the opportunity to develop expertise in their specialties. "How can anyone plan a career when you're essentially a Jack, or is it Jill, of all trades?" As Billie says, "I want to be in my specialty."

Most of them don't blame the Navy. As CDR Danston said, "I believe the Navy is action-oriented and wants us all to be as effective and competent as possible. It's simply the result of having no real plan for our employment." Another added, "The planning has been sporadic, a crumb here, a crumb there. The first step has to be provision for many career paths. The alleged integration of women without setting up career patterns is exactly why underutilization and channelization, as Tucker's study describes, is happening!"

The younger women are less charitable. They're angry. LTJG

Ferrebee said, "Each day at work and around the naval base brings favoritism and discrimination. It's difficult to say which is worse. Each keeps me uneasy."

Several junior women said the Navy recruits women on a pretense and tells them that they'll have great jobs. "And yet we find that all challenging jobs are reserved for men," said LTJG Ferrebee. "The Navy is just not telling it like it is, and it won't change either. The Navy is too tradition bound."

LTJG O'Sullivan added, "Even more damaging than professional suffocation is the widespread attitude that Navy women are 'mascots.' Our male superior officers don't take our efforts seriously; our male subordinates don't take our orders seriously."

They criticized the mixed messages we women receive. "Women are supposedly fully integrated in the Navy, but our authority as officers is constantly questioned. We're highly educated, but we can't use our education to its fullest capacity."

Ensign McIan, the most junior officer, articulated the Egalitarian's position: "I want the Navy to look beyond tradition. I want to see a Navy based on rational thought and not on the emotionality of male superiority, a Navy where men and women can work together, pool their resources, and be mission-oriented. The goal should be complete equality."

I felt strength from the group. Their comments definitely substantiate the major conclusion of my study which calls for further research! A new study group would reformulate the raison d'etre of women in the Navy in light of social changes in society and in the Navy; establish guidelines and criteria for the future of women officers and enlisted women; and delineate the philosophic base from which the Navy program for women should be developed. Is equality of the sexes or equality of opportunity for the sexes the goal?

I always return to the idea that understanding the values underlying policy, any policy, is critical in policy making. Policy making, be it about women or about war or about whatever, is driven by values. In the Interview Group, I heard women such as Ensign McIan motivated by equality; others, by security.

Okay, Fairfield. What else can Admirals Howeland, Hopkins, and Zumwalt want? These women stated the case succinctly. I'm proud of them for speaking up.

Just learned that Admiral Hopkins sent out a memorandum to commanding officers last month on the subject of "attitudes regarding Navy women." Unfortunately he seemed to separate the men from the women, addressing his remarks to the males' attitudes.

He said Captain Eleanor Marit was working on the women's attitudes! Someday we'll not think in such separatist, exclusive terms. A step in the right direction, nevertheless. Top management is finally putting some positive energy into the women's issue.

TF

One month later from Tucker

15 June 1972, Newport, R.I.

Dear Robyn,

Things are moving rapidly for the Navy, especially Women-in-the-Navy. "The good, the bad, and the ugly" best describes the scene regarding Navy women. I'll begin with an example of "the ugly": The results are in on CDR Louise Lauer's and my questionnaire regarding attitudes towards Navy women. We queried one-half (343) of the entire WAVE line officer population. The male officer sample (303) was taken from Navy students at the War College. The results weren't ugly, but several students designed a mock questionnaire, and passed it out to the entire student body not long after ours was distributed. To me, that questionnaire was ugly. Here are two of the four questions. The others are equally obnoxious:

I. Women who design questionnaires to prove that male naval officers are chauvinistic pigs:

   A. Should be horse-whipped.

   B. Need passionate love more than answers.

   C. Will probably gossip over the results.

   D. Have spent too much time listening to Women's Libbers.

   E. Probably dreamed up those questions over morning coffee in the restroom.

   F. Probably wouldn't understand the answers anyway.

II. Women change their minds more often than men because:

   A. There is less mind to change so it doesn't take as long.

   B. They understand less than men, so have less trouble doing so.

   C. Need passionate love more than answers.

D. They hear more gossip and rumor upon which to base their rather transient opinions.

E. They never really change their minds as that implies understanding and determination, both of which are beyond feminine capability.

F. No Answer — Rhetorical Question — Women have no minds.

You know my sense of humor disappears when dealing with any kind of prejudice, especially discriminatory actions toward women. That feminists sometimes have no sense of humor probably rings true! Perhaps you'd laugh at this questionnaire. If I thought the authors' intent was in good jest or sarcasm, I could smile. But these students are angry with the new attitude coming out of D.C. toward Navy women. They want to take it out on individual Navy women. Feels ugly.

The "bad"? The attitudes of male officers as reflected in the questionnaire which Louise and I administered:

A large minority are bothered by women as line officers. For instance, more than 45 percent generally or strongly agree that women should limit their aspiration to those jobs to which they've been traditionally assigned. Twenty-nine percent of the men agree that "Women as a general rule are not able to stand the stress and strain related to being a commanding officer." Another 20 percent were uncertain!

Twenty-nine percent of the men believe that "Certain necessary personal attributes for commanding officer are in direct conflict with femininity, and therefore women should continue to be excluded from command and key middle management billets." Another 16 percent were uncertain. On this same question, over 70 percent of the women strongly disagree and another twenty-three percent generally disagree. Women and men were far apart on many questions. Not surprising, but discouraging that so much work must be done.

The statement that showed the greatest disparity between men's and women's attitudes was, "Women officers should be given the same opportunities as male officers, including sea duty and flying status." Fifty-seven percent of the women agreed with this question, while 74 percent of the men did not agree.

We made a good decision to administer the survey, despite the flak we both suffered. The results give Admiral Howeland more data and more ammunition to say that women and men officers differ in their perceptions about Navy women. Hopefully the people admirals, including Zumwalt, are truly committed to change and will respond to the women.

The "good" is that women themselves aren't going to ease up on the institution and its rampant sexism. They're taking professional risks to get the word to the admirals. I've received many phone calls and letters since the article's publication. This week, for example, an ensign wrote saying she thought I might like to know of a discussion with the Superintendent of the Naval Academy and his wife last weekend in Annapolis. The Ensign had been invited to a luncheon as the girl friend of a lieutenant who's a friend of the Admiral's. When the Superintendent discovered this young woman was a naval officer, he asked about "LCDR Fairfield's study." He told the Ensign that he's a big supporter of my ideas, asked if Captain Eleanor Marit were interested in the study, and if she were taking action on it. The Ensign said she didn't know, but didn't think so. The Admiral told the Ensign he'd "talk with Eleanor the next time he saw her."

The Ensign wrote that her main goal in writing was to thank me for the time and effort "in what I believe is in my best interest personally and professionally and will make a difference for ALL women in the Navy." That's the good news, Robyn. I'm getting so many good vibes from women, especially the young ones who are wanting positive changes. The seeds are planted. It's a matter of time to see which little seedlings sprout. The climate's ripe for change. Women's equality is an idea whose time has come!

I'm having fun working with the Rhode Island Women's Political Caucus. Was elected to the Caucus' Policy Planning Committee. Great group of women, spearheaded by Shari Anderson, a Brown University professor's wife. I feel a twinge of conflict of interest, as defined by the Hatch Act which says the military shouldn't be involved in political activities. Yet a Rhode Island woman judge says we — she and I — don't have a conflict because the Caucus is bipartisan.

As you can tell, am upbeat again about my future. We're on the move. I'm doing what I can to bring about peaceful, sensible change from within. Now maybe I can spend more energy on my social life. It's been flagging, like barely existent, since the study's birth two years ago.

I continue to accept gibes and jeers from men about the *NavWarCol Review* article. You'd think that I'd stood in front of the flag on the College green and burned my bra. But that's okay, as long as we get policy changes.

Once a woman "gets it," in terms of discrimination and its effects, there's no going back. Once I acknowledged the anger and frustration about being turned down by the Academy and the CNO strictly because of gender, that was "it." Since then, I've been keenly aware of the gender-based innuendoes and biases surrounding me. More and more women are hearing that "click, click, click." How about you?

All for now. Take care of you and your family.

Love,

Tucker

Two weeks later from Robyn

July l, 1972, Bar Harbor, ME

Dear Tucker,

Though I see why that second questionnaire annoyed you, I wouldn't dwell on it. It seems pitifully immature, more like something a fraternity brother, or a high school student, would hand out to his classmates. Seems to be neither a sarcastic "good jest" nor even a righteously angry document. Just sadly stupid.

Comments on the designated "bad," the attitudes of male officers. You're right, no surprise here. I don't know where exactly these young males came from, though I seriously doubt that a high percentage are bleeding-heart liberals. They certainly seem to have incorporated whatever rhetoric they were brought up on or learned in the Navy. Their questionnaire measures that rather than carefully considered and reflected-upon opinions. Were the latter true, it would've been scarier. At least these fellows have the capacity for growth, I would hope.

And the "good": good that women aren't giving up. Again no surprise if you're the example. For years you've put pressure on the Navy, and it's finally beginning to pay off! Also this set of women can perhaps be more daring than their forebears because of the support for them in the real world.

Hang in there and keep on chuggin'.

Love,

The Outsider (and thank goodness)

Ten Days later from Tucker's journal

10 July 1972, Newport, R.I.

 For the record,

Don't be impatient. The wheels are turning faster now in D.C. You're in the loop, thanks to the May Inter-Service Conference and the study. No thanks to Eleanor Marit. Eleanor and I continue to remain at opposite political poles. She's truly "a man's woman." That's fine, unless one's job focuses on women's issues.

The word is that as a short-range approach Admiral Zumwalt has appointed an "Ad Hoc CNO Informal Study Group on Equal Rights for Women," chaired by RADM Howeland. Its purpose is to develop dynamic policies and programs to ensure equal opportunity and treatment for women. And we have some superb women in D.C. helping.

The Admiral must be using his ammunition, and more. Soon we might see a Z-Gram on women.

TF

One month later from Tucker's journal

8 August 1972, Newport, R.I.

For the record,

I'm thrilled! Today Admiral Z. issued a Z-gram on "Equal Rights and Opportunities for Women in the Navy." While the Z-gram itself isn't startling, its breadth and depth are a surprise. *Big* changes.

The Secretary of the Navy and Admiral Z. have "established a task force to look at all laws, regulations, and policies that must be changed in order to eliminate any disadvantages to women resulting from either legal or attitudinal restrictions."

Specific immediate actions are large: authorizing limited entry of enlisted women into all ratings; an "ultimate goal" of assigning women to ships at sea; suspending restrictions on women succeeding to command ashore; opening the Chaplain and Civil Engineer Corps; opening restricted line billets to women officers; offering paths to flag rank; and eliminating both the quasi-chain of command with WRs and the channeling of women officers to admin and personnel.

And much more! He addressed his conclusions directly to commanding officers, asking for their full support of the spirit and intent of "the new directions for women." God, I'm excited! I spoke with Jennie this afternoon. She praised my contribution; I praised her role in sustaining me throughout the storms. Called Billie and she's ecstatic. Must call Robyn and others tomorrow and spread the great news. I must write Tom, Billie, Robyn and Jennie and Pierre. Trust the process.

TF

P.S. "Nobody makes a greater mistake than he who did nothing because he could do only a little." Edmund Burke

One day later from Tucker

9 August 1972, Newport, R.I.

Dear Tom,

God, I'm excited! Have you seen Z-116? We've turned a corner in the history of the U.S. Navy! Women should be proud of their contribution, as I am with mine. As with any special interest group or minority the group itself has stood up and let their voices resonate. The women who supported the study and article stood up and "squeaked." So did the Navy women and men in D.C. who helped draft Z-116. So did the many women who have pushed for the ERA for decades. Hooray! We're moving!

To think I now have the possibility to be a restricted line intelligence officer, an attaché, a CNO briefer, and even a USNA faculty member! That's phenomenal and I'm thrilled! The internal fight about opening up the Academy to women is still unresolved. The Academies' restrictions to women will have to be removed, though congressional members and many senior officers will stoutheartedly defend against women invading them.

Separate subject: In following our own submarine building program, I sense we're in a race to outrace Soviet subs; i.e., each new Soviet sub class outperforms or counters a U.S. class, and vice versa. The Soviets, for example, are currently building the *Yankees*, more sophisticated than their *Echos* and *Hotels*, to outperform our *Lafayette* class SSBNs. These sub construction programs are more hushed up than their land-based equivalents.

Tom, whenever I focus on the intensity and size of the arms race, I get depressed. Will it ever stop? Now that the Soviets have opted for a blue-water Navy, how large must we expand? The big deal here at the College continues to be numbers of carriers. Any UNCLASS comments?

Haven't heard from you in a while. How's life? Joanna? I'm coming to D.C. next month to brief the CNO and his staff. Can we meet while you're on off-crew? Is the timing right? Would love to catch up, my friend.

I'm still flying around in the clouds.

Love,

Tucker

Two weeks later from Tom

20 Aug 72, USS Christopher Columbus, *Charleston, S.C.*

Dear Tucker,

This is an off-crew period, so I have time to write a short note. It was good to get your recent ltr. CONGRATULATIONS! I don't mean to dampen your euphoria but my experience with the Navy says, "There is many a slip twixt the cup and the lip." In 1950, two years after President Truman issued his directive desegregating the services, the Naval Base at Pensacola Florida still had "Colored Only" and "White Only" signs outside of its clubs! Not to say that Z-gram 116 and many of the other reforms ADM Z. has implemented through his Z-grams aren't steps in the right direction, but a lot of resistance to these types of changes makes me willing to bet that in twenty years we'll still see discrimination against women.

I too am feeling euphoric because *Christopher Columbus* just passed her second straight Operational Reactors Safeguard Exam (ORSE). This is an extremely arduous exam covering all aspects of reactor operations and maintenance, including oral and written quizzes given to all nuclear-trained personnel. Of course, it's really an examination of my management capabilities. Not only did we pass, we were so good we got an exemption from the next regular exam!

I was ecstatic, and after the inspection, over the 1MC told the whole crew about our success, ending my message with, "This was no small fucking feat."

The duty officer who was standing next to me said, "That's pretty good, Captain. There's only one woman guest on board!"

Tucker, you made an astute observation about the US/USSR submarine race. I don't fear the Russians. I'm sure that we're so militarily superior to them they'll never dare start a war with us. In addition, they're only a superpower because of their military. From what I read they only have a third-world economy. But our government continues to paint the Russians as 10 feet tall and about to attack us any minute. Therefore, the American people, through their elected representatives, are spending excessive amounts on the military in hardware races.

I feel pretty lonely these days as a McGovern supporter and am still wondering when Nixon's "secret plan" to end this malignant war is going to surface. We've been waiting for four long years and I see the damage that it's doing to civilian-military relationships every day.

Joanna and I are still on track and I think wedding bells will be ringing eventually. I feel I have insufficient time in my life now to give her and Carolyn and Willy but maybe I'm just "twice burned, thrice cautious." I admit it seems a little difficult to have a "built-in" family, but I'm coming to love the kids as my own.

As far as meeting in D.C. goes, what are your exact dates? I get there from time to time, and if I'm still in off-crew status, I may be able to adjust a visit to coincide with yours.

Hmmm, this wasn't as brief as I'd intended. I hope my comments don't dampen your enthusiasm over the Z-gram. Without it, nothing would happen. With it, there's opportunity.

Love, Tom

Four weeks later from Tucker's journal

21 September 1972, Newport, R.I.

For the record,

Last week I flew down to D.C. and briefed Admiral Zumwalt's staff on the results of the study and the questionnaire. They seemed preoccupied, but asked thoughtful questions. A good dialogue. Finally top leadership realizes the contributions we women can make!

AND, today I received a personal memo from Admiral Z. saying that he's "firmly committed to equal rights for women in the Navy and am convinced that we must find ways to more fully utilize their talents and capabilities. I am certain that the research you have done will be of value in the implementation of Z-116."

It takes so much to move our institution even a tiny bit to a different direction. But it can move. The Navy's made up of people, who are changing in attitudes and energies.

I must send Robyn a copy of Z.'s memo. That memo's a part of why I hung in. She and others always ask, "Why do you stay?" I stay because I love the Navy and fiercely want women to be included as first-team members. I stay because I believe in our mission. I stay because my job continues to be challenging. I stay "to serve at the pleasure of the President," in spite of my sometime disagreement with U.S. foreign and military policies. I just stay.

TF

P.S. D.C. is still abuzz with the Watergate break-in. It appears there's more to it than a third-rate burglary. How can people behave so stupidly? Politics!

Ten Weeks later from Tucker

5 December 1972, Newport, R.I.

Dear Robyn,

If it's not one thing it's another. I'm feeling good about the Navy's positive actions toward equal opportunity for women and gradually realizing it's a formidable task to bring about change for minorities (including women). As you probably have read in the headlines, we've had trouble with race brawls aboard the *Kitty Hawk* and *Constellation* these last weeks. Given the elitism and classism inherent to our Navy, the task of true integration of black and white sailors is horrendous.

Admiral Zumwalt and his entourage are overseeing not only the end of the Vietnam war and the continuing rise of the Soviet maritime threat, but also implementing new people programs, including integration of minorities. To complicate matters, they don't have full support from senior officers, particularly *vocal* senior retirees.

Two weeks ago I had a phoncon with CDR Bill Brown in D.C. He and I have been in close liaison about the women's study and its fall-out. "Tucker," he said, "How about you coming down here for a few days and helping us test out our new Race Relations Program. The training's purpose is to test a revised Race Relations curriculum. The training's students will be sort of guinea pigs. It's a hurry-up deal, based on the recent carrier riots."

"Bill, I'm not terribly in touch with our racial problems in the fleet. You know, I'm a white female officer who hasn't had much exposure to blacks."

"That's exactly why we want you, Tucker. Knowing your work with the women's program, you'll be up front and honest in your evaluation. You'll tell us your gut responses. I know you'll have some. By the way, you'll be one of 24 students and the only female. You can handle that, can't you?"

"Well, I'm used to being the only female, but what are the black/white and officer/enlisted ratios?"

"We're planning on seven officers, including you, with the rest enlisted. Most of the officers are white. Most of the enlisted are blacks."

He paused. "Tucker, actually there'll be another woman there, a black civilian DOD contract-type named Shirley Johnson, who will be one of two facilitators. The other facilitator will be a white male, Jim Huntington. You'll know at least one other student, Commander Bob Billings, from the War College. You can fly down together."

My first internal reaction was "No." My second, "Be open and sleep on it." My third, "Okay, it's only three days. I can do anything for three days." Duty sometimes takes over. My naval officer persona said, "Okay, Bill. You'll owe me one. I'll come down with Bob. Do we get to play at all in the evenings?"

"Sorry, my friend, this is an all-business affair. You'll be checking into the Holiday Inn in Crystal City which will be your only venue for the three days. You're to stay inside and eat only in its dining room."

"I've read about such training events. Is this some kind of sensitivity training? If so, I think you've got the wrong person. Especially if it's about racial concerns."

"Don't worry, Tucker. It'll be fine. Gotta go now and confirm the rest of your fellow students. See you soon."

The experience was unforgettable. As Bob Billings and I walked into the hotel lounge designated as our main training room, we both took a deep breath. Bob's a southern gentleman with the attendant stereotypical attitudes toward blacks and little experience with black Navy personnel. We found ourselves in a room filled with fifteen black senior and master chiefs, two white master chiefs and five other officers, all white. Soon the two civilian facilitators appeared, Shirley and Jim.

Shirley, an attractive black woman, expanded on our tasking: "We're trial-testing a Navy Race Relations program that will be taken to the fleet. Each of us should be honest and speak up about feelings. There'll be many group exercises intended to be both educational and attitude changing."

Jim spoke up, "As a psychologist I can say there are two conflicting schools of thought about change. The first says the best way to effect change is to work on people's attitudes. For example, once white people understand why blacks do what they do, they'll accept them. The second school claims that's a lost cause. The better way is to change the behavior. Tell whites what behaviors are expected toward blacks and the changed attitude will come later following the changed behavior. This curriculum supports the first school."

The morning went quickly. I was aware that everyone was on their best behavior. By the afternoon, differences of opinion developed among several of the officers, including me. Because of my immersion in the women's study, I felt a need to point out similarities between and among women and blacks as minorities in our conservative Navy subculture. After my second comment to this effect, Shirley lashed out at me saying angrily, "Commander, you obviously have no idea what it's like to be black. There's little comparison between women and blacks in terms of pain and suffering and discrimination."

I was surprised that this "facilitator" took such an active role in the discussions. Besides, facilitators are supposed to make things easier. "I must differ with you," I said to Shirley. "Furthermore, I believe that Shirley Chisholm disagrees with you. She has publicly stated that being a woman has meant more discrimination directed toward her than being a black. You don't agree, I take it?"

"No, Commander, I *don't* agree. I ask you to stop making the comparisons." Real hostility, as well as frustration and anger, came through in her voice.

The next morning the hostility reappeared.

We students were becoming fairly comfortable with ourselves and each other by the second day. Our first group task was to figure out why the Navy wasn't making its numerical goals for black officers at Officer Candidate School. Our group thought of several reasons. As a former recruiter, I thought the answer was simple: The first qualification to becoming a naval officer is a college degree.

"We may have 12% blacks in our country demographically, but how many are college graduates?" I asked. The group nodded. We estimated that probably less than 3% of blacks have a college degree.

I was the small group's spokesperson for its report-out to the large group. My report began with the point that it's a matter of *qualification*. "Many blacks aren't qualified to become officers because..." I was stopped in mid-sentence by Shirley Johnson.

"What do you know about being *unqualified?*" she shouted. "That's the whole story for the black person. We're continually told we're not qualified to do the job. How can you come up with such an answer, knowing that it's a vicious, unjust cycle?" She was definitely enraged. Seemingly she was angry at me for even mentioning the words "not qualified" and "blacks" in the same sentence. Her voice was getting louder and shriller. I looked around and could see a host of bewildered white men and a crowd of concerned black sailors. The only women in the tension-filled room were at odds with each other.

I tried to respond to Shirley's attack, which felt like a physical attack as well. With her eyes glaring, her hands flailed in my face. I said, "All I was saying is that because not many blacks have a college degree, they…"

"Commander, you have no idea what it is to be black, do you? You have no idea what it is to be told you are unqualified!"

I was about to tell her I did know something about being told I was "unqualified" when she lit into me with more of her diatribe. My polite white self, uncomfortable with the whole scene, withdrew in resignation. No wonder blacks have problems, I said to myself. I'm trying to be open and caring and I'm assailed by a person who's supposed to be making things easier for me.

I don't know what else she said after that, Robyn, except it felt like no other attack I'd ever experienced. Not only was I the victim of vicious remarks by a seething "facilitator," at the same time I'd developed a splitting headache, partly because of the tasking and company and partly because we'd been holed up in an air-conditioned, smoke-filled room for over twelve hours. My sinuses were rebelling. My senses were on fire. I just wanted to go home and forget about blacks and race riots on the fantails.

It was lunchtime. Bob and I sat down at a table for two in the hotel dining room. Shirley and several of the black men came in and sat at one of the tables adjacent to ours. I ate very little. I talked very little.

"I want to go home," I said to Bob.

"I don't blame you, Tucker. I feel the same. This scene presses me beyond my comfort zone too. I'm sorry I didn't speak up in your defense. But you and I don't really have the choice to go back to Newport, do we?"

"I suppose not. I can see why we're having problems with blacks, though. They seem so angry. Shirley seems in so much turmoil."

"Well," said Bob, "perhaps you and she are a metaphor for how whites and blacks perceive each other. You see her as a raving, emotional black person and she sees you as a polite, uptight, uncaring snob."

"Touché, my friend."

The afternoon sessions are a blur. I do remember that several of the black men individually came up and apologized for Shirley's behavior. They said it was way out of line, especially since she was one of the two leaders. Master Chief Brad White told me that he'd wanted to step into the fray and protect me, but had decided to restrain his instincts. "You realize, Commander, that we black men and you white women have much more in common than the white men and the black women, who have always had a more privileged life than we. We need to stick together."

It had never entered my mind that this might be true. "No, I've never thought of the black/white arena in those terms, Master Chief," I said.

"The next time she steps on your feelings, I'm going to interfere and stop the process," he said.

"No, Master Chief, the next time I'm going to be less polite and more aggressive. Politeness isn't working."

There was no next time. That night Shirley came over after dinner and apologized to me. She said she'd let her feelings take over and her actions were uncalled for. "Please forgive me," she said. "I have a lot of pent-up anger. Your attitudes and your comparisons of blacks and women trigger that anger."

I accepted her apology.

Robyn, I think I don't know much anymore, especially about other cultures, about civil rights, about other people's feelings. What's that phrase, "The more you know, the less you know."

What I do know from that experience: To stand up for yourself as a minority can be hell on earth. Shirley did that. She did it in an awkward way. But at least she did it! She's able to get her feelings out and put them right on the table. Perhaps I should do that more. My anger about the stupid restrictions and attitudes inherent in being a Navy woman is more bridled. Shirley wasn't willing to hear that women are similar to blacks, including being told they're "unqualified." She took a risk and confronted me with her feelings.

The experience was unforgettable. To help achieve equal opportunity for minorities can be as uncomfortable for majorities as for minorities. That's one big reason they don't participate! For instance, for me to confront my racist attitudes is not only risky, it's deeply painful. Yet it must be done by me and other whites. We must bring about change for blacks in the Navy and in the country. We must give of ourselves to better their rights. It's the right thing to do. Otherwise we'll only eternalize the "tyranny of the majorities."

That's my story, Robyn. We live in difficult times, reaping the benefits of the '60s' civil rights struggles and paying the price of years and years of discrimination against American blacks. Let's hope for better times.

I'm looking forward to our weekend next month. It'll be a real change from fighting the Navy's fights. All for now, my friend.

Love,

Tucker

P.S. Intuitively I believe the second school of change to be best for the military. It's sometimes too hard to erase bigoted attitudes through military training. If we, the Navy, expect non-racist or non-sexist behaviors, then issue directives and attitudinal changes will come to the majority with time and patience. As they say, "Grab 'em by the short hairs, and their hearts and minds will follow."

P.P.S. I must add that I'm far more comfortable with the thought of working for and with blacks than ever before. This training rubbed off!

Two weeks later from Robyn

December 20, 1972, Bar Harbor, ME

Dear Tucker,

Your letter arrived on Elizabeth's two-month birthday, a milestone indeed, as now she occasionally can see fit to sleep through the night. As I told you on the phone, for the most part Derry's very good with her and only an occasional overly energetic hug makes her eyes bug out. Now let me reply to your plight.

What amazes me about the Race Relations workshop is that the facilitator got so out of control and that no one, especially her partner facilitator, attempted to intervene. I can see where she was coming from, because I too don't see women being discriminated against in the same way blacks are. Maybe in the Navy the experiences of women and blacks are more similar in terms, again to use your word, of "qualification" requirements. But in society at large the black has a far rougher time than the female.

Back to your word "qualification." Years ago you'd mentioned that blacks were only qualified to be stewards or whatever, no questions asked. No wonder that woman was outraged when you used such an unfortunate word. But, Tucker, no offense, and this goes back to your OCS days, sometimes you do give off an aura of aloof superiority, which — if folks don't know you well, or, as in this case have an axe to grind — is hard to swallow.

The good aspect of that rather awful encounter is that you feel *you* came out of it in a different place and with a different perspective.

In terms of race relations in the Navy, you didn't really say what was the training's bottom line. As presented, it sounded to me rather unresolved and as though there's still considerable work to be done.

A mess indeed!

See you soon, love,

Robyn

Four days later from Tucker's journal

Christmas Eve 1972, Newport, R.I.

For the record,

What a scrooge I am! What an absolute, aloof, snobby jerk I am! Robyn's right. I'm so absorbed in my career and women's inequities that I miss hearing others' problems. Because of my own filters I haven't fully appreciated the problems of black men and women. While Shirley Johnson's anger shocked me and was out of line, instead of listening to her with an open mind, putting myself in her shoes and trying to understand her needs, I retreated into a defensive, holier-than-thou mode. Remember OCS, Fairfield? As Jennie would say, "Just *who* do you think you are?"

Why do I retreat and withdraw? Natural defensive posture? Probably when I'm scared I use it as a backup style, unwilling to reveal my true feelings. To be confronted with my own racism and prejudice stings. I realize I haven't questioned the Navy's racist thinking and policies all these years. Ouch. I've bought into *institutional* racism without even once questioning. A real block in attitude because I've questioned Navy policies for a long, long time. Why did I tacitly accept the Navy's racist attitudes? How stupid! I assumed the system was right.

In the Race Relations workshop we whites were asked to describe close relationships we'd had with blacks. I mentioned that my dad's longtime steward was "like one of the family," and that we treated him as "part of our immediate family."

"And, Commander," asked Shirley Johnson, "did he walk in the front or the back door to your quarters?" My heart stopped. "I, ah, I, I must confess," I said, "he came in the back door."

Why haven't I seen how dispassionate and inconsiderate I've been in my attitudes toward blacks? Here I complain about Navy men's attitudes toward women, and inside I haven't cared enough about blacks to question longtime racist policies. As long as I'm a part of this organization, I shall indirectly, tacitly, be asked to strive for the warrior's ways — cool, calculated, accomplished, and largely dispassionate, impersonal, but not prejudiced.

I'll work hard to become more caring and loving of others, especially those who don't fit the warrior mold. I shall give it my best shot to begin to step away from this mold and still get the job done. Be mindful of the task, Fairfield, but pay more attention to *how* the task is accomplished.

I'm beginning to understand my negative reactions toward Emma, my OCS bunkmate: Emma didn't fit the warrior mold. She violated unwritten Navy ways, which had become my own unwritten practices by the time I entered OCS. Furthermore, her lack of self-discipline was unacceptable. My own shadow, in Jung's terms, filtered my views of Emma.

You're a real damn dummy, Tucker. Shape up or ship yourself out of this organization soon. The Navy won't do it for you in this case. In spite of my gender, I now fit the warrior mold. I play the rules of the games. Playing the games gets me acceptance, and yes, a voice. But, does it get me peace of mind?

TF

Same day from Tucker

Christmas Eve 1972, Newport, R.I.

Dear Mother and Dad,

Your trip to Alaska sounds special. You both deserve lots of cruises after your many years of service to country. I'm still on a high over Z-gram 116. A real shot in the arm for all Navy women, both retired and on active duty.

Life is good here. I'm less pressured than last year at this time and am more balanced.

A strange circumstance which has to do with direct conflict between citizens and naval officers occurred last night in Providence. I've been participating in biweekly gatherings of the R.I. Women's Political Caucus policy planning group and have enjoyed the friendship and camaraderie of civilian women, who have a different take on the country.

Shari Anderson, the Chairwoman of the group, raised a key question last night. "I insist that each of us signs this telegram to President Nixon, demanding that he stop the bombing in Hanoi and Haiphong."

"That's a splendid idea," said the Vice Chair, Elizabeth Drake.

I felt the need to speak up and said, "In my heart of hearts I too want to sign my name. I've been totally against our Vietnam policy since June 1965. To continue losing young men and women over false premises and principles is unforgivable."

"Then why not sign it, Tucker? If your conscience says so, do it," said Shari. "We know that peace negotiations in Paris have broken down, but to restart a full-scale air offensive with B-52s seems unnecessary and wrong."

Shari's voice was getting louder. "Congress has adjourned," she continued, "and the President probably thinks he can get away with it. The public's in the Christmas spirit. But we've already lost several B-52s with this renewed bombing effort."

"I can't say that Vietnam has reinvigorated my patriotism," I said. "On the contrary, I'm ashamed of our actions. The President announced in January of 1969 that we're in an era of negotiation rather than confrontation. That was almost four years ago. His invasion of Cambodia in the name of withdrawal was wrong!"

"But I serve at the pleasure of the President, and as a naval officer I must honor his orders as my Commander-in-Chief. He's my ultimate boss in the chain of command. I cannot personally sign a telegram that publicly denounces our policy."

"That's silly," said Sheri. "You're a U.S. citizen. You have your rights too."

"Not when it comes to differences of opinion such as this," I said. "I'm sorry you force me to choose between the Caucus and my work as a naval officer. There's no question which must take priority. The Caucus has become too political for my own welfare and peace of mind."

I resigned from the Caucus last night. I was hoping that any political conflicts of interest wouldn't be brought to a true test. Sometimes it seems impossible to be both a naval officer and the person who I am — a woman, a liberal, and a concerned citizen.

By the bye, hope you'll be voting in the November election. I shall vote against President Nixon. Although McGovern seems far to the left, his policies and ideas are rational, and Nixon has been irrational and unresolving about Vietnam. Wonder how many more young men have gone home in body bags since Nixon initiated his "peace with honor"? And what about Watergate?

Enough of politics. Who knows, Dad, maybe you'll become a Democrat! I hadn't realized how very Republican our officer corps is until my tour here. Makes sense. We're a conservative bunch. Admiral Z. is forcing many to shake in their boots over antiquated, anachronistic attitudes and policies. I don't know how he climbed to the top so fast. He's not especially popular among our students, who see him as moving too swiftly and jumping down the chain of command to reach seaman at the boilerplate level, skipping middle and senior management. He has only eighteen more months to go in his tour, so I understand his speedy quest. That Zumwalt's watch coincides with the women's movement and its momentum is a blessing for Navy women.

Much love to you both.

Love,

Tucker

Four days later from Tucker's journal

28 December 1972, Newport, R.I.

 For the record,

I'm still pondering my discussion with Cynthia Aldrich in Providence last week. Cynthia, who calls herself a radical feminist, believes that women can't be in the Navy "because they aspire to and in some cases attain power. Those women already in the Navy must be harassed by Navy men in order to keep them down and under control."

Also, she said, "You can't have gay men in the military because they change the order of things; i.e., men's domination of women." Gay men, she says, have egalitarian relationships (theoretically), and what's more, don't serve men. Gayness itself, says Cynthia, is a challenge to the System which relies on force to stay in place. In the System there are only victims and oppressors.

This is both foreign and real for me. I know some radical feminists believe that men are out of control sexually, and that patriarchal training demands their sexual drives be satisfied. They also believe male violence is the basis of control of women. In order to change their status, say these radical feminists, women must be able to control their own sexuality and not allow themselves to be mere sex objects. Of course a radical feminist would never join the Navy!

Need to sit with it. A totally different perspective from my own moderate feminist view!

TF

One day later from Dad

29 December 1972, San Diego, CA

Dear Tucker,

Your mother and I talked a lot about your Christmas Eve letter. It was so like you. We read about your concerns over our Vietnam policy, your happiness over Zumwalt's efforts, your frustration over what you give up by being in the military, a great deal about national politics, and not one word about Christmas!

We found that surprising at first; then, after our discussion, agreed that your mind has always been a mind occupied by political ideas and events. We read your letter as saying you were thinking about us on this Holiday and wanted to share the things closest to you. There's a nice feeling in that.

From our Christmas phone call, I know you were with friends and had a Happy Christmas Day. It sounded as though they stopped all the strategic thinking at the College for a little while, and gave thanks for Him who was born to suffer for our sinfulness.

I understand your confusion over the Vietnam policy. The entire country is confused. Of course those in the military have sworn to support the decisions of our elected policy makers, but I'm sure many on active duty wonder just why we're there. I thought you handled yourself well at the meeting of the R.I. Women's Political Caucus policy planning group. (Boy! That's a mouthful.) Certainly you cannot sign a policy which disagrees with an action you've sworn to uphold, but I wondered why you resigned. Seemed overkill to me. Stay with them. Maybe you can influence the thinking, or at least the understanding.

From what you've written and told us, you're pretty high on Admiral Zumwalt as the CNO. A lot of retired military in San Diego and those I talk to on active duty worry about his chain-of-command problems. These "Z-Grams" seem to go right through the organization without input from the various layers of authority which must implement them. In my day that was a fairly certain way to ask for trouble. Hopefully he knows what he's doing.

Sometimes, Tucker, I think you write these things to test me, to see if I've softened up. I have to call 'em as I have lived 'em, and I'm pretty sure the law of "loyalty down begets loyalty up" hasn't been repealed.

Anyway, these thoughts seem so far removed from Christmas. Maybe it's just that I remember the Christmases I've spent far away from you and your mother, as you are having to do this year, and I know that what was important was not what our next war patrol orders would be, but rather my family's safety and security. Or, maybe now at my age, that's only what I think I thought about then, when in reality my mind was engaged in the immediacy of my surroundings. Oh well. What I remember now is what's important, and it has precious little to do with war and Naval organization at this time of year.

Your Mother and I send our love and best wishes for a Blessed New Year.

Devotedly,

Dad

Four days later from Tucker

2 January 1973, Newport, R.I.

Dear Mother and Dad,

My Temporary Additional Orders to Washington came through yesterday. I leave tomorrow for a 30-day tour in the Bureau to participate in the Secretary of the Navy's Study regarding "unisexing the laws." Except for two women line officers, all Study Group members are legal beagles. The Chair is none other than the Judge Advocate General. This group's a follow-up to the Z-Gram in August in which Admiral Zumwalt promised to conduct a study regarding equal treatment and opportunities for women.

I'm honored and excited to be asked. Captain John Lindsey, head of the group, is a pal from my ensign days. Very sharp. I probably won't have much time to write, so will call every week or so to keep you posted. I'll be staying in a studio in River House off Shirley Highway just over the Potomac as you head from D.C. into Virginia. Hope to car pool with someone.

The College is allowing me to take off for a month. Fortunately I team-teach in both my International Relations and Organizational Development courses.

Glad you're enjoying retirement. San Diego sounds ideal for you.

All for now. Love,

Tucker

One week later from Mother

10 January 1973, San Diego, CA

Dear Tucker,

Happy, Happy New Year and many Congratulations. Dad tells me that to be chosen for such an important study is quite a feather in your cap. From what you've told us when you were home, they chose the right person. Hope you can negotiate the many decisions that must be made without getting too upset at those who disagree with you.

Washington's magnificent during the Holidays. It can be bitterly cold in January, so I hope your studio apartment has good heat. Dress warmly. I probably sound like a nagging mother, and you have every right to say to yourself, "Wonder how she thinks I get along when she's not advising me?" Mothers think about these sorts of things.

If you get too chilly, try to think of some way to research part of your study in San Diego. How nice it would be to see you. Do take good care of yourself. You tend to be awfully hard on yourself. Remember, there are others in the Study Group!

All my love,

Mother

Four days later from Tucker's journal

14 January 1973, Washington, D.C.

 For the record,

Almost halfway through the work, and I'm totally exhausted. Long, long hours because the task is too large for the time committed. Fortunately the group works well together, with tasks assigned efficiently. We're ploughing through the laws (Titles 10 and 37) and of course discovering numerous statutory inequities to women in the naval services (both Navy and Marine Corps). The inequities for enlisted women are minimal. They compete directly for promotion with men. Even though, as with women officers, they do not serve at sea, they fare well in promotion.

The lawyers in the Group have their legalistic view, favoring "justice" and "equality," and that's fine. My role, along with Sue Callahan's (ad hoc from the Bureau) is to represent the views of women line officers. Having intensively studied policy options for women line officers, I see this SecNav study as an ideal vehicle for making real changes for women's promotion paths. At the same time, many traditional forces are less apt to recommend major change. Most of the senior officers (men and women) aren't ready to move to an egalitarian philosophical base, where women have the same opportunities as men. A knotty problem! The RC (resistance to change) factor's strong. Not to be resolved in thirty days. Maybe not even thirty months or thirty years!

Women as a gender *are* different from men. Should they therefore have a separate promotion category — open to men as well, but mostly including women — a category that recognizes Navy women who offer tremendous talent by serving as specialists in fields such as management, personnel administration, education and training, recruiting, and communications? This option assumes that some officers, men and women, will be "dry" (never go to sea).

Have written a policy paper so that the Group can argue the various options for use of women, if (1) Article 6015 of Title 10 is repealed (which we will recommend) and (2) women are fully integrated into male officer communities. The current Article 6015 lets the Navy deny women sea duty. The majority of the group believes in strict equality, which would mean that someday women officer candidates wouldn't be offered a career pattern that allows them to stay "dry." As lawyers, they take the meaning of equality seriously. I've tried to stay neutral and can argue either the Egalitarian or Neo-traditionalist's assumptions. I lean toward supporting the policy option which allows for a majority of women officers to be "dry." Let the majority stay dry!

Lt. Cdr. Sue Callahan, our Bureau rep, and other Bureau women officers appear unwilling to share their views on the above. A we/they attitude lurks in the room. This annoys me because we need their viewpoints to complete our task. Damn politics! We're all in the same bloody Navy, for god's sake! My War College Study, which discusses these options, has been available in BuPers for over a year and has been briefed at the Pentagon. Ah, well. Too many complex issues for the average bear to handle, I suppose.

Haven't been this tired in awhile. Must get more rest. This continuous, 12–14 hour grind is wearing me down. I'm only 36 and I feel 50, however that feels.

TF

Four days later from Billie

18 January 1973, JAX

Dear Tuck,

Good to talk last night and catch up. Sounds like you've been working through a lot of "stuff." I promised you more details on me, so here it is:

What a hectic time since I saw you in Germany last June! I'm amazed at how fast the Navy can move when they need something done NOW! Here I am, at Naval Air Station, Jacksonville, putting the finishing touches on an old WWII building which will serve as the POW Homecoming Center for approximately 33 POWs from the infamous Hanoi Hilton.

The Center, if I do say so, has been transformed into a nice reception area. At one end is the Press Room — desks, banks of telephones, and word processors. The press, both TV and newspaper, as ugly and disgusting as they have been, are now acting like decent people and are helpful and supportive. There's an open reception area, a private and nicely decorated lounge for family members to gather, and private interview rooms. Upstairs is another private lounge and a couple of "debriefing" rooms where DIA, CIA and others will talk to the returning men. There's a supply room containing refrigerators with soft drinks, beer, snack food, sandwich makings, plus the usual coffee mess and a popcorn popper. There's a second coffee mess upstairs, and yet a third in the press room. All of these things are to make the former POWs and their families as comfortable as possible.

Since my arrival in October, almost every moment has been devoted to this project. We work weekends as well. The overall Project Officer is Colonel Gerald Curtis, USA, from AsstSecDef for Public Affairs. I'm the OinC of the Homecoming Center, but both of our duties have been enhanced several times by SecDef. Colonel Curtis has taken over as the senior CACO (Casualty Assistance Calls Officer, have you ever been one? Probably not.) from the XO of the Air Station, and I've been assigned as his assistant. We've had several interviews with each of the families and other relatives who want to be a part of the homecoming. Someday I'll relate the horrendous emotional roller coaster these families have endured, and that Colonel Curtis and I are absorbing as we meet regularly to brief these families. Some stories are indescribable.

We are, nonetheless, ready to receive the POWs. Yesterday I purchased the Red Carpet to be put in place at the airfield, and the stand for both the still and TV cameras was finished this morning. Work is still in progress in the Navy Lodge and an older BOQ to provide on-base apartments for families. Most of the families want that. Somehow, Colonel Curtis and I are in charge of this renovation also. The intelligence guys are installing special flooring and ceiling tile to soundproof the debriefing rooms. They also have a truck outside bristling with electronic arrays to instantly transmit important information.

Next week everyone will be in place to practice the greeting procedure at the airfield. A MedEVAC will land, the proper people will be there as greeters, including the Jacksonville mayor. A couple of high school bands and the local Navy band will play. A Marine Corps drill team will line up on each side of the Red Carpet, the PA system will be tested. The whole nine yards, as they say. The hospital is primed and ready, the O' Club and main BOQ are spruced, painted, and ready, the Navy Exchange Restaurant has hired special caterers.

The population of Jacksonville and the communities surrounding the Naval Air Station are pouring out their hearts with offers of money, apartments, condos, beach houses, cars, limos, entertainment, food. Everything! My phone never stops ringing! DOD hasn't made a decision on whether to accept these offers yet. So I keep making lists —

Rumor has it that Secretary Kissinger will sign the Peace Accord maybe this month or next, and we can have our POWs back soon after. DOD wants to keep the reception centers open for six to ten months after the return to ensure a proper re-entry for the POWs. Right before Christmas I finally found an apartment to rent. Most of the boxes are sitting in the second bedroom unopened. Haven't had time to get to them. I haven't even set up my stereo.

Well, Tuck, it's a good thing we had a fantastic time in Europe because I think I'm stuck here for awhile. The weather is warm, a thunderstorm with rain arrives every afternoon at 1630. The NAS JAX people call it the "Civil Service Special" as everyone dashes to their cars. Speaking of cars, I bought a brand new Chevy Caprice convertible — a present to *me*. Cherry red with a white top!

I only hear or see sporadic newscasts. What's this Watergate thing? Don't let the politics get you down. Keep fighting for our equality!

Your friend,

Billie

One day later from Tucker's journal

19 January, 1973, Washington, D.C.

 For the record,

The pot's boiling over and the worms are sidling out of the bucket! John Lindsey sent a copy of our Group's policy paper to the Bureau Admiral for comment. The we/they posture is stronger than ever. Our Group's marching orders were to develop a legislative package that removes statutory inequities toward women. We *have* to address which promotion paths the existing line women should follow from a legislative viewpoint.

But the Admiral in response fired off one of his Silver Bullet Memos to his people and convened another Working Group to discuss our policy paper. He sees problems with career paths that are totally neutral for men and women, as our Group is suggesting. So do I. Yet, strictly from an equal treatment position, women shouldn't be allowed a "dry only" path if it's not also offered to men. Where's the solution? Maybe we're all too close to the issues, with vested interests and attitudes clouding any real solution at this time? I still feel that women are different but can be treated as equals.

TF

Eleven days later from Tucker

30 January 1973, Washington, D.C.

Dear Robyn,

I've had it with the Navy. We're in our last week with this Study Group and I'm wiped out. Let me relate what happened this afternoon and get it off my chest:

Captain Elizabeth Hastings, who detailed me to recruiting duty and whom I've always admired, now works in Plans and Policy in the Bureau of Naval Personnel. This morning she called the Study Group and asked that I come to her office. I had no idea what she wanted. I soon found out a few hours later. As she greeted me, I sensed hostility. Her cheeks were flushed, she seemed distinctly closed off to me. Then she blew:

"Lieutenant Commander Fairfield, just who do you and your Group think you are? What gives *you* the right to recommend that women officers will no longer be able to stay dry? Why are you delving into areas that are of no concern to your group?"

Surprised and stunned by this attack, I tried to gather myself together. I felt tears welling up inside. Stop that, Fairfield, you need your senses about you.

"Captain, I assume you've read the Group's policy paper that the Admiral shot out as Silver Bullet #7." She nodded, looking angrier than ever.

I continued. "A key question within the Group is — if Article 6015 is repealed, and if women are allowed to go to sea — what's the best route to afford women officers equal opportunity?"

"Tucker, your group is supposed to recommend a legislative package and not get into the workings of promotion categories and the like. You're way off the target. Why didn't you stick to the basics and not fiddle with the officer promotion structures? Women officers, long before you, my dear, have worked hard to be integrated into the Navy and carry the unrestricted line designator. You're trying to upset a system that's been beneficial to us as women. Why?"

"Captain, the group has thoroughly reviewed all the policy options for promotion categories, as best we can, and we're recommending an egalitarian system and philosophical base, with women serving in categories open to men, including the warfare specialties." The Captain seemed disturbed.

I continued. "Another, what I consider appealing option, would've opened up a dry category, or designator, for both men and women. But we were informed that your offices were against it."

"Yes, that's right. Tucker, why not leave things as they are, with line women filling important billets ashore, but with no sea duty requirements?"

"Because, Captain, that's not in the spirit of equality and this group's tasking is all about *equality*. Women are different. I agree. But that shouldn't allow 'dry' women to compete in the same promotion category as men who are required to go to sea, which is where we're headed if we remain in the unrestricted line designator."

It was clear from her stance, and my ramblings, that we weren't communicating. We both wanted to do right by Navy women, but we were approaching the issue from different perspectives.

"Tucker, I think you and the Study Group absolutely will have done a real disservice to women if you stay on the course you describe. I'm very disappointed in your performance, and feel thwarted by your little group."

Tears streamed down my cheeks. I was embarrassed. The Captain had taught at WOCS, and set forth the same rules that Lieutenant Winters had taught me. And, she was likely thinking I was "too emotional," whatever that means.

"I'm sorry, Captain, I've done the best I can and so have all the Group's members. I imagine you'll have an opportunity to comment on our Study and can recommend a less radical option. Too bad equality equals radical, isn't it?"

"Thank you, Tucker. Good luck back in Newport." We shook hands and that was that.

As I reflect on the scene, I realize I'd walked into Captain Hasting's office with a totally dysfunctional mind and body. My Aunt Fran, my most favorite aunt, had died unexpectedly yesterday, and I was still in shock. You remember how much I loved and admired her. She'd been ill with breast cancer and thyroid problems, but she was only 62. She loved life. Her wit, her laughter. Gone forever.

Also, I'm physically exhausted from the month here. And, last, I'm totally frustrated that Captain Hastings, Big Daddy Navy, our society, can't find a way to deal with women and equality. We are different. We do need sometimes to have different career paths, without being unfair to men. The Navy's caught in a web of old comfortable patterns — for women, for blacks, for all minorities! The outside is knocking and the Navy says, "Okay, we'll work the problem and create new policy." But then it seems bewildered as to how to fix the situation.

Robyn, I'll somehow come back from this. But for now I needed to get this on paper and write my faithful, loving friend.

Any thoughts on the above? I'll be back in a few days and take you out on the town if Ned will babysit.

Love,

Tucker

PART TWO

1973 – 1980

Chapter Eight

The Awakening

One week later from Tucker's journal

5 February 1973, Newport, R.I.

For the record,

Good to be home again and sleeping in my own bed.

I made another discovery flying in from D.C. What else is new? Maybe the droning of the engines prompts these revelations. Who knows?

Anyway, here it is: We in our military subculture run around with our blinders tightly fastened, afraid to look at the larger culture. We're like race horses, racing to win — to command. The horse's owner fears what might happen if the horse takes its blinders off and looks around. He might panic and lose the race. Military personnel who peer at the outside and notice what's actually going on around them terrify the Navy. After all, these observant individuals might panic, or worse, confront the system from within.

As an intellectual, I take off my blinders more often than the Navy likes. I see options for women. I'm finally noticing discrimination against all minorities. To send so many minorities off to Vietnam must've been an unconscious decision. The blinders were firmly fixed. Recruiters only cared about winning the war with whomever we could recruit or draft. A war we couldn't win.

The blinders are also securely fastened on Navy women's eyes. They believe they're already integrated into the Navy. The Captains Hastings and St. Martin have bought into the myth of integration. It's so sad that they have no idea they're wearing blinders in the first place. Nor do they want to know. Without the blinders, what happens to their identity?

Despite the scariness, I need to remove the blinders, to open up and listen when someone tells me I'm being racist and sexist.

TF

Two days later from Robyn

February 7, 1973, Bar Harbor, Maine

Dear Tucker,

You are *so* devoted to your ideals, and so persistent! Or is it just plain stubborn? I'm once again floored by how conscientiously the forward-looking, flexible, adaptable (ha!) Navy resists change. Actually, as a result of this latest collision with your superior (in rank only), Captain Hastings, a rather splendid comparison springs to mind:

Do you remember studying Plato a thousand years ago in Philosophy 101? Specifically, his Allegory of the Cave and its misguided denizens? Just in case Plato hasn't been at the forefront of your mind, let me refresh your memory. A bunch of people have been held prisoner in a cave since birth. They're not only prisoners; they're forcibly situated so they can only face forward. A light source (fire) behind them illuminates a number of figures passing before it. These figures emit noises and cast shadows on the wall in front of the prisoners. The prisoners, having no other source of sensory input, create their reality based on this shadowy illusion.

At one point, someone's released, turns around, and experiences the non-shadow-based reality. Plato says it would be difficult, if not impossible, for such a person to adapt to or accept the newly discovered situation. To remain in the familiar environment of shadowy illusion is more secure and comfortable.

Is there a parallel here? Or am I once again being unduly harsh? Maybe you should obtain a copy of the allegory and send it along to Captain Twinkletoes Hastings!

One of your remarks in your January 30th letter I especially liked: "Too bad equality equals radical, isn't it?" The turkey never even responded. I heard her crying, "No, no!" all over the place, but never heard why. Further, she never addressed the issue of equality. I see her as analogous to those benighted souls in Plato's cave...

Maybe the fire should be lit *under* her, and some of your other resistant officer-types, instead of behind them.

Yes! Take me out on the town. Ned will definitely babysit!

Love,

Robyn

Three days later from Tucker's journal

10 February 1973, Newport, R.I.

For the record,

My God, between me and the blinders, and Robyn and Plato's Cave, I think I've got it! It's too damn uncomfortable for the military to change its ways unless a fire is lit under the leadership. Years and years of military training and practice prevent change. Change occurs only by ripping off the blue and gold blinders, by edict if necessary, and by an intricate combination of civilian officials and activist citizenry. We've got a ways to go to reach true integration of women and minorities in the Navy. Not likely on my watch. Admiral Z., nonetheless, has climbed out of the cave, away from the illusory shadows, and is now asking others to join him, uncomfortable though it may feel.

New subject: dating Sandy. He seems okay with our arrangement. Perhaps he's gay. As I think about it, if Tom had been the one who turned me down because he preferred men and I found out he was dating women…oh, boy! I feel pulled in many conflicting directions, trying to meet the expectations of my parents, society, and the Navy.

TF

P.S. I've been so committed to work, to the institution, that I neglected to note a special day for me and for America. On 27 January 1973 a Vietnam "cease fire" was signed. Hooray for peace, though peace for the Vietnamese people is a long way off. The war of attrition, the body counting, the stupidity of this limited war have ceased. We'd better damn well be sure next time that U.S. intervention is "in the national interest."

Ten days later from Tucker

20 February 1973, Newport, R.I.

Dear Mother and Dad,

This year is looking good! I'm in a great mood over Vietnam's resolution, Admiral Zumwalt's people policies (especially toward women) and my job and social life. What else do I need?

You know about the first two, so I'll address the others. In addition to the everyday duties of teaching International Relations at the Continuing Education Center, I'm developing a new Seapower correspondence course. My true interest, however, lies with the two courses I'm teaching to our full-time students. One is a basic Internat'l Rel. course; the other, a new course in Organizational Development (OD). Admirals Zumwalt and Howeland soon intend to implement the world's largest OD program. OD helps managers diagnose organizational problems and move towards practical, realistic solutions. The nifty part of teaching OD is that the Navy has hired professors from M.I.T.'s Sloan School of Management to train us as the facilitators/instructors. That I'm learning a lot about me as well as about OD is an understatement. More about this later.

In the social life arena, I see CDR Sandy Vanderhoff off and on. He and I have had fun times of late, mainly getting together with other War College Staff members and their spouses in their homes or at the Officers' Club. (Wonder if they still count the liquor bottles. Those were the days!)

Last night Sandy entertained a bunch of us in his small but charming carriage-house. In my opinion he's the most eligible bachelor around. As you'd expect, he has reddish blond hair, a fair complexion and an abundance of freckles. He's always cracking a joke or telling a fun story; he swings a mean tennis racquet and plays a pretty good ragtime piano. Last, but hardly least, he's a true naval officer professional. What else could a girl want?

As you can sense, I find him appealing on several levels. And I think he enjoys me too! So, don't give up on me yet!

I do envy you your San Diego weather. Sounds divine right now, for it's been a cold, bitter winter in Newport and last week I was down with a bad case of pleurisy. Thought I was having a heart attack! But I won't have to march along the Base streets, piled high with snow, as I did at WOCS. By the way, they're planning to integrate the men and women's OCS. Should be challenging. I'm all for it. Now the Naval Academy will be a harder nut to crack!

Glad you joined the Yacht Club, Dad. Bet you're having a ball racing your boat in the Bay. Great to have year-round sailing there, unlike Newport and Norfolk.

Must close for now. Take care of yourselves.

Love,

Tucker

Five days later from Tucker

25 February 1973, Newport, R.I.

Dear Robyn,

That was quite the philosophical letter, my zoological friend. Your analogy hit the target for me and my Navy predicament. Here's what happened yesterday:

Some M.I.T. professors from your former Big City began the training in a course on Organizational Development, one I'm teaching at the College. Both faculty and students participated in a training exercise which centered on how organizational decisions get made. Except for yours truly, all were senior male officers (commanders and captains). We divided into small groups and were assigned roles within a make-believe company, the Johnson Wicket Company.

Each trainee played a make-believe management role (President, VP, Marketing Director, Production Director). I was VP in my little group. Within our group we had fiery discussions about how to improve the company's profit profile, our specific problem at hand. As you might surmise, your Navy and mine doesn't focus on profit, but we do spend a lot of energy on mission effectiveness. Same difference for the exercise's purposes.

I was so involved with content analysis and problem solving in the group discussions I didn't dwell much on the sense that I was overruled and overlooked by my group. After all, I had positional power. Then came the report-outs in the large group, the sharing of our small group deliberations. Lots of good learning about group dynamics and interpersonal communications.

After the report-outs, the professors, acting as consultants, gave the group their group process comments. When Dave, the lead consultant, said he perceived that, "Lt. Commander Fairfield was considered a non-person in her small group," my heart sank. Dave continued, saying that while I, as Executive Vice-President, had provided excellent input to the four-striper who was President of the Wicket Company, I was never heard by him or the rest of the group.

He said, "Whether it's Tucker's junior rank or her female gender, her comments were completely negated. We call that the 'non-person syndrome.'" The guys shrugged off most of this group process analysis, adding that they thought they'd listened to me.

Down deep I knew Dave was right on. Within a group of senior male officers, no matter how sharp and incisive I might be, because of my gender I'm a non-person, unless a more senior male officer has directed them to pay attention to me. Relatedly, women have been in the NavWarCol student body for several years, but speakers and staff *continually* address the student audience as "Gentlemen." It's as if we're not there...non-persons. Women have been and will always be non-persons among senior men, until we either are more senior in rank or agree to transsexual operations!

Robyn, I learned more about myths and illusions than about decision-making in this exercise. Must be serendipity that you'd dredged up dear Plato and his Cave Allegory. Those men in the OD course, along with many of the mock questionnaire's potential respondents, buy in to the myth that women don't have much to say in the work environment. I've listened to Navy men say they view us as mothers, sisters, lovers, wives or friends, but not as co-workers. The Wicket exercise epitomizes this narrow view of our gender. For my part, the illusion I maintain, for the sake of my own sanity and ego strength, is that I'm not a lesser voice than what I want or expect to be.

Carol Simpson, my sociology prof friend, says we women must create a "critical mass" to bring about this change. Currently we have about 10,000 Navy women in the force. That ain't a critical mass!

Other than dealing with being a non-person, my life's going well. Am having fun dating Sandy. His outward sex appeal scares me some, but I'm having fun, going to student parties. Yet I still can't seem to feel...you know...and can't believe I ever will. If I turned down Tom, how could I ever say yes to anyone else?

Will keep you posted. How's the family? Be good to yourself, my friend.

Love,

Tucker, the non-person

P.S. By the way, today is my PEBD. You probably don't remember. That's my "Pay Entry Base Date," the day I raised my right hand and swore to defend the Constitution against all enemies, foreign and domestic. Can you believe that was thirteen years ago! And that you and I are thirty-six?

One week later from Dad

3 March 1973, San Diego, CA

Dear Tucker,

What an upbeat letter was yours of 20 February. Looks like "God's in His heaven; All's right with the world." Was that Browning? Certainly sums up your letter.

Your mother and I assume those in Washington are still reacting to your work and others' regarding Navy women and to Zumwalt's initiatives. You know reactions to policy changes for women will not be unanimous. Perhaps the majority cannot see beyond the military as a "man's world." I like to tell myself that I can, but I think part of my feeling is caused by knowing that you have such capability. If you really decide to do something, people who get in your way run a risk of being run over. I haven't decided whether or not that's good or bad in the ultimate sense, but I do know that your presence can be very influential.

Too serious a way to respond to your happy letter! The courses you're teaching sound interesting. I have to tell you that when you wrote that the Navy intended to implement "the world's largest OD program" it occurred to me that it had been doing that for years. OD to me means "Officer of the Deck." It will always mean that, regardless of other uses for the letters. It would take a long time before I could think of those letters to mean "Organizational Development."

Times do change, don't they? How many of the professors you mentioned have had combat experience? Seems to me organizational development of anything military must start with the military's purpose: to prepare for war.

I'm glad your life is not all work. The young man you mentioned sounds as though he would be good company. Let us know if this gets serious. Your mother tossed that in when I told her I was writing you.

You're right about the sailing. I can leave the house, walk to the Yacht Club and be on the Bay in half an hour. There are several regular races around the buoys and on Wednesdays we have what's called the "Beer Can Race." You set out in your boat in the late afternoon from any Yacht Club on the Bay and race whomever is nearby and might be competitive. After a certain time, usually a half an hour, a gun sounds and you turn around and head home. The beer's optional as is the water balloon fighting which is a big factor on warmer days. The first one to get home wins. It's a race to nowhere and the club usually has a festive cook-out upon return.

San Diego is a great place for small-boat sailing, and I'm even getting your mother to go with me occasionally. What a life! Glad we're both enjoying it. Your mother sends all her love.

Devotedly,

Dad

Same day from Robyn

March 3, 1973, Bar Harbor, Maine

Hi Tucker, The Very Much Indeed — irrespective of a handful of supercilious white male nudnicks — REAL PERSON —

Man! Er, poor choice of words. You're so mild about the incident you describe. Maybe you're distancing. You politely analyze the attitudes and reactions of your peers and seniors who, apparently by virtue of Y chromosome ownership, have not only the permission but the right to relegate you to the status of a zero!

Tucker, it's not okay! It's also amazing that neither you nor the fellows in your mock company were aware of this denigrating process until the outside observer, a civilian I think you call him, pointed it out! That's what's *really* scary; and that lack of awareness explains in part how the military setup can indefinitely perpetuate itself. Apparently no one even recognizes the more subtle, or not so subtle, forms of disempowerment. Or, if they do, the disempowered — women and minorities especially — maintain the illusion that they're not lesser voices!

Tucker, listen to yourself! I know you're not into taking anything lying down or passively. But why is the narrow view of the female gender acceptable in this case? You've spent your naval life fighting this kind of discrimination. I don't believe you, or any of us in a larger sense, must live with this unsatisfactory illusion. Plato's Cave be damned!

And finally, congratulations, I guess, on your PEBD. Defending the Constitution against all enemies, eh? Define enemies. Might it be your bedfellow, Big Daddy Navy?

On a happier note. I'm glad you're having a good time with Sandy, but remember you don't have to do what your parents and others want. Be true to yourself. Do keep me posted.

Till soon, love,

Robyn

P.S. Elizabeth is getting her fangs much sooner than Derry did. She's drooling and gnawing and fussing and whining piteously. Gum massage is only soothing for so long. And besides it's hazardous duty!

Ten weeks later from Tucker

20 May 1973, Newport, R.I.

Dear Robyn,

Good to talk with you last week. I know you'll enjoy Williamsburg. I'm not sure that's going to be a vacation with Derry and Elizabeth along.

Have had another "heavy experience," so need to get your wise thoughts on same. Subject: motivation. The Organ. Dev. course stretches my boundaries, as you would say. The class' homework included writing stories using sets of pictures. Sort of Rorhschachy (sp?). The lesson's thrust was Motivation. According to the training, understanding one's self comes before understanding others. The leader must first learn what makes him or her tick before working with subordinates and seniors.

Psychologist David McClelland believes that the stories we write while looking at pictures of everyday scenes can measure three fundamental needs or drives. According to his theory of Thematic Apperception, a person's motivation is determined by Power, Achievement and Affiliation (Relationship).

Robyn, I essentially flunked the test, at least in my own eyes! I say this because my Relationship needs are so low that they're at the bottom of the lowest category on the statistical chart. What does this mean? Either my Relationship needs are being satisfied, or, I override them in favor of the other two drives, Power and Achievement. During the exercise we shared our stories' results in pairs. I shared with Commander Bob Billings, the officer who took the D.C. Race Relations workshop with me and to whom I feel close. He's a submariner and a warm, fuzzy-bear-type person.

Our story telling results were mind-boggling for Bob, too, who sees himself as a family man. Yet over the years riding the Navy's fast track, he's had tremendous work commitments. Our individual results suggest we both are hurting inside because of Relationship needs.

"Tucker," he said, "I can't continue to work such long hours and be deployed so much, away from my Catherine (his wife) and the children. It's killing my marriage and ruining my health. No wonder I have ulcers and Catherine has a heart condition caused by stress. We're too young for serious health problems."

Bob's jaw, indeed his entire body, quivered.

I tried to console him. "If you focus on Power and Achievement as high needs," I said, "the Navy hooks you, satisfying through rewards of top jobs and major responsibilities. It's not all bad. Look at the great billets we've both experienced." I was trying to ease Bob's pain, and mine too.

"I've been selected for captain, Tucker. I don't care if I don't make admiral. I need more Relationship in my life. And less Relationship with the GD Navy. Or a dumb ship, or shipmates. To be with Catherine and the children. That's what I think I want anyway. I don't know. "

I shared with Bob my astonishment that my stories barely depicted Relationship needs. What I didn't say was how conflicted I'd been in recent years on several relationship levels. First, who am I as a sexual being? If I'm a lesbian, and I think I am, how can I stay in the military, which denies its personnel this right, this path. And, second, why do I give so much of Self to an organization that won't put me on its first team? Yes, I love the Navy, but I love myself more.

Similar to Bob, my career "successes" have placed me in a position which fosters high Power and Achievement needs. When I'm a single, middle-aged retiree, however, will I regret striving for captain and admiral, having sacrificed Relationship along the way? Answer: Yes. I need to reassess career. I don't have a Catherine and children. I do have myself. My self would like a personal relationship someday. Maybe I can't reach my primary goal, to be the best naval officer that I can be. I'll have to be the best *person* I can be.

How's that for psychology 101?

Back to the stories. The individual must be the ultimate interpreter of the data. What did I see? Right now, my Power and Achievement needs are overwhelming my Relationship need/motive. Way, way down deep, within my psyche, within me, myself, and my shadow, I know that to so completely meet my Power/Achievement needs will no longer be truly fulfilling. Relatedly, women captains, as a statistic, have more than their share of major health problems.

I feel a shift, Robyn. Not out of the Navy, for I have too much time invested and I need to take care of my financial needs. Nonetheless, I'm going to worry less about the Navy's needs and more about my needs and others' needs — others such as blacks, other minorities, and my subordinates. While it's increased since

OCS days, my empathy quotient is way below average. And that's probably above average for a naval officer!

This new direction may cost me promotion, but I doubt it. My record and reputation stand high.

Funny, I seem to have lived out the passage of what the women's movement proposes. Movement leaders say women need to go out into the world, not always staying at home and tending the hearth. I've done that, and look where I am! A certain emptiness can build up when serving the needs of an organization. The key is balancing organizational needs with the needs and mysterious, meandering ways of the self (or soul). What do you think?

Do we tend to the philosophical and psychological, or not?!

Let's get together before I leave Newport. Am due for orders any moment.

> Love,
>
> Tucker

Two weeks later from Robyn

June 3, 1973, Bar Harbor, Maine

Wow Tucker —

A real triumph! Not so much in the exercise's results, but in the fact that those results forced you to take a hard look at yourself. I think this is an important juncture, Tucker. To some extent it happens to all of us at one time or another, and when it does, most of us take a look at ourselves and, like you, have an Ah-ha! experience.

As with your non-person experience a few months ago, it took someone on the outside, an objective observer, to provide the Ah-ha! perspective. We tend to get caught up in the minutiae of our daily lives, ambitions, needs, wants and lose the *gestalt* of what we're about and what our priorities really are.

If we don't get jostled, all of a sudden we wake up at age 90 and wonder, "Whoops!, have I missed something?" Especially in the military, where trudging mindlessly, but obediently, down the expected avenues is the easiest path to take. Indeed, not only the easiest, but the appropriate and dutiful course to follow. Whatever you decide to do at least *now* you're coming from a more aware place.

Whew! That was a heady one! Maybe that old Navy of yours isn't so bad after all; it keeps plugging away at you, making you constantly consider and reconsider. That doesn't happen as much to us more diaphanous beings lacking Big Daddy Navy's watchful eye!

I think whatever power and achievement needs you have help you guard against relationships. You're trying to sort out who you are and with whom you want what kinds of relationships. Such caution would naturally be reflected in your test results. So, it seems to me that it's not so much that you're not into relationships. Rather, at this point in your life you're wary. This brings us full circle to, now that you have awareness, you have choices. You can decide, "Fine, I like it like this. Or, I can make some changes or compromises in lifestyle, priorities, or whatever."

A note: Tucker, do be cautious about the popular psychology tests you've been exposed to. Take them at face value and verify with other criteria. Certainly don't change your life based on results of a few tests!

AAARGH! ENOUGH!! Probably your next letter to me will be on the order of, "Dear Robyn. The End. Love, Tucker," in order to minimalize the possibility of another meandering dissertation!

You're going through a lot, Tucker. Hang in there. We *are* getting old.

I just registered Derry for kindergarten next fall! Can you believe it?

Love,

Robyn

P.S. Bet you cheered about the recent Supreme Court ruling that women in the armed forces are entitled to the same benefits as those accorded male servicemen. Progress!

One day later from Tucker

4 June 1973, Newport, R.I.

Dear Billie,

I'm ticked!

Had a short conversation with Admiral Howeland today. He's thrilled with the progress for us Navy women and said we'll be integrating the Women Officers' School with the males' OCS by this fall. Can you believe that? It'll be very different, won't it? Normal and mostly right. Hope the physical training won't be too rigorous for the women. We'll need to develop some reasonable differences between men and women's criteria for physical stuff.

Admiral Howeland said resistance to having women at the military academies remains high. I told him that I'd listened to my dad many a time tell me women don't belong at his *alma mater*. I can understand that attitude. Men don't belong at my *alma mater*, but, it's not federally funded! At least we have a pilot program for women in the NROTC program.

Admiral Howeland assured me that my study had been a tremendous help in developing a "POA&M" for Equal Opportunity for Women. (By the way, that was a new term to me. It stands for Plan of Action and Milestones. Are you familiar with that concept? You're more into Pentagonese than I.)

Then I surprised myself and told the Admiral what I thought about the new leadership manual called *The N-Man*, which will be used in our Organizational Development program. Essentially it's a way of teaching the various styles of leadership, with the alleged "N-Man" integrating both men and mission and balancing the two as appropriate. My complaint to the Admiral, "How come you're calling this *The N-Man*? The title assumes women don't exist in 'this man's Navy' and I strongly object. Aren't we embarked on a program that includes women?"

"Tucker, you don't realize that the women's program will be implemented slowly. Furthermore, Admiral Z.'s Human Resource Management Program will focus on the Fleet. We don't have any women at sea and we won't for sometime. Be patient, Tucker."

I bit my tongue and held back angry words. When are we going to have N-People? We have a long, long road to trek, Billie.

Haven't talked with you since March. How's the POW Center? And how are you? I worry that now that we have no WAVES and no Director of the WAVES, we women will lose ourselves and our identity in the vast organization of the United States Navy. We're going in the opposite direction of civilian organizations that are instituting affirmative action programs for women. Does this bother you at all? The blunt fact — we're not integrated and probably won't be for years. It'll be long after we're retired and are rocking in our porch chairs and sipping those daiquiries you blend so well. What fun we had in Norfolk on those weekends at the beach.

Take care my friend and don't forget to play.

Love,

Tucker

Two weeks later from Billie

20 June 1973, JAX

Dear Tuck —

The Homecoming Center is getting raves for its handling of the former POWs' reception. My staff has been outstanding. Most of the returnees are on long leaves, a few remain in order to be more comfortable with their reentry. Colonel Curtis has returned to DOD and we confer daily by autovon. He's very professional. We have some excellent leaders in our Armed Services!

You're right, Tuck, this integration thing for women is going to be a long haul. It's societal. Our male leaders are comfortable with the way society views women, and so are many of our senior female leaders. It will change. Slowly. Yes, we'll be rocking on the porch before full integration comes to pass.

I'll be leaving here in December for leave and then to the Pentagon as the Community Relations Department Head for CHINFO. Now that I've had time to look around, this area of Florida is nice. Fernandina Beach, Amelia Island, and St. Augustine have beautiful beaches. The new Disneyworld near Orlando has been a big hit with the POWs and their families. And me too.

When are you going on one of your TAD trips to D.C.? I'll be back in my house by mid-January '74.

Your friend,

Billie

Four months later from Tucker's journal

1 October 1973, Newport, R.I.

For the record,

Am in the throes of packing up, one more time. Living in one town for more than four years has been special and unusual for me and for a Navy tour. Hope I can stay in San Diego four years.

I don't think the extra year has hurt my career, but who knows? At this point, am more concerned about competing with men for my next rank. The new law requires that line women compete with the men for promotion. A new twist. Subtle prejudice and bias against women already exist within our officer evaluation system and I worry about direct competition. Men have had difficulty accepting us as equals. They'll have great difficulty comparing

women with no sea duty experience against men. My departing
fitness report, for instance, reflects this problem. No way can I
compete with the male officer who's been a destroyer exec.

Never mind, Fairfield, your new life course is to deemphasize
Power and Achievement and more prominently feature Affiliation.

It's exciting to think that women officers' career paths will now
include commanding officer! My record surely will get me to
commander, but will it get me to command? My pals in D.C. say
everybody's fitreps are super inflated. Maybe mine won't stand up??
Can't worry a lot about that, though my competitive nature wants
to test myself in command. Hard to let go of the old high-
achievement pattern.

To be the best naval officer is no longer the best I can do and
be. Rather, I choose to be the best person, which means seeking a
more balanced course. Not easy. Turned down a top job at the
Pentagon for a Human Resource Management (HRM) billet in San
Diego. My detailer cautioned, "You're going directly against our
new career patterns for women officers. I should assign you as a
sub-specialist to an intelligence billet."

"I'll take my chances," I replied. "I'm weary of analytical work,
with minimum exposure to ordinary sailors and their problems. If I
screen for command, an HRM tour will be helpful. Besides I believe
in Zumwalt's HRM program. I get fired up about it!"

I didn't tell him about my quest to move away from power/
achievement. He wouldn't understand. I'm unsure I do yet, except
on an intuitive plane. Robyn's letter helped a lot. I'm at a crossroads,
with new feelings and directions.

TF

One week later from Tucker's journal

8 October 1973, Newport, R.I.

For the record,

Had an important dream last night: I was saying my goodbyes
at the College, when who should appear out of the mists but
Admiral Zumwalt. He said, "I have a special personal award for
you, Commander Fairfield, for your work that has helped to set
women on the right course in the Navy. I'm grateful to you." Then
the CNO placed a large purple and white medal on my chest and
smiled. "Thank you," he said.

Whereas I won't be receiving a medal for the Women's Study,
I've been awarded personal medals for work requiring much less

from me than the Study. The Navy's changing its policies for women reluctantly and no way would the institution give an award to someone for pushing the rivers about its women. Still have some achievement motivation, eh, Fairfield? Doesn't hurt to dream. Besides, you know the effort involved.

TF

Nine weeks later from Tucker

15 December 1973, Millington, Tennessee

Dear Robyn,

I'm completing schooling for my next tour in San Diego at the Human Resource Management School. Yesterday I finished the course's last assignment, "Operation Empathy," a day in Memphis during which we walked in others' moccasins. The operation was an honor and another peak experience!

The students drove to Memphis in pairs for an all-day experiment in the big city. My partner was "Mac" McDonald, one of my favorite chief petty officers in the class. Warm and fuzzy, yet tough when necessary. The event's purpose: for us to become more sensitive to others' concerns and feelings, especially those whom we wouldn't ordinarily meet. Mac and I decided we'd begin at the Memphis Zoo and then drive to the inner city, walk along the streets for awhile, and let the rest unfold.

I'd been to zoos many times, but yesterday for the first time I could put myself in the place of the animals. The big cats paced back and forth; the bears roared; the elephants stomped and chomped. All appeared sad and restless, wanting their freedom. While they were physically healthy, emotionally they were agitated. Man had caged them for man's sake. Mac experienced the same reaction.

After a few hours with the animals, we drove deep into the city. Reminded me of the last time I'd driven into an inner city and spoken at the all-black church in Philly. In both instances I was loath to stop and walk along the sidewalks. But Mac's a big man and I decided to get into the task, even though I felt uneasy. We were the only whites along the streets.

Soon it was lunch time and Mac said, "Let's find a restaurant."

"I don't know if I want to eat in an all-black place," I said. Mac talked me into it.

We found a restaurant which looked like a popular local spot. Only one table was available, with the rest occupied by blacks. I ordered carefully — a beer and a cheeseburger. Mac ordered the same. Robyn, I'll never forget the ill feeling that swept over me when I tried to eat the cheeseburger. I drank my beer, which seemed innocuous to me. I left hungry, not having related much to the people, though they seemed friendly and amused and surprised we'd chosen to eat with them. Unlike the zoo experience, I was the one who felt caged, trapped, alienated. To escape wasn't the goal of those with whom I'd supposedly empathized; it was my goal. I wonder, was my experience similar to how blacks feel sitting down in an all-white restaurant?

Mac and I drove around the city, seeking places to carry out our mission. After an hour or so, Mac said, "I think we should visit a gay bar." My immediate thought was, no! And then, why not? Here's a rare opportunity. To walk into a gay bar in San Diego would be risky. "I imagine it'll feel odd, Mac, but I'm game." We were both feeling adventurous, ready to continue our operation.

Mac seemed to know exactly where to find a gay bar. Funny, as I think about it. Hmmm. I walked into The Gray Fox with fear and wonderment. I'd never been in a gay bar, didn't know what to expect, and was relieved that Mac was accompanying me. Have you ever been in a gay bar, Robyn? This one was a spacious room, with tables for two, a small dance floor, and an elegant bar. We arrived around 5:00 p.m. and sat down at one of the tables. Though we were the only male-female couple in the place, none of the customers paid attention to us. They were mostly men, sitting at tables or dancing together to quiet music.

"It seems odd, but comfortable," I said. Mac nodded in agreement. For a straight, married sailor, he seemed completely at ease. The bar began to fill up with men in business suits, obviously stopping in on their way home from work. They looked happy and preoccupied with each other. Strangely, Robyn, they weren't any different from other men I know, except some were dancing with each other and that felt peculiar, even wrong. They were attractive, well-dressed, some downright appealing. They were uninterested in me, as a seemingly straight woman. They probably would've been uninterested if they saw me as a lesbian, given they paid no attention to the few women in the room. The women were also engrossed with each other.

As Mac and I became part of the scene and tried to fit into the shoes of these gay men and women, we both felt they were enjoying each other after a hard day's work. Smiling and at ease. We were the ones ill-at-ease, though, as I say, Mac seemed relaxed. I was anxious, but didn't feel trapped. Though this might have been an ideal time to tell Mac of my own sexual identity struggle, I never got the nerve...

Paranoia dominated my decision. Who knows whom he might tell, I thought. Yet we'd shared so much of ourselves this day and before, he probably would've understood and "empathized" as part of our experiment.

Mac and I discussed how to end our eventful day. "Let's visit 'a sleazy bar' and talk with the customers," he said.

"No, thanks," I responded, still wary. But I once again psyched myself up to live "in the moment."

After fortifying ourselves with appetizers from The Gray Fox, we said goodbye to our friendly waiter and took off to find a run-down bar. Didn't take long.

Sam's Bar, as you might envision, had pool tables and games and scruffy-looking men, sitting around drinking beer and hard liquor. I felt sick again. And trapped. Mac and I spoke with some of the customers. All I wanted was to go home. We left shortly. Those folks were definitely in their own cages (and cups!), but unlike the zoo animals, they seemed unaware of their surroundings. I could be wrong.

Later, I realized I feel trapped within, and in some way alienated from Mac, and, what's more, the institution he represents. I feel empathy and compassion for myself. It isn't self-pity. I realize I can never be fully me as long as I stay in an organization that damns gays and lesbians...compassion for others has prompted compassion for myself. Yet, despite a modicum of pain and sadness, I feel fortunate to be walking in my own shoes.

If we were truly a democratic, caring people, we would go beyond tolerance of others' differences and reach toward another level, acceptance. We would encourage integration and see each other as individuals, not as blacks, gays, women or alcoholics. We would be inclusive, not exclusive in our caring.

I'm sure you'll provide me some psychological constructs about all this. Maybe you and Ned might like to experiment with a similar operation.

Will write when I settle into the new job. In the meantime, I'm meeting Billie in the Great Smokies in two days. Am looking forward to some natural nature.

All for now. Here's to empathy!

Love,

Tucker

Two weeks later from Robyn

January 2, 1974, Bar Harbor, Maine

Well, Tucker,

How're you? I guess you're probably back from your trip with Billie by now and on your way to San Diego. I trust it was fun, though I doubt you did much camping at this time of year. Indeed, I wonder how you did, hating the cold weather as you do. Anyway, I hope it was a rewarding break.

We had a somewhat traumatic experience the other day. I have Elizabeth in a family day care situation, which has always been satisfactory. The woman (Deb) is pleasant, warm, and good with kids and there are only three in the group. A couple of days ago one of the kids split her lip and had to be taken to an ER. Deb engaged the services of a male neighbor to watch Elizabeth and the other toddler while she was gone. It turned out that the fellow had been the subject of multiple arrests for being a peeping tom and inappropriately touching children. Neither Deb nor I had known this, but one of the other mothers recognized him from newspaper articles. As far as we know, the kids were fine and Deb wasn't gone long. But the closeness of a potential horror story was very frightening. I think the young man is now out of the neighborhood because part of the terms of his parole was to have nothing to do with small children. Needless to say, Deb was also totally shaken up by the incident.

Again and again the Navy amazes me by offering potentially exciting personal growth workshops or courses. I've never really understood what kind of followup happens after the major presentation, either in terms of providing closure, or later when the participants venture out into the arena of Real Life. I'm impressed that someone thought it would be worthwhile to encourage an empathic attitude for you budding consultants. Do the head honchos indulge?

It seems these feelings of being trapped and sick reflect your struggles. You're caught in your cage of secrecy, where you cannot be yourself, cannot let people know who you really are, indeed it would be hazardous to your well-being to let that door open even the tiniest chink. This deception in turn causes the sick feelings. You feel trapped. By getting in touch empathically with others, some of your own issues have surfaced more clearly, more than you might have wanted! Aren't you glad you hit that workshop to identify all these upbeat responses?

Seriously, Tucker, you *are* going through a lot right now — personally, professionally, probably spiritually (should there be such a slot). I hope when you come through all this, you find whatever insights are required to live serenely. I also hope you have at least someone close by to share your thoughts with, as this heavy-duty kind of stuff can make a body feel not only down, but isolated and alienated.

You know, your life might have been less complicated had you elected to become an etymologist or a toll booth collector, or any of a number of other callings. Actually, it's not too late to change careers you know!

Till the next time,

     Love,

       Robyn

Three weeks later from Tom

20 Jan 1974, Washington, D.C.

Dear Tucker,

By now you must be in a new home in a new city in a new billet. Hope it's not too stressful for you. I've been thinking of you lately, so here's an update on my life. I suppose the Navy gossip vine has already wired you about my new duty station. Yes, I've finally arrived at our nation's biggest office building, though its 5-sides, 5-floors, and 5-rings seem to hide this fact. I believe it's attractively suited to its site on the Potomac across from the memorial monuments.

I wonder though if they're ever going to finish the Pentagon mixing bowl maze of roads and parking lots? I remember you saying you just learned one way to get here and then they changed it. No change in that! I ended up back on the Shirley Highway going toward Richmond yesterday in a snarl of ugly traffic.

My Chief has a great plan for the Pentagon on weekends. Says it'll reduce the national debt if we open it up as a skating rink! Think of the fun going round and round from one ring to another. Till then I must be satisfied with the athletic center; almost everyone uses it, even us workaholic submariners.

My title is Director of Tactics for Attack Submarines in the Office of the DCNO for Submarine Warfare. Of course the operational people at SUBLANT and SUBPAC are the people who really do this job. But we try to work with them providing the expertise of the operators stationed here. For instance the current DCNO is VADM Eugene Parks (Dennis) Wilkinson, the first Commanding Officer of the *Nautilus* and the cruiser *Long Beach*. I spend a lot of my time on the phone with submariners in Norfolk and Pearl Harbor.

For the first time I'm working with civilians, and we submariners have the best secretaries in the building — we usually manage to get the best of everything. My personal secretary, Linda, is capable of writing a complex letter if you just tell her the content. The civilians really provide the continuity and historical perspective around here. Unfortunately, they're treated poorly, and if they're attractive and/or have large boobs they're subjects of the usual sexism. I'm sorry for one particularly competent, well-endowed secretary in the Admiral's office whom the officers are always telling that it would really help their morale if she would just "stand up like this," as they bend their arms and push their elbows back as far as they can. I can't believe they make this request or that she tolerates it.

The Washington scene is currently dominated by the President's problems with Watergate. This is a difficult issue for military people who are required by law to remain loyal to their Commander-in-Chief, but can't help but be damned appalled by the whole sorry situation. What we're really worried about is that the President and his people will become so distracted that the security of the country will be endangered. So far that doesn't seem to be happening, probably because foreign policy is Nixon's strong suit and he continues to use foreign policy issues to try to look presidential.

My change of command went well, meaning uneventfully. Leaving Charleston was something else again. I really miss that town, its quiet elegance, the accepting way it dealt with integration, and the easy friendliness of its citizens, whites and blacks alike. I even miss the wonderful sign erected by the John Birch Society on Rte. 17 just outside of town, "When are we going to win in Vietnam and why not?"

But mostly, I miss Joanna and the kids. We talked about marriage when I got my orders but decided to wait and see how things go. She's not keen to move to D.C. and knows my work hours will be long. They're all coming the first weekend in Feb. for a visit so I'm planning kid things — zoo if it doesn't snow, Smithsonian, Natural History Museum, and the memorials including JFK's grave. In March, I start getting my nephews and nieces to tour around.

Oh yes, I forgot to mention that I'm renting a small 1840s townhouse in Georgetown. Seems living in Charleston gave me a taste for these historic row houses. Mine even has a bronze plaque that indicates the house is at least 100 years old and may have some architectural importance. The house has been nicely restored — red brick with black shutters, and a pretty garden in the back with a small fish pond. I await the spring to see what comes up and out! I've been busy furnishing in my small amount of spare time. So far, I have beds, a card table, and some chairs. Guess I better get busier. I'm hitting used furniture, about-to-be antiques stores next! Right now, I'm almost camping out. I don't mind and I suppose the kids won't mind either but I think I should do better by Joanna.

If you manage any trips here, I would love to see you. *Mi casa es su casa!* Would like to hear about how this Watergate mess is playing outside of the beltway. If you get a chance, write. I still hold a special place in my heart for you and always will.

Love,

Tom

Two weeks later from Tucker's journal

4 February 1974, San Diego, California

For the record,

What a change from the East Coast! Being in San Diego feels like being on permanent vacation, at least from my environmental surroundings. Palm trees, the San Diego Bay backdrop, and gorgeous flowers in February. Seems strange and a bit artificial. Sort of a man-made heaven.

My work life isn't a vacation though. Being Assistant Team Leader on a Human Resource Management Team challenges all my abilities and more. My boss and Team Leader, Commander Jerry Hadley, doesn't seem comfortable with his task, to be an in-house management consultant to commanding officers of ships and squadrons. He impresses me as nervous, yet kind and good. My other teammates are senior enlisted men who seem fired up about their work. Me too. I believe the Navy needs a shot of Organizational Development and in time we can transfer the total effort to leadership and management training of individuals. At least that's Admiral Howeland's plan. In the meantime, HRM teams provide consultant skills for fleet units, whether they want them or not, and some are resistant at best.

I think I'm in the right place. Our command atmosphere contrasts dramatically from the War College...more diverse people, more opportunity to work directly with Navy units. Hooray, I get to work with the Fleet! Less deep thinking and more hands-on communicating.

Good to be near the family too. Life is good.

TF

Two weeks later from Billie

18 February 1974, Alexandria, VA

Dear Tuck —

At least we exchanged autovon numbers last week, and I'm sorry I couldn't talk, but the VCNO walked in my office about that same time and I made the command decision to talk to him instead. RHIP, Tuck.

I'm back in my house in Alexandria, and in the middle of having my basement finished. A part of it will be a party room — paneled walls, standing fireplace, tiled floors, a bar/counter in the corner with a sink, small refrigerator, and stove. I'm scouring Thieves Market in Alexandria and other used-furniture stores for appropriate furniture, especially a round table for cards.

Here's the best part, Tuck, I'm also putting in a bedroom and bath. Now, you've got your own apartment for those frequent TAD trips to D.C. you seem to finagle more than anyone else.

I like my job, too. I'm in charge of the same Community Relations Department that I used to work for. I now know all the players in this business, both civilian and military, and they know me. It's a great community (sub-specialty), and it's a thrill to be accepted among these professionals. I know I don't steam the ocean and defend the sea lanes, but I help to "support the Fleet"!

I've enrolled at American U. again, and with a little luck, I can finish in a year. It's mostly project-oriented now, and I can use my CHINFO projects for my classes.

The only down note is the arthritis. My right wrist, both sides of my jaw, left knee, both thumbs are affected. My wrist goes from okay to unusable. Some mornings I can't button my shirt, or tie my tie, pull up pantyhose or turn on the ignition in my car. I'm taking gold shots and other anti-inflammatory medicine, but it's iffy. There's only one rheumatologist at Bethesda, and he's swamped. There's no real therapy for rheumatoid arthritis and each individual has a different reaction to the medicines. The doctor recommended to his superiors that the active duty RA patients be seen at the National Institute for Medicine RA Clinic. I have an appointment there next week. Those rheumatologists apparently are more aggressive in their treatments. We'll see.

One more health note — I'm at the time in my life where I have to hold what I'm reading at arm's length to focus on the print. I have a terrible time writing checks! So, I went to the eye doctor. He examined my eyes and then said, "Do you remember when you reached puberty?"

"Uh, yeah," I said.

"Well, congratulations!" he said cheerfully. "You've now reached maturity!" I'm now the proud owner (and wearer) of some Navy-issue half glasses! Are we getting old, Tuck!? I'd like to hear from you.

Your friend,

Billie

One week later from Tucker

25 February 1974, San Diego, California

Dear Buck,

Hello from sunny California! My parents and San Diego old-timers tell me February can be wet and windy in southern California. Thus far that's true, though the winds are a far cry from those powerful gusts blowing from Newport's harbor.

And how are you enjoying Pentagon duty? In many ways, I'd love to be working for you in OP-06. Thanks to "progress," some of my women officer friends now work in those offices, unlike nine years ago when I was turned away.

My career has taken a different direction. As one of two officers, along with five senior enlisted men (two submariners), on a Human Resource Management Team at the Center, already I know my new billet will bring major challenge.

Shortly after I reported in, my boss, Commander Jerry Hadley, informed me I would assume his task as lead consultant to the team's primary client, an aircraft carrier. His announcement surprised me. In HRM school they'd said recent graduates wouldn't be working directly with clients for at least six months. Furthermore, a carrier demands the maximum of consultancy skills. Jerry explained he was turning over authority and not responsibility for the success of the intervention.

He said, "I couldn't handle giving such poor HRM survey results to the Captain. Tucker, you must know, however, whatever happens with you and the team, as the Team Leader, I take full responsibility for the outcome. I can't feedback the data, Tucker. I just can't... "

Buck, I imagine you don't know much about this program, which affords assistance with human resource problems to the fleet. You're more apt to be thinking about the Soviet threat than our HRM focus. The primary means of "diagnosing" a command's people issues, as set forth by this organizational development effort directed by the CNO, is a lengthy, anonymous survey administered in the first phase of a client's HRM cycle. Then the HRM Team which is specifically assigned to a client command analyzes the data and feeds back results by workgroup.

This particular carrier's data, from the XO's workgroup level down, reflected major concerns within the command. Jerry said he had an additional problem with his function: "As a three-striper, I cannot tell any four-striper how to run his ship. I have a real problem with being a consultant who doesn't report directly to the skipper and who brings negative information to him."

I wanted to question Jerry's logic. Why should I, a lieutenant commander, be asked to perform this uncomfortable task? Instead, I listened to this man, who obviously had anguished over his decision. I listened in a way different from pre-HRM training. In the business, it's called "active listening." Jerry felt implementation of the HRM Cycle encroached upon a CO's prerogatives and responsibilities. He was comfortable with data analysis, but balked at interviewing, feeding back data, helping to set goals, conducting workshops, and working closely with COs and XOs.

I offered him a fresh-from-schooling understanding of the client/team relationship, suggesting that through our own command's chain of command, we had responsibilities to carry out because of our special area of expertise, human resource management. We were given authority by the respective Commander-in-Chief, who delegated to our commanding officer down to the Team Leader.

I'm unsure whether Jerry's "cognitive dissonance" arises from responsibility and authority issues or from discomfort with giving some very tough news to a senior skipper. A little of both probably. Nonetheless, unless I had strong disagreement, Jerry asked me, the team's most inexperienced consultant but second senior, to take over his role with the carrier. While I understood my boss's dilemma, I realized our team had to proceed with the task or else he'd be embarrassed and have to ask for help outside the team. "Let me sleep on it," I said.

The next day I told Jerry I'd take over the carrier assignment and do my best. He and I both knew the task should remain within the team, and he seemed relieved. Jerry exemplifies that solid, dedicated naval officer who finds himself in the wrong billet but carries on for the good of the institution. I'm sure you know many Jerrys.

So this gives you an idea of how my professional world has changed from teaching national strategy and seapower to handling everyday issues of Navy personnel. The job will be challenging and fun, especially after I acquire more consultant skills. As you've often said, a good line officer must do many things well.

The carrier story has a fairly happy ending. Captain Frank Kent, the commanding officer, a big man (character-wise), expeditiously accepted the client/consultant relationship and gave me full authority and support to conduct the HRM Cycle, with his personal chop and attention at all phases. After this private briefing to him and his XO, the skipper sighed and thanked us for the presentation. "A fine job, Commander Fairfield and Chief Shono. Your detailed analysis confirms my feelings about several problems within my command. Now, let's do something about them," he exclaimed.

The next phase with the carrier was rugged. A hard-charging young chief petty officer, Allen Shono, and I conducted a two-day workshop with the ship's department heads. That our beloved Navy remains classist, sexist, even ageist, became crystal-clear. The commanders grumped and blustered about the command's leadership and management issues, as defined by their CO and XO. I would've loved to have had another stripe and a half, and more consultant experience. These commanders didn't want to deal with the people problems, so they attacked the consultants. The old adage, "Kill the messenger," ruled. During this tour of duty I think it'll help to grow a stripe and (figuratively) wear thick armor. Hope to make CDR next year.

Keeping up with national and international affairs hasn't been high on my to-do list. "Lucky you" having that as your primary billet. Feels right to have U.S. participation in Vietnam over. While I don't have the best of personal feelings about President Nixon, he of course has my full support as Commander-in-Chief. This billet gives me minimum time to read the newspapers and think beyond my clients and their concerns. Hopefully life will settle down.

This letter should give you a sense of my professional world. Exciting and sometimes exhausting. Dad and Mother are delighted to have me in San Diego. My best wishes and my love to you and Helen.

Fondly,

Tucker

Two weeks later from Buck

5 March 1974, The Pentagon

Dear Tucker,

How delightful to hear from you from sunny California, even though rainy at the moment. Wet, cold, and miserable Washington could use an infusion of California weather. Don't know why I make a point of that, for I see darn little of the environs. This Op-06 routine requires early morning hours to get ready for the tank where the Joint Chiefs of Staff briefings take place. The day drags out as we debrief the staff who have labored many hours over the position papers we use in the tank to support varying service positions.

It's not a bad decision-making process. I wish the news pundits who write and talk about the alleged maneuvering of the Defense Department or the waste and confusion inherent to the military could witness the caring, debating, and agonizing which transpire over military policy matters.

Your letter sounds as though you might be in the midst of a classic dilemma concerning leadership, at least this is what we used to call it, till the "M" word became a magic solution. Now we manage rather than lead. Something good has left our system. Responsibility has become diffused, and it's more difficult to attach personal achievement to assignments. The escape hatches through the consultant route proliferate, and actual cause-and-effect is hard to identify.

You're seeing this phenomenon now on your carrier assignment; at least you're beginning to feel it happen. Your natural sensitivity to such things tells you instinctively that these problems belong to the respective Commanding Officer, and you feel awkward invading his sphere of influence. And you should. Your boss's high-sounding statement that he has "cognitive dissonance" with investigating anything within another's command sounds very right. I'm uncertain what "cognitive dissonance" is (you're the social science student), but I think he's saying he believes such practices are contrary to the tenets of command responsibility. He's correct.

But you have a separate problem. You were given an assignment to collect and/or report data in some form to the commanding officer. Your options were limited: either do it, prove to your boss beyond a logical doubt that you should not do it, or, ask for another assignment out of his command. It seems to me you handled your part of this well.

The difficulty occurred when the carrier CO had you and your chief petty officer work with his department heads. He should have been present and used the data to lay down the law that *his ship was not meeting his standards*. At this point the matter isn't a consultant's work (I prefer "outsider" to consultant). The matter is internal and should've been handled that way. Your discomfort typifies my own deep concern that we're diluting command responsibility by these outside influences brought to bear at command level.

In days gone by, operational, administrative, logistical, and readiness inspections by peers were routine and effective; they were accomplished by those who were engaged in the same type of activity as the command they inspected. The results went to the Commanding Officer and his Division Commander who probably ordered such inspections in the first place. These inspections were intended as constructive. Actually they were very competitive and resulted in each command feeling a need to excel since it was being compared with other similar commands.

Policy makers in all agencies of our government today feel intense pressure to quickly solve human relations problems brought on by what can only be described as radical societal changes. Whether right or wrong, these changes are happening and replacing mores and methods familiar for hundreds of years. The military is not a democratic society; it's a modified autocratic one. When we make attempts to spread the nearly absolute authority and responsibility inherent in a detached military unit among unattached agencies and activities, the whole psyche of militariness becomes fuzzy, and the lines of command authority are thus hazy. I'm sorry to see this.

I, too, wish you were here in Op-06. Your talents are much more useful here than in some management effort to help command do its job. But, you obviously manage well the situation at hand. I'll be interested to hear your personal feedback as you gather more experience in the HRM business. Is it doing any good? How should it be used? Is it seen as interference? Does it threaten command responsibility?

Remember me to your parents. Washington these days, where our government seems distrustful of itself, isn't really a happy place, except in springtime, when it becomes one of the world's elegant and gracious cities. How nice spring is nearly here.

Warm regards,

Buck

One year later from Tucker

26 February 1975, San Diego, California

Dear Billie,

How's my good buddy? When are you coming for a visit?

My job takes up most of my day, every day. I'm now an HRM Team Leader with lots of responsibility. We often have five or six clients, exclusively ships and squadrons, in various stages of the HRM Cycle. I believe we're making a difference. If people can communicate more proficiently, set goals and solve problems, we're bound to have a more effective Navy. How long have we heard our leaders say that *people* are the most important of our resources? This program upholds that belief.

Working with clients in their environments, on the ships and in the hangars, qualifies as a high point in my career. Wish you and I and other women had had the opportunity to serve aboard ships.

I've had only minor problems with clients discrediting me because of my gender. Perhaps the third stripe will help. The U.S. Navy's a meritocracy, and until otherwise notified, rank automatically carries respect, irrespective of race or gender. In this vein, how can I adequately say to you that I'm truly sorry you didn't make commander with me? Who knows what Selection Board members were thinking when they jumped over you.

I hate the term "passed over."

We're an "up-or-out" promotion system, but those who aren't selected are still worthy, sharp, human beings. The system, I guess, can't promote everyone.

You're one of the finest in my book and always will be. We had stiff competition as well. I believe your rheumatoid arthritis was the deciding factor for the Board.

This assignment pushes my boundaries. Feelings and personal behaviors, equally as much as intelligence, circumscribe HRM work. Perhaps personal growth has highlighted this difference for me. We consultants are quasi-psychologists, demanding counseling skills beyond those of a good naval officer. Therefore, I've come to "pick and choose my fights," and expend energies more prudently. Maybe I'm getting wiser too; after all, we're both pushing forty!

My social life is about the same — peaceful and quiet. I miss Sandy's companionship.

Have you noticed that Navy partying has cut back? Of course D.C. is atypical. Drug and Alcohol programs play a part, but I've noticed my command has fewer required social functions than previous duty stations. San Diego sunshine seems to call for a more active lifestyle than the East Coast.

How about an update from you? Are you having fun? Maybe we can meet halfway in Kansas. Colorado might be better!

Take care my friend.

Love,

Tuck

Two weeks later from Tom

12 March 1975, Bethesda Naval Hospital

Hi Tucker,

It's been a long time since you've heard from your deep diving pal. I hope all's well with you. It's not so well with me. You will note the stationery, compliments of Bethesda Naval Hospital. It comes along with the attractive baby blue back-vent gown and matching paper slippers. I'm in fact high up in the tower where the view is spectacular, but alas, it's pretty much wasted on me. I'm on the cancer floor. That's right, the cancer floor. But, look on the bright side, Pollyanna! I have time to catch up on my correspondence!

What happened? Well, about a month ago, I got some swelling and soreness in my left testicle. First it was treated for an infection (epidydimitis) and then for squash court trauma. Then they sent me here. Well, I wasn't in the examining room 5 minutes when the doc assembled his coterie of hangers-on (residents, interns) and said, "Hey guys, look at this! Set up the operating room for tomorrow. We've got one."

Most of my life, I've used the expression, "I'd give my left nut for that." Well, when it came time to give, I could hardly wait. All I could think of was, "Get this evil thing out of me." The trouble is, it had already spread to the lymph nodes on that side. And, yes, I had those out and biopsied too in a separate procedure.

Tucker, it's not easy to be cheerful. In fact, I feel damn mad. Contributing to my bad humor is that everyone from my doctor to my friends tells me it's important for me to have a good attitude. Well, I don't have a good attitude. My hair is falling out, I'm nauseated from the chemo and if I survive, which is highly unlikely (I've been to the library and looked the beastie up) I'll never have kids of my own.

I think this good attitude advice is given because if I have a good attitude, it makes everyone around me feel more comfortable. Hell, I know some guys up here with damn good attitudes and they're still dying. In addition, yesterday my doctor advised me to be nice to the corpsmen because, "They can make your life miserable." Can you imagine? I saw my chart last week and one of the corpsmen had written, "The patient was sassy today." Where else in the Navy would an enlisted man write of a captain that he was sassy?

Another thing that really bothers me — all the doctors are telling me I ought to plan to enjoy myself. What they really mean is, enjoy yourself because you're about to die! I cannot think of a single thing that I could do to enjoy myself. Enjoyment for me is to be well and free of cancer; nothing else constitutes enjoyment.

I'm letting all this steam out with you probably because my whole family has been visiting *seriatim* and I've been a brave Tom with a helluva good attitude. Also, I figure if I whine enough, you'll come to visit and catch me up on the current scuttlebutt and get me out of my funk. I don't think there's any pretending between us, Tucker, and for that I'm grateful.

You're probably wondering about Joanna, and yes, she and the kids have been to visit. Twice. I'm very glad now that Joanna didn't agree to marry me. Losing two husbands hardly would've been fair. I do think we love each other and I love the kids but it seems our caution has paid off.

Too funny. You remember meeting my fellow submariner, William Toliferro Collins, III, in Newport News? Well, it seems he was conveying my situation to the wife of another officer we both know well. Had run into her in the PX. He told her I was in Bethesda with cancer and of course, she said as everyone does, "What kind?" Well, he blushingly blurted, "It's in a private part," and back-pedaled his escape. As I recall, in his family one never asked for the breast, leg, or thigh of the chicken. One asked instead for white meat or for a lower or upper joint.

Come save me from my dark depression. I'm thinking crazy things, such as, "How come this happened just when I finished furnishing my house?" A variation on "Why me?" I guess.

I'm very grateful for my Navy medical care. It's bad enough having cancer, but to have cancer and think that the expense will break your family must really be awful.

Your high-up, down-in-the-dumps buddy,

Tom

P.S. Pierre reported to ComThirdFlt as Commander, DesGroup 5. You were right. He's a winner. Jennie's lucky (so is he).

Four days later from Tucker

16 March 1975, San Diego, CA

Tom,

What a shocker!! Glad to talk with you today and know that your spirits have revived somewhat. I can't believe this is happening to my best buddy. We always feel we're invincible and protected. I don't understand why you got hit with cancer. You've always been so strong and healthy. Of course, the possible nuclear connection springs instantly to mind.

Anyway, the doctors are right; the mind-body connection is direct. John Locke, the political theorist said it well, "A sound mind in a sound body is a short but full description of a happy state in the world." Knowing you, I'm sure you'll feel better if you can pull yourself up and out of your depression and concentrate on learning about testicular cancer. I think of you as a nuclear cold warrior who can lick everybody and anything! So please, Tom, be an informed patient and optimize your recovery chances, for everyone's sake.

As I told you, I'm coming to D.C. next month on TAD to help select civilian consultants for our next HRM contract. I'll be walking Bethesda's halls in the evenings, keeping you company.

Thanks for offering the use of your Georgetown pad during my stay. Just might work. I've always wanted to live in one of those historic houses. Your garden is probably spectacular in April. Tell you what. I'll bushwhack the weeds for you and urge on your roses.

I'll be sending you lots of good vibes. Constantly. Somehow you'll get through this damnable ordeal. It's not your time.

Love you a lot,

Tuck

Two weeks later from Billie

30 March 1975, Alexandria, VA

Dear Tuck —

Thanks for all your supportive phone calls and being concerned about me following my "passover." I'm kinda numb to say the least. I have good friends, you included, and they've called, dropped by to see me, taken me to lunch, invited me over for dinner and generally comforted me and held my hand. It's like a death in the family. CHINFO, himself, has been very supportive as well as the other staff members. My job's secure until my next assignment. I haven't fully analyzed what this means to me personally. Maybe later. Well, enough of this; life must go on.

I'm still in occupational therapy with my wrist. It's getting much stronger and I'm back to writing with my right hand. And yes, I think the fusion (synovectomy) and the conclusions of the Fit for Duty board had a great deal to do with my passover. To go with the operation was my choice, and I don't think I could've functioned well otherwise. The doctor who performed the operation is a pediatric orthopedic surgeon, and I think he did a marvelous job.

Did I ever mention my stay at Bethesda? Once again, the Navy didn't know what to do with women officers, so they put me on the VIP floor of the tower. In the room across from mine was Senator Mills. This was the guy who got into trouble with Fanne Foxe and made a jerk of himself in public. He's left-handed and took pleasure (almost too much pleasure) in teaching me to write with my left hand. Beyond the nurses' station was Thurgood Marshall. He had pneumonia, but was healing and we talked a little. The Commandant of the Marine Corps was in for a couple of days, not because he was sick, but because he had to have tests done on his stools, and his wife refused to keep the samples in her refrigerator! Every morning, with breakfast, they brought me the *Washington Post* and a single rose. See what VIP status brings?

I'm sorry about your friend, Tom Parker. I know you care for him very much, and it's hard to acknowledge such a terrible disease. We're just beginning to talk openly about cancer.

I'm all right, Tuck. I'll live. Hell, I have to! Ain't my time yet. I'm going to have to re-evaluate my situation. Can't get over feeling embarrassed or that I've done something wrong. I also feel that maybe I didn't do all I could or should and that my peers are better than I. Hell, whatta deal!

Your friend,

Billie

P.S. See you in two weeks. Your bed is awaiting in my basement.

Six weeks later from Tucker's journal

14 May 1975, San Diego, CA

 For the record,

Tom called today with horrible news. Pierre has been killed in a helicopter crash at sea, while transporting from one destroyer to another. Why Pierre? Why anybody? Jennie must be devastated. "To live without risk is not to live at all." But Pierre is gone...

TF

One day later from Tucker

15 May 1975, San Diego, California

Dear Jennie,

My dear, dear friend, I'm so sorry that you have lost Pierre. I know you're strong and will find courage and energy to remake your life once the overwhelming shock has passed. Life brings us mortals such unexpected sadnesses, as well as joys. One wonders what it's all about especially when something like this hits. I do believe some higher power lives in the universe and will help you through this tragedy. And I know you believe that too.

Jennie, you must give yourself plenty of time to rest and grieve, and let your friends and family comfort you during these difficult days. We do have a Navy family and I'm sure the part of your Navy family that's in Pearl will envelop you with love. Believe it or not, life will be good again for you, though at the moment you probably think otherwise.

I will miss Pierre. He was always so gentle and caring and understanding. His kind of man doesn't come this way often. His compassion was extraordinary, his human warmth and sense of humor were infectious. And, he was the professional beyond reproach. No wonder you loved him.

I don't have any more words to say how much I feel your sadness and pain. Just know I'm here and thinking about you and Pierre and all the good times we shared together.

Call or write when you feel up to it. Lots of love and hugs.

Tucker

Ten weeks later from Tucker's journal

1 August 1975, San Diego, CA

For the record,

My CO granted me time off to participate in the La Jolla Program, a 17-day group therapy experience that's held on the UCSD campus. The Program has a fine reputation and uses the facilitation techniques of psychotherapist Carl Rogers, or the Rogerian approach. Expect I'll acquire new skills in group dynamics and...learn a lot about myself! Starts next month.

TF

Two weeks later from Tucker

15 August 1975, San Diego, California

Dear Buck,

Time out for a letter to my favorite admiral (besides Dad) and mentor. At the moment I need to let off steam about the Navy, and you're one of the best listeners I know. My job lets me forget that I'm a woman naval officer; yesterday, however, I was reminded that Navy women have their designated place, and I'd better stop pushing the river toward equality.

Here's the latest from your activist commander. The best place to work with our clients is, at their request, at sea. Because of the Navy's longstanding regulation that women can't serve aboard ships, including TAD status, the women in my command cannot work with clients at sea. Twenty-five percent of the consultants are women, and therefore to disallow women working aboard the ships adversely affects our command's mission effectiveness.

Several months ago, after meeting with my commanding officer, I drafted a letter to the CNO via CINCPACFLT suggesting alternatives to alleviate this problem. My Washington friends had informed me that a Navy decision regarding article 6015 Title 10 (which precludes women serving aboard ships) was imminent. Either 6015 would remain as is, be modified, or repealed. The climate's ripe for change. The resistance to change, of course, remains strong, and it appears that the Navy has decided not to change article 6015.

In the CNO letter we suggested a reasonable solution, "To modify Navy policy, permitting Navy women to be assigned to all seagoing units on a TAD basis when their duties require, and the facilities and scheduled employment of such ships permit such an assignment." Navy policy already allows civilian female employees to ride ships in certain similar situations. My commanding officer, Admiral-selectee Jonathan Hampton, truly endorses the need for this action on several levels, including "in the interests of true equal equality."

But CINCPACFLT played it cautiously. "Returned without further action," was the first sentence of their endorsement. Their argument was invalid. HRM Centers have no mission requirements to embark HRM Teams in ships. Captain Hampton was furious, and said the rationale just isn't true. This situation illustrates why Navy men can so easily resent Navy women, yet we aren't given the opportunity to participate. In this instance, while my team members "understand" why I can't go to sea, they'd like me to share the workload equally. And so would I!

My immediate boss sent the CINC endorsement to me with the written comment, "Shot Down!! An idea before its time?!" I wrote back, "What a cop-out!"

Buck, when will seniors take off their sexist filters and start taking risks in support of equality for Navy women? Probably only when they realize that we must increase the numbers of women as an economic reality. Since 1972 the Navy has tripled the number of uniformed women because of two primary reasons: One, the press from our women's movement for equal economic opportunity, and two, the use of more women can be a major contributing factor in making the All-Volunteer Force work, in the face of a declining youth population. In other words, we won't have sufficient recruits unless we open up more opportunities to women. It's a simple choice. At some point, the DoD, the country's women, and the Congress will force the Navy to change 6015.

I know. Be patient. You may have considerable reason for agreeing with current policy re Navy women. But I know you're open to hearing all sides of an argument, and I needed to offer my (somewhat biased) views. In the meantime, I'll keep stepping into controversies about equal opportunity for Navy women. With the changing political climate insofar as women's equality, other fellow women officers are fighting for Navy women's equality, unlike in the early days. Feels good to have their support. Transitions are hard! Speaking of transitions, President Ford seems to be handling matters well.

Thanks for listening, Buck. You don't need to reply. I just had to spout off steam.

My best love to you and Helen. Enjoyed our short visit with

you at the folks' last month. You look more rested than I've seen you in awhile. Belgium and SACEUR must be agreeing with you.

Warm regards,

Tucker

Two weeks later from Buck

1 September 1975, SACEUR, Brussels

Dear Tucker,

Greetings from Belgium. Feels good to be working in NATO again. Wish you were working with me. Some fascinating developments since we left SACLANT in '69.

Your 15 August letter disturbs me. The refusal to change Title 10 to allow Temporary Additional Duty for women-on-ships when that duty is necessary to accomplish their assignments makes little sense to me. Either women shouldn't be assigned to such duty, or they should be allowed to accomplish their required tasks.

I suppose this illogic stems from caution regarding the women-at-sea program. If women can get a wedge in place with this TAD assignment, instantly they prove the ships still float and perform their missions with women on board. A major part of the argument against sea duty for women vanishes. Can't risk that, can we?

Maybe you took the wrong tack: Why not plead the case on the necessity for consultants to observe the ships in their operational environments. Leave women out of the argument. If it's unnecessary for you to observe the unit when the ship is operational, the whole purpose of the HRM program is a sham! As you know, I feel your intrusion into command responsibility is unnecessary, and the real reason for CINCPAC's disapproval may be his way of opposing HRM, not women-on-ships. The latter merely provides the opportunity.

This is pretty tricky territory, for CINCPAC would certainly reject any suggestion that he's blocking CNO policy. Nonetheless, many of us continue to wonder about social intervention within commands — to gather data, to assess opinion, to allow personal hair styles which sometime seem bizarre. We wonder if *real* leadership is made less effective by this high-level micro-management. By the way, this isn't too distant from the kind of micro-overseeing we observed during Vietnam.

Some years ago a survey group came to *Seaperch* to conduct an opinion poll concerning likes and dislikes in the Navy. As her commanding officer, I asked to see the questionnaire. One of the first questions was, "What do you dislike most about the Navy?" I disallowed the poll, and suggested they design a positive one which begins with the question, "What do you like most about the Navy?" After that, maybe we could talk. Back then, I had the authority to do this. They left in some disarray, not really understanding my objection.

My information about HRM makes me believe that some of what's happening isn't the direct result of CNO initiatives, but is actually the result of actions on the part of a group of young, somewhat inexperienced advisors who experiment with new ideas to see their effect. I suspect the Navy will endure this and outlast any real change to the inherent responsibilities in command.

Tucker, I think a change of scenery might do you a world of good right now. I have a little discretionary money for travel- and study-type projects. What would you say to an invitation to brief the staff here on what our Navy's doing in the HRM program, as well as the status of our efforts to make women an integral part of our military?

It would be a Navy staff, but international, not just U.S. You could draw on your study done a few years ago, and brief on the purpose of HRM consultants in our U.S. Navy, how they evaluate a command, how they can help, whether or not unit commanders are feeling benefited. I can issue an official invitation to you personally to expedite this idea. You'll have to be certain someone there doesn't decide to send someone else. To help with that, I'll drop a note to some people in BuPers, basing my request on your Women's Study and HRM expertise, and identify you as the invitee. If the idea appeals, give me your best judgment of the way to word my letter and to whom, so it doesn't get sidetracked. I can monitor it here, but I want to keep it away from the administrative managers who might have better ideas about the way to do this.

There'll be an added bonus. Helen and I will get a chance to catch up on your life in person, and we can make certain you'll enjoy some of the best places in the world to eat. You haven't lived until you've eaten at Jacques on the Grande Place in Brussels.

In the meantime, Tucker, you may be caught in the middle. Earnestly trying to do well the assignment you've been asked to accomplish, you have run smack into Navy politics. So, hang in there, let your CO handle the consultants-at-sea issue as best he can, and let your client COs be the final arbiters regarding people problems on their ships and squadrons.

Warm regards,

Buck

Two weeks later from Tucker

15 September 1975, San Diego, CA

Dear Buck,

Thank you for your kind invitation to come over on TAD to consult regarding women's issues and HRM matters. My commanding officer, Admiral-selectee Jonathan Hampton, and I discussed your idea and he sees no problems with your asking specifically for me. He said, "You're well known and respected on both accounts, Tucker. You're my top Team Leader and since our Center's the best in the business, you're a logical choice for the tasking. Do it!"

Captain Hampton said BuPers will support the idea as well. I enclose a rough draft of a letter you might include to the Bureau folks, copy to Captain Hampton and CINCPACFLT.

Due to my HRM Team's schedule, the best timing is approximately 9–16 November or 20–27 November. Hope one of these weeks works for you and your staff.

Thanks for your wise words re my struggles with getting women HRM Specialists to sea on a TAD basis. Patience isn't one of my strong virtues!

Hope to see you soon. My best love to you and Helen.

Very respectfully,

Tucker Fairfield
Commander, U.S. Navy

Enclosures

P.S. We can wet down my new stripe which I will put on 1 November.

One day later, Tucker's journal

16 September 1975, San Diego, California

For the record,

The end of a consequential day for me — the third day in the La Jolla Program. It's sort of group therapy for 17 days, led by high-level civilian psychologists. I'm finally beginning to, just a little, let in others' feelings and connect with them. A continuation of Operation Empathy, I suppose. It's a rewarding experience that I regret missing for lo' these 37 years. I must makeup for lost time, which will be exacting since my work environment doesn't exactly support getting into others' feelings to any great degree. How many Navy men even attempt to share their inner feelings? They're more buttoned up than I!

In our small group today we discussed being on the verge of great change. Our facilitator, Terry, shared her feelings about freedom to take herself and her own center wherever it feels right. Because of my profession, I don't have this freedom, and sometimes I want it. Yet perhaps I can create this sense of freedom as the Navy controls my career and, in many ways, my life. A challenge! To not be so influenced by the constraining environment which surrounds me, would take a lot of reframing within me. The only saving grace is the HRM program, but that too will pass.

This experience's unstructured approach can be wearing and uncomfortable. I wonder if I'll be able to appreciate the spontaneity and accept the lack of direction? My answer is usually to create tasks for myself, as they arise from the day's stimuli. I feel the need to share my "issues" with my group, particularly about the non-feeling Navy, but only because of others' stories and risks.

I feel — okay! I feel secure in who I am and what I have done in life and with life.The accomplishments are evident. The joy, the sadness, the pain, on the other hand, have been too closely held in and shared only with me, myself, and I. How much easier life would've been to have had someone to share the pains especially. Whatever the key, I would like to find a way to be not so alone with my sadness, or joy. Life's too short to cope with critical life junctures alone. Or, rather, life's too full of others not to have friends, close relationships, when the roads and waves get rough. I'm truly fortunate to have my friends — Robyn, Billie, Jennie, Tom, and Buck and many more. But they're not an everyday gift. I'd like an everyday gift. Yes, a partner.

My writing feels rusty. I'm dissatisfied with this note. Or, perhaps it's my incompetence in communicating my feelings. I sense that I'm actually loaded with feelings, but unable to express them. Will continue. Only five hours sleep last night and am weary.

TF

Four days later from Tucker's journal

20 September 1975, San Diego, California

 For the record,

More rested today, though still tired. Two major topics: (1) Liz and (2) my new small group.

I have really good feelings about my actions and reactions to Liz, another Program participant — to realize that I've been following my feelings with her and didn't reject her flat out. A strong mutual attraction exists between us, which could lead to, probably already has, a close tie. My first reaction? Push her away! This kind of feeling can only lead to disaster. Yet, there's more to it. To act on my feelings with her means being what I really want to be — free. Free and comfortable having relationships with women, rather than forcing myself into a sexual relationship with a man. I do love men, some men, but in a non-sexual way. I'm glad Tom understands!

I find myself pulling back from giving or receiving love which can have no long-term commitment. Especially receiving. To receive love is to accept an obligation, or so it seems. Yet I see such a strong need in Liz to be loved, and right now it seems wrong not to love her, at least during the Program. Maybe my love and friendship will give her the strength she needs to get to another place. She's where I've been and am trying to move away from.

(2) I may dive in with my feelings with my new group with its healthy dynamics. I'm still analyzing and evaluating; that's me and that's okay. But I need to take risks, and let them know my feelings. I regret I didn't use a pseudonym to protect my identity. Never know who might pass the word. I hate paranoia.

I'm acting out a role I've played for years, the Commander. Why not try some new behaviors?

TF

Two days later from Tucker's journal

22 September 1975, San Diego, California

For the record,

God! I need to put some direction on the 24-hour Marathon and feelings I experienced. The most moving experience in my life — bar none!

For the first time I witnessed real caring, and loving emotionally and physically (non-sexual), among men and women. We cried, we laughed, we hugged, and shared deep, deep problems. The combination was overwhelming. When we let our defenses down, after no sleep for eighteen–twenty two hours, plus intensive personal work and sleep deprivation all week, most were sad, and carrying heavy loads. My burdens seemed light!

What's my load? To prefer women sexually and in turn seemingly to be unaccepted by society-at-large. I write "seemingly" because this week's experience, sharing who I am, has given me another sense: People accept me and in fact are closer to me than before I shared my load. Strange. It's probably the environment.

Yet it's a burden, because loving women seems to play a significant part in who I am, and I can't or won't share this part in my everyday life. My intuition, however, says go ahead and get it out if appropriate. Certainly it's inappropriate at work!!

At the Marathon, I cried and sobbed with Wally. For him, for me, and for others. I'm not at all sorry to be where I am in life, yet I'm disheartened to be in a kind of bondage with an organization that gives me real pain, as well as with my own unuseful ways of being. It felt really good to cry. Joan's son committed suicide last year. What a tremendous burden!

Am unsure right now why I'm sad. Am also angry at "society," for putting me in this uncomfortable, uncommunicative state. I can't be me and I can't get my feelings out, except in terms of working for women and their rights. But women's inequality and lack of freedom are only two pieces of the anger.

TF

Three days later from Tucker's journal

25 September 1975, San Diego, California

 For the record,

Yesterday was a downer. The afternoon and evening I spent in a women's group, either angry, bored, or frustrated, and became more so as I continued not to speak up.

But the atmosphere, as created by the group's dynamics, wasn't accepting. Traditional values hung heavily in the air, especially from the older women. I sensed my input would've been misunderstood. I was confused. This was the gender that I've been fighting for, yet they seem so disconnected, so weak, and not at all attractive to me. I don't get it. How can they so adore men, while continually being subordinated to them?

"The male ego is too fragile to respond with an equal stance. We must submit to inequality," said one of them.

Their fear of getting too close to other women bothers me as much as their attitudes toward men. What a sad state for them, to be dissatisfied with both sexes. At least I can be close to women, I mean non-sexual closeness, and feel real equality, and I can have equal relationships with my men friends. These women, mostly married, don't seem capable of equality with either gender!

The group had a lively discussion of "open marriage," although the older women seemed not to condone the younger ones who were trying to live out this new approach to loving. I liked what the young ones expressed, though it seems a difficult road to take and not for me. In open marriage the primary relationship is maintained, with lots of communication and understanding about other relationships. Those relationships may or may not be sexual. The point is that no one individual can satisfy any one other's needs fully. Makes sense intellectually.

We're reconvening this morning. I may change the group's direction ("If not now, when?") and say to them that loving women can be very satisfying and sensual. This group of women represents the society that makes me angry, that sometimes puts me in such a lousy, isolated space. I suppose the way to bring about any movement is to share with them a few things. Get your courage up, Fairfield.

TF

Same day from Tucker's journal

I told them "a few things." They seemed to appreciate knowing me as a person and knowing that women can love, do love, other women and that it feels good. They wanted specifics about the sexual loving; I chose not to accommodate. Not my style.

They resented my statement about their appearing to take passive, weak roles. In fact I learned something very significant — lack of strength isn't the issue, but rather lack of assertiveness. There were many strong women in the group, but they're non-assertive.

But, and, they're still talking to me. What a surprise. It may be this idyllic group environment. Would society at large talk to me if...?

TF

Four days later from Tucker's journal

29 September 1975, San Diego, California

For the record,

I liked what Dick, our facilitator, said in the community meeting this morning. "Think warmly and feel rationally." Can't imagine the Navy doing that. Oh, well.

Had an important dream last night: My parents and I were in an encounter group. Mother asked me point blank if I were gay! Mother said Dad thought I was and it was important to know because Mother was having a baby, and they needed to give it younger parents. With great reluctance, I said "yes." She then told me that she and Dad would set up the paperwork designating that my cousin, Kay, adopt the baby and not me. Mother seemed most uncomfortable, but not shocked, with the idea of my preference for women.

My subconscious is working too hard!

TF

P.S. I met a new friend this week. Through a guided imagery exercise I found Laughing Owl, whom I see as my sort of guardian spirit and personal guide. He's Native American, majestic, and amazingly intuitive. Am I too old to have an imaginary friend? Feels right, anyway.

Same day from Tucker's journal

The community meeting was powerful. The two hours flew by. Much time was spent with Serena, who's lonely and alone in the community. Some of the comments to her were directly relevant to me and how I see myself. I know who I am: strong, yet weak in personal relationships; distant, yet close if I care to be; comfortable with people, but only at my own pace; and not needing to put forth just to put forth.

Another important thought was about going back to our everyday world and how to be ourselves, the selves we want to be. The key will be making this synthesis, the point where I can express myself but not compromise my position as a professional naval officer. I'm wondering if that's feasible. Are the two, the self and the naval officer, really compatible anymore? As I continue to grow, I find the blending of these roles more and more difficult.

Dick suggested we find a colleague or two who'd help change our environment, so that we could begin to create the same supportive, warm feeling, as we've felt here. For me that'll probably be accomplished after-hours with civilians.

Am looking forward to this afternoon's workshop on non-verbals and psychodrama.

TF

Next day from Tucker's journal

For the record,

The non-verbal workshop was dynamic. We said hello with non-verbal messages. I was relishing the hugging and smiling, when I came upon Carol, the Nun. Within thirty seconds, I was almost in tears. It was a very strange reaction, moving from enjoyment to sadness. I think our similar experiences triggered my response. She's married to a religious order; and I, to the Navy. We both have given up much freedom, as well as our very Selves, in different ways. My relationship, while less binding, is still bondage.

Later we reassembled with our first small group. I had a difficult time holding back tears and finally just cried and cried. I cried in happiness as well as sadness. Happy to have met such understanding, warm, remarkable people, and heavy-hearted to be saying goodbye, knowing that the everyday world cannot be so warm and loving. Sad to be unable to tell significant people in my life that I prefer women. Sad to be alone. Sad that I have at least five or more years of a very confining environment.

Later. I'm really sad the Program is over and that I'll not be seeing my friends. At the same time, I'm excited to go home, and I'm ready to move on to making a new life. Am uncertain where it will take me, but I have more faith that it'll be a welcoming and joyful journey. I feel much more alive. Must somehow continue to capture life in the moment, rather than always plan, plan, plan.

My Program friend, Leonora, a TA psychologist from Switzerland, gave me a beautiful book of poetry today. I will miss her. To know she knows I'm different but still loves me means a great deal. In fact, that's the Program's primary lesson — nobody shunned me because of who I am.

Lots of unfinished business to work on, soon...

TF

Six weeks later from Tucker

12 November 1975, Brussels, Belgium

Dear Jennie,

Have thought about you a lot these past months. Pierre's death is such a great loss for you and so many of us.

I'm in Brussels, on TAD to SACEUR! Buck asked me to consult with his staff on HRM and Navy women's matters. I'm conducting a series of lectures and workshops for his staff of 20 officers, representing personnel from all the NATO nations. Some come and go to my workshop but the majority are full time participants.

The consulting's going well. I spent the first two days on HRM, presenting the HRM cycle through enactment of a mock CO/XO Initial Visit, and then conducted several two–three hour workshops. The officers especially enjoyed the Time Management and Stress Management w/s. I think Buck sees the value of uniformed, in-house management consultants.

The SACEUR staff has just completed a two-week communication exercise (Operation COMCHECK) with CincSouth and the officers are in a relaxed mood. At the same time, I sense that as NATO officials, these staff officers are concerned about Soviet military strengths and capabilities, particularly its growing maritime threat.

By the way, my three stripes feel *great*. I made it!

Helen graciously invited me to stay as their guest in their spacious quarters, allowing me some special moments with Buck, as well as with her. Last night we three dined in this wonderful, bustling city and what an incredible evening! They took me to Comme Chez Sois, a family restaurant in the Bois de Bologne area with French, Italian and Spanish cuisine (as is typical of Brussels). I know you love food in all ways, so I'll try to recreate the menu for you:

> *Artichauts a la Mere* (artichokes stuffed with prosciutto); *Sauti de Veau Marengo* (veal stew with tomatoes and mushrooms); *Galette de Pommes de Terre* (crispy potato cake); *Salade verte* (lettuce and watercress salad), with Walnut Vinaigrette; *Tarte aux Pommes* (apple tarte); and *Fromage Assortis* (assorted cheeses).

And, three courses of wine: Vouvray Petillant, Cabernet Sauvignon, and Muscadet (I skipped the last wine though). Later, as we walked through the city's boulevards, I heard several languages. Brussels has been officially bilingual (French and Flemish) since 1970. Before this visit I somehow hadn't realized Brussels has been the headquarters of the European Common Market (ECC) since 1970. The broad boulevards (formerly city walls), the skyscrapers, the Parliament buildings, the King's Palaise, and the ECC combine in a glorious, industrious modern city.

I forget how just being in a foreign country stimulates all the senses. As my mother has remarked so many times, the traveling aspect of service life creates an individual with "broad horizons," a positive thing in her mind. The flip side is that the military, whose functions are protecting and preserving the country, engenders more conservative individuals. I also believe the peripatetic nature of military life nurtures shallow community roots. The bitter-with-the-better syndrome.

Tomorrow I brief re women's matters, and on my last day I play tourist — explore the shops, visit the historical military museum, the Church of St. Michael and Ste Gudule and, lastly, the "must see" Brussels' oldest citizen, the famous pissing nude boy, "Mannikin Pis." He's an angel-like child, four or five years old, about three feet high and peeing into a fountain. Buck says the sculpture is much ado about nothing, but everyone who comes to Brussels has to see him.

Wish you could be here! I recall your strong Norwegian heritage and regular visits to Norway. Perhaps you and I someday might take a Scandinavian vacation together? What a treat for me!

Must stop, my friend. A busy time tomorrow. I leave on the 15th and stop in D.C. to see how Tom's doing.

Know that I frequently send lots of love and good energy your way.

Love,

Tucker

Same day from Tucker

12 November 1975, Brussels, Belgium

Dear Mother and Dad,

Here I am in Belgium! Having a great time. Enjoying catching up with Buck and his life and family. Buck, with a bit more gray hair, is, as always, one of the most handsome and brilliant naval officers in our Navy; more distinguished than I'd remembered. We've kept our conversations on the light and upbeat side. We know we differ in certain areas. Yet the core values are the same — duty, country, and family. At least Buck and Helen and I agreed that these post-Vietnam years present challenges to our country. An understatement!

Mother, you would just bask in the beauty of the quarters provided for Buck and Helen. They lease an old Belgian home out on Avenue Franklin Roosevelt near the "Bois de Bologne" residential area of Brussels. It's a nice area, although not as palatial as some of the Brussels sections. The house is laid out with a gracious center foyer plan with an impressive wooden staircase leading to four large bedrooms on the second floor. The first floor has a receiving room or library (appointed with Buck's Navy memorabilia and many books), a big living room with a huge fireplace. There's a formal dining room which seats at least twenty at a long rectangular table, a pantry, and of course, a large kitchen. Opposite the main entrance double doors on the rear side of the house lead to a patio and a small English-style garden beyond.

The quarters' ceilings are at least 12 feet high, with massive moldings and rococo decoration. Now, envision Buck and Helen's lovely furniture and paintings and pictures throughout this home. The sense of it all is dignity and comfort, but not grandeur. Quite appropriate for a vice admiral. Buck has two stewards assigned for the upkeep and running of the quarters. As you might expect, he and Helen entertain frequently, an important part of his assignment.

For two days now I've briefed Buck and his staff on HRM matters. Tomorrow I'll brief on U.S. Navy women. SACEUR's Assistant Admin Officer, whom I'd met years ago at Bainbridge, will join our group as we discuss the changing policies and plans for Women-in-the-Navy (WIN). I prefer the acronym WAVES. Part of me will always be a WAVE!

Yesterday we celebrated U.S. Veterans' Day and Canada Day with a flag-raising ceremony at the Shape headquarters some distance outside of Brussels near the airport. The experience, 15 flags raised in sync, with the U.S. and Canadian national anthems played over the loudspeaker, brought tears to my eyes. Someday this mighty force for democracy will win! After the ceremony we returned to the SACEUR International Mess and raised our glasses to toast the U.S. and Canada. Yes, it was a wee bit early in the morning, 0900, but the cognac fired up the festive occasion. Their Mess operates similarly to SACLANT's, with an open bar and members signing chits and paying their Mess bills once a month.

One pleasant surprise of the visit — Captain Werner Wirsing, German Navy, serves as Buck's aide. Werner worked with Buck and me at SACLANT on the Brosio Study, and I remember him fondly. It was he who introduced me to the German custom of giving gifts to others on one's own birthday, including drinks and dinner. His birthday was two days ago, and tonight he's taking me and a fellow officer out to Le Cygne, a well-known, ritzy Brussels restaurant, where they supposedly have the best mussels in the world, served with freshly baked bread to dip into the sauce. I accepted with pleasure.

I will play tourist on my last day. Buck says he'll take time out to show me the world-class military museum, CinQuant Tennaire, named for a famous Belgian battle and which has every kind of armor, weapon, and battle *tableau* imaginable. Sorry you can't go with us, Dad. I head back via D.C.

Must stop. Will fill in details upon my return to San Diego.

Love,

Tucker

Six days later from Dad

18 November 1975, San Diego, CA

Dear Tucker,

We almost envy you that great visit with Helen and Buck. Your mother said we shouldn't envy, and that, of course, is right. But your letter was so full of happy excitement that we wanted to share it. I can just see Helen pulling off a magnificent dinner in those quarters. You'll remember from Naples that NATO duty includes much social activity. Just as you've entertained all your staff members, they start entertaining you and life becomes a bit hectic at times. If anyone can carry it off well, it would be Helen and Buck.

I don't completely understand what you're doing there. If it's to brief the NATO staff on the progress the United States is making (or is not making) bringing more women into its Navy, I can understand that. But it sounds as though you're getting into basic human relationships. Isn't that what HRM means? It must be fascinating to deal with a subject like that across the cultures represented by a NATO staff.

How're they receiving you? Some European men are certainly NOT brought up to receive such information from a woman, and I'll be interested to hear how you make out. I know Buck will not place you in a position that's difficult for you. I even wonder how he relates to your talks. He's not the most liberal person in the world when it comes to women in the military and the CNO's HRM program. I share some of his concerns. We'll have a lot to talk over when you get home. Nice to know we can do it face-to-face and I won't have to talk to you over the phone, or try to read between the lines in a letter.

Things go well here. Your mother's busy with her Book and Garden Clubs, and I'm enjoying sailing more every day. Maybe I'll get to become the Yacht Club's Commodore. No one has called me "Commodore" in a long time!

Come on home. Those Europeans have had you long enough.
We both send our love.

Dad

P.S. Will mail this to Tom Parker's address.

Ten days later from Tucker

28 November 1975, San Diego, California

Dear Tom,

So good to see you last week — and looking so much better
than in April. Wish I could visit more often. I'm glad you and the
doctors are pleased with your progress. I was quite impressed with
how you're managing your job while undergoing chemo. Must be
your "good attitude."

Lots of work awaited me upon my return. As I mentioned, each
HRM Team has an HRAV (Human Resource Availability) per
month, plus follow-up work with previous clients. Next week we'll
be working with a guided missile cruiser and two squadrons. So far
only one commanding officer (of a Fast Frigate) has flinched at
working with a woman officer.

"How can a woman tell me a damn thing about running my
ship?" he growled. I let it slide, and in time he changed his tune
and realized we don't tell him how to run his ship.

People seem more open and relaxed in San Diego than on the
East Coast. But the politics of Southern California lean toward
the right, unlike little Rhodey's more liberal tilt.

Speaking of politics, I want to tell you about an unusual incident
that occurred yesterday. Can't figure it. One of my fellow Team
Leaders is Commander Forrest Hancock, a guest at the "Hanoi
Hilton" for 7 years and who tells stories about confinement as a
POW which shock even our Vietnam veterans. Until his riveting
account and slide presentation, I hadn't heard first hand of the
ungodly torture the Vietnamese inflicted upon our prisoners.
Forrest, about 37 years old and normally weighing in at 180 pounds,
dropped to 90 pounds during solitary confinement, lost most of his
teeth and now has a beautiful head of prematurely white hair.

Having endured such excruciating pain and many near-death
experiences, Forrest doesn't suffer any fools. Yesterday, in the Team
Leaders' meeting, Forrest stood up and with an air of dignity took
on our commanding officer, Captain Hennessey, who tends to be
sort of rigid about Center procedures. The Captain was explaining

one more team procedural requirement when Forrest burst into a quiet, passionate rage. I'd never witnessed a junior officer chewing out a senior officer. Forrest, clearly troubled, pulled no punches. He said *exactly* what I was thinking, but would never have the gumption to say. Forrest even swore at Captain Hennessey. The Captain was clearly startled and angry at Forrest's actions, though he didn't bite back. I sensed the POW filter overrode others. The Captain probably thought seven years of hell is a long time in one's life.

In private, Forrest later confided to me that he's struggling with being a senior naval officer in an organization that carries on in such stupid ways. He wants to live each day in freedom and questions whether he can continue as an officer. Then, he said something I'll never forget. "Tucker, how can I be an authentic person and a naval officer? It seems impossible. I've lost my capacity to tolerate incompetency and inane regulations."

I understand Forrest's dilemma. After seven years of wondering whether he'd ever be safe and peaceful, why should he accept for one day the craziness and nonsense we innately accept as part of our profession. Sometimes I've asked myself the same questions. Is it possible to be the person I want to be and continue to be a naval officer? You know me better than most anyone, and know I've stuffed a lot of feelings. At the same time, I'm more vocal than the average bear and can, usually gracefully, get out my differences of viewpoint.

Tom, have you ever asked yourself these same questions? I bet not. You haven't been a POW and you're not a woman activist. You fit the mold of the finest of naval officers defending his country and rarely questioning the system. Like my Dad and many others. And we need you all.

Take care of yourself, my good, good friend. And keep playing squash. You've gotta be right. Whoever heard of anyone dying who played squash every day?

Love,

Tucker

P.S. I'm wondering if you're looking at our profession a little differently now that you're back on active duty but still undergoing chemotherapy.

Two weeks later from Tom

15 December 1975, Alexandria, VA

Dear Tucker,

I've given some thought to your question about being your own man (or woman) and being in the Navy. As you know I'm a political liberal, and I don't try to hide it. Most of my fellow officers don't share my political point of view (to put it mildly), but this disagreement has never affected my naval career as far as I know. Perhaps I've been blessed with outstanding commanding officers but I believe they've always judged me on my performance alone.

Admittedly I've suffered some insults. Early in my career a fellow Lt(j.g.) said to me, "Democrats should not be cleared for Confidential." Wonder what he'd think of my having a Top Secret? I hadn't even told him I was a liberal Dem. But as I said, the officers who wrote my fitness reports based them on my performance!

Not that I've admired all my commanding officers. One of them was a real Captain Queeg and one of them just wasn't very smart. Where I was lucky was that in both cases, these jerks were preceded by outstanding men who didn't suffer fools or foolishness themselves. So when I had a weak CO I knew it was only a short time before he or I left the ship. That no intolerable situation lasts very long is a great advantage in our outfit.

So the way I've put up with other irritating situations in the Navy is "Smile, Tom, things will get better." And in my case they generally did. I'm sure, however, this isn't true for everyone. Take blacks or other minorities who know, at least in today's Navy, they have to be superior to receive equal treatment.

New subject. I've about decided to retire. Although I appear to be cancer-free after my treatment with an experimental drug, bleomycin, my Drs. will only say I'm in remission. But I'm still eligible for the Temporary Disability Retired List (TDRL). This past year has been a critical year in my career. I should've been considered for command of one of the new Trident submarines but clearly my cancer treatment prevented that. It also prevented my being Chief of Staff for a Submarine Squadron Commander. These would be the best jobs for me.

Instead, I face another two years of chemotherapy for one week each month and enduring it, while vegetating on some staff here in Washington. The doctors say I must return to this 4-drug "antineoplastic cocktail" regime to be safe, and I'm ineligible for any more bleomycin because of its experimental status.

My career's essentially through. I asked my current boss what he thought my chances of making admiral would be. He replied, charitably I thought, "You have the same chance as any other captain." He probably thought I was lucky to have been selected for captain last summer considering my continuing treatment status.

So without much hope of making admiral some day, the benefits of retirement on the TDRL with 100% disability are very attractive. I'd get 75% retired pay — untaxable, social security benefits for me and also my family if I should marry, and several lesser benefits from the VA. Also, although it'll take up to 10 years for them to say I'm cured, the key word is "temporary" so I might be able to return to active duty before then if my remission continues.

What will I do if I retire? I think some type of volunteer job, maybe in Congress. A freshman (is it all right to say "freshwoman"?) liberal Dem. Congresswoman, Ann Haynes from Minnesota, serves on the Armed Services Committee and the Seapower Subcommittee. She needs someone to help her. She certainly isn't getting any from the services.

I want to work for a liberal for two reasons: First, I feel we're spending too much on defending ourselves from an enemy that isn't as powerful as we're told. The second reason relates to the first but is more insane: Why do we continue to build nuclear weapons when our arsenal is large enough to wipe out the Soviet Union and most of the rest of the world! Why we maintain and increase this nuclear arsenal continues to mystify me.

Some day, Tuck, we can have a long talk about this, but as I see it there's no logical explanation. As a nuclear warrior, I never knew who was deciding how many nuclear weapons we should have. We got forty-one SSBNs, but there's no justification for these numbers other than having more nuclear weapons, of every kind, than the Soviets.

I'm sure this Congresswoman would like to correct both of these problems.

My most recent news is that I've been accepted to a Masters program in Foreign Affairs at George Washington University. More good news is that, now that I'm in remission, people have stopped saying to me, "Be sure to have a good time." They never added, "before you die," but I could hear it anyway!

This letter's probably too long, but as Churchill wrote, "...if I had more time I would have written a shorter letter."

I'll let you know how my plans work out.

> Love,
>
> Tom

Nine months later from Tucker

13 September 1976, San Diego, California

Dear Billie,

Today I facilitated a Women-in-the-Navy Workshop, which we're now offering fleet-wide, distinct from Equal Opportunity (Race Relations) workshops. I'm still unnerved by the day, but maybe writing you will cool me down. How many more years do we women have to listen to stupid, sexist remarks? The workshop's participants were mainly former enlisted men, which may explain their high resistance to women as peers and shipmates, though I'm unsure about that...

The workshop design begins with setting ground rules that permit open expression of feelings. And we got into feelings! Before we'd consumed our first cup of coffee, my teammate, Henry Brown (a black senior chief), and I were blasted by negative statements about Navy women. To quadruple the numbers of enlisted women in four years has caused problems, and as you well know, much anger prevails about how to deal with these increasing numbers.

Having learned from our Race Relations training, the workshop designers combined the two basic approaches to bringing about organizational change. First, we share attitudes about the sexes; then, we present Navy policies and organizational expectations. For the first few hours, my adrenalin pumped overtime.

What most bothered me? That the CO and XO failed to respond to zinger statements from their subordinates. For instance, a lieutenant said, "Yes, I'm sexist, and I will be proud to remain sexist in the Navy." No response from the command. I had to respond, of course. "I'm a woman and will be proud to remain a woman in the Navy, in spite of prejudiced remarks like yours, Lieutenant, which are from this day on unacceptable by Navy policy."

What I would like to have said is unprintable — except here. "You're nothing but an asinine male chauvinist pig, and not worth my time of day." But that would've been unprofessional and out-of-character.

The CO and XO continually expressed sexist statements about Navy women. You and I both know it's still okay to be sexist in the Fleet, though not okay to be racist (progress?!).

One of the workshop diagrams develops the concept that men in the services for years have readily accepted myths and stereotypes about women. This is the real issue, one we won't eliminate overnight! The good news is we're at last accepting that uniformed women are here to stay, in the REAL NAVY, and talking openly about how to resolve problems.

In the afternoon we worked on specific items to be inserted into their Affirmative Action Plan, including watch assignments, professional assignments, uniform regulations, paternalism, and convalescent leave (for pregnancy). I'm delighted that women who become pregnant on active duty are no longer automatically discharged. Many senior officers and chiefs, however, are very unhappy with implementation of our pregnancy policy, and believe that enlisted women due to pregnancy have more lost time than men. Statistics prove otherwise.

Senior Chief Brown and I pointed out the milestones and changes for Navy women since 1972, including that the first class at the Naval Academy to graduate women reported to Annapolis this summer. The men dislike this and said so, "If women can't go to sea, why should they go to the Academy?" I didn't tell them that my dad often expresses the same view.

Sometimes, Billie, it feels as though we women are perennial guinea pigs, with the Navy getting its kicks tinkering with us. But at other times, I realize to move mountains requires much time and patience. As Lucretia Mott said, "Any great change must expect opposition, because it strikes at the very foundation of privilege."

Did I tell you I screened for command? I feel fortunate to be among the first women to have command opportunity. While my present tour has been a real learning base from which to observe and teach leadership and management, to know my next tour will be as a CO is kinda scary, partly because I will skip the XO tour due to affirmative action. Just as well. As you know, personality-wise, I'm more a CO than XO. Administrative details never have thrilled me! No comment from you, my friend!

I feel better having done a dump on you. I shall not continue to facilitate these workshops, even though I'm a natural and a subject-matter expert! Too emotionally taxing.

Will be back to D.C. on TAD in the next few months. We'll have to explore our favorite restaurants, assuming I have some evenings free. In the meantime I'm headed to Pearl next month on TAD with a sub tender. I'll see how Jennie's doing. She retired in the rank of Captain 1 Sept. Wonder if she's sorry she left the Navy now that she's alone.

Take care my friend. I'm looking forward to your visit.

Love,

Tucker

Two weeks later from Tucker's journal

27 September 1976, San Diego, CA

 For the record,

Billie and I had some good times this week. She's been TAD for a CHINFO function at 32nd Street. Stayed with me. She told a story about a discussion panel concerning women aboard ships held at the Pentagon. After listening to one male officer express concern about the lack of physical strength of women and not wanting to rely on women because of that factor, one young, slender female lieutenant stood up and said, "My three brothers and I grew up on a wheat farm in Minnesota. I carried my weight during the physical labor and never needed help. I know I can throw a bale of hay farther than most of you. Besides, it doesn't matter because if I'm standing beside you and a missile hits the ship — when they pick up the pieces no one can tell the difference. My guts will look exactly like yours."

TF

Chapter Nine

The Shift

Two weeks later from Tucker's journal

10 October 1976, Pearl Harbor, Hawaii

For the record,

I'm leaving early tomorrow, on my way home from TAD to USS *Sunley*, a submarine tender homeported in San Diego. The skipper, Captain Pete Dunlap, a nuclear submariner and friend of Tom's, asked for me personally to assist him in his Human Resource Availability follow-up work here, having begun the process with my team in San Diego. The days have gone well, using the HRM Center Pearl's rooms. I helped Pete's people rework their HRM Plan and facilitated ongoing Communications workshops. Communication, at all levels of supervision, continues to be the primary "people" problem area for commands. No doubt true for the corporate world as well!

Pete Dunlap's a real jewel, and between the HRM work and personal stories we've had a productive, fun time. He told me he hadn't made flag because he'd been too outspoken in the wrong places and times. Pete's pleased with *Sunley'*s progress vis-a-vis HRM matters in the last six months. The cycle's working!

I'm staying in the BOQ and tonight have thought about my days at Pearl Harbor Elementary, which isn't too far from here. The teachers were excellent; the quonset huts, unique and kinda half-roundedly barren, reminded one of WWII; the student camaraderie of all Navy juniors, special; and, me as May Day narrator, a little scary. "May Day is Lei Day in Ha-vah-ee."

Later on the plane home to San Diego

Need to write about the week's major event — being with Jennie. She's as lovely as ever — more than I'd remembered. Maturity, including her gray hair, agrees with her. Perhaps retirement too. Jennie and I had dinner Thursday night with CDR Sara Gordon and LCDR P.D. (Patricia) Hayward. We had drinks at The House Without a Key at the Halekulani Hotel, with two Hawaiian musicians playing romantic background music. *Lovely Hula Hands* and *The Hawaiian Wedding Song* are my all-time favorites. Then we walked over to the Hau Tree Lanai restaurant. Branches of three very old hau trees formed a canopy-like ceiling, reinforced by a permanent overhead. As we talked and ate, we could see the surfers in the distance coming in on their last rides at twilight.

We talked shop and politics, including the coming election probabilities. Sure hope Jimmy Carter can pull if off. We're due for a Democrat. (Not everyone agreed.) Sara and P.D. are challenged by their billets — personnel and intelligence — but they're unhappy with the sexism still prevalent in the Navy. Sara told of a recent event where her boss was making passes at her in his office. Times aren't all that different. After dinner and coffee Jennie and I said "aloha" to our friends and decided to go for a walk on the beach, which had emptied of people shortly after sunset. We walked slowly, talking about my screening for command, her grieving process, her new job with Coldwell Banker, and Women-in-the-Navy workshops.

Then, without skipping a step, I said out of the blue, "I feel an attraction to you, Jennie." No prep work, Fairfield!

Jennie stopped. I stopped. She looked directly at me and said, "That's mutual, Tucker."

My forwardness and her candor surprised us both. Of course I remembered Jennie's comment long ago in Newport, on the rocky Atlantic coast. She'd said she could be interested in me sexually but would go on another path. One of equal strength. And look what happened. She had a good marriage with dear Pierre. Why would she now choose to get involved with a woman? Beats me.

We walked a little longer. Then decided to sit down on the beach and rest for a moment.

I couldn't not say it. "Would it be all right if I just held your hand?"

Jennie placed her hand in mine. And it was magic. Bells, whistles, overlaid with serenity and heart-thumping fear. We watched the waves roll in and then looked at each other. I leaned over and kissed her! Then we hugged. Talked.

It was late. We turned around and began walking to the hotel and car. Our hands separated. What would people think?

Damn. Society is unfair.

Jennie drove me to the BOQ. Neither of us said anything profound. How I would've liked to have kissed her one more time.

She called the next night and talked as if nothing had happened between us. At the same time, she said we'd stay in touch.

I'm confused. Excited. And very likely in love with someone who will not be my partner.

Go with your feelings, Fairfield. That's your only option these days.

TF

Six days later from Tom

16 Oct 1976, Alexandria, Virginia

Ahoy there Tuck,

I'm home trying to recover from chemo-induced nausea. These days I start getting nauseated even before I get the injection. All I have to do is get within two blocks of the hospital. I tried to produce a counter mind-body reaction by thinking of my favorite food, but all that did was make me feel nauseated the next time it was served.

Rep. Ann Haynes, my boss since 1 Feb, finally received a letter from the Navy in response to her inquiry asking about the health status of nuclear submarine officers. So far, I personally know 12 nuke XOs and COs who have died of cancer and several others who have had some kind of cancer. This must be excessive since men their age normally have higher rates of heart attacks than of cancer, but I only know one who has had a heart attack. The Navy told Ann that, "The incidence of death from cancer for active duty nuclear submariners is far less than that of the population as a whole."

This statement is worthless on several counts: First, the comparison population should be men of the same age, preferably non-submariners in the Navy, not the whole US population which includes the elderly. Second, survivors should be counted. As naval personnel have immediate access to comprehensive free health care and are more healthy on average than the rest of the population, they should be more likely to survive. Third, those who have separated from the service should be counted. Everyone I know who has died of cancer retired prior to death because the retirement benefits to survivors are better.

Apparently the Navy cannot determine the health status of everyone who has ever served in nuclear subs. The Navy maintains a history of every piece of machinery and yet has no comparable records of its personnel. It's possible to determine the average hours until failure of every Navy pump, but it's impossible to determine the number of personnel who have died of cancer and served on nuclear ships. If the Navy were seriously concerned about the health of its nuclear sailors, it could flag their medical records and team up with the VA to obtain an accurate picture of what appears to be a serious health problem.

I've drafted a letter for Ann to send to the Navy pointing out the obvious problems and requesting a study that includes retirees and personnel separated before retirement eligibility. The situation may be an example of the impersonality of the military which tends to overwhelm individuals at times, or it simply may be that no one imagined service on nuclear subs could pose a health risk. You and your women's movement are right, Tuck, "the personal is political," but I'm still counting on our Navy doing the right thing by implementing a proper study.

Lest you think I only work on stuff that affects me, set your mind at rest. I'm also working on the big picture — why the US and USSR have 30,000 nuclear weapons and the implications of having them; military readiness; and YES, women in the military.

The most I've accomplished so far is to define the problems. Next I'll work on the solutions. Sorry, but here's another one of my lists:

1. The number of nuclear weapons is simply the result of an arms race. There can be no logic to justify building weapons that could destroy several times over, not only an apparent enemy, but also the rest of the world. Yet the US and the USSR continue to build nuclear weapons to attempt to ensure they have more weapons than the other in EVERY CATEGORY.

2. Military readiness suffers because it has no political constituency. Its natural constituency is the services themselves, but they're more interested in developing new weapons than in maintaining existing ones. Other than Admiral Rickover's Naval Reactors organization, I know of no military agency in Washington that's actually interested in what happens to the weapons they impose on the soldiers and sailors in the field. The big money is in new weapons.

3. From my current position with Congress I'm more able to monitor the problems of women in the military, because a lot of disgruntled women write to Ann. So far, there's little more we can do than approach the DOD on the problem's legitimacy. Usually

we receive a polite but noncommittal answer. I'd say we have a long way to go before the Navy achieves the spirit of Z-gram 116. Widespread corporate resistance to accepting women's equality in the military prevails. The predominant opinion blames the victim. If the women weren't there, then the problems wouldn't be there either. I try to maintain contact with active duty personnel and especially count on friends like you to keep me informed about what's really going on in the field.

I'm going to Mich for a week. Nothing special. Just catch up with my family. One nephew has joined the Navy and will be in the Navy band. I think I'll talk to one or two nieces about going to Annapolis or NROTC. I can be nothing but grateful for the education and opportunities the Navy's given to me.

Keep in touch. Come to visit. You can visit even if I'm not dying!

> XOX,
>
> Tom

Nine days later from Tucker

25 October 1976, San Diego, California

Dear Jennie,

First of all, I miss you. Seems strange, since I didn't miss you like this before two weeks ago, and I hadn't seen you for a long time before. I feel cheated to be unable to continue our conversation and relate in person.

Secondly, I'm still befuddled and amazed at whatever happened between us. For me, I did what I've been honoring lately — go with my feelings, especially when they're so intense. Rarely, in fact never in my life, have I had such a pull toward someone, and I wasn't about to suppress it. If you hadn't responded, I probably would see you as my stereotype of a neat woman who, like me, has missed a lot by not at least experiencing women. Yet I'm definitely not the person to change another woman's behavior. I have sufficient resistances of my own!

I do have a sense that you and I were meant to have a relationship, and I believe we could have a wonderful one which would be significant for both of us. If it scares you, sorry, but that's how I perceive the situation. You turn me on more than anyone ever.

You've certainly made an impact on me, because I've had quite a few fantasies about what life might bring. In fact I haven't thought about anyone so much in a long time. Since Tom. Scares me a little, so I'll have to turn down the volume until I talk to you in person and can get a more rational perspective. You took me by surprise, I must say. Am amazed at my openness, yet that's more and more who I am and I like that about me, and about you.

At the same time, I'm aware of the restrictions on any intimate relationship we might explore. Nonetheless, fear of reprisal, of NIS, seems to be taking a passenger seat next to these powerful and wonderful feelings you've stirred in me. Life isn't always as we would imagine or predict. My life at age 39 is a great one. And I envision you'd only make it more so.

Would like to see you soon, but I realize you have a new job and other commitments and indeed I do as well. I'm eager to see you in San Diego, so do think about a visit. In the meantime, I'll call you, because I seem to miss you...either that or it's that I feel as though we have so much to share and I have a need to do that now. I do wish you were here, or that we were on a long vacation together. Then I could talk to you in person and get some immediate personal responses from you.

I trust myself, and I trust you and somehow know whatever happens will be good for both of us. I really like what I see in your eyes and identify with the warmth and love that you radiate. I meant to tell you I especially love your beautiful, in-set hazel eyes and your graceful hands.

Hope this letter makes a little sense. Difficult to write about feelings. I'm glad we re-connected and I'm looking forward to a special relationship, whatever that turns out to be.

Take good care of your lovely self and see you soon. Aloha.

       Love,

       Tucker

Three weeks later from Jennie

                       15 November 1976, Honolulu, Hawaii

Dear Tucker,

I'm not sure where to begin, which accounts for my not sending you a reply sooner. Your letter was a bit rambling and I cannot, and don't want to, respond item by item. So, I'll just plunge in.

I too was deeply moved by our evening together last month. It's the first time I've let myself really feel anything other than grief and loss since Pierre's death. I believe your vulnerability touched me deeply and in turn invited me out of the closet, so to speak. It was wonderful to relax into being desired and desirable, and there's no doubt in my mind that it was mutual.

Having said that however, dear Tucker, please try to understand, I do not want to commit to anything right now. These feelings are too new, too raw. You should also know that I've never forgotten our discussion back on the rocks in Newport. At that time it seemed really important to put my career in the driver's seat. My head, not my heart, ruled. But now a lot has changed.

Looking back at my marriage to Pierre, I'm beginning to see where some of my resistance came from, although at the time I didn't want to look very deeply into my own self.

That I am curious about loving women — a woman — you — I cannot deny. That I am wanting it to be more than an exploration, I truly don't know.

I find it deliciously exciting to get your special letter and yet I'm at a loss as to how to respond, except to say that I am willing — be honest — I want, to see you again *with no expectations*. I hope it's possible to go slowly, feeling our way — oops, probably wrong choice of words, or perhaps a Freudian slip! — into whatever is possible between us. I'm just finishing up my classes here with Coldwell Banker and then I'll have to jump into building a clientele. Lots of hard work and a major energy and time commitment.

But all work and no play makes Jill a dull girl as they say, so perhaps I can give myself a little vacation around the holidays. They can be a difficult time anyhow. I could come to San Diego for a week or so. Let me know what works for you since I can probably be more flexible than you. Hopefully you don't have to hold some skipper's hand while he initiates his HRM cycle on the day after Christmas.

So, my dear, despite this probably mixed message, I want you to know that you pop up in my mind's eye at odd moments of the day and night. I will try to address more of your points at a later date. This is all I can handle right now.

Let me know about Christmas.

      With lots of feelings,

      Jennie

Six weeks later from Jennie

3 January 1977, En route to Honolulu on Flight 2356

Dear Tucker,

Wow, I think I'm on overload! Thank you for being a wonderful hostess — and lover. I loved getting all the personalized tours of San Diego. The zoo really is wonderful. No wonder it has such a grand reputation. And like Honolulu there's no shortage of good places to eat. It was especially nice to drive up the Coast and eat at The Chart House, right on the water. Can you imagine what that would be like in a big storm — the waves could crash right through the windows! Rather like how my energy level feels when I think about coming up against you. Wow!

I'm overwhelmed with this sense of "coming home" when we make love. I've heard about it, but haven't experienced it before. Is this the bottom line when one woman loves another?

And that brings me to a reality check: I'm home here in Hawaii at least for the time being. Much as my body craves seeing you weekly (daily!), my head reminds me that I've only begun to make a new home for myself here in Honolulu; I'm still coming to grips with who I am without the Navy, without my stripes, and yes, without Pierre. I'm enjoying my new-found freedom immensely. You must remember it's also freedom to be with you when we can work it out. We've discussed how this is a time of new exploration for me, on so many levels. And I think the same is true for you, my lovely Tucker.

So I would suggest we be resigned to/excited by a long-distance affair for the time being while we both integrate this incredible meeting of minds and bodies. Who knows, maybe someday our love letters will be the basis for a best seller!

It was most enjoyable and special to meet your friends; you've met some wonderful people in San Diego — course there's that core of Navy folks whose paths we keep crossing. Reminds me, Tom and Joanna seem very happy together. Wonder if they'll get married soon?

Since Pierre died I haven't dated anyone, except for you. Is that what we're doing, dating? I think I'd like to open my vistas a bit and see what else is out there. Tucker, please try to understand, I care about you more than I probably want to admit to myself, but I must be sure. To step into this lifestyle without being absolutely sure of what I'm doing seems stupid and only hurtful to you in the long run.

Take care. Know that I care deeply about you and am grateful for your opening me, and you, to a whole new spectrum of possibilities.

With love and caring,

Jennie

Ten weeks later from Tucker

15 March 1977, San Diego, California

Dear Robyn,

It's been too long since we've connected. Why do Americans correspond less and less? Thirteen cents a letter is a good deal. Probably our accelerated pace and need for instant gratification. No excuses.

I've been thinking of you and your family and wondering how you're balancing career and children? Have you metamorphed into Superwoman yet? You'd be a great counterpart to Clark Kent! I don't envy you...most of the time. On the other hand, this professional woman lifestyle can be a lonely experience.

My career and Navy women in general are striding along smartly. I can't tell you how good I feel about the changes for military women coming so rapidly!! We even have our first admiral. Our organizational ambiance is shifting to women as real contributors. We've instituted workshops throughout the Navy, similar to those in the civilian world, addressing women's equal opportunity issues. And, to be racist or sexist is no longer okay, though I know some Navy women continue daily to experience sexual harassment.

Navy leadership is considering changing the law (Article 6015, Title 10) which prohibits women serving aboard ships. While our pilot test of women serving at sea (on the hospital ship, USS *Sanctuary*) went well, a high resistance factor to the women-at-sea program remains. By the way, the *Sanctuary* evaluation concluded that, "In general, the enlisted women's performance on watch is on a par with or, at times, superior to that of men with equal experience and time in the Navy. The striking difference is that women perform their assigned tasks with inspiring enthusiasm which invites a man to do his best." Not surprising, eh?

Several friends have instituted a class action legal suit against the Secretary of the Navy which will test the constitutionality of Article 6015. Talk about courage! Navy women, like civilian women, are learning to use our legal system to achieve equality of opportunity. We know that successes will come slowly. One day at a time in sisterhood!

But integration is a slow process. As you remember, I'm stationed at a recruit training center, one of three in the country, and some days I get downright annoyed with young male recruits (they look like babies!) who salute and greet me with a "Good morning, sir," or "Good afternoon, sir."

I typically don't confront them, but yesterday I said, "Young man, do I look like a sir?"

He replied, "No, sir, you don't. But what do I call you?" I said, "Ma'am would do fine." I've finally gotten used to "ma'am," certainly a better description than "sir."

It's the little touches that need changing. Most enlisted personnel, for instance, are trained to answer the phone with their duty station and name and then, "How may I help you, sir?" As long as I'm in a good mood, I let it go. Imagine how most men would react if daily they heard, "How may I help you, ma'am?" We're going to recruit a lot more women in the Navy before traditions and mores become inclusive.

Enough Navy. My West Coast assignment has brought me closer to your civilian world. I'm involved with the Unitarian Church as well as some women's activities. Of course, there are regular family functions with my folks. So I do have a life outside the Navy, more than in previous years. Because of my expertise in military women's matters, I've given talks at several local universities. San Diego State University has one of the oldest and largest Women's Studies Departments in the country, and I've made some good friends with department faculty.

Yet I find myself in a sort of social dilemma: As you know, since my experience with Tom I've had no sex life except for dates with men, and thus honored the Navy's policy toward gays. In retrospect, this decision seems dumb juxtaposed with my wish to explore relationships and move away from power and achievement. In the last several years, the reality I've been observing is that civilian heterosexual and gay worlds have usually separate social gatherings, mixing only at office and family social functions. Seems wrong and unnecessary to me, but that's the way it is.

Because of this reality, as far as partying and meeting people, lately I feel like neither fish nor fowl, nor kangaroo (as you once joked). Relatedly, I was going out with a great guy, a former POW, and having fun; but, as soon as he learned of my "status," he stopped asking me out. We're still good friends but he's looking for something else in a date. So, in choosing to remain asexual and single, I cut off opportunities to meet interesting women and men except as friends. Friends are of course important! Military policy expects that active duty gays and lesbians, heaven forbid they might exist, be nonsexual and that they completely reject this part of their identity.

Other women officer friends have chosen this same asexual way of life and therefore I have companions for the movies, theater concerts, and desert and whatever. I still, however, would like to have a partner someday. If the truth be known, I've fallen in love with Jennie Dumonte, whom you met several years ago. She's a widow, retired from the Navy, and living here. If I go down deep (as you would have me do), I realize I've been in love with her since WOCS days. That Jennie is open to experiencing a relationship with me seems like a miracle! My connection to her probably is as close as yours is with Ned. Magic happens!

But, as with Ned and you in the early stages, Jennie isn't ready for a committed one-to-one and wants "more freedom" for growing. And besides, part of me is downright scared.

Life's a real conundrum at the moment. I plan to stay in past twenty and go for captain. Are promotion and greater responsibility worth this solitary confinement of any sexual drive? Any suggestions, my friend?

As usual, please keep the above dilemma *confidential.*

And as usual I delved into some fairly heady issues with you, the nature of which has changed only slightly since our early correspondence! Where's my maturity? We're both approaching the big 4–0! Or are you there? You're a lot older than I, as I remember. A joke!

Would treasure an update from you. In the meantime, lots of love to you and your family.

Tucker

Two weeks later from Tom

27 March 1977, Alexandria, VA

Dear Tucker,

It's time I updated you on some of my life events. The most important is that Joanna and I have set Thanksgiving Day to be married. Maybe that's a little corny but choosing a day set aside for giving thanks might give us a beneficent start. My last (Hooray!) chemo week is in Sept. The only good thing about the chemo is that it acts as an insect repellent. Once in a while, a mosquito makes a mistake and takes a bite and you can almost see the little devil spit it back.

I intended not to marry until at least five years out from my surgery, but Joanna convinced me that, as life's uncertain for everyone, we should go for it. We've surely given our relationship an adequate "shakedown cruise." With the decision actually made, I find I am truly joyful. The ceremony will in Charleston and will be small, with close friends and family, and Carolyn and Willy standing up for us. Of course in my case, family alone can almost fill an average size chapel! I always imagined my best man would be someone other than one of my brothers to avoid the difficulty of choosing among them. Pierre likely would've been that choice but sadly his death makes that impossible. I asked Jennie to come but at this point she's uncertain. Joanna and I hope you'll make it. If you can come, maybe you can talk her into it.

Second, I'm fed up with working in Congress. There's an old saying that if you want to continue to respect two things you should never see them being made. One is sausage; the other, laws. No one in Congress can contain the military. The present system works like this: the military says it needs something; then Congress holds some "mock" hearings and accepts the military's logic no matter how unreasonable. This disgusting situation exists because of the close liaison among the military, defense industry, and key Congressional leaders. Prior to the military making its request, Congressional leaders are informed of the money to be pumped into the economy, especially into their districts, and everything is agreed to. The unsuspecting members of Congress who might be in opposition, such as my Congresswoman, only hear about the deal when it's made public and by then it's too late.

I really admire Ann Haynes but, because of her junior status and liberal politics, she gets no cooperation from the military. Having me on her staff has helped her become more knowledgeable but not more influential. The military looks at me as sort of a "dirty trick" she plays in an effort to gain credibility. That I'm a volunteer somehow makes my motives even more suspect.

So I'm going to leave her staff after I receive my M.A. from GWU in December and will try to return to active duty. The way the TDRL works is that the military member (on the list) is examined at 18 mos. to determine physical status and then again at three years, after which that status becomes permanent. I remained on the list after the 18 mos. exam primarily because both my Dr. and I thought I was only in remission. At the three-year exam, Jan '78, unless things change, I'll have a hard time convincing myself that I deserve 100% disability permanently. And I don't know what my Dr. will say. A "statistical cure" isn't even suggested until you've been disease-free for five years. See my dilemma?

If I'm cured I don't want a permanent disability status that I really don't rate; at the same time, if I'm sick I'd certainly want that status. So what I'm going to try to do is return to active duty and wait to clarify my health question. If my cancer returns, I can always return to the disability list; if not I'll proceed to a normal 26-year retirement. Coming off the TDRL I'd normally get some cushy job in Washington, maybe in Congressional relations, but my association with the Congresswoman and the enemies I've made in the Navy will probably preclude this. I hope to use both what I've learned in grad school and on the hill, maybe as something like liaison officer to the Arms Control and Disarmament Agency. I know I won't make flag, but I must let that go.

So, Tuck, "the times they are a 'changin.'" I'll keep you informed particularly if I return to active duty. Keep sending up those good thoughts for me. I still need 'em. I hope you've learned the Hawaiian wedding song by now. I want you to play a duet with me at the reception!

Love from your still pickin' and strummin' Tom.

One week later from Robyn

April 5, 1977, Bar Harbor, Maine

SIR!

I found your gender-title anecdotes extremely entertaining! Talk about literalistic, concrete interpretation of etiquette, orders, or whatever! Talk about losing touch with common sense and the context of the real, or rather, broader world (no pun intended)! Or, as you call it, the "civilian" environment. Speaking of which, you sound as if you're re-emerging from the rarified military atmosphere and positively squinting in the bright San Diego sunlight! Welcome aboard! Note the Navy jargon designed to ease the transition.

Your ongoing dilemma has been reactivated by contacts in your new, expanded universe. I refer, of course, to your choice between close relationship vs. raw ambition. Tucker, I can't really make recommendations since, despite our friendship, we clearly come at this adventure called Life from different places.

Having said that, here's one bit of sisterly advice I might pass along: Maybe you should relax and let happen what will. I understand you feel you need to be always wary when expressing your feelings. It seems to me, however, this need to analyze every situation can only have the effect of distancing potential relationships or stunting them, before they can begin.

Maybe that's a slightly harsh take on the situation, but as I see it, you need to prioritize some decisions. A compromise isn't possible and you seem to want some kind of closure. In this case, your integrity's pressed to its limit and something must give — your career or the rest of your life. As in Big Daddy Navy or Jennie. Your choice.

Life isn't easy. You were probably born fifty years too soon (through no fault of your own, of course). Some day, some time, all this stuff will be sorted out. But not in time for you (us). And, P.S. I'm NOT a lot older than you, you ageist creep!

So, Sir, how you proceed is up to you, and you alone (alas).

We're fine and thriving, and I'm continually grateful that Ned and I decided to move from the big city to the likes of beautiful, spacious Maine. Come for another visit and we'll treat you to a soccer tournament (Derry's team is 8th out of 9.)

Roger, then, and over and out, SIR.

Love,

Robyn

Six weeks later from Jennie

27 May 1977, Honolulu, Hawaii

Dear Tucker,

This has been an extraordinarily busy time: Having graduated from real estate school, and that was pretty demanding, I find that setting up a real estate practice takes a lot of grit. Making cold calls to prospects isn't fun, no matter what anybody says. But I have one property in escrow and another family looks about ready to make a bid on a beautiful waterfront home on Waikiki. If that one happens I can easily afford a trip to D.C. and that's one reason for this letter.

I have on my desk the invitation to our WAVES' 35th Reunion in Washington in August. Knowing your enthusiasm for women in the Navy, no pun intended, my dear, I'm sure you won't miss this. I too would like to go. I must be honest, I also want to spend some time with you. Perhaps you could arrange for a few extra days of leave. I probably can find someone to cover for me for a week.

You must know you're never far from my thoughts. But I'm also aware that my decision to stay here has been a good one and one that I'm going to stick with for the time being. I often think back to my Christmas visit in San Diego. What a good time we had and what a delightful city that is. Tucker, I'm happy here. It's beginning to feel like my home, so for the time being I see no reason to consider any moves. As far as I know you don't know where your next duty station will be anyway.

Need to type up flyer info for a new listing. Think about August in D.C. Probably not a great name for a song, but it could be a good place for a rendezvous.

Hear from you soon I hope.

> With love,
>
> Jennie

Ten weeks later from Tucker's journal

7 August 1977, en route to San Diego

For the record,

What a week! Not only did we WAVES celebrate ourselves and our unique history, but Jennie and I had a glorious time together, sharing a room at the Mayflower.

While my feelings of love for her are unparalleled, I still feel somewhat confused and cautious. The confusion is more fear of allowing myself to be vulnerable to giving myself in the deepest way to a woman while I'm on active duty. The caution. Well, I'm violating the UCMJ and I could be court-martialled. I'd resign first. If the circumstances were otherwise, there'd be no question what I'd want.

The week topped off with my detailer telling me that I'm slated for a command in Pearl. Is that ever luck, happiness, and karma!!

Life's great, except I'm very tired, and I already miss Jennie's body and soul. I hope she'll be able to attend Tom's wedding in Nov. I don't think I can wait to see her until March! For sure! It's ironic that now I'm leaving S.D., Tom's been assigned here. Wonder how he'll find returning to active duty and also returning to being married?

TF

Seven weeks later from Billie

28 Sept. 77, Monterey, CA

Dear Tuck —

It was great to see you. I had a marvelous visit in San Diego, and since many of our friends are settling in San Diego, I know I'll visit often. It's not that long a drive from Monterey. The tedious part is "El Lay." Anyway, thanks for the side trip to Ensenada, the beach party on the Strand, and that terrific dinner at the Top O' the Cove in La Jolla. San Diego might be a Navy town, but it has a few other things going on.

As does Monterey. I've rented a small house on the top of what I suspect is Steinbeck's "Bumbleberry Hill" overlooking Cannery Row and beautiful Monterey Bay. Every morning as I leave for work, I look down on the Bay and say, "Those poor slobs back in D.C." Monterey, Pacific Grove, Pebble Beach, Carmel, and Carmel Valley are breathtakingly beautiful. Big Sur is beyond belief!

My job as Public Affairs Officer for the PG School is so-so. The Admiral read my record and saw the security assignment at Pearl, so I'm also the Security Officer. Public Affairs here is certainly not as hectic as in the Pentagon. As I said in S.D., this is a passover assignment, an idiot job. As I survey the staff at the School, however, with the exception of one or two officers, I'm not alone in the passover department. I now know what the PG School Staff means to the Navy. Not much. The real movers and shakers are the students and faculty. No other female officers are attached to the staff, but several are assigned to the "Fleet Numbers" command, a sort of computerized weather command that translates satellite weather data for the fleet.

I'm settled in for the duration and looking forward toward retirement. I'm getting gold shots at Ft. Ord hospital. I have a very efficient Public Affairs staff. We publish a newsletter, do radio and TV broadcasts for the Armed Forces Radio and TV, do the school brochures. I've assigned the Chief to research the history of the Hotel Del Monte (the main building here), and I liaise with the Peninsula Chamber of Commerce community relations committee. Very mundane stuff. Oh, I forgot, I've contacted the Pacific Fleet scheduling officer to see if some ships can lay over at Monterey — show the flag and all that.

I try not to be down in the dumps, but sometimes it's an overriding feeling. I know, I know, I told you in San Diego I was okay, but I can't help feeling down. As I said, after all I've done for the Navy, here I am — out to pasture like some old mare in

Kentucky. To keep my spirits up and to keep me busy, I joined the Monterey Little Theater. Not on stage, but behind the scenes. I'm the props manager, help paint scenery, and other jobs. It's helped me socially, and I've met some good people.

I bet you're excited about your orders to Hawaii and command. I know I am! That means I can come to visit. Speaking of visiting, how about running up here one weekend?

Your friend,

Billie

Four months later from Jennie

2 Feb 1978, Honolulu, Hawaii

Tucker Dear,

I'm so thrilled that you will actually *be* here next month! I've cleared my calendar for the couple of days surrounding your arrival and the Change of Command.

And as your realtor of choice I want you to know that I've found a darling rental for you within 3 miles of Pearl, in Aiea. It'll be an easy commute so you, my workaholic friend, can go early and stay late but not get frazzled on the drive home. Besides, occasionally someone might be waiting with a cool drink and a back rub. Who knows?

Am enclosing the data on the house and a rental agreement. Check it over. I've filled in what I can and highlighted what info you need to provide. If this sounds okay, send back the paperwork and a deposit check and I'll do the rest. You see, my XO tour has stood me in good stead, to say nothing of being a realtor!

Hope your closing days in San Diego are going smoothly. I seem to remember that "stuff" always used to appear at the last moment. I'm sure you can handle it.

See you SOON!

Love and hugs (there are never enough of those),

Jennie

Chapter Ten

Command

Six weeks later from Tucker's journal

17 March 1978, Pearl Harbor, Hawaii

For the record,

A PEOPLE PLACE

If this is not a place where my spirits can take wing,
　　　Where do I go to fly?
If this is not a place where tears are understood,
　　　Where do I go to cry?
If this is not a place where my questions can be asked,
　　　Where do I go to seek?
If this is not a place where my feelings can be heard,
　　　Where do I go to speak?
If this is not a place where you'll accept me as I am,
　　　Where can I go to be?
If this is not a place where I can try and learn and grow,
　　　Where can I just be me?

This poem by W.J. Crockett was the theme of my assumption of command today. Instead of discussing Navy policy, or new personnel, or the disbursing system, I spoke of my own philosophy about people, and how our command can be a healthy, productive place in which to work. The poem gave me freedom to speak about the unspoken in our profession — crying, feeling, being. What we naval officers don't often address publicly or privately.

What a thrilling day! The flags flew gently in the Hawaiian tradewinds, the weather was perfect, and we all looked elegant in our Dress Whites. I'm surprised so many friends and family members, in addition to Jennie and my parents, came to the ceremony. I can't believe both Robyn and Billie flew over. Robyn and Ned decided to get out of wintry Maine and capitalize on the time as vacation. Billie took leave. Tom flew in from San Diego, with Joanna home with the children. What a special treat. Mother and Dad came over from California and are staying at the Hale Koa, our military hotel. And Captain Hastings, now Rear Admiral Hastings, made an extra effort and flew in from Washington for the ceremony and other official matters.

Many from other area commands attended, as well as commanding officers in the area. Several admirals too. Some in the audience squirmed a lot during the speech. Then there was Captain Shirley Blackburn, who sat in the second row behind my parents, and made faces during my entire speech! She seemed to loathe every word I said. Ah, well, she and I never have understood each other!

Fairfield, *you are the commanding officer* for over two hundred and fifty men and women. The ceremony made it so. Women made it so, by working for equal rights. The Navy made it so, by preparing me for the job and opening up opportunities for women. I made it so, by hanging in and working hard for eighteen years. As they say, "You've come a long way, baby."

The only key persons missing were Buck and Pierre. Buck's too busy in Charleston with his new investment business, and Pierre, he's off somewhere working as a guardian spirit no doubt. On the other hand, I somehow felt he and Laughing Owl were with me today helping me smile at Shirley and others who have taxed my patience (and I theirs) through the years. I do think of the Navy as my big family, and in families some members are cooperative and loving; others, resistant and downright nasty.

I felt all kinds of feelings throughout the ceremony — joy, pride, openness of heart, and excitement. Simultaneously, I felt twinges of anger and heavy-heartedness. In the speech I spoke about everyone, majority and minority, being accepted as humans who have feelings and questions and tears; yet, I can never, ever, share the feelings I have about the Navy's policy toward gay people within our Navy family.

Seems hypocritical, Fairfield, and that's not your character.

But it's also the way the ball bounces, and the policy reads. I only hope and pray that it's possible to continue to compartmentalize my thoughts about being a lesbian in an institution that denigrates the "lifestyle." Probably a hard task ahead — being a role model for my command personnel while living an allegedly sinful personal life. I certainly cannot live with Jennie during this time. Too risky and too scary.

Fortunately, I have a strong sense of self, a few friends, and Jennie, to see me over the bumps and lumps that are bound to come. Why must the Navy be so narrow, so righteous, so stick-in-the-mud, so anti-individual in certain areas? As Forrest asks, why can't an officer be an *authentic* person?

Hey, this isn't a time to be annoyed. Be joyful. I'm a commanding officer! Takes me back to when I observed Dad aboard his ships being treated like a king. Doubtful I'll be treated like a queen, but I'll be given the respect that the office commands. I do rate a command car and driver and my very own secretary!

Many are counting on you, Fairfield. Enjoy, work extra hard, take it a day at a time, and enjoy being with the love of your life.

TF

Two months later from Tucker's journal

17 June 1978, Pearl Harbor, Hawaii

 For the record,

No one said it would be easy. But no one told me I wouldn't have an Executive Officer to help create a new command, including all policies and attendant Instructions and Notices. Within a month, my XO was ordered to work for a three-star and guess who's holding down both jobs. Wouldn't be so bad, but I don't shine at details (and the devil's in the details, Fairfield). It's difficult being simultaneously the good and bad cop. Am really fortunate to have strong support from my boss. But he's leaving soon and the next one may be less supportive of this new, unpopular concept — consolidation of personnel, disbursing and transportation functions within the Navy. Change causes pain and resistance.

I'm blessed also to have closely observed the actions of COs and XOs during my HRM days. My only regret is that I haven't served as an XO! The Navy's personnel system demands that officers work their way up the ladder from Division Officer, Department Head, XO, and then CO. I skipped one big rung due to affirmative action and the times. Equal opportunity is great, but it has costs. I feel totally comfortable in the role of CO, but less so with XO responsibilities.

Dad has always said, "Expect the best of your personnel, and you'll get it. If otherwise notified, then you can take action." So far command personnel, military and civilian, men and women, put forth their best and we make things go! I'm forever gratified that we have such fine Navy men and women. The machinery, from recruiting to schooling to shipboard and shore duty, works very well. The country doesn't understand what's required to operate this outfit and other military units, yet I know we're appreciated by most citizens. Keep the faith!

TF

One month later from Tucker

18 July 1978, Pearl Harbor, Hawaii

Dear Buck,

And how's retirement in Charleston? I bet it's a real shift from SACEUR and so many years in the U.S. Navy. Hope you're enjoying your new career as an investment counselor. Dad has adjusted well to his retirement. Oodles of hobbies keep him out of mischief.

Wish you could have attended my assumption of command. I think you would've been proud of me, notwithstanding your hesitancy years ago to recommend I join the WAVES. Who would have dreamed that I, a woman, would someday assume command of a naval shore activity?

Command is everything I anticipated, and more. I feel privileged and honored to serve both my command personnel and those whom we support. Big Daddy Navy (in the institutional sense) did a good job grooming me and generally I feel qualified.

Our major mission is to maintain both personnel and disbursing records for our customer commands, which creates one of my immediate problems — I'm not as well-versed in personnel and administration matters as most other officers serving in comparable billets. Strategic planning and international relations aren't the best of backgrounds; I find few in my everyday encounters who care to discuss the pros and cons of our current policy in the Soviet Union.

My chief problem, beyond handling people issues within the command, seems to be an unwarranted urge to know the details of my people's jobs, at least down to the Chief Petty Officer level. Yesterday, for example, one of our customer COs, Captain Jack Scott, dropped in and started chewing me out over pay record entries made by the disbursing clerks. I have a hard enough time figuring out my own pay record, let alone explaining the whys and wherefores of entries to some irate captain or commander who thinks our disbursing clerks have erred in the Navy's favor! But as

Jack talked, my management background began to kick in. I calmed him down and called in our Disbursing Officer, a bright supply corps lieutenant, who nonchalantly explained the entries under question. Luckily we were correct.

My first reaction to these incidents, and they seem to be *constant* because we're shifting to new ways of administering personnel and pay matters, including the use of highfalutin' computer technologies, is to learn everything about each facet of the command. That approach is burning me out. My second is to realize that my forté is management and leadership, and I need to be both CO and XO for the time being. (Fortunately I have a superb Command Master Chief, and if necessary my own supportive boss, to help with the toughest people problems). Therefore, I must depend upon the department heads and division officers to be the specialty experts.

Maybe this is similar to going from CO of a diesel to a nuclear sub. My friend Tom Parker talked about this large shift in attitude when he moved to a nuclear submarine and could no longer know the entire boat and its workings.

Thought you'd like to hear of some of my command problems. Won't bore you with any more details, for undoubtedly you can imagine them. I've discovered the art of dictating which saves me much time. I couldn't be CO and XO without my little microcassette recorder and outstanding secretary! Have had to allay my natural inclination to keep abreast of world affairs for now and instead concentrate hard on getting this command off the ground and properly functioning.

Would love your insights about "Command." That's a huge subject, but I think you know what I'm asking. Though your many commands were shipboard, except for the War College, I expect the same concepts prevail.

What's your daily routine like? Exciting and rewarding I hope. Helen must be adjusting to changes too.

My very best to you both. Take good care of yourselves.

    Love,

      Tucker

One week later from Buck

25 July 1978, Charleston, South Carolina

Dear Tucker,

So very good to hear from you. For a time Helen and I thought we'd get to Pearl to see you assume Command, but the gods decreed otherwise, and we found ourselves in New York attending a command performance of a Mutual Fund Board associated with this investment business. It's essential to know as much as possible about the various opportunities for investment before I can in good faith recommend them to others.

The more I see of the uncertainties, complexities, and hit-or-miss philosophies in this world of investing, the more I miss the Navy's steady, predictable, level playing field. I know I'm prejudiced, but sometimes I have the strangest feeling that my value system has been turned upside down, with making money the *sine qua non*. And morality, peaceful human relations, and joy in life have become highly secondary. I must be wrong in feeling this way; I certainly hope I am.

So they gave you the job and took away your exec. The Navy hasn't changed much since I retired. Kinda places you in a no-win situation, doesn't it? If you do a great job without an exec, some will believe you don't need one. And, if you do poorly, you'll take the blame, whether or not an exec is in place. You have to view the situation as a challenge. In time the exec billet will be filled, and you'll be a stronger commanding officer, having had both the executive and the staff responsibilities.

You handled the irate captain well by referring him, in your presence, to the individual who was actually responsible for the system which led to his complaint. You pinpointed the source, yet maintained the responsibility. Sounds as though you did this instinctively, not by your usual systematic research which establishes options and chooses the most probable. Due to the exigencies of the moment, your decisions will often be "seat of the pants" judgments of this nature.

It seems, too, you never even thought of shifting the blame to someone else. That effort, when attempted, results in the downfall of more potentially outstanding COs than any other single cause. The essence of command is the acceptance of the responsibility for the professional actions of those within the command. You cannot avoid this. And if you try, it boomerangs. I believe you'll have no trouble here, Tucker. Your nature is to gather unto yourself as much responsibility as you can and exercise it.

Your trouble comes — and it will, it comes to all of us — when you delegate a task and then get involved in *how* to accomplish this task. (In submarines the most common example of this is the Engineering Officer who becomes Commanding Officer and then can't stay out of the Engine Room. In aviation, it's the Executive Officer who becomes the Commanding Officer and then can't stay out of the XO's basket.) You don't delegate until you know where to delegate; then you evaluate by accomplishment, nothing more. If the delegatee doesn't accomplish well, he or she soon finds less work to do, and sooner rather than later, is reassigned.

Sounds simple, doesn't it? Organize by function, not by personality; match personality (ability) to function; delegate with clear orders; and then step aside until the time for hearing the report. Judgment then takes over, decision follows, and the process is repeated. With those elements in place, anything is possible. This is the way units selected for recognition and awards of excellence are commanded (whether they be ships, squadrons, personnel commands, tanks, submarines, and, yes, governments). The process builds unit loyalty, pride, and belief in the mission.

I know you know all these words, Tucker, but for someone as energetic and bright as you, to implement this process and leave your reputation in subordinates' hands, is one of the toughest things to do. You're aware that it takes you less instruction to understand the purpose or need for any task than it does for most individuals. That's why you're the Commanding Officer! Yet, you must let your people do their tasks their way, even if you know a better way. Gradually you can get them to discover that better way and believe they figured it out all by themselves. Then they're disciples. If you force a better way on them, they're slaves.

Over the years we've talked about leadership styles and the inherent danger of trying to emulate someone else's leadership style unless it's a natural inclination. If your boss gives you instructions about HOW to do your job after you've been given the job to do and understand what's needed, BEWARE. Of course you listen attentively, but your footwork must be very fancy, avoiding alienation and at the same time indicating you appreciate the suggestions but would like to try things your way. We've talked, too, about the absolute maxim of praising in public and correcting in private. Those who do otherwise are reinforcing their fragile egos at someone else's expense.

You seem to recognize that many of the details in accounting, bookkeeping, and the minutia of record keeping, you'll never know, and will never need to know. The results of those functions, however, you must carefully evaluate.

Tucker, put your own stamp on this thing. Do it better and differently, if necessary, than it's been done before. Accept the responsibility for the job, gracefully accept the praise, when it comes, in the name of your people, and should criticism come your way, shield your people from it publicly, but privately let them know that keeping them out of trouble will get old in a hurry. Delegate and trust, evaluate, and praise or change. With your innate sharpness and common sense, the personnel management business will be a pleasant walk in the park.

And, when this command tour is over, let's hope your next assignment will tax your ability to the hilt...perhaps strategic planning or policy determination for Women-in-the-Navy. I understand the Navy has revived many of the functions of the old Director of the WAVES job and made the new billet of captain rank. A good spot for you maybe.

Charleston seems to be getting more attention from the Navy all the time. Can't you arrange to check up on some of the personnel management functions here, just to see how the other half lives? Helen and I would love to see you, give you a look at "retirement," which believe it or not, you, too, someday will face. Doesn't seem possible now, but the time will come.

Warm regards,

Buck

Five weeks later from Tucker's journal

30 August 78, Honolulu, Hawaii

 For the record,

I just read Judge John Sirica's opinion issued 27 July regarding the legal exclusion of women from sea duty, as written in Section 6015 of Title 10. Several courageous women, some of whom I know, are fighting via a class action suit to repeal 6015. I probably wouldn't take on the Navy in the courts; I prefer to work within, through persuasion. Younger women, however, are more aggressive and willing to risk their reputations big time, and these women hit pay dirt!

Judge Sirica declared that 6015 denies Navy women "their right to the equal protection of the laws as guaranteed by the fifth amendment of the Constitution." The women won their case, our case, my case!

Sirica doesn't adjudge that the defendants (SECDEF and SECNAV) let down the gangplanks to women; instead he instructs military leaders that they cannot enforce 6015 as "the sole basis" for excluding Navy women from sea duty. Methinks our Navy policies may not change for awhile — "the mills of God grind slowly" — but 6015 no longer will be the primary barrier which excludes us from serving at sea. Hooray!

The decision's tenor and implications are significant:

- Sirica says individuals should be free to take part "in an essential national enterprise to the limits of their abilities. This aspect of a naval career is not something plainly reserved for one gender rather than the other." By god, I think he's got it! Wish he'd taken this logic to a broader plane, but that's the law — specific to the case.

- The judgment emphasizes the cost effectiveness of sending women to sea. We, the Navy, for moral and financial reasons, must move ahead and overcome traditional ways of thinking.

- Sirica comments about the "justicability" of the case. The defendants claimed that because military affairs are implicated, this case raises a nonjusticable political question. In other words, the courts should keep their voices out of executive and legislative political matters. Sirica, on the other hand, concludes that courts shouldn't abdicate their responsibility to decide cases "merely because they arise in the military context." Courts, he says, should declare whether internal military policies and decisions are lawful. Makes sense to me, though I know many admirals and generals and senators would like to make their very own policies, without alleged "judicial activism."

- Sirica also shoots down the Navy's argument that 6015 should be upheld "because any degree of integration of men and women aboard Navy ships is apt to cause morale and discipline problems among crews." He quotes CINCLANT who essentially says COs already have ample authority to tend to any discipline problems that may arise. I say "yes" to that; by its nature, the military can readily control disciplinary problems. Morale directly relates to leadership ability.

While Sirica leaves policy making about Navy women at the discretion of military authorities, this decision, as I read it, opens the doors to women so that finally they'll have equal opportunities in the Navy.

Congrats to the brave plaintiffs, Kathy, Joellen and the rest. I predict their efforts will aid in speedy passage of an amendment to 6015 and allow *some* women to serve aboard *some* ships. A watershed for Navy women! All women!

Changing laws doesn't change attitudes. My friend Pat Thomas' recent survey out of the Naval Personnel Research Development Center, which asks similar questions to those in my survey, shows that women today perceive themselves as more subject to status ambiguity and institutional sexism than six years ago. Not surprising. As more women become conscious, they're saying the Navy discriminates against them as a category of people. As the opportunity gap between genders closes, all professional women for some time will feel rising resistance from men.

I feel another magazine article rising up within me. Maybe the *Proceedings* will take it this time. The climate's more open.

"Equal protection under the law." Thank you, Founding Fathers, for our Bill of Rights. Thank you Judge Sirica!

TF

Two weeks later from Tucker's journal

15 September 1978, Honolulu, Hawaii

For the record,

Jennie and I had a difference of opinion — we don't fight, we just differ. While I'm deeply in love with her, sometimes her conservative nature aggravates me:

I received an invitation to the SUBPAC Fall Ball and, of course, will accept and attend unescorted in my CO capacity (or, maybe CAPT Harry Shaw, a good friend of Tom's and a widower, will escort me). At dinner last night I was speculating to Jennie about the various reactions were I to take her as my "date." The conversation went from joking to serious. My issues were around justice and truth and hers were about supporting the system, the Navy, and traditional values. At the end, I raised my voice, "You're my partner and I want to take you!" She replied calmly, "Tucker, you know that can't be and that's how it will always be. Stop dreaming."

TF

Two weeks later from Tucker

30 September 1978, Honolulu, Hawaii

Dear Buck,

It's been a little trying, this command tour, and I need to vent a little, and perhaps get advice from someone who knows the ways of our unique (but sometimes frustrating) institution. And, you know me and my *modus operandi*. Goodness, it's been thirty years since my dive onboard the *Seaperch*. Amazing!

Life in Pearl has been hotter than the devil, in other ways than temperature and trade winds. My job has heated up. Seems I displease my immediate superior, to understate the situation. My new boss, Captain Pat Patterson — Naval Academy grad, basketball hero, and destroyerman — has served with few women. This morning he called me into his office and dished out harsh words. Took me back to my ensign days in Newport and the little Abie story ("Don't trust anyone, not even your own father…").

The Captain said he'd received complaints from several peers regarding my command's services and had heard that I was "holding too many goddamn staff meetings instead of taking immediate, decisive actions."

"What's your main problem, Commander?"

I told him I have insufficient personnel to perform the job well. *That's* the main problem. I said we were constantly in an OJT mode as we develop this different type of command with new procedures and Instructions and Notices. This analysis set him off like a firecracker.

He said, "No, Commander, your problem is that *you* are not leading. You need to be more forceful and decisive with the troops you do have assigned to you. Big Daddy Navy on the seas, in the skies, and in BuPers isn't going to be sending you any more bodies. You and I have asked for more billets and bodies for you and we've been turned down. Besides, remember the Can-Do spirit and mission accomplishment. Support the Fleet and all that."

Then, Pat Patterson pounded his fist on his desktop. Bam! Bam! Bam! I stood in front of his angry energy, trying to contain my own feelings.

"Get mad, Tucker! Act like a goddamn commanding officer!"

Captain Patterson said he expects me to perform just like his destroyer COs who'd worked for him when he was Squadron Commander. "They were great!"

I wanted to repeat to him that from my perspective my major problem wasn't an inappropriate leadership style, but rather a real shortage of experienced personnel, like twenty percent short, including an XO. This would've sounded like a broken, whiny record and upset him even more; I stayed with the subject of leadership style. At first he didn't want to hear a lecture about the major styles of leading. (I realized later I was acting like an HRM consultant and not a subordinate CO.) Then, he engaged in the moment.

"I've been reading about Leadership Styles in one of my Master's courses. What's your style, Tucker?"

"Participatory, Captain. I like to get everyone's input and not come down too hard on the leader aspect of leading. Make it a synergistic, positive experience for all. Power-with, in lieu of power-over."

It wasn't a happy scene, Buck. As he slowly came down from the overhead, we had a fairly rational conversation about leadership. He said his preferred style is obviously Authoritarian. I can accept that. I know it's what the majority of naval officers prefer. But it's not my way of leading, even though he wants it to be.

He changed the subject. "I dunno, Tucker. I've never worked with women officers before, and rarely with enlisted women. I know how to relate to a woman as a wife, a sister, a mother, a friend, but not as a subordinate CO. It just feels odd."

I could tell he'd much prefer to deal with guys. I responded with some understanding comment and said that we women should be treated the same as men. I added, however, that research tells us women executives and leaders typically manage and lead somewhat differently from men.

"That's one reason you're uncomfortable with me, sir. I don't pound desktops and I rarely raise my voice or swear."

The conversation ended more pleasantly than it began. But, Buck, I know I'm on trial in these coming months. The Captain expressed something important. As if I didn't have enough to fret about, my boss thinks I'm too wimpy. While it's fun and challenging to be among the first, it can be damn difficult.

And, if you really want to know the interpersonal dynamics of my situation, I think, despite all our Women-in-the-Navy workshops, Captain Pat Patterson doesn't accept that he can't call me "honey" or call women in general "bimbos," as he's wont to do. I invariably respond with a comment that annoys him. He's frustrated when he can't hook me with sexual comments.

He's also dealing with a woman who isn't absolutely turned on by his attractive looks and charm. That's not to say he isn't a terribly appealing man to me, especially in Tropical Whites with his salt-

and-pepper hair and athletic figure of six-foot-five or so. I happen to be uninterested in sexual nuances that go beyond the friend stage from men within my same command structure.

Buck, do you have any advice? Whereas Captain Patterson and I respect each other, on an important level we don't connect. Please don't advise me to get mad and change my leadership style. While my backup style is indeed Authoritarian, I operate in it only in crises. I know, the command and its commanding officer are in crisis and maybe I should try pounding on desktops for a few weeks. Yet for me to come down hard on overworked, underpaid troops seems out-of-line.

I truly hope life is good for you these days in retirement. Do fill me in when you can. My love to you and Helen. Wish you were here!

> Warmest regards,
>
> Tucker

Two weeks later from Buck

14 October 1978, Charleston, S.C.

Dear Tucker,

I'm sorry you're dealing with the likes of your Captain Patterson. For what it's worth, here are some of my reactions.

Leadership for me is not something to be placed in neat categories. Some people can be rather successful as bombastic, loud leaders; others, trying that technique, fall flat. I've always thought that to attempt to change one's natural style (which I read as personality) into something else because of some book or classroom trainer or professor, is a huge error. In the end such attempts just seem insincere. Accomplished actors can pull off such stunts, but the daily business of command responsibility requires a rock-hard, consistent honesty, showing neither favoritism nor circumstantial change of leadership. Your people understand that. They may wish you were less of a son-of-a-bitch (if that's your style, and for you it obviously isn't), but they'll work harder for you than for some quiet, reflective type who tries to be a son-of-a-bitch because someone like Pat Patterson has told him or her to change from reflective to bombastic. By the way, I see you as neither reflective nor bombastic.

But leaders come in all shapes and sizes. Leaders are people who can get people to trust them. When they say something's going to happen, it happens. They don't threaten. They establish reasonable methods for doing what has to be done, set aside quietly and without prejudice those unable to handle these rules, and work consistently with those who can. Sometimes harder discipline is required, and if so it's administered quickly and evenly. If people understand the rules, they'll understand the discipline and the need for it. If the rules are not understood, the leader is at fault.

Arleigh Burke has always been my model of a leader. I know that to be true for many officers. He had time for his people. When he disagreed with them, he told them so. You always knew where you stood with him, and a mistake wasn't an irrevocable error which put you in some category from which you could never escape. In short, you trusted him and he trusted you. Haranguing, shouting, ridiculing people and groups of people in front of others, and emotional profanity were not his style. But if he quietly said, "I am unaccustomed to work of this low caliber," you were ready to cut your throat, or more effectively, work all night to make it right for him. We don't have many Arleigh Burkes.

I don't know this Patterson fellow. But, Tucker, I know you and you have the smarts to adjust to the scene. Don't change your style, but I would pay attention to what the organizational climate is, within and around your command, and adjust your actions accordingly. You might try being less analytical and academic about how you operate as a commanding officer and be more in the moment. Go with your instincts as well as your head.

And, for heaven's sake, don't use the phrase "participatory leadership" around Patterson. That's a red flag for his military mind set. I know you'll figure it out.

And, yes, the majority of shore commands are short on personnel these days, due to a downsizing in our military budget and force structure in this post-Vietnam era. I recently read that U.S. military spending has dropped from $386.8 bil in '68 to $307.9 bil in '71 to $239.3 bil in '74 to $228.3 bil in '77. Of course, the Shore Establishment is taking the big hits. I'm just sorry you have to be caught up in this drawdown of people and money.

Well, this discussion about our Navy seems a bit removed. Helen and I are comfortable here in Charleston, but I know that golfing and the cocktail circuit will not satisfy me for long. I have a bit of an in with the investment world here. Am having to take some formal courses in the legal aspects of managing other people's money and to study in-depth the various investment and credit instruments. Margin trading, for instance, is no playground for a fool. Maybe the next time we write I'll have some basis to tell you my version of the economic times ahead, or at least my guess about current stock market ups and downs.

Sometimes I think you, too, have given this Navy of ours as good a shot as it deserves. Maybe you should be having thoughts about "what next." Whatever it is, I hope you find a niche that uses the unusually capable person you are. Don't handicap yourself too much in your next endeavor. Check out the environment carefully.

Charleston continues its well-established ways. Tradd Street will always be Tradd Street. The investment business sometimes seems more like playing games than anything else, but when you're trying to maximize estate planning for others the "game playing" metaphor is hardly apt. Perhaps I just miss the Navy. Helen occasionally asks, "What's wrong with you?" I'm not conscious of anything being wrong, yet when I analyze her question and its timing it's always just after some event or news concerning the Navy has come my way. I guess what was "wrong with me" was that I was off somewhere reliving a life I found decent and very right. Please pass on my best wishes to your family when you communicate with them.

Warm regards,

Buck

Two weeks later from Tucker

27 October 1978, Honolulu, Hawaii

Robyn, my friend (and therapist!),

Rousseau got it right. "Man is born free, and everywhere he is in chains."

By law, I'm defending our Constitution and freedoms, while ignorance and prejudice constrict my own spirit and my own freedom.

Damn it, Robyn, would you believe my dream of command nearly became my worst nightmare — forced resignation and everlasting pain due to "homosexual tendencies." Robyn, I think my world's coming to a dreadful end. I've learned that the SOB I call my Commanding Officer, who seems to think he's a king if not God, is having or has had me tailed to see if I'm up to any "bad things." Here's what happened:

At the end of work today, Senior Chief Sam Watson, my boss's Special Assistant for Plans, knocked on my office door and sauntered in. He stayed only long enough to announce that last month Captain Patterson had assigned him to follow me after hours to "try to nail her for homosexual actions." The Senior Chief failed in his mission. "I knew this was an illegal order, ma'am, but I didn't want to piss off the Captain, so I didn't go at it very hard," he said. Because he likes and respects me, he came in to warn me that the Captain is displeased with the command's performance and looking to relieve me any way he can. I thanked him for his candid remarks and he departed.

Robyn, I know my command will do fine. We're on the right track, with measurements of mission effectiveness rising every day, thanks to exceptional hard work, training, and strong leadership at all levels. What I don't know — will I be okay? Will I bear up?

I feel like Daddy's little girl who, in his eyes, committed some terrible act, got caught, and was banished to another kingdom, far, far away from her family and friends. It's now clear this might actually happen. The very possibility makes me feel distant from my extended Navy family and, sadly, from even those who know my story, love me, and know I've given my all to the Navy. What would Buck think of me now? What would my parents think?

Because of Captain Patterson's actions, I feel betrayed by my Navy, just as the Navy would feel betrayed by me were I to walk out of the closet. It's a lose/lose deal, isn't it? No one can win if a Commander like Patterson uses such undignified, probably illegal tactics. Everything's coming apart, especially my psychological stability. To involve my command in a witch-hunt like this is stupid, insensitive, and poor leadership on Patterson's part.

I feel ill, on the verge of helplessness. I'm scared.

It's similar to being a Havenot in the Starpower simulation game we played at HRM School in Memphis. The Havenots can never, never climb from the bottom of the heap and reach to the stars because the rules are rigged by the Navy, the military, and the politicians who have set it up for straight white men to succeed. The Haves keep pushing minorities away in the name of national security and mission accomplishment and morale and discipline. I should feel lucky to have been born white!

Judge John Sirica ruled last summer that no one in the military should be kept from achieving to the limits of his or her abilities. The rules and laws for women in the workplace are changing and their opportunities improving accordingly. For instance, the proportion of women in med and law schools is climbing steadily. But what about gays and lesbians? "Fags" and "dykes?" Are we supposed to have no personal, intimate relationships and remain celibate? What they really want is to force us all out of the military.

My relationship with Jennie has absolutely nothing to do with my job performance, other than I'm happier than I've ever been in my entire life and therefore more productive. She and I see each other regularly and I know someday we'll live together. Not now. I know that because of prejudice, some would think less of me if they "knew."

I detest living in constant fear of discovery. I abhor the bigoted attitudes of the power elites; remember C.W. Mills in PoliSci 101? Captain Patterson, even though I give him feedback, continues to label women "bimbos and broads." He calls gays, "fags and lesbos." He thinks he's being funny and one of the boys.

I suspect the country can handle only one social movement at a time. The Civil Rights Movement shocked the '60s; the Women's Movement, the '70s; and with any luck the Gay Rights Movement will change the '80s. But, as you know, a major problem for military gays, unlike blacks and women, will be their inability to speak out without getting court-martialled or administratively discharged.

Robyn, I cannot put on the battered, tattered blinders, return to the Cave, and reclaim the old illusions. What do I do? In this instance, I will try to determine my legal rights, in a quiet way. Surely there's something in the military code of justice that gives me some recourse. If I accuse Patterson of illegal action and I'm discovered as having an improper relationship with another woman, then I'll be discharged. I suppose I could lie, but I don't do lying well.

I imagine you'll advise against that dingy, stuffy old Cave. Maybe it's time to say goodbye.

I don't know if I can bear the emotional load much longer. The irony? The responsibility of command is a piece of cake compared with this other worry, and so far my own abilities and Navy training conjoin and bring solutions to the toughest of management problems. It's even fun!

Damn. *It's my Navy, too!*

Hey, our 20th reunion is next year. Hope I can get away and renew myself.

What's with your life? How're the children and Ned?

Love,

Tucker

Ten days later from Robyn

November 7, 1978, Bar Harbor, Maine

My God Tucker!

Of all the disasters you've experienced, and all the discussions we've had about Navy things, this latest episode is the most appalling! Your Navy, our Navy, is a modern-day Gestapo! For one thing, why is it any of their business *what* you do or *where* you go after hours?

Secondly, if Patterson had questions about your behavior, lifestyle, whatever, why didn't he confront you directly instead of having you tailed? I'm unsure but I bet that sort of thing, as you say, is illegal. If your friend Watson "likes and respects" you so much, why did he tail you even "not very hard?" Why didn't he come directly to you instead of spying? I find these antics to be twisted, devious, and sordid!

I would think that your level of personal paranoia has escalated exponentially! Whom can you trust? Where can you turn? Will every blink of your eyes be monitored and judged? And by whom? Will your performance ever be assessed fairly and objectively? I'm sure you know all the blather about the quality of your command has nothing to do with your job performance and effectiveness. I'm even further stunned by the bigoted, short-sighted attitude shown by Patterson *et al.* apparently representing and sanctioned by The Institution.

Of course your relationship with Jennie has nothing to do with your job performance. As a matter of fact, with all the tension you're experiencing, a loving relationship should improve job performance.

You're indeed in a dilemma, and your living "in constant fear of discovery" as you describe yourself will doubtless hasten the onset of an ulcer, or worse. What can you do? Where or how can you get some relief?

I know your dad is not only another generation but old-school Navy. But you seem to have a pretty close relationship with your mom. Have you ever considered coming out to one or both of them? Or is that too close, too threatening to consider?

Also, Buck occurs to me. I know he's another generation and old-fashioned Navy, but there's a little more distance than with your parents. He likes and respects you both personally and professionally. Could you ever talk to him frankly? Being an insider he might have some suggestions on how you can handle this, or what options you might have.

Tucker, a couple of things: I do think you'd feel more comfortable, less in fear of being "discovered" by important people in your life, if you take the initiative and share who you are with people who already like/love and respect you. Your parents, Buck, other friends. They might be more of a resource for you than you think.

In terms of the Navy, I really don't know. I think you're right. It would be premature to come out. The naval structure isn't ready and you'd risk being discharged by tight-assed bureaucrats. Hopefully your words of the Gay Rights Movement being a part of the '80s will be prophetic.

You commented you should feel lucky to have been born white. While that certainly is a plus in this society, you were also born female and gay. Society has a lot of growing to do. Indeed, that's the answer to your conundrum! Not that it's much help! We were born some 75 years too early. One day, these issues are going to be resolved within our American democratic experiment. But probably not this afternoon. Meanwhile, we all have to live and cope and work for personal resolution as best we can.

Tucker, you're spunky. "Damn it, it's my Navy, too!"

Keep me posted on how all the above unravels and, Tucker, give me a call if you ever want to discuss this stuff directly! Elizabeth wants you to know that the tooth fairy gave her an extra nickel for losing both front teeth at once. A big fat quarter! Hang in there.

>   Love,

>   Robyn

One week later from Tucker

>   *15 November 1978, Honolulu, Hawaii*

Dear Robyn,

Thank you, my friend, for your support and concern.

No, the Navy is not a modern-day Gestapo, except as it deals with gays and lesbians. Policies are based on false stereotypical assumptions and cultural myths. Similar to women's policies, time will niggle away at these false assumptions. Feelings of aversion and pity toward gays and lesbians, rather than tolerance and acceptance and affirmation lurk behind the policies. But, to be in the military is to give up one's privacy rights and many other individual rights. The government gets to tell me what's right or wrong about my sexual behaviors and go after me if I exhibit the "wrong" behavior, a values clash between privacy rights and majority, heterosexist beliefs.

The odd thing is, most officers respect the privacy of others' personal lives and don't intrude unless behavior affects job performance. For instance, in my last job I counseled my assistant, a married Commander, about his ongoing affair with another woman. At the War College one of my immediate bosses, another married Commander, was having an affair. Nobody reported either of these situations. Another odd thing — most commanders feel a need to take care of their own and protect their troops. But gay behavior is so unacceptable and immoral to some commanders that it doesn't fit within these parameters, at least, for the Patterson-types.

I know it would be wise and right to share my story with loved ones. Too scary to do at the moment. Maybe someday.

The Navy seems to want to shame me into celibacy or out of its officer corps. I absolutely feel guilty about my feelings toward Jennie, yet the positive parts of the relationship far outweigh the negative. I get to *be me* with her. Although, since the surveillance incident, Jennie has been acting kinda funny with me. She has withdrawn some and is more distant — maybe I'm projecting.

Ever since the incident I've had a recurring nightmare about "being caught." I may be distancing her as well. Personal relationships may be the essence of living, but they can cause real pain and worry.

Naval aviators have an expression, "Watch Your Six." In other words, when you're up there flying, with the enemy surrounding you and you can't see him at the six o'clock reading, behind your plane, BE AWARE! Guess I need to be more concerned about where Jennie and I have dinner and always wary to Watch My Six.

Yes, I can retire in 1980. That's not my choice. I intend to make captain and serve several more tours. We'll see. My dad had a bleeding ulcer some years ago. Is that a genetic thing?

On a brighter note: Congress has amended the combat exclusion law concerning women onboard ships. We'll be able to serve on non-combatants and support ships! Ensign Mary Carroll, the first woman ensign to serve under this new policy, is reporting to *Vulcan*, a repair ship. Can you believe it?

Don't worry about me, Robyn. You know I'm a survivor. I just get ticked at the Navy's prejudice and stereotypical behaviors. And it is my Navy.

What do the John Birchers say about our country? "America, Love It or Leave It." I love the Navy and I don't want to leave it.

I'll call if life gets more complicated.

Love,

Tucker

Two weeks later from Jennie

December 1978, Honolulu, Hawaii

Dearest Tucker,

This letter is so hard to write but write it I must. Ever since you told me about Pat Paterson putting a tail on you to look for "homosexual behavior," I've been in a stew.

That I love you I have no doubt. That I want to spend the rest of my life with you in it, is also a given.

But because I love you so much I cannot bear to see you so paranoid about, so distracted from, the career that you love. Here you are with a command — the assignment you've worked so long to achieve!

I know you see yourself as a risk taker but the stakes here are too high. I'm well aware of the Navy's position on this issue and while I personally don't agree, I'm unwilling to be the instrument of change. Nor do I want you to be!

We must call off our relationship NOW. It will give us the opportunity to get some perspective on all of this — God knows, I never had to deal with this while I was on active duty!

If we're meant to be together, then someday we will be. But for now...With love and concern,

Jennie

Four weeks later from Tucker's journal

Christmas 1978

 For the record,

Dad gave me a special present, a newly published book, *Famous American Admirals*. And he's in it! The inscription, at this point in my career, tears me up:

> Don't know why my name was included in the book, but thought you might like it for your library. Perhaps in the next edition they will have you in as a lady Admiral! In any event, I thoroughly enjoyed my naval career and wish you all success in yours.
>
> Merry Christmas,
>
> Dad

TF

Three months later from Tucker's journal

31 January, Pearl Harbor, Hawaii

 For the record,

Billie and I roamed around the other islands this past week. Super relaxing. Billie seems to be her happy self again and pulling out of her malaise about health and careers issues. It was good to talk to Billie about my feelings of loss and despair over Jennie. Billie said, "Just give it time, Tuck."

And now I'm totally engrossed in research for my *Proceedings* article. The editors this time asked me to write something about Navy women, and between command duties I've been immersed in conducting interviews with fleet-types. Yesterday I spent an afternoon aboard a guided-missile cruiser homeported here with the skipper (good friend of mine) and some of his more senior enlisted. I posed questions and then let 'er rip. I need to sort out some of their thoughts. Here's a taste of yesterday's discussion:

A Warrant Officer, Jim Smedley, with twenty-five years' Navy experience, said, "Let 'em [women] learn to love their cruiser. Their destroyer. Let's do it right. Let's go whole hog. Don't be a bear, be a grizzly." He said the Washington power structure's giving out strong, mixed vibes about integration of women and needs to be clearer with policy. Many admirals are against the women at sea program. "Either let 'em do the damn job or don't let 'em in at all," said another senior enlisted man.

One officer argued that 90% of the solution for the Navy is the mental makeup of the woman reporting to a ship. If she wants to do the job, then she'll fit in. A woman going to sea will have to have self-confidence and "have her shit in one bag." She must neither be defensive nor reject Navy ways of discipline. And, "She must confront sexist behaviors," said a black Master Chief.

During the interview the men resorted to humor when we discussed the issue of sex and women aboard ship. All the men could get serious as well and agreed that just because they might get horny, with women in close quarters, is no reason to restrict women. "Why in the hell should women be deprived of serving aboard ship because of me? Yes, give them the opportunity. The women will get horny too." They admitted that the situation might look different if the women were their shipmates and partners and buddies and in their home [ship]. "But, the biggest problem for the Navy," said one Warrant Officer, "will be the Navy wives."

All of the men in the wardroom had served with women and all felt that only a few enlisted women truly wanted to go to sea. (Most men don't want to go on long deployments either!) Women officers might be a different story. My personal survey tells me that about 10% of the enlisted women want to go to sea. But these All-Volunteer Force women didn't come into the Navy expecting to go to sea, so we can't disparage their attitudes.

The bottom line for these men about the issue of women at sea is that of any squared-away sailor: "It's gonna be whether she gets qualified to relieve that watch...whether she can do the damn job." As we talked, I began to sense tremendous frustration from these men about the sweeping changes happening within our Navy regarding us women. They want to support us. No doubt about that.

Yet, as more and more women report for duty aboard ships, the men have real concerns about a breakdown in discipline and, yes, about sex aboard mixed-crew ships. From the men's comments, enlisted women in certain local commands are using their gender to override good military behaviors and bearing. Women, particularly enlisted, manipulate their male superiors into protecting them from rules and regulations. "Hey, Chiefie," kind of stuff.

It's the male/female dynamic. Rules are rules, but some male supervisors bend them when women, especially the more attractive, enter the scene. Obviously our Navy-wide Women-in-the-Navy Workshops haven't solved this problem. I personally have little sympathy for these disciplinary problems. Either supervisors lead their men, and their women, or they themselves need shaping up by their seniors.

I realize, however, that if women remain a viable part of the fleet structure, the ones who misuse their feminine wiles will have to be dealt with firmly. Our Code of Justice doesn't have an exact article for the woman who uses sexual attraction to get a man's favor or to overlook her sloppiness. But charges must be made against such improper actions. I, as a woman, have never encountered insubordinate Navy women; but I take no guff from women and this sexual dynamic is missing.

The Master Chief of the Command summarized our discussion in this way, "Women are gonna have a place, an opportunity to serve. Whether they're capable, I don't know. I personally think they can serve well aboard ships."

My own reactions to Navy men who are asked tough questions about Navy women: generally speaking, they genuinely want women to be given equal opportunities, including sea duty. They don't know how it'll all work out, but they're unhappy and even angry with the current situation — women staying ashore their entire careers and filling "cushy jobs" while men fulfill their sea duty obligations. Men (and women too) have grave reservations about women truly wanting to serve aboard combatants, but they're willing to entertain the possibility.

By 1985, we're anticipating we'll maintain over 45,000 women on active duty. Seagoing sailors, officers and enlisted, are worried about bringing in so many women and not having them share sea duty requirements. The seavey/shorevey rotation will get fouled up. Personally I don't see a problem for a while, but those numbers will begin to hurt the seavey/shorevey concept unless we send more women to sea. Aren't you glad, Fairfield, that you're not in BuPers crunching numbers!

Though the tenor — sometimes two-faced and often sarcastic — of these and other interviews causes concern, I appreciate these guys' openness. They acknowledge that most Navy men see us Navy women as a big joke, and don't ever talk seriously about women as their peers and part of the first team. Their one-liners fit perfectly with Pat Thomas' survey data which says there's a growing pessimism among Navy women about acceptance by men. Three-fourths of the respondents in 1978, compared with two-thirds in 1972, believe that they're held back in their professional development, "because of ingrained beliefs held by men that women are not capable as managers."

Several areas of concern regarding our Women-at-Sea program: the women petty officer base is insufficient; the program's internal-Navy publicity is inadequate; and the new women officers' surface warfare career path has major problems. Ah, well. We'll muddle through as we always do. After in-depth talks with senior Navy men about women in the Navy, I know our great Navy has significant challenges ahead as we try to integrate so many women so fast. Luckily, it's peacetime.

TF

Two weeks later, note attached to one dozen pink roses on Tucker's back porch

14 February 1979

Tuckerlove,

Roses are red
Violets are blue
I'm going crazy
Without you!

I never was very good at poetry but perhaps you get the idea. This separation is not a good idea — at least for me. Can we talk? Maybe walk on the beach tonight or this weekend, whenever. If you want to.

Yours,

Jennie

Eleven days later from Tucker's journal

25 February 1979, Honolulu, Hawaii

For the record,

Spoke with Tom last night in San Diego about my research and he reassured me that men don't want to be at sea either. He said, "for us lifers, it's a job. Something we're good at; something they pay us for being good at."

He told a sea story about the time aboard USS *Sanddab* when they had an opportunity to extend their WestPac cruise to visit an exotic port. In a moment of weakness the Captain decided to take a vote. It came out overwhelmingly that they should go home. Even the Captain admitted he never intended to do anything but go home. He only wanted to know how many people he was going to disappoint. Tom added that many of his close friends have confided to him, at one time or another, that during those six-month cruises they ached to be home with their families.

For Navy Juniors, our mothers raise us and we sort of come from single-parent families, because our fathers are at sea...and soon, some few Navy mothers will be at sea! For sure, my mother had to be both mother and father for so much of her child-rearing days.

Just the way it has to be, in peace and in war and in the Navy.

TF

P.S. Happy PEBD!

Three weeks later from Tucker

18 March 1979, Pearl Harbor, Hawaii

Dear Dad,

The command is (finally) beginning to run well and I thought you'd enjoy an upbeat report. We've written and implemented our major Instructions. Captain Patterson found five more able-bodied seamen to ease my personnel problems. Next month I'm getting an XO, a mustang who knows the personnel business. Hooray!

Participatory leadership. I'm still operating within that model, as I've discussed with you, but I task more specifically and allow less process than at first, and use the authoritarian approach as required! These are youngsters, including department heads, who need significantly more explicit direction than I'd realized.

Believe it or not, I struggle with working with some women officers in the command who see their position as a job and not a profession...and go home at 1630 to tend to their children. A new Navy!

Captain Patterson relaxes more with me and seems pleased with the command's improved mission effectiveness. The black clouds have faded for the moment, although yesterday we had an altercation about uniforms. He sets the Uniform of the Day for the Base and insists that women cannot be authorized to wear *both* skirts and slacks. "Uniform is uniform. Look it up in the dictionary, Commander." The real truth — he doesn't like slacks on women.

During FitRep preparation he asks all his officers, before finalizing his own marks, to fill in their own marks and comments as if they were writing their own FitRep. A hard but educational experience for me. I'll institute this system with my own officers. First time in a long while I've been at 5% overall. I marked myself 1%.

Yesterday I counseled one of my Department Heads, Lt. Anne Ferguson, on a basic management principle that's difficult for some to grasp. The lieutenant strongly disagreed with a command decision, believing her department had gotten the short end of the deal. She couldn't rise above her status as department head and see the total command requirements. I advised her that an officer usually wears at least two management hats, and in this case she not only manages her department but is an integral member of the command's management team.

I said, "To me, Miss Ferguson, what separates an outstanding officer from the mediocre often rests on this very point. The officer understands and accepts that beyond her management level is the next, and the next. The good of the entire command doesn't always jibe with the good of any one department. The top officer amicably and easily changes hats and perspectives."

Ah, command decision making can be tough.

Lots of love to you and Mother. Hope you're both well.

Warm regards,

Tucker

Three weeks later from Dad

3 April 1979, San Diego, CA

Dear Tucker,

I'm pleased, Tucker, that Captain Patterson has eased up on you. Knowing you, you've made the necessary adjustments to set the command on a steady, successful course. I'm certain you're learning that many aspects about leadership are impossible to teach in a classroom, or in a CO's office. If individuals haven't been raised to understand and apply certain ideas instinctively — the fundamental values of caring for their people, evenhanded discipline, trust in command — they'll find the ideas hard to grasp. Your Lieutenant Ferguson, for instance, is unwilling to trust command decision-making and accept that there's a larger view than her own department.

I don't see her problem as two different kinds of leadership. I see it more as a loyalty and command responsibility issue. Perhaps, Tucker, she represents a little bit of Tucker Fairfield coming back to bite you. By that I mean that you're not one to accept a decision which you believe to be wrong. Your quick mind sees beyond the immediate cause and effect of most reactive decisions. You keep the big picture in front of you and determine or judge when small decisions work toward or away from that big picture. I know you. You're very vocal about the larger vision and have gained a reputation that doesn't have much patience with those who don't see things your way.

Strong people are like this and many strike out because they cannot cope with allowing the less far-sighted individuals to have a piece of the policy cake. They have to prove themselves right even when the decision goes against them. Their being right becomes more important than the Command policy. I'm not implying that you're among the self-righteous. But surely you know these kinds of leaders are everywhere, not only in the Navy, but in government, industry and even in churches and seminaries.

I always go back to Arleigh Burke's definition of command loyalty: "You may never knowingly allow your Commander to make an error. BUT, if after you've done all you can, by advice, by example, by logic, by plea, to prevent that error, and your Commander persists in making it, then your options are clear. You may embrace the Command decision and do your very best to make it work, or, you may remove yourself from the umbrella of the Command protection. You may not remain under that umbrella and continue to work against the decision."

That is *the* maxim of leadership, in all its forms. If the leader cannot develop that attitude within the organization, he or she will, at best, be only average.

Enough about management.

I'm about to become a member of the Yacht Club Board.

Take care of yourself, Tucker. And enjoy your command time.

Devotedly,

Dad

Two weeks later from Tucker's journal

16 April 1979, Pearl Harbor, Hawaii

For the record,

As I sat at my desk reading the proposed discharge papers for two young women seamen, I asked myself, what can I say to make them feel less scared, less humiliated? How can I send them out of their Navy and still have them feel pride about their Navy and, even more importantly, pride in themselves?

I looked up and saw the two young women walking into my office. They looked so frightened and sad. At the same time, they looked squared away. I asked them to sit down and walked to the door, then carefully and gently closed the door to the outside world. This will not be the usual check-out debriefing, I thought. What can be said? They're embarrassed; I'm embarrassed for them. They'd overstepped the bounds.

"Good morning," I said, thinking it was *not* a good morning at all, for them or for me. Seamen Rankin and Johnson were both about to burst into tears and looked completely ill-at-ease.

"It's okay to cry," I said. "This is not a happy occasion for any of us." With that, Seaman Rankin took out her handkerchief and wiped away the streaming tears.

I shifted into "the Commanding Officer mode" and advised them that the Navy issues definitive regulations about women and men who relate sexually to the same gender, at any time and any place, but particularly in the barracks and in close quarters. I said that it appeared they'd both violated these regulations, and that we describe their alleged behavior as "conduct prejudicial to good order and discipline." I asked if they'd understood the consequences of their behaviors, and they said they hadn't meant to become so involved. "It just happened," they both proclaimed simultaneously. I wanted to tell them it was okay. I wanted to make it better for them.

I knew then, and now, that the impersonal discharge papers that called out discharge "for reason of homosexuality" would likely haunt them for many years. They seemed to be the all-American types. Unsophisticated. Small town.

What a waste, I thought. What a dumb policy! What a discriminatory policy! It's almost always the young and the foolish who get "caught," I thought. What about human decency and equal rights? It's wrong that these young women be discharged for homosexual behavior when we, the Navy's leaders, often look the other way if and when there's unacceptable heterosexual action in the barracks, including adulterous acts. None of these behaviors is acceptable under regulations, but there's often a wink and a nod if it's *straight* behavior.

"Under Navy procedures and policies, we must process you for separation from the Navy, unless the allegations are groundless. Are they groundless?" I asked.

"No, we did in fact get carried away with ourselves," said Seaman Rankin.

"Didn't anyone ever tell you, 'don't ever fool around in the barracks?' " I said, somewhat annoyed.

"Oh, yes, ma'am. Several petty officers told us in boot camp," said Seaman Rankin. "We both know better."

"I don't know if you're lesbians or not. You may not know yourselves at this point in your lives. I don't want to know."

I continued. "I have no other choice. It's gone too far. The NIS agents say they have too much on you. Unfortunately, I can't look the other way and must sign these papers. As CO I have to support the policy."

I told them it was ironic that while the Navy had made so many positive changes towards achieving equal opportunity for women, the institution chooses to keep coming down hard on lesbians and gay men. Then I added, "It's a shame the Navy refuses to insist on equal protection and privacy rights for its gay members...*some day it will be different.*"

"But," I said, "the good news is that recent policy changes allow us to give you both an honorable discharge, as opposed to a dishonorable one."

"That's great," said Seaman Johnson.

"You should be proud of your fine Navy records. I know both of you were in line for promotion to Third Class petty officer next month. It would've been my real pleasure to put on your crows. You know that?"

"Yes, ma'am," they chimed in.

Suddenly I felt sick to my stomach and terrible all over. Why should they be discharged and I stay? Because they were not "neat and discreet," as Jennie would say.

"I don't want you to feel badly or have any lasting humiliation when you get to your home towns. This just happened. *Some* day the military won't be so blatantly discriminatory against its gay service members who usually serve with distinction. *Some* day these personnel will be allowed to serve with the same pride and dignity and self-respect as the majority members."

And to myself I thought, *some* day maybe I'll be able to feel that I served with dignity and pride.

I counseled the young women that everything works out for the best and that there's got to be good reason for their discharges at this time. "At least you won't have to worry anymore about being discovered, and I hope civilian life will be kinder to you both."

And that's that. Only it isn't, Fairfield. I'm still stewing about those young women. They seemed so young and ingenuous. Neither deserves a black mark on her record — her very life.

Can I maintain my balance, my integrity, when I too have committed the same alleged "Navy sin" — only in the privacy of my own bedroom? Hypocrisy is not my style.

TF

P.S. Feels as though I'm sailing under false colors!

One day later from Tucker

17 April 1979, Pearl Harbor, Hawaii

Dear Tom,

Thanks for listening to me last night. You'll always be my good friend and buddy. After talking with you, I'm wondering whether, by not pushing for a more extensive investigation into the young seamen and their behaviors, I took the wrong actions? Because of my own "values," perhaps I acted negligently in not going the extra mile with them. On the other hand, they had proper legal counsel, a woman civilian lawyer, working their cases.

You know how I detest inane regulations. And this one fits that category, plus it's discriminatory. Military justice shouldn't be that far from social justice in its intent and practice. Ah, yes, we must have good order and discipline.

Other than this messy incident, life's very good. I truly enjoy command, now that the kinks are out of the mechanics of it all and our policies and instructions are in place and working. My Executive Officer's outstanding, though he still has some resistance to his CO's management style! He's beginning to come around and I predict he'll thank me someday for having to learn new ways of leading and managing.

Am surprised you're considering early retirement! Why not enjoy some of the benefits of senior rank? How about a tour as an NROTC Commanding Officer? Hope your thinking has nothing to do with your physical health...I forgot to ask about you, I was so caught up in my own "stuff."

When you have a moment, I'd love for you to elaborate not only on your future personal plans but also more on your thoughts about gay military personnel, if for no other reason than that you're a man and you've no doubt met with different experiences than I, especially at sea. I rarely discuss the subject, and then only with my closest women friends. I suspect your experiences and assumptions could greatly help me through any future brush with gay personnel in my CO tour.

Jennie and I have planned a special trip to Norway next month. She'll be looking for cousins and her mother's friends. I'll be looking for down time and fun!

Will you stay in San Diego to retire? Hope so, for I'd like to get there on my next tour, though D.C. is likely.

My best love to you and Joanna. How's my favorite niece? And of course Willy, that adorable little devil.

Love,

Tucker

One week later from Tom

24 April 1979, San Diego, CA

Ahoy there Tucker,

Joanna and I were just about to call you when you called with your distressing news. Since we had a big single-issue conversation, I didn't get around to our mundane family items. I got your letter this morning too.

Tucker, I understand the source of your distress; you feel guilty; you feel like a hypocrite. But I want you to try and step back and be a little more objective; those feelings are just add-ons to what we all feel when we lose competent people for irrelevant or arbitrary reasons, or for unevenly administered regulations. Don't feel like the Lone Ranger. Here, for example, is what's happened to me:

When I think back on it, homosexuality has always been close by during my naval career. On my first ship, the cruiser in Norfolk, the Exec, a Commander, was believed by everyone (and known by some) to be homosexual. His performance didn't appear to be affected and as far as I know he had a fairly successful naval career.

On my second ship, the destroyer here in San Diego, one of the yeomen was giving "hand jobs" to the crew members when they came back from liberty. When the Naval Investigative Service (NIS) got wind of it, the Captain was informed, the yeoman was administratively discharged, and the other men were transferred. The only ill effect on the crew from this incident, however, was that we lost an experienced yeoman and several other crew members. Their shipmates were sorry to have them leave.

When I first came into nuclear submarines, I experienced a couple of incidents where NIS informed us that they suspected homosexual activity on the part of some sailors. The first happened while I was on *Starfish*, an attack nuke. The sailor in question, a first-class electrician, was supposedly dating a seaman from another sub. We made the sailor available to NIS and their agents apparently convinced him they had a solid case. I told him he could either have a general discharge, or fight the charge in court. He elected to take the general discharge and left the ship shortly thereafter.

Before he was discharged, I asked him what had happened to the other guy. He told me the other guy fought the charges and they were dropped. I decided that I'd handled that case pretty poorly because our sailor was doing his job well and had been a positive contributor to the command. In other words, his conduct hadn't been prejudicial to good order and discipline.

The second incident occurred while I was CO. NIS approached me and said they suspected homosexual conduct on the part of one of my sailors. I'd learned my lesson and this time I made the sailor available but sent his Division Officer with him. I instructed the Division Officer to intervene any time he thought the rights of the sailor were being violated, and at that time he should suggest to the sailor that he get counsel. Apparently the Division Officer objected to the way NIS conducted business and advised the sailor to get a lawyer as soon as NIS asked the first question. NIS was aggravated, dropped the questioning immediately, and tried to pressure me to advise the sailor not to retain a lawyer. I wasn't about to do that, so NIS no longer pursued the case. The sailor continued to contribute to the ship. In fact, he was so happy about how we'd protected his rights that he became a truly outstanding performer. The rest of the crew knew about the whole incident and didn't make it a big deal.

I've decided doing your job competently is what counts to the crew, especially to the crew of a submarine. They accept a lot of weird conduct from outstanding performers. For sure they can be merciless teasers when they sense a weakness or difference in anyone. And I mean something as innocent as being a vegetarian. But in the cases of homosexuals I know about, I think the crew was against NIS and on the side of their shipmate. After all, who knows best who's a threat to good order and discipline, the crew with whom they've been submerged for months or these sex police?

In contrast to NIS's devotion to "rooting out these wicked violators of decency," let me tell you how we handled a different "violation." When the *Farragut* was at Cape Kennedy for her practice missile shoot, one of our First Class petty officers went ashore, got very drunk, and looked into a bedroom window. He saw a woman getting undressed and getting into bed beside her husband. Our hero waited awhile, walked 'round to the front porch, found a window he could open and climbed in the living room. Like a good boy, he took off his clothes and folded them, neatly placing them on a chair. He then went into the bedroom and tried to get in bed on the woman's side. She woke up. *Screamed.*

All hell broke loose and he was arrested. The Captain, however, told the Exec to get him off. The Chief-of-the-Boat and the Exec went down to the police station, argued that boys will be boys, sailors will be sailors, and drunks will be drunks; they promised that the Navy would mete out punishment, and got him off the civilian charges. Completely! As I recall, the punishment we then gave him was losing liberty for the reminder of our port call, one more day!

Some kind of double standard here I'd say! Although I can't defend what our potential assaulter did, I will defend trying to keep my crew from the clutches of NIS. I'd have to be convinced the accused was causing a problem on the ship or harming his shipmates on or off the ship, a situation I've neither seen nor heard of insofar as gay sailors.

Hope this gives you some perspective, Tucker.

And now for news from the home front: Your favorite niece said you had to know that she was selected to be captain of her soccer team and she'll get to play the clarinet (following your no-strings lead) in her school orchestra after all. Also, she got your card from Honolulu and will write you soon on the pretty Hawaiian note paper you gave her. Our 9-year-old captain of industry piped in that he had to tell you that he has two more dogs on his dog-walking list, bringing the total to four. I never thought that I would see Willy willingly, if not eagerly, employ a pooper scooper on a regular basis! He complains bitterly about owners who don't feed their dogs in a way that produces firm poop.

Joanna's fine, and sends her love. She's been promoted at the library. Odd, but in a way you seem to fill a hole in the kids' lives. I always knew that they, especially Carolyn as the oldest when Harry was killed, continued to feel some loss even though I doubt they were consciously aware of it. I think the kids recognize that when you're here and paying attention to them, it's because you want to and not because you have to.

The kids and I have had a great relationship. I've been wonderfully rewarded and can't imagine that biologically Parker kids would be better. And yes, do try to get stationed here next. By the way, I thought that was a fine answer you gave Willy when he asked you why you aren't married.

Re: retirement number two in the offing. It's still undergoing on-again, off-again intrafamilial inspection. I feel that my previous retirement time for the cancer treatment, while outfitting me with a possible halo effect for having survived, will not help me make admiral. It's hard enough to make flag and many don't make it who are really outstanding. Any deviance from the expected path is usually the kiss of death and my two years on the disability list were certainly a deviance.

I've been a captain now for six years. This duty on the 3rd Fleet staff has been good, and I think I've done a lot for Readiness, but I don't see myself really making a great contribution or changing much from now on. When we're junior officers, we think we'll make big changes when we get there but no one ever seems to get there, no matter how high they go. I know I should want to relax and settle back and enjoy the pace, much slower after the growth years of the nuclear sub program, but I just don't want to. Well, I guess this is an off-again day. Want to try to talk me into an on-again one?

Joanna's staying out of it pretty much, but the kids say, "Don't go to sea again!" I'm also trying to assess how much my disaffection with the Vietnam war has affected how I feel. As for my health, as far as I can tell I'm totally recovered, well, except for lacking one of the two sperm-producing parts, and thank you God for giving me two! Did I tell you that when I retire I'll likely have 10% permanent disability pay for donating that part to my country? What a deal! What an incentive! I wonder how the VA decides how much to award? What's the payline for ovaries? Is there gender bias here?

I hope I've at least cheered you up. Although I guess there's plenty to be depressed about in this letter too. As you say, "you gotta take the bitter with the better."

　　　　　　　Luv ya!

　　　　　　　Tom

Three weeks later from Jennie

　　　　　　　　　　　May 20, 1979, Tonsberg, Norway

Goddag, Tuckerlove,

I miss you. It's too bad you couldn't have stayed longer. I've had the most extraordinary time with Grete, the daughter of Mother's life-long friend, Liva Tonnesen. She took me to Horton, the site of the Norwegian Naval Academy where Mother grew up before and after WWII. We walked between the two lines of barracks where the cadets lived and at the end of which is the apartment where Bestapapa, as the Commandant, lived for over 15 years.

We were able to visit what used to be the Officers' Club where Mother told me she'd attended many balls with dashing cadets and their friends. I could just envision her with a group of formally dressed young people arriving in their sleighs on a cold winter's evening for the Holiday dance. The ballroom has been maintained beautifully and a large mahogany bar and formal dining room add up to a place where a young girl's dreams would certainly be stirred.

We also peeked into the Base chapel, more of a large church, where Mother was baptized. You remember she was born in Horton before Bestapapa got orders to go to Oslo. It wasn't till after the War that he assumed command of the Naval Academy.

Grete has a beautiful home in Tonsberg. A narrow cobblestone road on one side and the fjord on the other. The dining room and living room overlook the water and a lovely garden in which tulips and lilacs are blooming profusely. See what you're missing?

We did have a marvelous time though, didn't we? I loved showing you Bergen and Trondheim. It was such a treat for me to reconnect with Uta, my second cousin. And you got to experience those incredible Norwegian breakfast buffets! Well, we'll have a lot to reminisce about in our old age, won't we? It's fun building a memory bank with you, Tucker. Maybe one day we can keep that bank deposit box in one home instead of two? (Did I really say that? Something to discuss when I return.)

Are the pictures back yet? I'm eager to see them. Oops, time for one of Grete's incredible dinners, so I'll sign off. See you in a week.

Much love, Jeg elsker deg

Jennie

Four months later from Tucker's journal

14 September 1979, Honolulu, Hawaii

For the record,

I've been invited to present a paper at a University of Virginia Symposium, to be held at the Grand Cayman Islands in January. Sounds like a boondoggle, except each participant must deliver an extensive paper with research and new ideas on naval and maritime matters. They want me to research the role of Women-in-the-Navy in the '80s and '90s.

Should I accept? I would have to considerably expand my research and spend many after-work hours on the project. Yet this could be a breakthrough arena for women. Important attendees and other presenters will hear the work. And my command has shaped up and requires less of my time and energies.

Wonder where the Cayman Islands are? Somewhere in the Caribbean I think.

TF

Three months later from Tucker

Christmas 1979, Pearl Harbor, Hawaii

Dear Buck,

It's been much too long since we've corresponded. I do miss your intellect and presence, although you're always with me in spirit. As you know, you've been a special person for me over the years. Today I need to write to you in both the role of my good friend and prime mentor. You've always been there to listen to my feelings and ideas, at least in the Navy environment. And for that I will be forever grateful. So here goes:

My past year in command has led me to the highest of heights in rewards and successes, and to the lowest of depths in personal struggle and pain. Paradoxically, the Navy, my profession, has provided this range of feelings. I've never been totally comfortable sharing feelings about my personal life. Probably my military upbringing. Stiff upper lip and all that.

Many factors have mitigated against my success in command, not the smallest of which is our post-Vietnam political environment that has afforded shore activities insufficient resources to get the job done. This means that my command has twenty percent (20%!) fewer than the numbers of persons the experts say we should have assigned. We've been particularly short in the senior enlisted ratings, petty officers and chiefs, and overloaded with female seamen apprentices.

Those Democrats don't get it when it comes to the needs of the Defense Department. I'd like to see Commander Jimmy Carter run this command with any real distinction! With the help of fine officers and enlisted personnel, I've at least kept the command above water.

I'm not getting to the primary issue. Am seriously considering retiring early. During my HRM consultant stint, I worked closely with a carrier's O-6 chaplain, an outstanding officer. He once remarked, "Tucker, at any one time, five percent of the men on this ship, *any* ship, will not be functioning in their jobs. Dysfunctional, if you will. They'll have some acute personal problem that preoccupies their thoughts." Before this statement, I hadn't thought in these terms about the work environment and have found the concept helpful in command. Further, in recent weeks I've been one of those five percent, and the concept has given me some solace. Buck, without much support from anyone, I've had to confront my demons, as we all do throughout our lives.

Needless to say, what I'm about to write is a private matter that's formidable to talk or write about. The nub of it: For several years I've known that I'm more attracted, sexually, to women than to men. I arrived at a point where I no longer care if the Navy, or society, believes homosexuality to be immoral. After much struggle and soul-searching, I'm now in a relationship with a wonderful woman. She happens to be a former naval officer and a widow of one of our finest officers.

This predicament has brought me great pain. Within the last few months I've had to discharge six personnel, men and women, within my command "for reason of homosexuality." I need not tell you what deep agony and conflict those discharges caused me. Early in my tour, I felt even more torn up when a Senior Chief told me that my boss had put a tail on me in an attempt to relieve me for cause of homosexuality. Since this episode, he and I have had a good working relationship, largely because my command has proven to be the lead among its peers. He has no reason to relieve me.

I write you some of these details as a preface to my current personal crisis. I'm at the point wherein it feels too hard to continue with an organization which is hateful to gays and lesbians. I would never "come out" and cause a fuss for the Navy. Yet you know I'm an activist and it'll continually be more uncomfortable to bite my tongue and accept the Navy's policy that gay men and women are unwanted. I've given a big chunk of my life to our great Navy, and it will be rugged to stop at commander. I figure — since Dad was an admiral, I should at least be a captain. Probably a Navy Junior syndrome. I don't know.

Why am I writing this to you? Because I respect your advice and opinion. I'm wondering, what *do* you think about the Navy's policy regarding homosexuality? You know that if I were to make captain with the next board, I'd face a Background Investigation. I'd probably survive it, as have others. But should I lie about my sexuality when it comes to my NIS interview? Perhaps I should; I've done so for fellow officers.

I've faced many dilemmas with the Navy. I know you've met more. But this situation is almost unbearable. Is retiring the easy way out? Is it the coward's way out? I've never thought of myself as cowardly.

I haven't found the courage to share this situation with my parents. Dad strongly feels I should stay in and make captain and accept greater responsibilities. And, of course, I think he'd like me to make flag! Fat chance. I'm too political and infamous!

Buck, I finally got to the issue. Few in our culture "get it" about the gay population. It took me a long time, in a long search. Our Navy subculture is even more uptight about the subject. We, the Navy, have made significant changes within our people programs. When will we recognize that military gay people are ordinary human beings who just want to do their job? Why do we have to be so damn righteously against homosexuality? Why do we force out people like me? When will the country's gay movement educate Americans about gays as the women's movement has been educating them about women?

It's special to be in Pearl Harbor and to be in command. I enjoy every day, notwithstanding the stressors!

How're you and your lovely family doing? Are you enjoying retirement? Bet you have many activities to keep your mind active. I think of you whenever I read about our deployments in Diego Garcia, and other times as well!

Take good care of yourself. My love to you and Helen. When you find a moment, I'd appreciate your thoughts on my personal dilemma.

Warmly,

Tucker

One week later from Buck

New Year's Day, 1980, New York

Dear Tucker,

This Christmas has brought more joyous gifts than your Christmas letter, but none causing the range of emotions that letter stimulated.

What do I say? My first reaction is a humble one. You've conferred a signal honor by trusting me with such all-important information, and I feel a huge need to respond with as much thought, honesty, and trust as you demonstrated.

My next thought was escapist. It said, "What the Hell! All of us are floating around together on this spaceship among the stars. We're all different, products of our genes, our upbringing, our various environments. What difference does it make if Tucker is outside the norms? Just as she is more intelligent than the vast majority, just as she is more intense, competitive, and dedicated to producing only in the top one percent in everything she does, why should it be a big deal that her truly private moments are spent differently from most others? She IS different. That's what makes Tucker Tucker, and what creates a very high order of satisfaction with her work."

Then reality set in. I couldn't evade the stark truth that Tucker's difference had and would create problems for the peculiar society she'd chosen: Although providing plenty of maneuvering room for the individual thinker, the great United States Navy —with all its heritage, jealousies, conservative beliefs — requires that originality be injected carefully and along a procedural path much more constrained than the decision-making patterns of most organizations. Taking on the whole establishment isn't one of those paths. Regardless of the worth and contribution of individuals, if they're perceived as antithetical to the grand notion of a mission-oriented, duty-driven, "What's-good-for-the-country" philosophy, then they cannot occupy important places in the system, and in some cases, no place at all.

How can I tell Tucker this so that she will hear it as truth, and not as merely another cog in the system falling into place against her? By being direct and truthful, I decided. Evasiveness with Tucker is an insult, she sees through it; pabulum-type, "Don't worry, everything will be all right" statements will rightfully infuriate her, and any attempt to rationalize will do her more damage than good in the long run.

The professional dilemma she senses is accurate, alive and well. There's a thing called "service reputation" which is impossible to chronicle on service records, very difficult to identify or isolate, but is startlingly important when selection boards meet and when screening is done for command positions, when choices are made for personnel assignments. It's much more than an old-boy network, easily defeating obvious attempts of "old boys" to ramrod a favorite into important assignments. It's the intangible opinion of an officer which develops over time as a result of the manner in which that officer is perceived to work within or outside the system. Sometimes it's simply spelled "loyalty."

Our press and those unfamiliar with the closeness of military life use sarcasm and cartoons to paint "service reputation" as an insidious favoritism, as a time-honored method to maintain the status quo. That sort of outside opinion probably created the famous remark usually attributed to President Franklin Roosevelt, "The Navy is like a feather bed. You can punch it down in one place but it will pop out in another." Strangely, the Navy didn't think that a bad description. To change the fundamental naval structure takes great effort; it also takes a *long* time.

In your Christmas letter, Tucker, I sensed deep anger directed against that system, an anger directed at a lot of things: the Defense Department, the command selection system, the personnel distribution system, Vietnam policy, even the Democratic Party and President Carter came in for sly digs. Anyone reading your letter would wonder why you keep yourself involved in such untenable circumstances. Someone like me, who knows you, admires you, and doesn't want to hurt you, will want to dig more deeply and assess causes and possible cures. But, even those like me, who don't want to lose your talent, can never agree to fundamental changes in the Navy in order to keep that talent.

I see your very personal decision regarding sexuality as causing you much more anguish in the Navy than outside it. It will be a long time, if ever, before the military organizations, designed to inspire and train individuals to die for their country, and perhaps more importantly, in a strange way, to die for each other, can be comfortable having within their midst, known gay individuals who threaten that special feeling of camaraderie, esprit, and morale. I don't argue that such individuals cannot perform well in the system. You and many others throughout history have proved otherwise. But this occurred when their sexuality was unknown. Once known, regardless of their sterling performances, they inhibit the system's performance. It's not an environment which nurtures them.

Tucker, as much as I admire your ability and your logic which says that the important thing is that you do your job well, my sense of the system's reality is that once your chosen lifestyle becomes known, and it will, the pressures on you will be unbearable. Not only will you continue to face the hypocrisy of carrying out orders which you personally violate, but there will be built up such an adverse "service reputation" concerning you, that your happiness and sense of accomplishment will vanish. Your energies will be spent fighting back. Nothing will be left for the Navy.

Your letter ends with a litany of questions. I suspect you know the answers as well as I. Even if legislative or court decrees force the Navy to lift the gay ban, leaders will gather data and build a case to prove that the military goals of readiness, unit cohesion, and devotion to duty are unacceptably disturbed by homosexual influence. Most Americans believe that, and the final outcome will be a return to some form of stating rules for belonging to the military, with the onus for abiding by the rules on the individual and not the system.

I truly believe that, Tucker. And believing it, I don't want you hurt by it. Can you not say to yourself that your timing was off? If you believe that some day the country will be more accepting of such differences in its armed forces, can you not say that you were born too soon, and ease up on yourself with that logic. You're far too valuable to continue to wear yourself out against a system which will grind you down, if it hasn't already done so.

So my regretful conclusion is obvious. I believe you *should* bring your parents into this as soon as possible, anticipate disappointment from them, particularly your dad, and begin to take the steps toward retirement. In no way is that a cowardly way out. You have given much. I personally attest to that. You should have no feelings of avoiding the battle, or leaving because the going has become too tough. You have served well. The time has come to move on.

Tucker, what I've written is rough to read, I know. Perhaps you shouldn't have asked me. But as I said at the beginning, the fact that you did is something I shall always cherish. Put it behind you, smell the roses, enjoy life and find a vocation that lets you wake in the morning unworried and unstressed. You surely owe yourself that, given all you've endured the past years.

> With affection,
>
> Buck

One week later from Tucker

> *9 January 1980, The Grand Cayman*

Dear Jennie,

I'm settled into my hotel room for the evening, wishing you were with me in this ever-so-romantic, peaceful spot. My flight out of Miami was a little scary in an old and downright rickety two-prop jobber-do. Flying so close to Cuba that we saw her lights glistening in the night renewed old memories of the Missile Crisis.

Upon our arrival in Grand Cayman, we were driven to the hotel by Joe, a black man with a veddy British accent. His flashy islander's shirt definitely outclassed our Aloha shirts. As we drove to the hotel, I observed that the island is sparsely built up compared to Hawaii. Joe pointed out the many banks along the way, explaining that Grand Cayman (British West Indies), has the same financial status as Switzerland and encourages the wealthy to maintain their bank accounts here.

The hotel, small and picturesque, sits back about 100 yards from the sands of the Caribbean. I'm looking out from my second floor window down onto the large lanai with a big wooden bar and kidney-shaped pool. Not bad for an ordinary line officer. Where are YOU?

The conference is well-organized with some top Americans attending. The conferees are about twenty-five in number. Many brought their wives. I'm the only woman presenter.

Tonight I'm wearing my new mauve negligee set which Mother gave me especially for the occasion. Special and feminine. Mother, in her dreams anyway, would probably like me to meet a dashing bachelor on this faraway island and be swept off my feet. I'd rather have you here as my "companion." Oh, me! I'll have to settle for enjoying the elegant surroundings, the excitement of the moment, and preparing for my presentation tomorrow.

To be in this gorgeous place giving talks about strategic naval and maritime matters feels extravagant. The remote atmosphere, on the other hand, gives these very responsible people time away from their busy schedules and duties. I'll include myself; command has taken its toll.

Know you are missed. We should definitely plan a mini-vacation.

Love you,

Tucker

One day later from Tucker

10 January 1980, Grand Cayman Island

Dear Robyn,

I'm basking in the afternoon sun and sands of the Grand Cayman. Today I presented a paper, "Women-in-the-Navy in the '80s and '90s," to a University of Virginia Symposium of many important folks. In the middle of my presentation I thought about *you*. Well, sort of. I flashed back to the "non-person syndrome" which we discussed many years ago.

The conferees included admirals and deputies and lawyers, all men. The one woman is the Undersecretary of the Navy's wife. As I presented my research their politeness was overshadowed by their body language which told me only a few truly wanted to think about Navy women. I represent either negative stuff or nothing at all. The non-person thing. Most would rather have been talking about the other subjects of the day — Principles of Naval Warfare, Technology and Force Structures, Changing Ocean Law, the Soviet Navy, and so forth. I couldn't help observing that several of these

men were Navy Juniors, like me, but I'm sure they'd had a totally
different life experience within the Navy. Sometimes I have a weird
ah-ha! that mature men love to play Strategic Thinking and
Planning in the same way they loved to play Cops and Robbers or
Cowboys and Indians as little boys. I rather liked Cowboys and
Indians myself!

Notwithstanding, several conferees got noticeably excited about
my research and conclusions. That feels good because the paper is
a culmination of deep thinking and research and I too am upbeat
about its usefulness and implications. In the right offices the paper
will be very useful. This seems to be the wrong audience.

My speech was hard-punching and didn't mince words. You
would've been proud. My strength seemed to come from within; it
was as if you and Jennie were at hand, guiding my delivery. I told
the conferees I believe the Navy has made more progress re its
uniformed women in the last decade than in the previous three
decades. Then I went into the status of the law, which is still a
major stumbling block.

Remember I wrote you in Nov '78 that article 6015, which
disallows women from sea duty, was amended and now the law
permits women to be assigned permanently to certain auxiliary and
support ships? The Navy's current thinking places women on
support ships, including tenders and salvage ships. Current long-
range planning doesn't have them aboard combatants, except in a
temporary duty status. Current plans have the women on board
non-combatant ships returning ashore in the event of a hostile
situation, since the law prohibits women from being in a combat-
mission environment. The question one must ask: If women are
permitted only on noncombatants in peacetime, and the Navy
recruits them in large numbers — 45,000 by 1985 — will they not
be a liability in event of war? Support personnel in peacetime often
are assigned to combatants in wartime.

As an aside to the sea duty issue, a Coastie admiral came up to
me at Happy Hour tonight and said he supported me and Navy
women and men who are trying to move the Navy into a new era.
He explained that the Coast Guard has women, several of whom
will soon be skippers, serving onboard its cutters. I asked him,
"What about the implications of wartime, when the Coast Guard
comes under the jurisdiction of the Secretary of the Navy? Wouldn't
they be illegal under 6015?" He said the Coast Guard isn't worried
about that, "We're just ahead of our times. The Navy ought to read
your paper and get with the program!"

You'd be interested to know I talked about the issue of the attitude of the American male toward sexuality. I mentioned a destroyer commanding officer, whom I'd interviewed for the paper and who referred to "the basic sexual immaturity of the American male." His point supports a Traditional view of male and female roles as the major barrier toward full integration of Navy women. I told the conferees that for many male officers the introduction of women into a destroyer officer wardroom would cause distraction and discomfort. In the eyes of these men, the Women-at-Sea program is a lip service "nice-to-have," but in reality it's an equal opportunity program which has a very low priority juxtaposed with current Naval problems. Also, there's deep reluctance to compete with women. It seems, Robyn, to have women on board, especially in higher positions, somewhat deflates the macho male stereotype and the individual's self worth!

Complex, eh? I'm sure you have a more in-depth psychological explanation.

Must stop. I need to get ready for our cocktails and dinner. Wish you and Ned (and Jennie) were here to enjoy the atmosphere and good food and wine. This Caribbean island is an uncelebrated spot which may someday become crowded with American tourists.

Take care. Best love to Ned too.

> Love,
>
> Tucker

One week later from Tucker

18 January 1980, Honolulu, Hawaii

Dear Buck,

Your New Year's Day letter stirred within me a vast array of feelings, with a huge sadness predominating. Seems ironic…the mentor recommends to his protegé that she retire early. I trust your wisdom, Buck, yet disagree with your analysis. I cherish your continuing concern for me.

Having thought about your letter a lot, I need to respond. I hold major differences with the assumptions you and naval leaders put together about "dealing with the gays." Your assumptions are passé for me. Remember the women's study and how I argued for policy options based on assumptions and values? You and I agreed a decade ago with the Neo-Traditional assumptions about women.

Today the Navy is moving rapidly to the Egalitarian option, with differing assumptions.

From your letter, which I truly appreciated, your assumptions about gays-in-the-military stand apart from mine, no doubt because (1) I've lived as a lesbian for several years and (2) I'm a woman. You believe that allowing open military gays will destroy the morale, good order and discipline, and *esprit de corps* of our great Navy.

You mentioned "taking on the whole institution." Perhaps that thought comes from observation of my work for Navy women. That's a valid conclusion. At times I felt I was taking on the whole system; ergo, my reputation as a feminist activist. I've never felt my work was antithetical to the institution and would do it over in a minute.

But I'm not about to take on the Navy and its policies toward gays and lesbians. I'd be a fool! I may be stubborn, but not stupid. While the gay rights issue is at a different place in time than women's rights, I believe to lift the ban on military gays is not antithetical to the Navy's missions. First, however, within the entire country, prejudice and (dumb) illusions about gays must change. Personally, like most naval personnel, I live a quiet private life and a very active Navy life, mainly working to move the command forward in the interest of Navy goals. We've "bonded" within our command, and our morale is high despite tough growing pains.

You mention service reputation. Notwithstanding any thoughts about "Is she a lesbian?" or "Why is she so much the feminist?," I know my own reputation is mixed. The controversial aspect relates to standing by my convictions and going against the tide to support a person, a regulation, or a situation that I believe needs support. Has to do with not automatically replying, "Yessir", until the decision is made. The positive sides of my reputation speak for themselves. What irks me: "Is she a lesbian?" or "Is he a gay man?" should not be a part of service reputation or a civilian's reputation. For the moment, if the answer is known to be, "Yes," it's a huge potential negative.

Am I angry with the Navy? I would say no. Rather, I'm disappointed and frustrated. I feel let down as an individual and as a commanding officer. I'm not alone on the latter. For too many years I've observed the strains and stresses of overcommitment on the faces of individual sailors and officers who put in extra hours to "get the job done." Perhaps my frustrations and disappointments have blossomed into a mild case of anger.

Enough. Enough. Misdirected feelings toward you! Must be that I'm sad you advised me to leave (as would Big Daddy Navy if the opportunity presented itself). Many years ago you advised, for different reasons, that I not join. This time I shall more carefully weigh my good friend's counsel. Many thanks for your openness and sincere caring about my immediate dilemma.

Somehow I don't feel as alone anymore. My love to you and Helen.

With affection and sadness,

Tucker

P.S. Please don't discuss any of this with my parents, at least the sexuality issue. I can't yet tell them of my conflict.

Same day from Tucker's journal

For the record,

It was hard restraining my feelings and thoughts in answering Buck. He knows that military studies show there's no rational basis for the ban on gays. He's a logical man. Why, therefore, does he require me and other gay people in the military to lie about our sexual orientation? Why ask me to leave when I'm one of the Navy's hard-charging leaders within my peer group? What I believe to be a wrong-headed policy toward gays may be the *real* source of any anger toward the Navy. I keep that stuffed deep within and pray it disappears.

As long as Americans remain negative toward gays, stereotypical images will persist and allow the military to maintain anachronistic policies that cause gay people to be unnecessarily on constant guard.

I can feel my blood pressure rising! I'm angry at those who buy in to prejudiced reasoning. That kind of narrow thinking is what creates difficulty in building *esprit* and camaraderie with anybody who might be different. It's the same prejudice that withheld equal opportunity from American blacks and women. Whereas it took many, many years of women's and blacks' activism to attain a modicum of equality, I'll be dead and gone before the American military drops the ban on "people like me." That's what Buck meant by being born too soon. Impossible for an activist to accept.

Buck's euphemistic "chosen lifestyle" reveals his lack of knowledge about being gay. I wouldn't have intentionally selected this path; my god, look what it hath wrought! I worry a lot about Jennie and me and about witch-hunts.

Lifestyle as used today conjures up dreadful scenes, including promiscuous gay men in the baths. "Chosen lifestyle," a loaded phrase for sure, needs to be dismissed from the vocabulary. It's a major insult to gays. The counter argument says, "Well, one is born black, but not gay or lesbian." I strongly disagree with that statement, though the scientific data is still not in.

Buck's right, I must tell my parents soon. Seems a formidable task.

TF

Three weeks later from Robyn

5 February 1980, Bar Harbor, Maine

Dear Tucker,

And the beat goes on. It's the same issue again, and again, and again! Your comments about the male psyche are right on. The Navy, indeed the military in general (no pun intended), emanates from a long tradition of males scrapping, beating their chests, and generally posturing in ways both absurd and arrogant. For what? Gaining territory? Status? Power? Females? Ego? Perhaps a more civilized and sophisticated definition would describe a fraternity of old-boy-slap-on-the-back-brothers-forever type organization.

Bear in mind, Tucker, it's only within the last sixty years that American females were deemed worthy enough to vote. How long ago was it that only boys were taught to read and write? In how many societies are women still property and still subject to all kinds of mutilations and physical abuses, such as clitorectomies in Africa? Female infants today are left out on hillsides in China to perish. In like jobs men get higher salaries...and on and on. As I've said before, the Navy represents a microcosm of our society and a distillation of deep, historical tradition. Because the military environment is condensed and hierarchical, issues surface more forcefully and urgently.

In sum, men and women worldwide, even in our own forward looking, insightful, and equal opportunity country, remain at an immature, perhaps barely nascent level insofar as relating to, living with, and accepting each other as equal human beings. Thus, we come around again to the point that the military, partly because of what you call the warrior culture, intensifies the way the rest of us live out our values.

So, Tucker, a complicated combination of historical and societal factors form your Navy men's resistance, almost built into the genes, at least the ones on the Y chromosome! It's similar to arguing for or against the existence of God. (Remember those days?) Beliefs run deep, emotional and not very rational. Maybe there should be a separate (but equal of course) military for women.

God, Tucker, I give up! Maybe you should too.

Till soon,

Love, Robyn

P.S. Remember that ugly maroon velvet Victorian couch we inherited? Elizabeth's ferret has totally destroyed the seat by burrowing through it — velvet, horsehairs and all. Even chewed the frame. Pity.

One month later from Tucker's journal

28 February 1980, Pearl Harbor, Hawaii

For the record,

My detailer called again today. He's working up my case and is detailing me to a captain's billet at the Pentagon in June, with the assumption that I'll make the cut when the Promotion Board reports out in October. If I make it, that's another five years of obligated active duty.

My other option: within two weeks, to submit my papers for a 30 September retirement, twenty-one years for pay purposes, and he'll leave me in command over the summer.

The good news about retiring — I won't have to fret about an NIS clearance, I won't have to ask Jennie to move, and I can be moving toward peace with my love. The bad news — I'll never achieve my goals of making the grade of captain and having a major command. Tough decision, Fairfield. What would the Ambassador's wife say?

TF

Ten days later from Tucker's journal

10 March 1980, Honolulu, Hawaii

 For the record,

Last Thursday, no doubt about it, a peak experience. I came out to Mother and therefore to Dad for she'll tell him. I spoke with Robyn; she advised that I record my feelings about this watershed.

You might say I had preplanned the happening. Mother and Dad are visiting me and attending a Sub Vets' Convention. Buck pushed me over the cliff in January to go for it and come out to my parents.

You know, Fairfield, this is absolutely a stupid reality! Why should children and parents be put through such an ordeal? Societal norms. Why should lesbians and gays be locked in the so-called closet, holding on tightly to a huge secret they feel they can't tell their loved ones? Societal norms. Dumb! How archaic, anachronistic, controlling, and some profane words.

I could only deal with telling Mother, who is by nature liberal and accepting of diversity. So, when Dad decided he was going to the Sub Base for an officers' luncheon, I said, "This will be *it*, Fairfield." A host of feelings washed over me. My strongest physical feeling was anxiety. FEAR. On the other hand, I felt strong and brave and pleased that I would finally take the risk to come out to Mother.

As Mother and I ate our lunch on my lanai, fear took hold. We talked about trivialities, given my decision. While I wanted to jump in with my announcement anytime, I couldn't. My heart pounded so hard and fast, it ached. This has got to be the most difficult task of my lifetime, I thought. After eating our sandwiches and cookies, we agreed the sun was getting too hot and gathered ourselves into the comfort of my cozy family room. My strength returned!

I blurted out, "Mother, I need you to know that I now live a different so-called lifestyle." Mother pulled herself away and dropped her eyes. "I have a relationship with Jennie and I love her more than anyone in the world." I suppose that was an obtuse way of saying I'm living as a lesbian, but Mother's no dummy. And I detest labels.

A long silence. Mother looked stunned. Then, Mother replied that she and Dad had often discussed my social life and why I hadn't married long ago. They'd been wondering lately about Jennie. Yet Mother's true reactions were hidden, not unlike her usual persona. I sensed she was simultaneously taken aback and feeling genuinely motherly and supportive. To discover a daughter is lesbian isn't a happy feeling, I'm certain. At least for my parents and their generation. Nor is it happy for the child!

She finally said softly, "It's not as if you haven't tried."

My response — relief and sadness. My scared feelings dissipated with her remark. A deep sense of freedom swept over me. My life's Big Secret was out to my mother, and soon to my father.

That night in bed I relived the moment: My sense of self was multifaceted. I'd been true to my authentic self and in that regard I'm a proud self, proud to have had the wisdom to follow my heart which took me to women and to finally be courageous enough to tell my mother. I feel guilty. Guilty about violating societal norms, disobeying the Navy's laws, rejecting the heterosexual model. My self is a grown-up daughter who's taken charge of her inner life, just as she has for many years taken charge of her outer life.

My father, whom I couldn't directly tell, represents to me societal norms and Navy laws that have kept me closeted and paranoid for a long time. No way could I share my conflicted, guilty self with my father. I couldn't be vulnerable to one who is invulnerable and somewhat insensitive to diversity.

Feelings? I'm sad that I don't feel comfortable in telling my father. Sad that he and many others cannot comprehend that two women could love each other in a complete, intimate relationship. I feel angry that my *own father* is a part of the anger and resentment I have toward the Navy and its negative, unproductive view toward gays and lesbians.

I feel brave and pleased that I confronted Mother with an issue that potentially creates discord — *verboten* behavior in our family. It took 42 years; better late than never.

I feel relieved to have knocked down the wall of secrecy between my parents and me about my personal life. I feel concern for my parents' fears. I know they'll be upset with this news for sometime, maybe always. I don't want to hurt them.

I feel shame.

I feel balanced.

I feel relieved.

What a complexity of feelings!

Mother's final remark implies failure or defeat and that her expectations haven't been met. I haven't succeeded. She's disappointed in me. And, the unspoken, she's terribly disappointed that she didn't have grandchildren.

I've been told to live by a set of norms that intrinsically, and biologically, don't fit for me. Authority figures and institutions have asked me to do the impossible. I have done it fairly well, until recently anyway, given the parameters.

Robyn made an important point. Yes, Mother's disappointed. But the feeling extends beyond being disappointed for herself. She's also disappointed for me. She knows what a wonderful life marriage has brought for her as a woman and for many reasons she'd like that for her daughter. She's disappointed that this same pattern has not been, and will not be, replicated in me. She's sad she cannot fully know me, given my differentness. "And, my friend," said Robyn, "I imagine there'll come a day when she'll come to honor and love that quality in her own child that is different from her own self and most others' selves."

TF

Two days later from Tucker's journal

12 March 1980, Honolulu, Hawaii

For the record,

Another difficult day with my parents. I told them I'm strongly considering retirement. Mother was understanding, but Dad was opposed, even though Mother had told him about our coming-out conversation.

I know he's disappointed that his daughter would opt out and not make captain. Me too.

I explained that a primary reason to retire is my need to establish roots. "I'm tired of packing up and moving, and packing up and moving and packing up...I want a place to belong. A real home. I thought it was that I don't want to leave Jennie. But it's deeper, broader — a need for an identity, other than commander, a need to be part of an accepting community. I no longer feel like I'm a solid member of our Navy community. Because of my love for Jennie, I'm finding it impossible to be at peace in the Navy."

Dad was agitated. He argued that I was "downright foolish" to give up the financial security which would be more certain with the rank of Captain. I said I knew that and would pay the consequences. "Money's never been a driving factor for me to stay, Dad. The challenges and the pleasures have been my motivators. The challenges are ever present, but the fun gets harder and harder to come by."

He said, "The homosexual thing can be managed. The Navy takes care of its own. If you're quiet, they'll leave you alone." He said that everyone must make his own decision about when to retire, but he thought I was cutting off my career in its prime. "I think you have a good chance for flag, Tucker."

"Thanks, Dad, but I'm too politically left — and an intellectual! And we only allow one woman at a time to serve in a flag billet."

As I write, I realize Dad's doubly disappointed in me because I have brought him and Mother no grandchildren. I should at least bring him the satisfaction of not giving up the ship.

TF

Two days later from Tucker

14 March 1980, Honolulu, Hawaii

Dear Robyn,

You've followed me and "the Navy thing" for twenty years. The end is coming. Today I submitted my resignation, effective 30 September.

Much turmoil within. Why didn't I reach my goal, success in my chosen career. Maybe success isn't reaching the top rung, but rather knowing when to step aside for others to compete for the top. Or, perhaps success is being honest to my Self and not my career.

I've outgrown the Navy. Long ago I felt like I was married to the Navy. As of this date we have irreconcilable, irresolvable differences.

Besides, it's no fun to be unwanted. And unless I continue to lie low, my real self, were it divulged to Big Daddy Navy, would be persona non grata.

I'm not that innocent ensign of so many years ago. Today I intentionally choose no longer to defend my psyche against unjust, exclusive attitudes and actions. Oh, yes, our Navy, along with our society, will gradually become a place where I can grow and be. But that's a long way off.

One of the reasons I would stay is to pave the way for the many junior women who've implored me to stay. But the mantle must be passed on. The second reason is Dad's wishes.

Remember that young ensign who thought the threat was communism? This middle-aged commander thinks the more elusive, scarier enemy is within. To wit: American extremism on both sides of the political aisles is as insidious and as threatening to the country and our people as is the Soviet Union with its nuclear warheads aimed at the United States. Only moderate minorities, those included as the extremists' enemy targets, would agree with me.

Those same minorities understand that the myth of "Join the Navy or the Army and be all that you can be" supports the false assumption that all recruits are white heterosexual males.

I'm probably sounding whiny and sour grapesy. So be it. The positive side of the decision is that I can be safe with Jennie, my life partner.

In the Navy we have an expression called "the J (Jesus) Factor." Oftentimes you've lined up your weapon's sights, ready to fire a missile or torpedo or bomb, and you know you don't have all the digital or navigational data. At the very last you reach up for the J Factor, that which will give you the rest of the information, the unknown, the missing factor in your equation. My dad evoked the J Factor innumerable times during his highly successful war patrols in WWII; otherwise, he and his submarine would have been among the 52 boats and the many submariners never to come home.

Just good luck you say? Robyn, this J Factor isn't exactly luck; it's something enigmatic, even mystical, which brings the fortune and the power to hit your target and keep you safe when fighting your enemy. Since '75 I've transcribed this Factor into my Guardian Spirit, Laughing Owl, who's been sitting on my right shoulder in critical times and keeping me from falling on my sword through all kinds of crises (as you well know)! Laughing Owl tells me he's tired. He's worked long hours, especially during my command tour, and is ready for a long rest. So, best I pack it in and send us both on leave for awhile.

Sounds a little hokey pokey? I don't know. These ideas keep my spirit in touch with something larger than myself, larger than the everyday routine and connect me with life's Mysteries.

A sense of belonging? That'll return, as it came for me in those formative Navy years; the feeling may be less intense, but I'll find that peace again.

Perhaps I stayed too long at the dance? So what. I had a great time in spite of some awkward dancing partners.

I trust that you and Ned are totally happy as Main-ee-acs. Keep August open for a trip to Hawaii for my retirement. Jennie and I are truly looking forward to your visit.

Love and hugs,

Tucker

Four months later from Billie

15 July 1980, on the seas

Dear Tuck —

Now that I've done it, I feel everyone should do it. Whatta relief! As I said on the autovon, go with your heart. The regret, the nostalgia, knowing that you still have a career — these are only temporary feelings. It's the *relief* that gives you a rush!

I had a very nice, quiet retirement ceremony on the beautiful grounds of the Naval Postgraduate School — clear blue sky, green, green grass and trees, brilliant flower beds with lots of buzzing bees, dress whites, all the accolades and short speeches (a CDR retired with me), nice reception in the expansive lobby of the Del Monte. Then, hot damn! It's over! Just like that! Twenty roller coaster years! My sisters and brothers-in-law attended, and got it all on tape. I did not cry, or even feel sad. I felt — relief!

You know where I am now? In Puget Sound, moored at Friday Harbor, sitting in the cockpit of *Osprey*, a 46' single-masted sailboat called a Tatoosh. My sisters both married sailboat freaks and they chartered this boat when they discovered I was retiring and taking a job in Seattle. After the ceremony we had a raucous time in San Francisco and even a more raucous time driving up the gorgeous Northern California, Oregon, and Washington coasts.

They helped me find and move into a small house in the Ballard area of Seattle overlooking the Sound. Then we stocked up the car and boarded the boat at Anacortes. I hardly have had time to think about the fact that I'm in retirement now. Except that I'm still in a relieved state. This little cruise through the San Juan Islands has been a real tonic. My sisters wait on me hand and foot. They thought I was tense, uptight, and downright dour, and they set out to restore my positive outlook and my sense of humor. We have laughed, told old family stories, and have generally worn out my brothers-in-law. It's fun!

I thank the Navy for all it did for me. It offered me travel, responsible jobs, leadership positions, good times, good friends, good money, damn good sea stories, and a confidence that's hard to shake (although it was shaken). As I told you, I'll be in Seattle for approximately a year as a consultant working in community relations and demographics in preparation for moving a portion of the Fleet to Puget Sound. Good ol' CHINFO contacts, they mean something after all. And I certainly will come to Hawaii for your retirement! I understand you couldn't get out of the command responsibilities to get to mine. It's okay. But, don't back out, girl. The best is yet to come!

I think of the Navy as a phase. I don't know how long I'll be on this Earth, but life's made up of phases, stages, and passages. The Navy brought us to maturity. Now it's time to step away and begin the next passage. As with all of our life phases, they must intermingle to make the whole. Listen to me. I sound like some damn philosopher!

My sister's mixing daiquiries and my brother-in-law's firing up the grill, even on a sailboat. Whatta life! When I get the date of your retirement, I'll be there! Except I'll fix mai-tais!

Your friend,

Billie

Five weeks later from Tom

20 August 1980, Washington, D.C.

Dear Tucker,

By now you should have received my formal regret to your "passing out" ceremony. How things have changed since, well, you know since what. I'm sorry to be missing your grand finale. I love these retirement ceremonies. There's the basic script: "I never could have done this without the wonderful support from my (crew/wife/family/staff)."

"Behind every good sailor is a good (crew/wife/family/staff)."

"My ships made every commitment and I owe it all to my (crew/wife/family/staff)." Then the retiree embellishes the basic text with some effort at originality, perhaps reciting poetry ("I must go down to the sea again...") or including well-known nautical quotes like, " Damn the torpedoes, full speed ahead." Or, "I have not yet begun to fight."

For mine I had the most devilish desire to say something like, "Despite staffs that didn't know a warhead from a watermelon, crews that never wanted to go to sea, ships that were falling apart, and a hopeless family, my ships made every operations commitment and I somehow managed to survive long enough to retire!"

Seriously, these ceremonies do serve a useful purpose as do all ceremonies that mark a transition. Tuck, I wish you the best of days with the best part of your life to follow. You deserve it. I know you think the Navy let you down in a most hurtful, personal way by not accepting you as a whole person.

I know it's unfair. I sincerely believe though that you've contributed to change. There have been real advances in opportunities for women in the Navy, and eventually, one's sexual preference won't mean a damn. Success will just amount to how well you do your job.

How am I? Well, I've made it past the mystical five-year cancer survival period. When I got the cancer, I said, "Why me?" Now that I'm apparently surviving, I say, "Why me?" It was so close and I was so lucky. If I'd gotten my cancer a year earlier, I'd be dead. If I'd gone to another place for treatment, one not hooked into NIH, I'd likely be dead. I understand the experimental drug, bleomycin, which I was given after the cancer returned, and another one recently approved, cisplatin, are now the drugs of choice for the very malignant form of testicular cancer I had, and if it's caught early enough, all men who get this cancer are surviving.

I've heard from Ann Haynes that the Navy finally has asked a Yale researcher to look at the health status of men who have served on nuclear subs. I hope they do it right this time.

Joanna and I and the kids are having a great time and we're riding out living with an adolescent and her 10-year-old younger brother. My job? Well, I'm trying. Being a stockbroker should be easy, but I find it hard to call up strangers and ask them for money and even harder to ask people I know. Not a good combination. Fortunately, Dean Witter's entry-level pay, my Navy retirement pay, and Joanna's salary are keeping us going pretty well.

Have a big, wonderful, knock-em-dead day, kid. And for sure, keep in touch.

We luv ya!

Tom

From Tucker's journal

August 1980, Pearl Harbor, Hawaii

For the record,

Yesterday was a beautiful, sunny day in Pearl. I spoke outside to an audience of hundreds seated on an expansive green lawn. I shared the grandstand with Admiral Gilligan, a fellow classmate at American University, whom I'd invited to be guest speaker. Others on the stand were all men and naval officers.

The podium was framed by several monkey pod trees blowing in the soft afternoon winds. From up on the stage I could smell the sweet odor of plumeria which decorates the front of the Headquarters Building. As I looked out over the audience, the back rows of the seats were under some coconut palms and I had a passing chuckle that coconuts might tumble onto the guests. As I sat, awaiting my turn, I could look out over the "haze gray and underway" ships at Ford Island piers and beyond to the high reaches of the magnificent Pali, which so long ago was so frightening to me as a little girl.

I said goodbye to the U.S. Navy, to Big Daddy Navy, with whom I've had a volatile, exciting relationship since birth. With fronds and flags flapping in the breezes, I delivered a combined Change of Command and Retirement speech. My troops stood at ease in the back of the audience, looking sharp and well-turned-out in their dress whites. My parents, as well as Jennie, Buck and Helen, Billie, and Robyn, were smiling at me from the audience. Tom, Joanna, and, of course, Pierre, were missing.

I thanked the appropriate people who'd assisted our new command in its birthing process and who'd helped in my own career. I spoke of the reasons we had succeeded as a command — well-defined goals, commitment and cooperation, and support from others. "Finally, we've succeeded because we've taken care of ourselves in the process."

I read the Crockett poem, A People Place, which has become important to me through the years and that I'd read upon assumption of command.

I said that I'd sometimes had difficulty in the 20+ years of active duty accepting the Navy's norms and values and that I'd almost resigned twice. But the Navy, while remaining conservative, had allowed me to be myself, to maintain my own integrity and, yes, to make some impact on its values and norms, especially regarding women's policies. I said, "The Navy was a place evidently where I could just be me, and I did try and did learn, and I did grow. And, my feelings have often been heard."

I was presented a personal medal, the Meritorious Service Commendation, to add to my others. I then read my orders, and was relieved of command. Then, as I gave my last salute, I walked through the bridge of sideboys, both men and women, to the other side and retirement.

And how do I feel the day after?

I feel like the confident, proud naval officer who has said farewell to an organization which handed me both great joy and deep pain and sorrow.

I feel like the successful daughter who has accomplished some of what her parents had expected through the years, but not all. I topped out too early for Dad.

I'm proud that, in an environment in which I'd become more and more uncomfortable in the last three years, I accomplished three primary goals: to be the best that I can be, to survive, and to help change things for Navy women in the future.

I feel sad that in truth, unlike in my speech, the Navy is not a place where I could be accepted as I am, where I could grow and be me. A song plays over and over in my head: "Don't ever take away my freedom, don't ever take it away." My freedom *to be*...was taken away. I know, my friends know, that the rigidity of the Navy distresses a significant part of me. In those early years, and even later, I'd been sufficiently naive to believe that my inner self could flourish, despite a fairly negative environment for strong women, and an absolutely bigoted environment for gays and lesbians. An expert at compartmentalization, I was able to select situationally when not to be me so that I could withstand.

I'm not surprised I chose to tell a little white lie yesterday. The Navy hasn't been a place where I could be me. Why did I lie? It was *my* farewell. Because I will always stand up for the Navy and its general direction. And, in so many ways, individual Navy people — Dad, Mother, Jennie, Buck, Tom, Joanna, Pierre, and Billie, and on and on — have been my support system, my family. God Bless America. God Bless the United States Navy!

I feel disappointed in myself for not reaching the rank of Captain, given that Dad made Admiral. I'm scripted for success. While success may mean something else, I'm not finishing what I started.

I feel anger.

Though I have wonderful Jennie as a partner, I feel alone and disoriented inside. Tell the truth, Fairfield. As I'm moving into unexplored territory psychically, I'm scared. Who will be my mentors?

I feel apprehension about the future. Will I have enough money in the golden years? Can I take care of myself without the Navy and its protections? Without my Navy family? How will it be without the structure from top to bottom?

I feel movement, away from a fulfilling life and into the unknowable.

I feel freer than yesterday and that's scary.

I feel excitement that I will have full control of my life, something I have never, ever had. Who knows, as I seek a new sense of self, I might find where I do truly belong.

What I know in my heart:

> For what is a man profited, if he shall gain the
> whole world, and lose his own soul?
> *The Bible*, Matthew 16: 25-26

TF

One week later from Robyn

2 September 1980, Bar Harbor, Maine

Dear RP (Regular Person),

How're you surviving your new existence? I just wanted to thank you again for including me at your retirement ceremony. For one thing, it was fun to meet the friends I've been hearing about for so many years, as well as your parents and Jennie. The kids have talked of almost nothing else to anyone who hasn't already heard the adventure a zillion times.

And, despite my opinion of the Navy as an institution, which hasn't changed by the way, I found the ceremony impressive and moving. The to-be-expected pomp was managed with a low-key dignity and simplicity. Somehow the ritual's formality seemed just right and was awe-inspiring in that special setting!

But I can't resist one final diatribe: For all our conversations over the years, you said some things in your speech which I don't believe, and don't believe that you believe either, as in *having the opportunity to be yourself, maintaining your own integrity, and being able to freely express your opinions and ideas*. I assume that your speech, at least in those areas, was simply for the protocol of the retirement ceremony. You were articulate and clear, but you spoke the party line. Which is fine, but IT WASN'T YOU! I suppose it would have been politically inappropriate for you to have told it like it really was. Anyway...

Now comes the hard part for you. What next? Who to be for the rest of your life? Whatever the struggles you engaged in, the Navy was, nonetheless, with you in some form or other, night and day, for twenty-plus years. I'm sure your feelings run the gamut for having taken such a dramatic step.

You're on the brink of your next adventure, and while brinks are always rather alarming, they're also very stimulating!

So Tucker, Congratulations! Congratulations on your retirement, on your decision to retire early, on your surviving the Navy all these years, on your insights, on your new life, and on just being you!

Enough!

Write or call when you get settled, or whenever. Now that you're a Regular Person perhaps we can get together more often.

Take care. Ned sends his love.

> Love,
>
> Robyn

Same day from Jennie

> *2 September 1980, Honolulu, Hawaii*

Tucker, dearest —

I know you'll receive many notes and letters commending you on a career well done and a retirement ceremony *par excellence*, but I bet nobody writes one that tells you how beautiful you looked in your dress whites with all those medals sparkling on your beckoning (to me) bosom.

I felt the depth of your love for your Navy and I know also the pain that it has caused you over the years. You will be remembered, my love, for your dedication to women, for your integrity, for your hard work, for your persistence. Who knows, maybe someday a woman officer will come up to you and say, "So you're The Tucker Fairfield. Why, you're an icon for Navy women!"

But before we get to that — welcome to retirement. May it bring you fulfillment and happiness and may it bring us a new life together — living, loving, and laughing our way into old age.

> With much love,
>
> Jennie

Three days later from Buck

> *5 September 1980, Charleston, South Carolina*

Dear Tucker,

Helen and I are back in our routine of "retirement," whatever that is. I know it to be a word not a condition, as you'll soon begin to discover. Your energy and intelligence will hardly let you retire in the do-nothing-but-smell-the-roses sense.

We appreciated ever so much your letting us be a part of this grand event. As you know we debated about taking such a long trip, but Helen said I'd never really shown her Honolulu, though I'd talked about a Hawaiian vacation over the years, and I just wanted to be there when you hauled down your flag.

It has been quite a journey for you since that trip on my submarine, thirty-two years ago. I tried to convey some of my thoughts when we said goodbye in Pearl, but during the flight back, and since getting home, Helen and I have talked about you a great deal. We end such discussions expressing pure admiration for the grace and dignity you've shown as you encountered "Daddy Navy" in his many roles and images and as you've made your mark.

You did that, you know. Made your mark. Whether you realize it or not, few could have made the lasting impact on basic officer education, women's rights, equal opportunity, notions of command style, and career paths for women. Others have tried, of course. Some have been defeated and left early, most have given in to political safety in order to move ahead. Your handling of the delicate equation which balances professional rules with personal drives has been exemplary. To use your phrase, you "have been you."

I had an opportunity to relive with your parents some of your triumphs and trials of the past years. You must know how proud they are of you, and how much they enjoyed basking in the glow of your ceremony. I hadn't realized, until later at the reception, how many of your friends had made that long trip to Honolulu to be with you on this occasion. That tells a lot. You've touched many of us and we are the better for it.

Tucker, let's not lose touch, now that Daddy Navy is no longer the catalyst that ties us together. Guess the name "Mommy Navy" doesn't make sense yet, does it? When you decide how retirement will play out, come East for a visit. I suspect that Washington, D.C. will still demand some of your time, for I doubt that leaving the Navy will end your involvement in women's matters.

Thank you for letting Helen and me be a part of this important day. And from us both — a sincere WELL DONE!

Warm regards,

Buck

EPILOGUE

August 1997

Epilogue

~~~~~~~~~~

Robyn Greeley — August 1997, Bar Harbor, Maine

It's been a long time since Tucker retired from her Big Daddy Navy. The Navy seems to roll on in its typical autocratic, myopic way. Recently, the papers have been full of Navy scandals, misuses of power, cheating, sexual harassment cases, and gay rights cases. I believe the position of Navy women today, though, has a lot to do with the efforts of Tucker and those men and women in the '70s who opened up women's opportunities. Tucker and I have maintained contact pretty well, considering the geographic distance since her conversion to Regular Personhood. Wellesley class events and connections make it easier.

Thinking about Tucker, I suspect one never totally loses an identity connected to being a naval officer. For instance, a couple of years ago, during the Gays-in-the-Military debate, Tucker lost her military ID card and freaked out, way out of proportion to the (easily rectifiable) loss itself. I knew the card represented a focused, concrete symbol for all the agony Tucker was experiencing over the American military and public attitudes toward gays and lesbians.

Tucker still sees the Navy as a family. And, while she's come out to her biological family, her Navy family (as an institution) has expressly told her and other gays that this is a part of their identity it doesn't want to know about. This leaves Tucker in a position of being perceived as a partial person or even a non-person by her Navy family. The Don't Ask, Don't Tell, Don't Pursue policy denies Tucker and other military gays general access to sharing a significant part of their identity.

Loss of the ID card was a dual pinnacle for Tucker: a pinnacle of satisfaction on the one hand, and a pinnacle of total despair on the other. The positive part represented her satisfaction with an organization she'd identified with closely as both a military brat and a naval officer. She'd certainly benefited from it in many areas, and she still holds this organization in great esteem. The negative pinnacle resulted from feeling that the institution had let her down by forcing her to deny, ignore, and hide a vital part of her being.

Except for the occasional former naval officer identity crisis, the Navy doesn't hold much interest for me. I continue to maintain a small private practice which allows me plenty of time for writing and illustrating and enjoying my family. Ned continues to have a busy practice. Derry plans to stay in the Northwest where he recently obtained a doctorate in Environmental Studies. Elizabeth's teaching in Santa Fe.

With the ocean right here in Bar Harbor and a big garden, it's fun to try and live off the land. Such self-sufficiency is somewhat squelched between November and April, however.

Billie Baker — August 1997, Norris Lake, East Tennessee

Greetings from East Tennessee. I've traveled down many roads since I retired from the Navy, and now I've finally returned to the place where I started. Well, not exactly, but not far as the crow flies. I'm quite content being back in Tennessee.

After my retirement, I spent a few years in Seattle, and then in Washington, D.C., working as a consultant for the Navy. I worked on various successful public affairs projects which included a lot of travel. Then, my sister and I established our own computer and graphic design business, which designs, produces, and prints brochures, annual reports, and advertising booklets.

In 1990, some cousins, my sisters and brothers-in-law, and I purchased an old fishing lodge and marina on Norris Lake, the first lake in the TVA system, near Andersonville, Tennessee. Norris is the most pristine of the lakes, with breathtaking scenery and great fishing. We used *very inventive* financing, and nearly wiped ourselves out financially. But the Lodge was refurbished beautifully, five new and very modern cabins were built, and the marina was rebuilt and expanded to twenty-five slips and moorings for eight houseboats. The Lodge has an excellent restaurant and a loyal following. We host barbecues, fish fries, and, for entertainment, present a bluegrass band. Today the Lodge is booked solid, and my family is extremely busy in the day-to-day operations.

The Navy wasn't only good to me, but good for me. When I joined, I was so young, naive, and lucky. The Navy taught me to think, to produce, to be absolutely correct in every detail: My family has been amazed at my constant attention to the little details of the "lodge and marina" business. In addition, my Navy experiences — the travel, dinners, receptions, dress uniforms, calling cards, social engagements with international navies — combined to shape me socially in a different way from my friends and family here in Tennessee. I make business and social decisions quickly and accurately. I find I'm tough and don't back down easily. All of this makes me the "leader" of our little group.

My arthritis has advanced such that my physical activity is impaired. The Navy's outstanding health system provides for my complete health care. As a result, I've experienced the latest treatments available for arthritis and I'm not as crippled as perhaps I might be.

The Navy in its technology and strategic awareness is a very professional organization. At the same time, since its members come from our larger society, the institution reflects all the ills, as well as the goodness, of this society. To address some of the knotty problems in accepting women as equal partners has taken so many years. And many more years may have to go by before women truly are equal partners. It all depends on our leaders, both military and political, rising above society and showing the way. The same goes for Tuck's favorite subject these days — the unjust ramifications of the DADTDP policy as it's been implemented.

Hey! I had a great time in the Navy! Lots of fun! Met some really super, tremendous people! A few bad apples, but what the heck! East Tennessee's a spectacular place. I invite ya 'all to visit.

Tom Parker — August 1997, Washington, D.C.

Joanna and I moved back to D.C. in 1981 not long after Tucker retired. A friend in Ann Haynes' office called me to say there was a position on Sen. Carl Johnston's (Dem.-Mass.) staff that I might like. As Dean Witter and I had mutually concluded we should part, I jumped at the opportunity. Carolyn, 14 (going on 21), wasn't pleased to make the move but it was OK with 10-year-old Willy. Unfortunately, the Senator couldn't find a way to achieve the goal of nuclear arms reduction in the face of opposition from the Department of Defense (DOD). After two years, I felt lucky to get an appointment to the Arms Control and Disarmament Agency (ACDA) in its Congressional and Public Relations Office.

The Reagan Administration directed ACDA to achieve real arms reduction and focus on strategic and intermediate-range nuclear weapons. There was little chance of achieving reduction, however, because the Administration insisted that any treaty be verifiable by on-site inspection. Everyone knew the Soviets would never agree.

I traveled frequently for ACDA, to Geneva and to other nations and within the U.S., attending conferences and explaining our arms control policies. In all, I enjoyed myself. During this period, Tucker and I kept in touch and we continued to exchange views on the state of the world and the Navy within it.

In 1985, when Mikhail Gorbachev assumed the post of General Secretary of the Soviet Union, the arms control arena changed dramatically. One of Gorbachev's acts was to propose a comprehensive list of arms control measures; he said the U.S. could devise the verification procedures and the Soviet Union wouldn't object. Suddenly everything was possible. I worked on the first real breakthrough, the Intermediate Nuclear Force (INF) Treaty. The Soviets accepted all of our demands which called for elimination of intermediate nuclear weapons and rigid on-site inspection procedures. This was followed by the first Strategic Arms Reduction Treaty (START I), which called for significant reductions in strategic nuclear weapons. After ratification and implementation of INF and START I, we began work on START II, which envisioned even greater reductions.

The Navy finally released a report on submariners who served prior to 1983. The report showed that officers, but not enlisted men, who'd served on nuclear missile-firing submarines had significantly higher death rates from cancer than men the same age in the U.S. When the study was published in a professional journal in 1989, the officers weren't included. In 1996, a new contract was awarded to New York University Medical Center to follow-up death rates among submariners. I'm still wondering why they don't include men like me who got cancer but survived.

After President Clinton's election in 1992, I became involved in his attempt to cancel the DOD directive on gays in the military. Whereas my relationship with Tucker over the years probably heightened my interest, I like to think I would have acted without this incentive. My primary reasons for believing the DOD directive should be canceled, then and now, are my beliefs that it's a Constitutional violation of civil rights.

During my 26-year Navy career, I encountered a couple of incidents involving homosexuals, and these cases were handled quietly and without major disruption. I knew that the Uniform Code of Military Justice contained a prohibition against sodomy, but charges were rarely brought under this article because sodomy is difficult to prove and applies equally to heterosexuals and homosexuals without regard to marital status. Probably because of the difficulty in enforcing the sodomy regulation, the three branches of the military had procedures allowing them to discharge homosexuals administratively rather than taking them to trial by court-martial.

When I researched the matter in 1993, I was surprised to discover that, in addition to the individual service directives I was familiar with, DOD had written its own directive in 1982. This was what Clinton proposed canceling. Why had DOD considered it necessary to write its own? I didn't know a single uniformed officer who felt that the tools we had to deal with homosexuals before 1982 were inadequate. I thought this DOD directive had onerous characteristics. The most onerous was that it started out saying, "Homosexuality is incompatible with military service." Even the directive's authors knew this was wrong. They knew of many homosexuals who'd served this nation honorably and with distinction, many buried in Arlington Cemetery. They knew also that homosexuals have served and are serving openly in the militaries of other nations.

The second thing I really didn't like about the directive was that, in defining homosexuals, it stated then — and now — that homosexuals are those who "engage in homosexual conduct, desire to engage in homosexual conduct, or intend to engage in homosexual conduct." Since when does the United States punish people for desires or intentions instead of actions? In my opinion, this is a blatant violation of civil rights.

I read several studies on the issue and wrote an op-ed piece for the New York Times that was published at the height of the debate. This basically said the DOD Directive was unnecessary and the President was justified in canceling it. This brought me a lot of notoriety, but appeared to have no affect on policy. The President was faced with overwhelming opposition in Congress and seemingly in the country. So for the first time, but not the last, he backed down in the face of concerted opposition.

In September 1993, both houses of Congress approved a law that's tougher on military gays than the Clinton/Joint Chiefs compromise. The offensive Directive wasn't canceled;

homosexuality is still "incompatible with military service," but the practice of asking recruits whether they're homosexuals was abandoned. The policy became known as "Don't Ask, Don't Tell, Don't Pursue (DADTDP)."

I knew Tucker believed in President Clinton when she came to Washington to help him on this issue. I helped her all I could. Alas, another losing battle for her. President Clinton's capitulation was, of course, more painful to her than to me.

Amazingly, the discharge rate of personnel under this Directive actually has increased since DADTDP and personnel suspected of being gay continue to be asked, pursued, and harassed in disregard of the policy!

Although we're on different coasts since our respective retirements, Tucker has remained a close family friend. She's still "Aunty Tucker" to the children. Willy graduated from the Naval Academy in 1992 and is the Chief Engineer on a Sixth Fleet destroyer. Carolyn graduated from law school, clerked for a Supreme Court Justice, and works for the Justice Department. Joanna and Tucker maintain a frequent e-mail correspondence via Joanna's library computer. If anything, Joanna (and also Carolyn) are more supportive than I of gays in the military. I think it will be a long time before Big Daddy Navy accepts gays on the same level as heterosexuals. I'd be satisfied for now to see the DOD directive rescinded and to await the inevitable "catchup" with the rest of society.

Tucker's phrase, "Big Daddy Navy," always has a mixed meaning to me. The Navy was in many ways my Daddy. And a good one. The Navy educated me, trained me, provided stimulating career opportunities, promoted me, fulfilled my needs for ritual and discipline, took care of me when I was sick, tolerated my outspoken criticisms without reprisal, and provided me with a generous pension. I'm proud now to see Willy, a nephew, and two of my nieces in Navy Blue and Gold.

Buck Buckingham — August 1997, Charleston, South Carolina

I was glad to hear from Tucker after her blow-up with me in the Spring of 1993. Her outburst seemed more to hit out at the first convenient target than genuine anger at me. She'd known for too long that I oppose her strong stands on women and gay people in the military to suddenly have that a reason for such emotion. We've always been able to discuss these issues without the emotion she showed in her visit here, so I have to recognize that it was caused by something else.

Tucker's an intense individual. She often pushes too hard for her beliefs. She's no politician. Standing firmly and unequivocally for what she believes seems more important to her than negotiating for the best possible result. Her extreme disappointment at observing the high expectations raised by the President's campaign rhetoric change to the political reality of the Don't Ask, Don't Tell compromise had to have some outlet. I was in the line of fire when she exploded. She needn't have apologized as she did, but certainly her letter cleared the air between us.

I find myself often playing the "what might have been" game regarding Tucker. What if she'd obtained her Doctorate and concentrated that mind of hers on academic pursuits; what if she'd added a law degree or an M.B.A. to her credentials and turned her originality to the legal profession or the business world? Why in the world did she tackle issues of individual rights in our society's most difficult environment, and grind herself down trying to change the military? She's a mixture of conservative values as they apply to duty, honor, country, and liberal values as they apply to individual rights. Her insistent idealism is most often too far ahead of reality.

Not much point in wondering what might have happened, but I wish she could relax a bit now and not feel the issue of gays in the military as her personal crusade. Although Tucker would deny she feels this way, her arguments often seem to place the needs, wants, or desires of individuals well above the requirements of the military, its mission and purpose. At times she seems oblivious to the fact that the military is not a democracy. In order to protect the rights of individuals, the military sector of any democratic society must be autocratic and not run by a majority vote and consensus leadership.

The military's success depends upon its ability to instill trust, faith in leadership, responsibility for each other, a command bonding quite different from company loyalty or academic collegiality. The introduction of remarkably different patterns in any fundamental human trait — extreme aggressiveness, extreme passivity, extreme timidity, extreme assertiveness, and certainly extremes in sexual behavior — tear the social fabric of a military organization. They threaten the stability of a military society, and create command problems which should not be part of command decision-making.

If women in combat or openly gay people contribute to the prevention of conflict by enabling a better preparedness for conflict, they should be a part of the military. If they do not, the military shouldn't be restricted from screening them out, just as it screens out those too tall to fly military aircraft or too large to fit through a submarine hatch. The objective is the most effective military organization, not the most compassionate social organization. These are the grounds on which the debate should be based regarding qualifications for the military. The grounds are not morality or civil rights or equality; the issue is what enhances the purpose of the military.

I tell myself that Tucker cannot hear me when I make this argument, for she responds with the moral or civil rights or equality arguments. Yet, when I tell myself this, I have to question my own rationale, for Tucker is a very intelligent human being. She's capable of hearing and interpreting the most complex issues. Why, then, can she not see that the Don't Ask, Don't Tell policy is a huge compromise for the military to make, and that military officialdom will honestly try to make it work.

But policy has to have the cooperation of all who say they wish to be a part of a military organization. By their opposition the gay community demonstrates it puts first its own needs over the needs of the military. Reality is the other way round. If gays cannot understand and live with this, they shouldn't be in the military.

I can conclude only that Tucker has been so disappointed by her inability to make a deeper dent in the tradition-bound Navy, that she must continue her fight outside the organization. Surely she realizes that her ammunition outside is much less effective than was her demonstrated capability within the organization. If she couldn't be happy on active duty she certainly cannot be happy trying to change the system from the outside. Her hitting out at me didn't change my admiration for her inherent capabilities one whit. It did make me want to shake her and say, "Tucker, wake up; it's over; leave it alone; relax and expend your remarkable energy in fruitful pursuits."

As for me, I stay away from these things. I long for the Navy culture at times. I keep track of events through various journals and writings. I reminisce with Helen occasionally about the wonderfully varied and exciting life we lived while in the Navy, and exchange social events with friends where we talk about those times. My time is spent keeping current with investment opportunities for my clients. Charleston's an ideal place to enjoy life, and is a quiet and dignified page from a past culture, moving with firm steps into the culture of tomorrow whatever that will be. I wonder when Tucker will reach that quiet period in her life?

Tucker Fairfield — August 1997, Honolulu, Hawaii

Since my Navy retirement I've been active and well. Jennie and I have enjoyed some wonderful times together as well as with our friends and families. I'm fortunate to have a deep, loving partnership with Jennie and a fully supportive, loving relationship with my parents. I've maintained my special, long-term friendships with Robyn, Tom, Buck, and Billie.

Upon my retirement Jennie and I bought a small business and sold it at a good profit four years later. Operating a small business is very different from being a naval officer! Since the sale of the business, Jennie has been involved with volunteer work for homeless women and lately with writing her memoirs.

In recent years I've been teaching political science at the university level. In my favorite course, "Sex, Power, and Politics," we address the central dilemma of modern feminist thinking — the need to make gender both matter and not matter at the same time. I ask the students to "take a stand on whether women should assimilate into a culture or choose to be and act culturally different from the dominant gender." My considered stand on this pressing question, as well as on whether gay men and lesbians should assimilate into the culture, is this: To become the healthiest of cultures and communities, people should integrate, not assimilate, into a culture. Assimilation implies loss of identity. Diversity must have a place at the table.

For a short period in 1993, during the national debate on gay military personnel, my relationship with Buck was tenuous. In March of that year, on my way to participate in discussions about the Don't Ask, Don't Tell, Don't Pursue (DADTDP) policy, I flew to Charleston to visit Buck and Helen. My emotional temperature was high, and I blew right through the overhead at Buck's comments about Navy women and military gays.

Dad had advised that I not become involved in any lobbying efforts in D.C. about DADTDP. He said, "A year from now no one'll know who said what. Tucker, you can't possibly influence the decision." Buck had concurred that my insistence on taking the trip was unfortunate. During the several months prior to the trip, Buck and I had exchanged several letters, as in many previous years. As usual, we wrote about a gamut of subjects; the major topics of this series were women in combat and military gays. The assumptions and values supporting our thoughts on recommended policy options were dissimilar.

Given our strong philosophical differences and the Don't Ask, Don't Tell environment, I'd considered not taking the trip, or at least not visiting Buck. But I truly wanted to see him in person, and besides, the plane reservations had long since been set. In addition to my lobbying efforts, I was looking forward to a Wellesley class gathering and visits with Robyn and Tom. So, I decided to fly via Charleston to Washington.

In preparing for my trip, I'd gone through a profound experience: As I was packing, I couldn't find my military ID card that had given me privileges at military bases for more than 45 years. Never had I lost this card. A real fright engulfed me. "What if I can't find it? What will my parents think? What will the Navy think?" I fussed and stewed for hours.

Finally, the anger passed and I moved from despair to awareness. I reflected on having served many years in a military that (1) allegedly is all the best that America can be and (2) defends the democratic ideals of justice, equality, and freedom. This same military was now vigorously restating throughout the media that the "gay lifestyle" should not be condoned and gays and lesbians are "incompatible with the military." The message to military gays was and still is: "We define you as unsafe to our missions and straight people are incapable of bonding with you. Either lie or get out."

I related the ID card incident to Robyn via e-mail and told her that I believed the inattentiveness that had caused me to lose my card reflected the Self who desperately wants to be done with an institution that, intentionally or not, continues to inflict great pain upon me and my lesbian friends. I wrote that I needed to end my long-time relationship with Big Daddy Navy — I could no longer love an institution that excludes me from its family because the family member happens to have a same-sex relationship.

My message ended with a question, "I can easily go to the nearest naval base and get a new ID card, so what's the Big Deal?" Her response the next morning and prior to my departure, addressing what she called the two pinnacles of satisfaction and despair, summarized my relationship with Big Daddy Navy. Had I fully absorbed her feedback I might have known that my meeting with Buck, who for me symbolizes the Navy, was likely to be volatile.

Upon my return from the trip and after President Clinton's DADTDP policy decision, I apologized to Buck for my outburst and explained that the negative vibes about gays and lesbians during the military debate had propelled me into an estranged state. He'd received the brunt of my frustrations and anguish over the impending decision. I wrote, "Buck, your support throughout these many, many years doesn't deserve my discourteous, unbecoming actions. Please accept my apology."

And my relationship with my Navy? I've come to be more involved with other activities and more objective about Big Daddy Navy. As I observe today's Navy, a sadness comes over me: While the Navy's operational commitments have been met with successes and pride, emphasis on the social aspects of the institution, particularly since 1991, have outplayed mission accomplishments, certainly in the eyes of the public and media. Just as we'd let go of one Navy scandal, we'd have to absorb another. Then, in 1996, came the tragic and symbolic death of the CNO, Admiral Jeremy "Mike" Boorda, with women's issues cited as contributing factors.

I've observed Big Daddy Navy in the last decade as muddling through social issues in a difficult, transitional era for each of the military services. Whereas the old ways of dealing with social issues don't work effectively, I believe Big Daddy doesn't truly wish to change sufficiently to allow in the changing mores appearing in the larger society, including diversity and equality of opportunity.

Many more women serve in our military services than in the '60s and '70s, with stellar job opportunities, far exceeding my dreams of probabilities. (You may not believe this, but I have reservations about women serving in direct combat roles, probably due to my generation and a touch of the cultural feminist's views.) The following 1997 statistics reveal the current status of women in the Navy:

- Over 52,000 women, representing 12.3% of the total active force, serve in the Navy. Women represent 13.6% of all officers and 12.2% of the enlisted.

- Seventy-two percent of Navy enlisted personnel and 81% of Navy officers are serving in mixed-gender commands.

- Between 1992 and 1995 the Navy downsized by almost 25%. Although the number of women declined, the percentage of women in the Navy increased slightly.

- In Fiscal Year 1995 women represented 18.2% of officer accessions and 19.9% of enlisted accessions. By the year 2000, women will represent approximately 20% of all accessions.

- There are now six women line admirals in the Navy, including one three-star.

- Since the repeal of combat exclusion in 1993, 43 combatant ships and 26 combatant aircraft squadrons have transitioned to mixed-gender crews. An additional 16 have women line officers aboard. The Navy now has more than 541 women officers and 3,621 enlisted women serving in combatant units.

- By 1998, 27% of incoming surface warfare officers will be women.

With few exceptions, these women successfully meet their challenges and commitments; all the while, the old attitudes about women in our Navy, and about the seas and ships and naval aircraft and the female gender, persist in parts of the Navy and society at large.

Given the volatility quotient of gender and sexual matters, deep-seated and chauvinistic attitudes within the Navy, and changing times and belief systems, something was bound to blow. And Tailhook blew in 1991. Insofar as the damage to its public image and the social strains experienced subsequent to Tailhook, the Navy has suffered one of its most unsatisfactory, tragic periods. Yet, beneath unseemly headlines, I know my Navy is operationally on track.

In contrast, I believe the blinders are securely fastened, and Big Daddy's relationship with Navy women can be described as uneasy at best; and with closeted Navy gay men and lesbians, just plain uncomfortable. As long as important elements within the Navy choose to act from both lack of knowledge and prejudice toward certain groups of people, as reflected by the fairly inept implementation of DADTDP, I choose with regret to be distant and — now and then — angry.

Author Rita Mae Brown describes tragedy not as foul deeds done to a person (usually noble in manner) but rather, as "irresolvable conflict. Both sides/ideas are right." In light of Ms. Brown's definition Buck Buckingham and Big Daddy Navy are as "right" in their beliefs as Tucker Fairfield (and vice versa), and my relationship with the Navy is a tragedy for both the Navy and me.

The primary issues we've raised on this journey, however, are not about rightness or wrongness; rather, they are the communications problems and values differences among various communities within an important American institution, reflective of the total society. My fantasy (and some say, "That's all it is, Tucker!") is that richer dialogues among the diverse members of Big Daddy Navy's great organization will occur, and the healing can begin. In the meantime, whereas my friends and family encourage me to take on a more restful retirement, where justified I'll continue to work for social justice and freedom.

This above all: to thine own self be true,
And it must follow, as the night the day,
Thou canst not then be false to any man.
                                    Shakespeare, *Hamlet*

GLOSSARY

Glossary

Airdale. Slang used for a naval aviator.

Aye, Aye. "Aye" derives from Middle English and means "yes." Today the phrase aye, aye means "I understand your orders and will carry them out."

Big Daddy Navy. Tucker Fairfield uses this phrase to embody the organization and concepts of the Navy. In *My Navy Too*, Admiral Buck Buckingham symbolizes these organizational beliefs and ideas.

Billet. Military personnel experts refer to a specific job within a specific naval unit as a billet. Each naval unit or command is allotted a certain number of "billets." Detailers then assign people to these billets.

Blue Water Navy. Traditionally, since the days of Alfred Mahan, the purposes of the U.S. Navy have included maintaining autonomy of sea forces and decisive fleet engagements in deep waters; hence the phrase Blue Water Navy.

Blue and Gold Crews. SSBNs operate with two crews which rotate their schedules on and off the submarine. Tom Parker served as CO of the Gold crew on *Christopher Columbus*.

Boomer. The nickname for fleet ballistic missile submarines (SSBNs).

Brown Water Navy. During Vietnam, the U.S. Navy had to restructure its forces and create types of vessels needed to operate in and around a country with inlets and rivers. This Navy is called a brown water Navy.

Bucket Hat. Headgear for both enlisted and officer women; hats with sides turned up. Male officers wear hats with bills on them. The white hat is worn by enlisted from seaman apprentice to First Class Petty Officer.

Career Patterns. Officer career patterns or paths, known as professional development paths, usually fall into well-defined sequences of duties. They are followed as closely as possible by the detailers. Tucker Fairfield was fighting for regular career paths for unrestricted women line officers.

Combat exclusion law. Section 6015 of USC Title 10 barred women from assignment to ships. In the fall of 1978 Congress approved changes to the law, permitting the Navy to assign women to support and non-combatant ships, putting the Women-in-Ships program into force. Surface Warfare and Special Operations communities opened to Navy women. In November of 1993 Congress repealed the combat ship exclusion law and the assignment of women to combatants took place quickly. In 1991 Congress removed the prohibition on women flying aircraft with a combat mission and in 1993 the Secretary of Defense opened combat aviation to women aviators.

Commandant, Naval District. Designates the officer commanding (according to numeral) any of the several Naval Districts of the Continental USA, Alaska and Hawaii. All naval districts except the Naval District of Washington have been abolished and their functions turned over to appropriate naval station commanders. In time of war, naval districts will be reestablished. Each naval district is commanded by a commandant, a flag officer of the line eligible to command at sea, who directly represents the Secretary of the Navy and the CNO.

Commissioned Officers' Mess Ashore. The commissioned officers' mess is often referred to as the Officers' Club. Available for members, officers of the base, and officers afloat, as well as reserve and retired officers. Open messes customarily serve meals and have bars; some operate recreational facilities such as swimming pools and tennis courts.

Cumshaw. Acquisition of material in whatever manner is possible; often involves bartering.

Dead Horse. With a set of Permanent Change of Station (PCS) orders, one may draw a "dead horse," which is up to six months' advance pay to be paid back by the individual over an extended period.

Dept. of the Navy. The Department of the Navy, or the naval establishment, consists of three principal parts: the operating forces; the Navy Department, the central executive authority of the Dept. of the Navy; and the Shore Establishment.

Detailer. An officer or enlisted person in the Bureau of Naval Personnel or NMPC responsible for the assignment of other personnel.

Flag Officer. An officer of the rank of Commodore or Admiral or General.

Fleet. An organization of ships, aircraft, Marine forces, and shore-based fleet activities, all under one commander, for the purpose of conducting major operations.

Havelock. An official garment that is part of a Navy woman's uniform and that covers the head and neck, protecting from the elements. Fits over the bucket hat.

J (Jesus) Factor. Navy officers use this phrase to describe that extra factor which will accomplish the mission when no more data can be figured into the problem.

Line Officer. Unrestricted line officers within the Navy are those officers who are either surface warfare officers, aviators, submariners, or SEALs. Until recent years women officers were designated unrestricted line officers. Tucker Fairfield's (and Beth Coye's) study was entitled, *The Restricted Unrestricted Line Officer.* The "dry" women line officers of today have been moved from the unrestricted line and are designated Fleet Support Officers, within a restricted line community. Since the 1990s more and more women are participating in the unrestricted line as surface warfare and aviation warfare officers.

Master Chief of the Command. Senior chief petty officer who acts as ombudsman for enlisted personnel and reports directly to the CO.

Mustang. A naval officer who came up through the enlisted ranks.

Naval War College. Located in Newport RI, the college is predominately for naval officers, but is attended by all services and consists of both a junior and senior course. The courses were initiated in 1886 with the lectures of Alfred T. Mahan, and further the understanding of command and staff responsibilities, as well as naval strategy and its employment in future warfare.

Navy Junior. Term of affectionate humor or identification used to refer to the child of a career Navy person.

Navy Regs (NAVREGS). An important official document outlining the organizational structure of the Department of the Navy and providing the principles and policies by which the Navy is governed. Defines the responsibility, purpose, authority, and relationship of each bureau or office of the Navy Department.

Overhead. The underside of a deck forms the overhead of the compartment directly below, never called a ceiling. Often used as in the phrase, "he went through the overhead."

Power. Of the innumerable definitions of power, Tucker Fairfield would favor Carolyn Heilbrun's in *Writing a Woman's Life:* "Power is the ability to take one's place in whatever discourse is essential to action and the right to have one's part matter."

Quarterdeck. Deck area designated by the CO as the place to carry out official functions; the station of the Officer of the Day in port.

Scuttlebutt. (1) Originally a ship's water barrel (called a butt) which was tapped (scuttled) by the insertion of a spigot from which the crew drew their drinking water; now applied to any drinking fountain; (2) In the old days, the scuttlebutt was a place for personnel to exchange views and news when they gathered to draw their water; hence the term scuttlebutt is applied to any rumor.

Skipper. "Scip" meant ship in Old English, and scipper meant a ship's captain. By 1390 the English were pronouncing the latter word skipper and using it for the captain of a small merchant vessel. It now refers to the captain of any ship.

Square Away. Put in proper order; make things shipshape. Also, a squared away, shipshape person.

Submarine. The Navy has both attack and ballistic missile submarines, depending upon their primary mission. The last of the active diesel submarines was the USS *Blueback.* The Navy's approximately 80 nuclear attack subs (SSNs) may be compared to the "fleet" boat of WWII since their main job is to attack enemy ships and submarines. The number of SSNs is being reduced to 55 to comply with the bottom up review. The SSNs' principal weapon is the high speed Mark 48 torpedo. Some SSNs carry Harpoon and Tomahawk missiles for use against surface targets. The latest of the SSNs are the 6,900-ton *Los Angeles* SSN 688 class and the 9,130-ton *Seawolf* SSN 21 class. The SSNs, as were the diesel subs, are mostly named for fishes.

The fleet ballistic missile submarines (SSBNs) have a strategic mission. They are in constant patrol in the world's oceans. Earlier SSBNs were armed with 16 Poseidon missiles; the new *Ohio* class ships carry 24 Trident I missiles. They also carry torpedoes, mainly as defense weapons. The *Ohio* class SSBN 726 is the newest addition to the Navy's missile deterrent, carrying 24 TRIDENTS. This class will be the backbone of the strategic submarine force through the end of the century. Like battleships and some missile cruisers, the TRIDENT SSBNs are named for states. We have 18 *Ohio* Class SSBNs.

The Threat. Before setting a national policy or planning a military attack, it's customary to examine the nature of any opposition that might arise in relation to such issues. In planners' parlance this process is known as examining the "threat." Planners want to be sure that their scheme provides enough forces to overcome the most likely opposition or threat; at the same time they don't want to waste forces or effort. Throughout *My Navy Too*, the various naval officers write about the threat, as observed by the characters.

To Sail Under False Colors. Pretending to be something you aren't, to be a hypocrite. As seen in the swashbuckler movies, the pirate ship at the moment of attack lowers its friendly or neutral flag and hoists the deadly skull and crossbones. The unwritten law of the sea, of course, required that all ships display their true flags of colors so that they could be recognized as friend or foe, but the Jolly Roger was by its nature exempt.

Uniform of the Day. Uniform is prescribed for all naval personnel within a command or geographical area. Usually the Plan of the Day (POD) for ships or stations lists the uniform for officers and enlisted personnel.

Watch Your Six. In the Navy, especially among aviators, Watch Your Six is used as TO BEWARE, referring to hostile fire at the position of six o'clock (directly behind the pilot).

Wetting Down a Commission. This old naval custom, dating back over a century, consisted of giving a party to a naval officer who had just received his commission. The parchment commission was formed into a cornucopia, filled with champagne and drunk from as it was passed from hand to hand. In today's Navy, it's customary for naval officers when they are promoted to give a party to celebrate their next stripe.

Z-Gram. While Chief of Naval Operations, Admiral Elmo Zumwalt issued terse, direct memos considered by some to be models of conciseness and clarity; to others, they were thought to violate the chain of command. These were called Z-grams and became naval slang for such model memos.

ACRONYM LIST

Acronym List

ASW — Antisubmarine Warfare. Weapons systems or operations against hostile submarines.

Autovon — Automated Voice Network. The military's official long-distance telephone carrier.

BOQ — Bachelor Officers' Quarters. Known as BOQs, these quarters are provided for transients and permanently assigned bachelor officers.

BuPers — Bureau of Naval Personnel. Now called NMPC. Responsible for the procurement, discipline, promotion, welfare, morale, and distribution of officers and enlisted personnel.

CHINFO — Chief of Naval Information. Navy's top public affairs officer. This billet is filled by a flag officer.

CNO — Chief of Naval Operations. The senior military officer in the Department of the Navy.

COB — Chief of the Boat. The senior enlisted man aboard a submarine and the boat's ombudsman for enlisted personnel.

COD — Carrier on-board delivery plane. Specifically designed for delivering mail and personnel to and from carriers.

CofS — Chief of Staff. The senior officer of the staff. Responsible for keeping the admiral informed of the condition and situation of the command.

CINCLANTFLT — Commander-in-Chief of the Atlantic Fleet. The operational and administrative Commander of all ships and naval bases within the Atlantic Ocean area.

CO — Commanding Officer. The head of a naval organization, both at sea and ashore.

DACOWITS — Defense Advisory Committee on Women in the Services. Established in 1951, its composition is twenty-five civilians and retirees appointed by the Secretary of Defense. Influential as change agents for equal opportunities for military women.

DADTDP — Don't Ask, Don't Tell, Don't Pursue. The national policy regarding military gay and lesbian personnel agreed upon by the Congress and President in 1993. The military's new regulations on homosexuals were implemented on February 28, 1994. Despite its seeming intent, since 1994 the rate of gay and lesbian discharge has increased to reach a five-year-high of 850 persons in 1996, the highest discharge rate since 1987 and up 42% since 1994. And, though women comprised only 13% of the active duty force, they constituted 29% of those discharged under DADTDP in 1996.

DCNO — (Plans and Policy) (Op-06). Develops and disseminates plans and policies. Principal adviser to the CNO and Secretary of the Navy on strategic planning, nuclear weapons systems, national security affairs, international political-military affairs, technology transfer, foreign military assistance, and naval operational information.

EMI — Extra Military Instruction. A phase of military duty in which an individual is deficient. This training device improves the efficiency of a command or unit and must not be used for punitive action that should be taken under UCMJ. Must not be assigned for more than two hours a day. May be assigned at a reasonable time outside of working hours.

FitRep — Fitness Report. A regular fitness report, or officer evaluation, is submitted annually or on dates specified for each officer grade and also upon the detachment of the officer or his/her reporting senior.

HRM — Human Resource Management. In the '70s the Navy instituted the largest Organizational Development effort. This program of planned change assisted COs in implementing their own people programs, including management and leadership training, race relations, drug and alcohol programs, and intercultural relations. Seen by supporters as a way of helping commands achieve their goals and objectives, with the ultimate goal of Command Excellence.

JAG — Judge Advocate General (Corps). An officer specializing in legal work in the Navy. JAG also refers to the senior legal officer in the Navy.

MAA — Master at Arms. Member of a command's police force.

MSW — Master of Social Work.

NIS — Naval Investigation Service. The office in charge of all Navy intelligence activities. Formerly ONI.

NROTC — Naval Reserve Officer Training Center. Located on over fifty college campuses. A source point for naval officers to be trained in matters relevant to their serving the Navy. Others sources are the Naval Academy and the Officer Candidate School in Pensacola, Florida.

OinC — Officer in Charge. An officer responsible for a special operations detachment or small unit otherwise without a commanding officer.

OJT — On the job training. Due to the high degree of personnel turnover within the Navy, a considerable amount of OJT takes place in lieu of classroom training.

ONI — Office of Naval Intelligence. Formerly the office in charge of all Navy intelligence, counter intelligence, criminal and security investigations. Changed to Naval Investigative Services Office (NIS) in mid-sixties.

PEBD — Pay Entry Base Date. Date a person is sworn into the Navy and usually the date of years in service for pay purposes. Fogies (pay advances) are given every two years on a person's PEBD for the first twenty years.

PCS — Permanent Change of Station. Personnel transferring from one permanent duty station to another go under PCS orders.

POD — Plan of the Day. The schedule of day's routine and events ordered by the XO; published daily aboard ship and at a shore activity.

RHIP — Rank Hath Its Privileges.

SACLANT — Supreme Allied Command, Atlantic. The only NATO command located in the United States.

SECNAV — The Secretary of the Navy. Highest civilian official within the Navy. The CNO reports to the SECNAV and the Secretary reports to the Secretary of Defense.

SUBLANT — Submarine Forces, Atlantic.

SSBN — Ballistic missile submarine.

SSN — Attack Submarine

TAD — Temporary Additional Duty. Naval personnel sometimes are sent on assignments in addition to their regular duty for short periods of time.

UCMJ — Uniform Code of Military Justice. All service personnel, upon enlistment, are subject to the jurisdiction of the UCMJ. The basic criminal laws of the Navy are stated in the UCMJ. It's a "uniform" code of law because Congress made it apply equally to the Navy, Army, Air Force, Marine Corps, and Coast Guard. Under this code, the various services bring criminal charges against personnel who violate military law. Under the UCMJ, service personnel are required to obey all laws established by Congress for the regulation of the military and all lawful orders and regulations of the service and of its superior officers. In the event of violation of the code, a service person receives punishment at the captain's (CO's) mast, or if the offense is more serious, through Navy court-martial.

WAVES — Women Accepted for Volunteer Emergency Service. The WAVES, or the Women's Reserve, were established by legislation on July 30, 1942. Mildred McAfee Horton, President of Wellesley College, was the first Director of the WAVES. The woman who coined the term WAVES wrote to a friend, "I figure the word 'Emergency' will comfort the older admirals, because it implies we're only a temporary crisis and won't be around for keeps." On June 12, 1948, Congress passed the Women's Armed Services Integration Act (Public Law 625). President Truman signed it on July 30, six years after President Roosevelt had signed the bill that allowed women to enter the Naval Reserve. The primary purpose of the 1948 Integration Act was to provide a nucleus of women and an ongoing means to call upon large numbers of women in event of a national emergency. Navy women until 1972 were affectionately (mostly) called Waves.

West Pac — The Navy sends their ships on cruises to the Western Pacific for six months' duration in various ports, exercises, and operations.

WOQ — Women Officers' Quarters. In 1960, at OCS, there were two WOQs, #112 and #113.

XO — Executive Officer. The exec is responsible directly to the captain for all administrative work of a command and crew training. He/she is presumed to be able to take over command in case the CO is incapacitated.

Some of the above definitions and acronyms were taken from:

Ebbert, Jean and Marie-Beth Hall. *Crossed Currents*. New York: Brassey's, 1993.

Hendrickson, Robert. *Salty Words*. New York: Hearst Marine Books, 1984.

Wedertz, Bill, Ed. *Dictionary of Naval Abbreviated Terms*. 3rd Edition. Annapolis: Naval Institute Press, 1984.

About the Authors

Lead Author and Editor:

Commander Beth F. Coye, U.S. Navy (Ret.)

CDR Coye brings to the subject a lifetime of relevant experiences. Her academic background includes a B.A. in Political Science (Wellesley College), an M.A. in International Relations (American University) and a Certificate in Naval Warfare (Naval War College). CDR Coye has taught at several colleges and universities, including the Naval War College, Newport, RI; Mesa College, San Diego, CA; San Diego State College, and the University of San Diego. Her academic fields include American Government, Women's Studies, International Relations, and Human Resource Management. Having served twenty-one years as a U.S. Navy line officer, CDR Coye has published several articles including in the *Naval War College Review* and the Naval Institute's *Proceedings*. Since her Navy retirement, she has served on numerous boards and is currently Co-President of the Rogue Valley Unitarian Universalist Church. CDR Coye writes the letters and journal of Tucker Fairfield and is overall editor and creator of *My Navy Too*.

With:

Vice Admiral Marmaduke Bayne, U.S. Navy (Ret.).

VADM Bayne served as a naval officer commanding submarines when on duty at sea, and was involved in politico-military affairs or military education when serving ashore. He commanded the United States Middle East Forces. During that time he and his wife lived in Bahrain in the Arabian Gulf. He has been Executive Assistant to the Secretary of the Navy; Aide to the Supreme Allied Commander Atlantic and the Commander-in-Chief, Atlantic Fleet. During his last tour on active duty he served as Commandant, National War College in Washington, D.C. and as the first President of the National Defense University. Since retiring from the Navy he has served on many Boards and Committees, most recently as Trustee: New York Life's Mainstay Mutual Funds, and as Co-Vice Chair of the Board of Trustees of Union Theological Seminary in Virginia. He is a member of the Board of Visitors of Georgetown University's School of Foreign Service. VADM Bayne writes the letters of VADM Arthur "Buck" Buckingham, and RADM Hank Fairfield and his wife Emily.

Esther Bain Bell

Ms. Bell worked briefly after graduating from Wellesley College with a B.A. in History. Subsequent to her marriage she worked as an elementary school librarian, a marketing administrator, a small business owner, a real estate agent and, finally, a massage therapist. She has three children and four grandchildren. She is currently working on family histories and memoirs. Ms. Bell writes CAPT Jennie Dumonte's letters.

Captain James T. Bush, U.S. Navy (Ret.)

After graduating from high school in Detroit in 1947, CAPT Bush enlisted in the Navy and a year later was accepted as an NROTC student at the University of Michigan where he graduated with a B.A. in political science. During his first Navy tours, he served in the Atlantic and Pacific fleets on cruisers and destroyers. Subsequently he served in the submarine force, both in diesel and nuclear submarines. He was Executive Officer USS *Triton* and USS *John C. Calhoun*, and Commanding Officer of the USS *Simon Bolivar*. Tours ashore include: Staff, Commander in Chief U.S. Naval Forces, Europe, and the Pentagon. While on shore duty he earned an M.A. in International Relations from the University of Southern California. For two years he was on temporary disability retired and worked as a volunteer on Congressional staffs. Returning to active duty, he served on Second Fleet staff. Upon his retirement, CAPT Bush worked for a congresswoman and senator. Since 1982 he has been Associate Director, Center for Defense Information. He and his wife Patricia write the letters of CAPT Thomas Jefferson Parker.

Patricia J. Bush, Ph.D.

Dr. Bush spent her early married life raising children and moving frequently. Eventually she resumed her education and career and currently is Professor *Emeritus*, Georgetown University School of Medicine, and Visiting Scholar, United States Pharmacopoeia. A pharmacosociologist, she is the author of *Drugs, Alcohol, and Sex* (Marek) 1981 and the co-author of *Death in the Locker Room* (Icarus 1984). She has edited three books, most recently *Children, Medicines and Culture* (Haworth 1996), and has published more than 80 book chapters and journal articles, primarily on the medicine-use process and children's health behavior, including several in the popular press. She has a B.S. from the University of Michigan, an M.Sc. from the University of London, and a Ph.D. from the University of Minnesota. Professor Bush assisted in the editing of *My Navy Too*.

Kitty R. Clark

Ms. Clark received her B.A. from Wellesley College in Zoology. Subsequently, she worked as a researcher in human development. During this time she married and started a family. In 1975 she received her Masters in Social Work from Simmons College and then worked at an inner city mental health center for 15 years. Ms. Clark is an illustrator of children's books and currently enrolled in Vermont College's Master of Fine Arts in Writing for Children. Ms. Clark writes Robyn Greeley's letters.

Lieutenant Commander Sandra L. Snodderly, U.S. Navy (Ret.)

Ms. Snodderly is a retired Lieutenant Commander, U.S. Navy, having specialized in Public Affairs. Ms. Snodderly holds a B.A. and an M.A. and is a very private, upbeat lady who has a passion for sports watching and crossword puzzles. She writes LCDR Billie Baker's letters.

Colophon

The text of *My Navy Too* is set in 11 point Goudy on 12.5 leading. Other fonts used are in the Tiffany family.

The text stock is Eureka Recycled Opaque. It is acid-free for archival durability, and it meets or exceeds all guidelines set forth by the U.S. Environmental Protection Agency for recycled content and use for post-consumer waste. The binding is Perfect Bind.

The printer is Commercial Documentation Services, Medford, Oregon 97501 (Allan Barnes, Account Manager).

The cover, page and publisher's logo design and production are by Dan Schiffer, Digimedia, Jacksonville, Oregon 97530.

The book was produced on an Apple Power Macintosh 8500 using Adobe PageMaker 6.5.

Trademarks: Apple and Macintosh are registered trademarks of Apple Computer, Inc. PageMaker is a registered trademark of Adobe Systems, Inc.